The End of the Universe

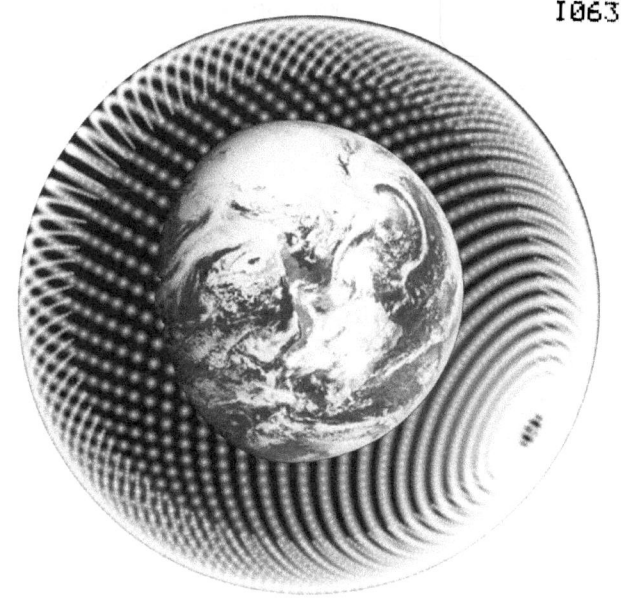

by

Kenneth J. M. MacLean

ISBN-13: 978-0-9794304-0-4

Also by K.J.M. MacLean: *The Vibrational Universe*

Distributed by: Baker & Taylor, Ingram Book Group

The Big Picture is an imprint of Loving Healing Press

Contact the author at www.kjmaclean.com

Contents

The Very Near Future …

The President of the United States exited the White House and stepped onto the back lawn. He lifted his head to the stars, trying to find the Big Dipper.

Then the stars disappeared.

The night sky was replaced by a flat, dull gray nothingness.

"What the hell?" President Sam Rosen rose abruptly with a rush of nervous energy. He looked toward the Secret Service agents. They were staring, dumbfounded, at what once had been the stars.

Sam walked quickly back toward the building. He heard the screeching of tires and crunching of metal. An excited babble of shouting arose from the downtown DC streets that surrounded the White House. Somewhere in the distance a siren screamed.

The president grabbed his dataset from his pocket and frantically dialed his science advisor…

Part I – HOLOGRAM

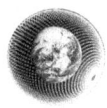

Chapter 1

Dr. Jack Martins sat in his basement holographic lab with an unlit cigarette in his mouth. Surrounding him was an astounding collection of mirrors, lasers, and other equipment that reached from the massive black granite holo bench almost to the ceiling. It had taken him 25 years and over $250,000 to accumulate this collection of state-of-the-art holographic gadgetry.

A shiny, silvery sphere three feet in diameter was suspended from almost invisibly thin wires attached to a ceiling beam. The sphere had a completely uniform, light-sensitive coating on its surface. It hung halfway between the top of the bench and the high ceiling, which was painted black to avoid all reflection.

Jack's swarthy face was covered in a stubble of beard. He looked haggard. His thick jet-black hair was uncombed. The setup was so familiar he didn't even see it. For the 2,078th time he had failed in his attempt to produce the world's first spherical hologram.

After 25 years he knew he should give it up. But he knew he wouldn't. Mechanically, Jack prepared for the next exposure. He tweaked the placement of a couple of the mirrors that would reflect light from the lasers. The silver sphere was coated chemically so that it could be reused over and over. This was itself a significant breakthrough that he had never bothered to share with the holographic community. He had ignored them completely. Jack Martins was a loner and liked it that way. He would spring his creation on the world, fully developed, and create the maximum impact.

Jack placed the artificial plant—which he had used now in almost 600 recordings—back on the recording area of his holo bench. "I really need a cigarette," he muttered to himself. But the sensitive optical equipment made smoking impossible. He dimmed the lights and began the exposure. At that moment something furry jumped up onto the table, jarring the plant and disturbing the meticulous placement of mirrors.

"Dammit Ivan! What are you doing, cat?"

Ivan the cat sat complacently amidst the wrecked experiment, calmly cleaning himself. He looked into Jack's eyes as if to say, 'you left the lab door open you fool.'

Jack noticed something interesting. The wavefronts of light, which he had never successfully coordinated to strike all points on the surface of the sphere at precisely the same moment, were now perfectly modulated.

"Stay there cat." Excitement burst from every cell of his being. Ivan looked up at his supposed master, bored. Jack knew that this cat, like all creatures of his kind, would do what he wanted when he wanted. Just like me. We're well matched.

Ivan the cat leaped off the table and onto a chair. Jack allowed the exposure to run for the requisite 90 seconds and turned off the lasers. With trembling hands he picked Ivan up off the chair and removed the plant. He set up the system for playback, leaving the mirrors in exactly the same place. With Ivan stretched out on his shoulder Jack illuminated the sphere. Because of the ultra-thin suspension wires it seemed to float in mid-air in the middle of the darkened room.

An image of startling clarity burst forth from the surface of the sphere and enclosed him. It was an image so clear and crisp it was more real than reality itself.

Ivan jumped off his shoulders, digging in his claws to get better purchase. He propelled himself out of the room and up the stairs. Jack rubbed his bloody shoulder and stared at the image. It filled the room with impossibly rich, saturated colors that were more alive than the colors of life itself. The room was now transformed into an exact replica of the lab as it had been recorded. Jack saw himself bent over the equipment and Ivan leaping off the holo table. The plant was spilled over onto the table. The holo bench and his setup, as well as all of the recording equipment he used to document his research, were all outlined in breathtaking clarity. The "real" basement that existed before he turned on the playback was now replaced by an even more detailed image of the recording from the spherical hologram.

Jack moved to the image of himself standing next to the holo bench. In the image he was looking down at Ivan, who was in mid-air. Was it solid? Jack hesitantly pushed his hand toward the image of himself. He reached for the cigarette and saw his hand go through it. There was an evanescent feeling of *solidity* to the thing. With a little amplification would his hand feel and touch it?

Equations filled his mind. What would happen if that three foot spherical hologram were much larger? Jack stood there feeling justified for all the hard work and the money he had invested.

He remembered the paper that had inspired his experiments with spherical holograms. Research into black holes suggested that the information capacity of any system is related not to volume, but to surface area. It was an amazing concept that said, "If you want to find out the physics of a system you have to look on the boundary, not inside." It was divergent and counter-intuitive and it appealed to his contrarian personality. Jack abandoned making holograms in the traditional way, which used flat light-sensitive plates. He started to construct his holograms on the surface of a sphere.

Jack remembered when he had first come across the Holographic Principle.[1] It proposed that everything we see around us might be holographic in nature. Including all of the laws of physics. If that were so then the universe itself might have a holographic boundary. The surface of a sphere is the two dimensional boundary of a three-dimensional sphere. If the universe itself had a holographic boundary it would exist somewhere out in space. It would surround the entire universe. But where would that boundary be? Jack had already answered that question theoretically in his controversial papers. Now he had a spherical hologram that might back up his claims.

In theory, all of the 10^{100} bits of entropy in the universe could be packed inside a sphere about a tenth of a light-year across. However, that sphere could also be 13.5 billion light years in diameter, the size of the observable universe. Or even bigger. But what if it wasn't? What if there was an area of space out there that holographically created our physical world? What if the light recorded by our telescopes came not from faraway stars, but a holographic illusion? It was a fantastic concept that everyone said was totally absurd.

---

[1] Introduced in 1993 by the theoretical physicist Gerardus 't Hooft. See Appendix A for further information.

The people who pilloried him hadn't read his work and weren't intellectually capable of understanding it even if they did.

Jack looked around his basement at the reality his spherical hologram had created. The detail, clarity, and crispness of the imagery was imprinted three-dimensionally over the physical reality of his basement. It looked more real than reality itself.

At first Jack's idea was pure speculation, not science. So he collected astronomical data. He used sky survey databases and deep field data supplied by the Hubble Space Telescope and others around the world. With his assistant's computer programming help he created a theoretical, holographic model of the starfield called the Martins Sphere. His model told him that the starfield and the physics as observed from earth could be described on the boundary of a spherical hologram. This Martins Sphere would have a radius of approximately 4.618 light years from the sun. "Such a holographic representation of the Martins Sphere," he wrote, "would correspond precisely with astronomical observations."

Jack Martins had reduced the size of the universe from an almost incomprehensible 13.5 billion light years to an area just larger than the distance from earth to the binary system of Alpha Centauri, the closest star to Sol. His paper was rejected by the mainstream scientific press. But it was so revolutionary that it found an audience among those Jack called forward thinkers. After that the shit hit the fan.

He had been pilloried not only by the media but by the orthodox scientific community. The idea was too preposterous. The *New York Times* called it "a child's fantasy." *Astronomy and Astrophysics*, in its rejection letter, wrote that "Martins' paper was written by someone demented." Religious leaders also weighed in. They were affronted that their idea of a Supreme Being could be so minimized and truncated.

Jack Martins was acknowledged as the world's most brilliant cosmologist. His lectures and appearances at scientific conferences always attracted luminaries in the field. When he spoke the world listened. But did they understand? Of course not.

At an astrophysics conference at Harvard he heard one of the organizers say, "What has the troubled and unstable genius come up with this time?" Internationally his work was considered revolutionary but unsupportable.

Jack was honest with himself. He didn't know if he believed his own theory. The universe as a holographic illusion? Why? How? He had brass co-hunes they all said, the brash and brilliant Jack Martins. Too bad he was such a fruitcake.

Jack strode over to the lasers and turned off the display. His body passed through his own image. Again there was that feeling of almost reality. Did he feel something or was it his imagination? There was only one way to find out: build a bigger hologram. Or go out into space and see if he was right.

Jack made meticulous notes as to the placement of every mirror, laser, and gadget. By God, wait until they see this!

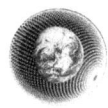

Chapter 2

Washington DC, six months later

Burt Froebel, Jack Martins' graduate assistant, tweaked the holographic setup in the large auditorium. They had brought their ten foot spherical hologram "to blow the socks off those VIPs," as Dr. Martins put it. Tomorrow was the demonstration in front of a selected panel of politicians, scientists, and media. The Air Force was also sending two representatives.

The night before Jack Martins didn't come back to the hotel until 6 a.m. After drinking several cups of coffee he pronounced himself ready to go.

Burt had learned never to ask questions about the volatile scientist's personal life. He merely shrugged. "Let's kick their butts sir."

Martins grinned. "I'll see you there. Make sure everything is ready."

Burt arrived at the auditorium at 6 and fiddled with the setup until 6:54. Everything was set. People began arriving at 7. At 8:15 Dr. Martins had not shown up and some of the VIPs were beginning to grumble. A minute later his boss strode into the auditorium in a rumpled suit. Without preamble he strode up to the podium.

"Ladies and gentlemen, distinguished guests. The press and many of my own colleagues have pronounced that I am a fruitcake. Well, take a look at this." He signaled and Burt activated the hologram.

It was an image of Ivan the cat in the middle of a jump off Jack's holographic table. When the image appeared it filled the entire auditorium. Several persons screamed because the auditorium with its conference chairs and stage simply disappeared. The audience was now in Dr. Martins' basement being attacked by a huge housecat. Several of those who were facing the animal fainted in shock. Most of the attendees were disoriented and a few of them lost the contents of their very expensive breakfast. "Turn it off!" someone shouted.

Burt Froebel was amazed. Even though he had seen the hologram dozens of times, the astonishing reality of it still blew him away. Excited and angry shouts were coming from the assembled dignitaries. His boss ignored them and began to speak.

"Ladies and gentlemen, you have now seen the power and the reality of my spherical hologram. The math suggests that with a larger sphere, the objects in the image you saw could become as solid and real as the physical universe itself. What I have presented today shows us that the Martins Sphere concept is a distinct possibility.

"Have you not wondered why life has evolved only on one planet? We have postulated an almost infinite universe with trillions of galaxies and 30 billion trillion stars that is entirely empty of intelligent life. Does that make sense? Do you build a parking lot the size of North America for a mom and pop grocery store? Of course not. Does it not make more sense to think that the universe is much, much smaller than we have imagined? That life has evolved on only one planet because there is only room for one planet that can support life? Our only option is to validate or invalidate my hypothesis by actually going out into space."

Dr. Jack Martins then walked off the stage. Burt knew that his boss had enjoyed shocking the hell out of those VIPs, and especially the scientists present.

The two Air Force reps came up to Martins but he waved them off. "I have someone to see." Martins walked out of the auditorium, leaving him to answer questions.

A ramrod-stiff man in uniform trailed by another man in wire-rimmed glasses approached him. "I'm Major Cosgrove and this is Major Chen," Cosgrove said. "Your boss is an asshole."

Burt smiled. "Yes major. He's a first class prick and a world class genius."

Cosgrove was taken aback by this statement but Major Chen grinned. "Dr. Martins is the kind of asshole the Air Force might be able to use."

"I'll tell him," Burt said. "I've already anticipated your questions gentlemen. This technology has no military application. What you see here is exactly what you get. If we make any breakthroughs I will make sure to inform you right away."

Major Chen handed Burt his card. Major Cosgrove spoke. "Make sure you do so Mr. Froebel. Or things may get difficult for you. I don't trust Dr. Jack Martins."

Burt grinned. "Neither do I major."

Cosgrove frowned and Chen laughed. They both walked away. After that he was bombarded with questions from the scientists and from the press.

After everyone left Burt had to pack up the equipment and see that it was delivered to Martins' home. Ninety minutes later Martins walked in.

"Where did you go?" Burt asked.

"None of your business son."

Burt smelled perfume. "How do you fit all of this stuff into your basement?"

Martins frowned. "Just barely. The university won't expand my lab space."

Burt held up his hands to ward off another outburst against the university president. "Two Air Force majors were here. I told them this technology has no military application."

"Good boy."

"Fuck you professor. I also told them I would inform them of any new major developments."

"You had no authority to do that."

"You left me to handle everything sir. I handled it."

Martins frowned but then his face broke out into a smile. "So you did. Thank you Burt."

Burt could never tell whether those lips were curled in a sneer or a smile.

Soon after that demonstration came the media explosion, the controversy, and the notoriety. The consensus of the media was expressed by the *Washington Post* in an editorial. "Dr. Jack Martins has taken humanity back five centuries to the belief that the earth is the center of the universe and the stars are just lights in the sky." The Martins Sphere was appalling, scary, and totally unacceptable to the popular imagination.

Jack Martins was the most interesting and irritating person Burt had ever met. Two weeks after they returned to Carleton his inebriated boss walked in to the lab on a Monday morning and began to ramble on about his life.

"I've always been interested in holograms. I fiddled for years with the mathematics of projective geometry. In particular, the placement of holographic images upon various curved surfaces. I've been making holograms since I was 14."

Burt knew that a hologram is a laser created photograph that generates a complete three dimensional image of an object or a scene, normally using a flat photographic plate.

"As a teenager I wondered what would happen if that information were recorded on the surface of a sphere. Would a spherical hologram exhibit any unusual properties? I soon discovered how difficult it was to make such a hologram. But I was not discouraged. The challenge suited my contrarian personality. The greater the difficulty the more I was determined to overcome that difficulty. I was so confident of my eventual success that I wrote a paper explaining the Martins Sphere theory. Shortly after that, viola."

Burt remembered that famous paper. At the very end Martins wrote, "What if the Hubble Sphere (the visible universe) has a radius of only 4.6 light years? What if the starfield we record with our instruments proceeds from an invisible holographic boundary? Is it possible that the universe we observe in the night skies is actually a mirage? And if so, what, if anything, lies beyond it?"

"When I showed my unpublished paper to a few of my colleagues my conclusions were summarily rejected."

As his boss babbled on Burt lost interest. He knew what happened. In typical Martins fashion the professor pilloried anyone who did not accept the entire paper. He alienated almost everyone at Carleton University who might have looked with favor upon it.

Even so, the work circulated within certain sectors of the scientific community as a sort of revolutionary underground polemic. It was somewhat like Mao's little red book in some academic political circles in the 1960s and early 1970s. It found its way onto the WorldNet where Burt saw it. Eventually word reached the ears of a few prominent politicians, scientists, and the Air Force. These VIPs had gone to DC for the demonstration.

The assembled public servants had been awed by their DC demonstration. But it didn't change their minds about Jack's radical ideas. Most of the scientific community still pronounced Martins' work to be "brilliant but unsubstantiated." The *New York Post*, in a headline titled "Martins' Delusional Universe," showed Jack standing next to Alfred E. Newman of Mad Magazine. The caption read, "Egghead Says Universe Isn't Real." Late night comedy hosts had a field day. On the Tonight show Brian O'Connor cracked, "We didn't really land on the moon did we? Maybe it was just an *illusion*."

Burt Froebel shook his head just thinking about it. He was a very level-headed person but it was guilt by association. He had been tarnished with the same mad brush as his boss. Now he had to keep Dr. Martins happy because he couldn't find work anywhere else.

Jack Martins reveled in the attention. His boss had pronounced that those who could not see the brilliance of his ideas were "fools."

Burt realized his boss was still speaking. The man was hung over but Burt had never seen him incapacitated either physically or mentally.

"...even if my theory turns out to be wrong the intellectual stimulation it provides transcends the occasional bouts of depression that I have, over the years, staved off with womanizing and drinking."

It was a soul-wrenching admission from someone who kept himself very tightly wrapped. Burt thought he should be honored by this confidence, but there wasn't much honorable about Professor Martins. Or so he thought until the janitor came in to clean the room that evening.

That Monday morning Burt came in early to the lab, as usual, to check on the latest run of data. Martins was constantly tweaking his model based on new observations. The lab door crashed against the wall. Burt scrambled to his feet, knowing that his boss was probably in a bad mood. "Dr. Martins, what do you make of this?" he said, showing him the printout of last night's run.

Jack Martins shrugged out of his coat. He crushed his cigarette on the floor with his foot and shoved his assistant out of the way, quickly perusing the data. He was a big man, 4 inches over 6 feet. Jack was solidly built with a square jaw, a determined chin, and unusually large hands. Bushy black eyebrows overhung large eyes with black pupils. Thick jet-black hair framed a strong face with a wide brow. It was a compelling face, the face of a man with a purpose.

"Nothing new here, what's the matter with you?" he said, fulfilling all of Burt's expectations. Dr. Martins was hung over again this morning.

Martins was surly all day. Burt pushed in new astronomical observations into their database and the boss looked for inconsistencies in his Martins Sphere model. The man was irritatingly opinionated and regarded everything he said as the Word of God. Burt kept silent, not wanting to set him off.

11

At the end of the day the janitor walked into the lab with his bucket and mop. He saw Jack Martins crush a cigarette butt on the worn linoleum floor. "Hey, professor! Crappin' on my floor again?"

Jack looked up. His haggard face with its heavy eyebrows broke into a grin.

"You're a mess, professor."

Jack sagged. "That I am, Lawrence. When am I ever going to get my life together?"

"Don't be so hard on yourself Dr. Martins," Lawrence replied. "That loan you gave me and Jessie really helped…"

Jack waved him off irritably. "I was happy to be of assistance. You pay me back whenever you can."

Lawrence the janitor shuffled off contentedly, whistling.

Bart was shocked. Jack Martins, *helping* someone?

Curious, Burt talked to the building receptionist, office workers, and even the window washing crew. He discovered that his bad-tempered boss was the most popular person in the entire Physics/Astronomy complex. Apparently he had done little favors for people over the three years he had been a part of the Carleton University faculty. Martins was universally liked by the lower orders. He talked to them and kept track of their lives.

This made Burt see his brusque and unforgiving boss in a new light. Was Jack Martins really a teddy bear at heart? He had almost never received a word of encouragement from his brilliant boss.

The next morning Burt arrived early at the lab. He had to have the coffee pot ready at 7:30 every morning. Dr. Martins had been drinking more than usual lately. He needed coffee like most people need sleep.

As he worked Burt recalled his first meeting with the controversial professor six years ago when he was an undergraduate. It was at a panel discussion at the University of Michigan in Ann Arbor, "The Origin of the Universe." Burt drove all the way from Midland, Illinois to see his hero. Dr. Martins appeared in rumpled clothing and unshaven, with an unlit cigarette between his teeth. The young student had been shocked. He turned to the man seated next to him.

"Is that Dr. Jack Martins?"

The man's face hardened. "That's him all right. Brilliant but unbalanced. He's been kicked out of three universities."

"What's wrong with him then?"

"He's a maverick. Resistant to authority. Self-destructive."

Martins dominated the panel discussion. Afterward Burt approached him. "Dr. Martins you were brilliant. I…"

Martins cut him off. "Yeah sure, kid." In the crowd of attendees, almost a third of which were women, Jack Martins' voice lifted above the others. "Does anyone know how a man can get laid in this town?"

Burt laughed out loud at that memory. He provoked a sharp glance from his boss. Martins had entered the building and was at his desk with a mug of steaming coffee in one of his big hands.

"Have you heard about the military's deep space probe to Alpha Centauri?" Martins asked abruptly.

"No sir, what's that all about?"

Jack grinned. "We must have scared the shit out of somebody. They've already sent an unmanned probe on a trajectory to Alpha Centauri and out to the Martins Sphere barrier."

Burt was surprised and not a little pleased. He wondered where Martins had gotten that information. It sounded classified.

"You don't really believe that the radius of the universe is only 4.6 light years, do you sir?" Burt was pretty sure he would receive a sharp snub.

Martins gulped his coffee. "I don't believe in anything this early in the morning."

Chapter 3

D R. Jack Martins sat alone at a table in Densinger's Campus Bar and Eatery, getting quietly drunk. The place was crowded tonight and the decibel level was deafening. Sound bounced off the brick walls and hardwood floor, making conversation a matter of who could shout the loudest. Jack didn't have anyone to converse with so he didn't care.

An empty pitcher stood on the small round table top. Jack poured the remaining contents of the second pitcher into his big beer stein. He stared blankly at the side of the stein. A man held a woman's hand in front of a castle with a village in the background. Upon it were words in German. "In himmel gibt kein bier, drum trinken wir es hier." Which meant, "In heaven there is no beer, so drink all you can while you're still around." It had a hinged top in the shape of a cupola, which he could flip open or closed with his thumb. Idly he flipped the top up and down. The rim of the heavy ceramic stein was chipped there. He always brought the stein to Densinger's when he wanted to get wasted. Jack tipped the stein and drank deeply, then again. He lit a cigarette and inhaled the acrid smoke deeply into his lungs. A beautiful young woman was standing at an adjoining table talking to two seated young men. She looked bored and dissatisfied.

Jack crushed his cigarette on the floor and walked over to the woman. He placed his hand gently on her upper arm. "Come with me. These kids don't know how to treat a lady."

The woman shook herself free from his grip. "Get your hands off me!"

Martins gave the lady his best smile. She softened a bit. "Never fails," Jack muttered to himself.

A tall, well built young man stood up suddenly. He grabbed Jack's left shoulder and whirled him around. "That's my date grandpa." The boy made a fist with his right hand. "I'll give you a break this time. If you ever touch Kathy again I'll turn your head into a Dali painting."

"Very clever kid," Jack sneered. "You couldn't tell the difference between a Dali and a Hiermonious Bosch."

Jack saw the young man's face cloud in confusion. He laughed and took Kathy's hand, gently leading her away from the table. "Your date seems to have a banana in his tailpipe. Would you like me to take you out of here?"

Despite herself she grinned. The older man's smile of childish innocence caught her off guard. He had swarthy but ruggedly handsome features. She surveyed Jack and liked what she saw. He was well set up with wide shoulders and a narrow waist. She liked his attractively disheveled hair and his piercing black eyes that seemed to see right through her. He had a magnetic masculine attractiveness. "Well, all right. Ernie has been…difficult lately."

Jack knew what to do. He gently but confidently placed his arm around her and began to guide her out of the big campus bar.

Ernie propelled himself forward, blocking Jack's path. "Please Ernie, just leave it alone," Kathy said. "I was going home anyway."

Ernie's face was a crimson study in insult and anger. His fists clenched at his side. He looked about to burst a vein in his temple. "You're not going home with *him*," he said, and took a step forward toward Jack.

Two gigantic bouncers charged over to restore order. One of them spun Ernie out of the way with one hand and carelessly grabbed Jack with the other, separating Kathy from him.

Jack looked upward from his 6 feet 4 at the biggest fellow he'd ever seen. "You've got your hands on my date," Jack said gallantly. He was unconcerned with Hulk Hogan hovering at his side. The bouncer was gripping his shoulder with a meaty hand that could probably melt iron. Jack gave Kathy a wink and saw her giggle. He turned his attention to Hogan, who was just about to shove him ignominiously out of the place. But Jack couldn't let that happen. Kathy's eyes were on him and his mind had cleared. His senses had sharpened and his heart rate slowed. A feeling of strength and power flowed though him. He grounded himself. Despite the huge bouncer's best efforts Jack could not be moved. The martial arts lessons he had painstakingly mastered were serving him well.

Jack spoke coolly. "Excuse me son. I was just about to leave under my own power."

The big man's eyes flared. "Don't get smart old man or I'll bust yer face." His companion looked like Paul Bunyan without the axe. "Yeah that's right, we saw the whole thing. You started it."

"I have my tab to pay." A crowd had gathered around. Out of the corner of his eye Jack saw Spenser, the president of the university. What was the Old Man doing in this campus bar? Then he remembered: it was graduation night. At Carleton the tradition was for the university president to come down to Densinger's and give the kids a rousing send-off. In the old days Spenser even got drunk with them. But the crusty old curmudgeon was now well past his glory days.

As Spenser approached a devilish smile slowly crept over Jack's features. He bowed slightly with just a hint of mockery. Hogan was still beside him. "Good evening sir," Jack said. Spenser grimaced and his eyes blazed as he recognized the offender. "This is the last straw, Martins!" His voice could easily be heard over the din of voices and the loud bar music. "Your tenure is up for review. This time I'll see to it you're expelled."

Paul Densinger, the bar owner, hurried over to the scene. He was a small man in his mid 40s. "I don't ever want to see you in here again Martins."

Jack kept the irritation he felt inside. He feigned astonishment. "But whatever for, sir?" He was playing to the crowd of young people. Jack loved this place and didn't want to be persona-non-grata. Often he'd just come here and drink, not even trying to pick up one of the lovely young things who frequented the bar on any given night. The energy here was exuberant and the patrons full of life and promise.

Jack heard a few chuckles. "Throw this man out of here," Densinger ordered Hulk.

The bouncer smiled aggressively. "Sure boss." But before the brute could get into action Jack stomped hard on his instep. He glided away like a ballet dancer and smiled at Kathy. Jack took a step toward her and felt an arm reaching for him. He jumped into the air and with his right foot, planted it in Hogan's solar plexus. The bouncer's wind was knocked out and he crashed to the floor. Jack whispered to Kathy. "Meet me outside sweetheart." He was gratified to see her smile and he stepped toward the door. Bunyan had helped his friend to his feet. The two beefeaters were about to rush Jack but he held up his hands. "I'm leaving."

Fortunately for him these guys were well trained. Jack knew that a good bouncer was known by the fights he prevented, not by those he started. Jack was sure he wouldn't want to meet any of them out on the street. He had gotten lucky and surprised Hulk. In a real fight Professor Martins would have probably wound up at Midland West Hospital.

Jack could tell the men desperately wanted to engage him. The Hulkster had recovered his wind and yearned to turn Jack into a pretzel. "If I ever see you again…" Jack had already turned and was walking quickly toward the front door.

He saw Kathy waiting. Suddenly, he was hornier than he'd been in a long time. He moved closer. "Come home with me sweetheart." His voice was a little slurred.

Kathy jerked back. She had forgotten that this good-looking charmer was drunk. She smelled the stale odor of beer on his breath. Now she noticed the stubble of beard and his unkempt appearance.

"I don't even know your name," Kathy said, looking him over critically. "I don't think I like you very much at all." She stepped away from the older man.

Jack sagged. "That's OK beautiful. I don't like myself very much either."

Jack drove home, still smelling of beer and cigarettes. He was about to throw himself into bed when he heard a frantic pounding on the door. He walked slowly downstairs, his muscles aching. It had been a while since he had used himself so strenuously.

The pounding was getting louder when Jack opened the door. A thin, plain looking young woman stood on the porch. She had frazzled hair and looked desperate. She held the hand of an anxious little child who was probably no more than four or five years old.

"Excuse me sir, would you please take my child for a few hours?" The woman looked nervously over her shoulder. "I know it's late but I just moved into the house across the street. I saw your light on and I don't know what to do…."

Surprising himself, Jack found himself smiling. He spoke calmly and reassuringly to the woman. "Come on in." He opened the front door wider in welcome.

Now what did I do that for? Jack laughed at himself mentally. 'It's a woman. You just can't resist a damsel in distress.'

"I'm so sorry to bother you this late," she said, brushing tangled hair away from her face. "It's just that…"

Jack smiled again. He felt a kinship with this woman, whoever she was, a feeling of shared misery. "You don't have to explain. It's a man and he's probably drunk." And so am I.

He led the woman and her child to the sofa. They sat down. The little girl sank gratefully into the cushions, her small figure enveloped by the large cushions. The woman sat nervously at the edge.

"Sorry it's so messy in here," Jack said. "I'm a bachelor and definitely not a neat freak."

She sighed with relief and smiled apologetically. "Why do I always…oh, I'm sorry." She tried to straighten her clothing. "I'm Paula Leonard, this is my daughter Susan. I live in the apartment complex across the street."

Jack knew all about that. The apartment complex had been the brainchild of the progressive Midland City Council. A result of their campaign to provide affordable low income housing.

Jack sat on the wing chair about five feet from his guests, giving them a little space.

"My boyfriend is drinking and he's starting to get violent. I didn't want Susan to see anything…" The woman trailed off and shrugged her shoulders helplessly. "I'm new here and I didn't know where else to turn." Jack noticed that her eyes were very large and very blue.

"That's all right. If you like I'll go over there and kick his ass." Jack laughed. "I've already had a fight tonight."

Paula's eyes widened. They were beautiful eyes, Jack thought. He noticed things like that. "You have?"

Jack nodded. "Over a woman. But it turned out that she didn't like me anymore after she got to know me a little." His voice was bitter. "Let me go over there and pound some sense into him," Jack suggested. He felt the injustice of a smaller woman dominated by a physically stronger man. He wanted to do something to make the world a better place.

"No, no, that wouldn't be good at all," the woman said quickly. She felt that she may have gone into the fire from the frying pan. This man was drunk too. But something about him calmed her. He seemed…intelligent, but basically harmless. She perceived an underlying warmth of character beneath his masculine bluster.

"Have you called the police?" Jack asked.

Paula hung her head. "Even worse." She looked up. "You see, I've tried to tell Thorpe that it's over. He insists on coming around anyway. He followed me here, of all places, from Chicago, where we used to live together. If I could just stay here for an hour he'll drink himself into a stupor. He'll be asleep on the couch."

Jack spent an hour and a half with the woman. He made mother and daughter a sandwich. After fixing a pot of coffee and talking for a while, Paula calmed down. Susan fell asleep.

"She's cute," Jack said. "She has your eyes."

The woman started, then she smiled. It was a bright smile and her plain face became beautiful. "How could a man not want to see that smile all the time?" Jack said, thinking aloud.

"You're the kind of man I need," Paula said. "A man who notices things like that. A kind man, not someone who uses me for sex and then hits me."

Jack gulped. At least he could say that he never laid a hand on a woman in anger. His dad had taught him that. He wanted to help her, to call the police, to do something. But he had fucked up every relationship he'd ever been in. He was afraid that if he got involved in Paula's troubles he'd just make them worse. "Honey, I'm not the kind of man you want."

She smiled again, her head tilting a little. It was a feminine gesture that called to his maleness. He could see why Thorpe wanted her.

Jack didn't like the direction his thoughts were taking.

"Uh, well, maybe you should try going home now."

Paula's smile vanished and she shrank inside herself. Jack cursed himself for a fool. "I didn't mean it that way." He tried to explain that he didn't trust himself with women.

"Of course," Paula said. "I'm sorry to trouble you." She woke up Susan and lifted her into her arms, then walked quickly toward the front door..

"No trouble at all," Jack said, opening the door. "Do you want me to walk you home?"

"No, that's all right."

Jack watched as the woman, the child in her arms, walked across the street and entered the apartment complex. He stood on the porch in the cold

October air for a few minutes, listening. He heard nothing so he walked back inside and up the stairs to his bedroom.

As he took off his shoes he thought about Paula Leonard, and Kathy at Densingers, and the strippers at the Heavenly Bodies, and Amara Thompson, his department head at Carleton University.

"You're a dammed fool," he told himself. "But at least you did something good tonight."

Jack threw himself into bed and slept soundlessly until the alarm went off at 6:30. His tenure hearing was in two days.

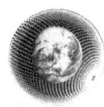

Chapter 4

THE next day after classes Jack got into an argument with Alex Krajicek in his office. Krajicek was the senior member in the department and one of his biggest critics. Jack stepped into the old-fashioned book-lined room and noted its very nice view of the Diag, the Central Campus greensward. His own office faced the parking lot, not that he cared. Jack knew that Krajicek was outraged that he had taken what should have been groundbreaking work and turned it into food for gossip. Alex had apparently called him in for a man-to-man.

"Look," Krajicek said without introduction, pointing to the Star tabloid lying on his desktop. The headline read, *Scientific Theory Says Aliens Control Earth.* "This is getting out of hand, Jack. It's time to stop this foolishness."

Jack sighed. "Alex, I've been able to build a spherical hologram. From it I have been able to confirm the validity of the Holographic Principle. I have proven that the information content of a system can be described on the boundary of that system." Jack could see that the older man was already tuning him out. He plowed ahead anyway. "Simple extrapolation from a working spherical hologram and painstaking analysis of astronomical databases have confirmed my original proposal. Such a boundary, at approximately 4.618 light years from the sun, would exactly account for astronomical observations."

Jack went over the math and explained his reasoning but Krajicek had stopped listening. Finally, he gave up. "Voyager 1, the furthest human penetration into space, has only traveled about 12 billion miles from earth. That's less than 1/500th of one light year. All of our observations of the universe have come from essentially one tiny area in space: the earth and its solar system.

We don't really know what's out there. We just *assume* we do. Taken in that context, the suggestion I'm making isn't so farfetched."

The man studied him silently for several moments. "You're *serious*, aren't you?"

"Indeed I am," Jack replied. "I've decided to finally submit the paper for formal publication in the Carleton Review. It's been almost four years now since the paper was written. I think it's about time this university formally validated my work."

Krajicek laughed. "No you won't. I'm on the departmental review committee. If you think that nonsense is going to pass muster you're nuttier than I thought."

Jack tried once more. "Is it so radical to propose that the universe is not as large as we think it is? All we have is the evidence presented by the electromagnetic radiation that hits the detectors of our telescopes and our instruments."

Krajicek looked at him queerly. "Of course it is Jack! What you're saying doesn't make sense. If the universe really is a gigantic hologram then who put it there? And why?" The older man spread his arms out as if to say, 'I'm trying to be reasonable.' "That's why we have these stupid headlines." The department head pointed to the offending tabloid. "You're opening a philosophical can of worms that has no business being opened. There's just no reason to seriously accept such arguments, Jack." Krajicek spoke resignedly, as if explaining to a brilliant but recalcitrant child why $2 + 2$ doesn't equal 5. "Your assertions belong in a science fiction story or a fantasy novel. Isn't it much more reasonable to apply Occam's Razor? Isn't the simplest explanation the most accurate? And that is, that the evidence before our eyes is simply the reality? That's what any sane, rational person would think."

Krajicek stared at Jack, assuring himself that the man before him was serious. "Cosmologically speaking, your paper doesn't add up."

"All of my calculations are based upon solid ground," Jack countered. Krajicek dismissed this with a wave of his hand.

"You've made a series of brilliant but far-fetched assumptions about the nature of reality," Krajicek replied. It was the standard rote objection to his work.

Jack was tired of such prattle. His lips curled. "You haven't even read it." He watched with satisfaction as the other man's head jerked slightly backward. "And even if you did you couldn't understand it." Jack knew full well that Krajicek was weak in math. It was said that most of his papers were written by his graduate students and the math checked by Brad Doherty, his long time administrative assistant. How the man ever achieved his doctorate was a mystery to Jack.

Krajicek shot back quickly. "You're a fruitcake Martins! The only place that paper will be published is in 'Popular Science,' or maybe on some new-age internet website."

Jack tried once more. He reeled in his frustration with a visible effort. "I believe the paper will find acceptance among those who can look outside the box. You weren't in DC when I gave my demonstration Alex. If you had been you wouldn't dismiss my theories so glibly." He paused. "You've heard that NASA has already launched one of their new deep space probes to test out my theory."

Krajicek snorted. "To test out your theory? That probe is going to Alpha Centauri to prepare for a possible manned mission."

"Yeah. But they're sending it out to the Martins Sphere barrier after that." Jack was smug.

The older man was really irritated now. "That theory of yours is nothing but pure speculation, Jack. Philosophizing! Remember what Gauss said: 'If a philosopher says something that is true, it is trivial. If he says something that is not trivial, it is wrong.'"

Jack lost it. "Fuck you Krajicek. You wouldn't recognize a new idea if it fell down on your head."

The look of hatred on the face of his colleague told Jack he had made another enemy. Krajicek stomped out of the room and Jack lit a cigarette. He ignored the "No Smoking" prohibition within all campus buildings.

"I think I'll get drunk tonight," he said to himself.

When Jack got home that night after 2 a.m. he stumbled over to the computer in his first floor study and picked up his messages. Jack didn't have telephones or even a mobile device.

He didn't have many friends.

There were three messages, two of them from the department head. "Jack, what are you doing tonight? Call me OK?" and "Jack, at least have the courtesy to return my call. You said you'd be home tonight."

Amara Thompson was the biggest problem in his life. Like almost all of his problems it was female. Thompson was gorgeous, intelligent, and had a thing for him. She was the only woman Jack had ever seriously considered. Amara was the only one who could match his wit and his intelligence. They both had congruent interests. Sometimes during the work week they'd have lunch together. Often the two would become so immersed in conversation that their food would grow cold. He recalled the only time he'd invited Amara to his home.

It was just after he'd completed his first spherical hologram last fall. He was so excited that he dialed her office number without thinking. "Amara Thompson, Physics and Astronomy," the smooth voice said.

"Amara!" He was surprised to hear her voice. Jack realized that he'd unthinkingly chosen this woman to share one of the most important victories of his life.

"Jack?"

"Uh, hello Amara. I was wondering if you'd care to come over to my lab and see the results of my latest experiment. It's pretty exciting." He realized how lame that sounded and kicked himself mentally.

"Jack, you don't have a lab. You haven't been drinking have you?"

Jack caught her inference and was not offended. "Uh…no Amara. I've got an optical laboratory in my basement. I've just successfully completed a remarkable experiment that I'd like to share with you."

Jack could feel her excitement. "On one condition. It's almost 5 and I'm hungry. After, you have to take me out to dinner."

"Deal."

"I'll be there in half an hour."

Jack gave her directions and went downstairs to prepare. A while later he heard the doorbell ring and ran up the stairs two at a time. Jack pulled open the door. Amara stood on the porch in the cold, smiling shyly.

"Come on in." He took her coat and hung it up in the hall closet. He noticed how great she looked in black slacks and a fuzzy red sweater. Her hair was tied in corn rows.

They made small talk as he led her through the living room and the kitchen and down the stairs to the basement. "Don't you get warm in that thing?" Jack asked, indicating the heavy sweater.

She laughed. "The walls in my office are so drafty I'm always cold."

Jack opened the door and Amara gasped. The large basement with its 15 foot ceiling was filled with an astonishing and complex array of lasers, mirrors, and other equipment she could not recognize. Jack had searched all over Midland for just such a space for his holographic work. He was delighted to have discovered a house that had been previously owned by a businessman who had used his basement for a warehouse. The house was on Traver Street in a secluded area inhabited by quiet academics who all worked at Carleton. The house and the location had perfectly suited his reclusive personality.

"My God, Jack. It's incredible. What do you do down here?"

"I make holograms. But not just ordinary ones. I have just completed a spherical hologram." Jack spoke with a smile of enormous satisfaction that replaced his normally taciturn expression.

"What's the big table for?" Amara asked. She indicated a large, black topped table with thick legs. Mirrors and lasers sat on the table. Above and surrounding it there were more mirrors and lenses and a host of other equipment. The basement was covered from the floor to the ceiling with apparatus.

"That's my holographic bench. It consists of solid granite one inch thick. I've rested it on large wooden legs that have been set in concrete into the basement floor. As you can see, it is supported in nine different places."

"What's so special about the bench?' Amara asked.

"It's important to eliminate even the tiniest extraneous vibration when performing this work."

Amara noticed a silvery sphere about three feet in diameter. It was suspended above the table and secured by two extremely thin, rigid wires. "That's your new invention?"

"Yes."

Amara laughed. "It doesn't look like much."

"Wait until you see what this baby can do." He began to fiddle with the setup.

"What's so special about a spherical hologram?" Amara asked.

"It turns out they have remarkable, unanticipated features." Jack walked her to a small bench at the back. "This was my first holographic bench. I built it when I was 14." It was a simple setup with a single laser, two mirrors, a beam splitter, and two lenses. He showed her how light from the laser could be split to form an object beam and a reference beam. He picked up a pencil off the desk and placed it in front of a photosensitive plate. "The light comes from the laser and is split with the mirrors. One of the beams shines on the object that you want to image and bounces off, hitting the plate. At the same time the other beam is directed onto the plate. When the two beams of light hit each other an interference pattern is formed on the plate. When you shine light on the plate you can see a three dimensional image. When I first saw one of these things as a kid I became immediately fascinated with them."

Jack shined laser light onto a coated plate. A three dimensional pencil appeared in front of it.

"It's like magic!" Amara spoke brightly, on her face a look of childlike innocence and happiness.

Jack had never been with a woman who allowed herself to completely let go. As he looked at her something within his heart ached. The kind of women he went out with were not like this at all.

Jack pointed to the recording plate in back of the pencil. "Recording an image on a flat plate is a rather straightforward proposition. The beam of light that comes off the object you want to photograph, and the reference beam, can easily be brought together simultaneously onto the plate." They walked back to the front of the room and Jack pointed to the sphere. "But how do you get the target beam and the reference beam to cover all areas of the sphere?"

Amara contemplated that for a few moments. "It would be very difficult."

"Precisely," Jack said. "But it's also very difficult to figure out how to cover the sphere with a perfectly uniform, light sensitive coating." It took me ten years just to do that." Satisfied with the setup, he began to switch off the lights.

"Are you ready to be alone with me in the dark?" he teased.

She gave him a look that challenged and invited him. "I think we might manage that."

Now the lights were off and Jack activated his hologram. Tthe laboratory sprang to life around them. But it was a different lab than the one she was in, an astonishingly lifelike three dimensional reproduction that almost completely filled the room. "Jack it's…it's incredible," she breathed.

"Isn't it? Now walk a few steps back and forth and see what happens. Remember that although you see the lab as it was when I recorded this image, things have been moved around a bit since then."

Jack stood at her right and Amara hesitantly took a few steps to her left. "I don't remember this chair being here," she said, walking right through it. "Oh! What's happening? I feel like a ghost who can walk through walls."

Jack laughed. "You're quite correct. That chair isn't really there."

"What's that fuzzy area?" Amara pointed to a slight fuzziness along the periphery of the image.

"You see it too?" There was a barely discernible perturbation at the periphery of the hologram. "I thought it might have been my imagination." He made a mental note to investigate it later.

"So that's why you invited me over here," Amara said, pouting a little. "You just wanted me as an observer for your experiment."

"Well yeah, a little." Jack was feeling a little uncomfortable. He never felt uneasy around women except for this one. "But I really wanted to see you. You're the first one I called."

Amara smiled. "All right Jack."

He walked forward a few steps to the table, turned off the lasers, and switched on the lights. "What do you think?"

"It's remarkable. You owe me dinner."

"Just like a woman. Eminently practical."

"That's right. Feed me."

That was almost a year ago. He'd taken her to the Mediterrano, an Italian restaurant. They talked until the place closed and then went to his place.

That night was the best of his life. They made love over and over. The feel of her body against his was indescribable. After, they talked until the sun came up. In every particular they were ideally suited.

"You're perfect." Jack startled her and himself.

Amara told him about her childhood.

"I was raised in Detroit and went to public schools because my family couldn't afford to send me to some of the good private schools in the area. What I couldn't learn at Finney High I found in books. I have a natural head for math and figures. When I got to the University of Michigan I found a home. It wasn't very long before I graduated magna cum laude with a degree in business administration and a minor in statistics. I got my MBA there as well."

It was clear to Jack that she was a go-getter, and had a driving ambition to succeed. Jack told her about his childhood, how he was raised in a rich family and attended the best prep schools. "I eventually found my way to MIT where I learned to drink, do Qui Gong and karate, pick up girls, and get into fights." Jack told her of his trips into south Boston, how they'd gotten involved peripherally in the drug trade, and their street fights. "I even did some jail time. Despite the inattention to my studies I graduated with top honors. Three years later I got my doctorate from Brown in cosmology. I was proclaimed one of the brightest young stars to emerge in the past fifty years. Great things were expected from me, Amara. But in the eyes of my colleagues and critics I have failed to fulfill that promise."

Amara told him about her family. Jack was a bit embarrassed.

"I don't keep in touch with anyone. I don't even have a mobile." This was unreal to Amara, whose family was very important to her. "I'm a loner Amara. I've made a goodly sum from the university. Coupled with my salary and the income I receive from the sale of my articles and papers, I'm well off financially."

"How did you get the money to build your lab?"

"I was the sole beneficiary of my father's estate. I used that money to build this optical lab and make a 20% down payment on the house."

"Your father must have died young."

Jack grimaced. "He did. When he was only 37 he had a fatal heart attack."

"Jack, I'm sorry."

"No need Amara. I'm satisfied with my life."

He could tell Amara wasn't so sure about that.

Jack was still standing by his computer downstairs after getting his messages. Amara's feelings for him had not changed despite his erratic behavior and his refusal to continue what they started. She didn't really know him, she only thought she did. He would make a terrible companion. For some reason she continued to look at him as if he was better than he really was. Jack knew that for all his success getting women into his bed he really didn't understand them. Or himself either.

The next morning at 7:30 Jack cleaned himself up and put on some fresh clothes. It was the morning of his tenure review. Who would be on the committee? Probably a lot of people who didn't like him.

The Tenure Review Committee would meet in Room 243 of the Admin Building, affectionately known to the tenured and nontenured staff at Carleton as The Gulag. Jack knew he'd have to pass Amara's office at the head of the hall. He hoped it would be vacant. At Carleton all departmental administration was centralized. If you wanted to know what was going on in your area you had to get off your duff and take a walk. It was a system, Amara told him, that worked well.

Jack got out of the elevator on the second floor and walked surreptitiously past her open door.

"Jack!" She noticed him immediately. Like all good department heads her desk was placed to afford a clear view of all who passed through the hallway toward the only exit.

Jack groaned and walked in. "I called you twice last night," she said, a little hurt.

"I was, er, out late."

"Yes, we all heard about your…exploits at Densingers."

Was that last night? Jack couldn't remember. He'd been out late two nights in a row.

"Did you take her home?" Amara asked.

"Her?" Jack didn't know who she was talking about.

"Your damsel in distress," Amara replied in accusing tones.

Kathy! "Uh, she decided that she didn't like me very much so I just…"

"OK Jack." Amara's eyes welled with tears. She brushed them off her cheek and a few drops fell on the keyboard.

"Let's not have this conversation again," Jack pleaded.

"I love you," his boss said, tearing Jack's heart out once more. Every time she said that it reminded him of the truth. They both knew it. Jack said nothing, his emotions in turmoil.

Amara looked up at him. She spoke roughly, still fighting back tears. "Your meeting with the Tenure Review Committee has been pushed back to 3 p.m." She was clearly implying he should be on time.

Jack fumbled for a response. "Right." Jack stared at the floor, unable to meet Amara's eyes.

Amara jerked her head around and back to her monitor screen. "Get out of here Jack."

Jack showed up at his hearing on time. The policy at Carleton was clear; Jack knew it by heart. "A tenured professor who brings disgrace upon the university or who fails to uphold proper moral, ethical, and professional standards of conduct is liable for immediate dismissal from the Carleton University faculty." But this hearing would be different for Dr. Martins was no ordinary faculty member. His academic reputation had spread across the globe and reflected well upon Carleton University. That would be in the back of everyone's mind this afternoon.

Jack settled into his chair facing the panel members. His interrogators sat in a semicircle at a raised conference table, looking down on him. Alan Krajicek, his department head, was here of course. Krajicek looked like a shepherd about to fleece one of his sheep. He was probably President Spenser's man. Well, let them kick me out. I'm tired of the academic life.

Krajicek leered from his position to the left of the committee chairman, Professor Emeritus Jackson Brundage. Brundage was an astrophysicist who Jack knew to be fair-minded. On the far left sat a young guy Jack had never seen before. To Jackson's immediate right was Winston Pollard, a no-name ladder climber in the mathematics department. Pollard was eager to make a name for himself at Carleton. He'd get no sympathy there. Professor Hideki Matsui sat at the end, maybe his only true friend left. Matsui was a meticulous researcher and loved by all of his students. A man of unquestioned integrity. When Jack first came to Carleton he tried to turn over a new leaf and emulate the professor. But his personality just didn't suit and he gave it up.

As Jack surveyed the panel he saw the guiding hand of Amara Thompson, whose influence extended well beyond the confines of the Physics/Astro section. Two of the five board members could be said to be sympathetic and the third, neutral. A pretty good set-up for the odious Professor Martins if he handled it right.

Jack smiled and nodded toward Matsui. The hearing began.

Brundage spoke first. "We have a special letter from President Spenser that I am required to submit into the record." He shook the paper in Jack's direction. "Would you like to see it?"

"No thanks. I already know what's in it."

Jack was asked about his actions at Densinger's, his propensity to hang out at student bars, and his liaisons with undergraduate students. There were complaints from faculty about his rudeness, his drunkenness, and his cigarette smoking in university buildings. The most damming charge was a sexual harassment complaint from a female student, which had been filed with the Student Affairs office.

Jack was keeping his temper throughout the litany of the complaints against him even though Krajicek had been sniping at him the whole time, supported by Pollard. At one point Chairman Brundage asked him a question. "Why don't you find some woman your own age?" The chairman spoke mildly.

Jack growled, beginning to lose control. "It is not the business of this board to be pontificating about my private life."

Brundage bristled. He respected Martins for his brilliant work but the man was being impossible. "It is when your conduct adversely affects others. There are some serious incidents here professor."

"As I'm sure you've found out at your other, ah, places of employment," Pollard contributed.

Jack was tired now, tired beyond caring, a tiredness that seeped into his bones and sucked the life from him. When he felt like this not even his holographic work could bring him out of it. A cloud of depression blotted out all joy. That old self-destructive impulse rose up in him again.

Krajicek gleefully read the sexual harassment charge and the statement from the young woman into the record. "You're a disgrace Martins!"

Brundage was about to censure his colleague when Jack spoke. "Let he who is without sin cast the first stone." This peroration upset Pollard, who was a devout Christian.

Jack reached into his pocket for his cigarette lighter. He placed it on the table, indicating quite bluntly that he was ready for the proceedings to come to an end. He could tell even Matsui was tired of his act.

Fifteen minutes later Jack was dismissed by Brundage. "Professor Martins, you have not made a favorable impression with this board."

Jack shrugged dismissively and walked out. They hadn't even mentioned his brilliant work. Ignored were the rave reviews the cosmology department at Carleton University had received in the latest nationwide survey. Professor Martins had been prominently mentioned.

A week later the board came back with its recommendation. Professor Martins was on probation. One more severe incident would result in his immediate dismissal.

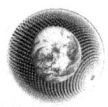

Chapter 5

Nine months later

YOGESHDalal had just gotten off work. He was the staff aide to Congressman George Dempsey (D, Mich), chairman of the House Appropriations Committee. Dalal was a slightly built man of medium height, the junior member of the Congressman's staff and his science advisor. In his briefcase he carried the famous Martins Sphere document. He was charged by the Congressman with the responsibility of evaluating it. Since Martins' demonstration last year the document (and several summaries) had been circulating rapidly through the city.

Congressman Dempsey briefed him during the morning staff meeting. "Martins' spherical hologram demonstration shocked everyone who was there. The descriptions of the presentation have rocked the entire DC community, Yogesh. This has lent credence to Martins' crazy theory that the universe itself might not exist. Rumor has it that some heavy-hitters in the Rosen administration have backed a hush-hush military project associated with Martins' work." The congressman paused for a moment and frowned. "NASA launched one of those new probes last year. Something happened out there in space, Yogesh, that has scared the crap out of the military big-wigs. Now there is serious talk of a manned mission to Alpha Centauri. The wheels grind pretty slowly around here, young man, so whatever happened out there must be BIG. Hell, we haven't even put a man on Mars. Now they suddenly want to go out to the stars? It doesn't make sense to me." He jabbed his finger in Yogesh's chest. "The military and the boys over at Langley want the Alpha Mission real bad. They're putting pressure on the president and everybody in

35

Congress, including me, to fund it. I want you to tell me whether this Martins thing is bullshit. I don't understand science and neither does anyone else in this office. So get to it. I want your evaluation by the staff meeting tomorrow morning."

Dempsey went over to his desk and handed Dalal a manilla folder. "Read this. There's Martins' original paper, a summary of Martins' original work, some scientific analysis, and a timeline of what's happened politically since it came out."

Dalal felt a little intimidated by his boss and he listened carefully. When the congressman gave orders he expected them to be carried out without fuss.

"The leadership has rushed a bill out of committee to fund the new Alpha Centauri Mission. You've been here long enough to know that this a politically sensitive vote for my Rust Belt constituency. People are out of jobs and now we're going to spend billions on some cockamamie space mission? You take a look at that and tell me whether this Martins Sphere thing makes any sense scientifically."

Dalal took the folder and peeked inside, seeing a lot of equations. "All right congressman. I might have to stay up all night to figure this out."

Dempsey was gruff. "Do whatever you have to do. Abraham, President Rosen's Chief of Staff, wants my answer tomorrow. The bastard came to my office yesterday evening to personally put the squeeze on me." He dismissed his aide and walked briskly back to his private office.

Yogesh exited the corridor in the Rayburn Office Building and was met by a blast of hot, humid evening air. He hardly noticed. Compared to Delhi the temperatures here were moderate. He was hungry. Yogesh decided to mix business with pleasure. The Madras Masala was just two blocks over from his apartment complex. In the restaurant Dalal grabbed a table at the back and ordered. He enjoyed the atmosphere and the background conversation in the lilting accents of his native Hindi.

After finishing an excellent meal of chicken vindaloo Dalal settled back to study the documents.

Was the Martins Sphere just another crackpot theory? Did Martins' proposal have real scientific merit? He sat in the restaurant for over five hours, drinking tea and nibbling on nan, until the documents were fully understood. Yogesh wrested enough information from the equations to get a good idea of the author's intent and his conceptual framework. It left him feeling excited and disturbed.

Martins' argument for a truncated Martins Sphere—a universe that was a mere 9 light years in diameter—was presented so trenchantly it upset him. Martins' model was compelling. The paper had the feeling of truth, even if that truth was in opposition to everything science currently believed about the size of the universe. Throughout the history of science great minds proposed revolutionary ideas that seemed impossible at the time. Until they were borne out by experimentation.

Yogesh read the rest of the papers in the manilla folder. Most interesting were rumors about an exotic new space drive technology that the military had already used to send out an unmanned probe to Alpha Centauri.

Had the probe discovered something threatening to earth? Could it be that Martins was actually right? No. The universe is the universe, not a holographic illusion. He would not accept it. Reading between the lines, however, it was clear that the probe was not just scientific in nature. There was an underlying element of fear behind the probe launch. Was this just military paranoia? Observers speculated that the probe was launched primarily to test Martins' theory. The Alpha Centauri Mission project had then been hastily added on after the probe encountered something out there. If that were true the military must be afraid of something.

Yogesh became aware that he had been sitting hunched over in his booth for several hours. He stretched, relaxing tensed muscles. The clock read five minutes until midnight; the restaurant was getting ready to close. Yogesh paid his bill and left a tip commensurate with his rather meager salary. He walked quickly back to his one-bedroom apartment in a seedy neighborhood a mile south of the Rayburn House Office Building.

Yogesh read over the documents again until 3 a.m. He prepared in his mind what he would tell his bosses tomorrow and fell asleep on the couch.

At 7 a.m. he reported to Victorio, Dempsey's Chief of Staff and campaign manager. The two would then meet privately with the congressman before the general staff meeting at 8 a.m.

Dempsey's Chief of Staff was an Apache Indian, a descendant of a fierce tribe of warriors from the American southwest and northern Mexican desert. Victorio had wide, flat, aboriginal features and a naturally fierce countenance. Behind those eyes was a burning intelligence.

Yogesh gave his report succinctly and concisely. His tired body and mind came to attention under Victorio's gaze. "Very well, Yogesh. Your recommendation is that the Martins proposal is scientifically sound enough for the Congressman to risk his vote?"

"Yes Victorio." Dalal replied as if he were a child to his teacher. Victorio was large-souled; an imposing figure who inspired Yogesh to do his best.

"Come then, let's meet with the Congressman." Victorio rose fluidly from his seat and ushered Dalal into Dempsey's private office.

"Well?" Dempsey asked as Yogesh entered the room. The older men were not familiar at all with science. Yogesh knew that his word would determine the congressman's position. He had never before seen Demspey so on-edge.

"Sir, I'm very impressed with Martins' arguments and his model. My recommendation is that Martins' work is scientifically solid, brilliant even."

Dempsey sat at his desk, gazing intently at his junior aide and waiting for something important that was still unsaid.

"Your 'aye' vote on this Alpha Mission is politically defensible from a scientific standpoint," Yogesh added.

Dempsey smiled broadly. "You personally feel competent to defend my position scientifically, even to some of my hard-headed constituents? And to the press?"

Yogesh gulped. "Yes sir."

Dempsey knew that the Martins papers had been read in every important political circle. There was growing support for a manned mission to Alpha Centauri anyway. But nothing was going to happen on the manned project if stay-at-home, rabble-rousing Democrats began to howl. As chairman of the House Appropriations Committee his support for the Alpha Centauri Mission was critical. Over the years he had engendered good will on both sides of the aisle. Where he went, others would follow. Therefore his approval would sway votes. He had to be right.

To Victorio he said, "Tell Abraham that I won't object to this mission. He's got my vote."

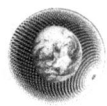

Chapter 6

P RESIDENT Sam Rosen looked up from his daily briefing book. It was a closely spaced, twenty page summary of the worldwide events of the past twenty-four hours. The Middle East was on the front pages again. Almost all of the briefing was about that interminable conflict, which he had helped to diffuse during the previous election cyle. With his nelp the parties had finally agreed on a permanent solution, but of course there were still radicals on both sides.

President Rosen looked at the last page, which mentioned something about a Martins Sphere. What was that?

A separate document was attached. The president postponed his meeting with the ambassador from the European Union to read it. His science advisor had been urging him to do so for weeks and had doggedly paper-clipped the document to his briefing papers every morning. Rosen had a Masters degree in international relations and couldn't make any sense of the mathematics or some of the important scientific concepts. He hastily called in his team of science advisors.

"Hal, get the SAB in here right away."

"Yes sir. Ambassador Dugens is a little irritated right now. I thought you should know."

Screw Dugens. The man was here to whine about the dollar again. "Tell Dugens that I'm eagerly waiting to hear from him but a national crisis is taking shape that requires my immediate attention. Take him outside and show him the parade. He'll like that."

Hal Blanchard, his liaison for European affairs, laughed. The parade the president just mentioned was an international youth conference for peace and understanding. On this hot summer day there were a lot of good-looking girls wandering around in shorts and tank tops, in preparation for a tour of the White House. The ambassador from the European Union was known for his affinity for young women. Blanchard grinned. In Europe they understood such things, but not here. He decided to take Rosen's suggestion.

Meanwhile, the Science Advisory Board had assembled in the president's study. Sam Rosen walked in and saw his old college buddies sitting in chairs in front of his desk, eating sandwiches. Dirk Wheeler, John Cho, Peter Bambridge, and Lev Katzenbaum had cushy four-year appointments. They were on loan from their universities. The Board members had only to dish up a few papers every year and serve on a few select panels.

"Lev, can you tell me anything about this Martins thing?"

Katzenbaum, a very tall and bony man, snorted. "First you have to understand a little bit about holograms in general." Lev's old friend had little interest or understanding of science and technology so he briefly explained what a hologram was. He knew Sam wouldn't understand anything about boundary phenomena or the Holographic Principle so he just explained it in general terms. "To make a long story short Martins is basically saying that you can describe reality itself, and everything about the real world, with a hologram."

"That's fascinating Lev, but I don't understand why this hologram stuff of Martins is so significant. It's just some wacko theory isn't it?"

"Basically, yes. However, Martins is a compelling and very popular writer. His work has fired the imagination of a certain segment of the public. It's been on the news. The late night comedy shows have joked about it, so people know about it."

The president was confused. "People actually take this seriously?"

"Some important and influential people do Sam, and these people usually lead the social discussion. Unfortunately organized religion has fervently attacked Martins, inflaming opinions. Those concerned about the reemergence of religious conservatives have defended him. This has led to a public debate that the scientific community is now joining. All of this talk has led to the further popularization of his crazy theory."

Sam Rosen grinned. "This is a great country isn't it Lev?"

"Don't get me started Sam. There's one other thing you should know. The Martins Sphere idea just happens to coincide with the logical progression of our space program. With the development of the new deep space propulsion engines, NASA had already planned a series of unmanned deep space probes. The scientific community is very excited about that."

Katzenbaum briefly consulted his three companions before continuing. "If Martins was just a theoretician, Sam, he'd be dismissed as a nut. This guy has figured out how to record a holographic image onto the surface of a sphere and how to extract the information. It turns out that such a hologram has properties that were wholly unexpected. During the DC demonstration last year Martins brought in a spherical hologram. Everyone just shit their pants, including yours truly. It was a recording of a cat, taken in Martins' lab. The cat was leaping off a black granite table next to a potted plant. When Martins illuminated the hologram the familiar comfort of floor, walls, and ceilings disappeared. We were *there*, in Martins' lab. It was the most astonishingly *real* image I've ever seen. Like a high-definition rendition of real life."

Everyone in the room had gone completely silent, mesmerized by the account.

President Rosen looked at his watch. Dugens was probably steaming right now. "Just tell me, in one or two sentences, what this guy discovered and why everyone's so upset about it."

Katzenbaum looked to his friend John Cho, a portly man who favored expensive clothes and strong cologne. Cho could see the president fidgeting. "Martins proposes that the radius of the entire universe is actually only a little over four and a half light years. He says that the stars we see in the night sky are just a holographic illusion."

Rosen jumped back in his thickly padded chair. "This guy is taken seriously?"

"I'm afraid so," Cho said, leaning his forearms on the table. "At least by those who can understand his paper."

"We've all read it," Bambridge commented from his position next to Cho. "The man is a true genius."

"Sam," Dirk Wheeler said, "there's really no reason to believe his crazy assertion about the size of the universe. It's just that his work is so brilliant, *anything* Martins says must be taken seriously."

"That's right," Bambridge echoed.

"But it's crazy!" Sam retorted. "There's no evidence to suggest that the universe as we know it is a fake."

Lev Katzenbaum shrugged. "No one has ever directly observed an electron, or a proton, or a quark. But we believe they exist all the same. Martins has proposed that the starfield as we observe it *could* be explained holographically. The development of his spherical hologram, Sam, lends credence to his theory. You had to have been there to understand just how real his hologram was. If a little ten foot spherical hologram could generate a reality so palpably real, what would happen if the hologram was nine light-years big?" Katzenbaum shook his head. "Martins claims that the only way to disprove his theory is by physically going to that area of space. After what I saw I'm inclined to go along with him myself."

"The guy's got cohunes as big as bowling balls," Wheeler muttered. "He refuses to back down no matter how loudly and forcefully he's criticized."

Rosen pondered this quietly for a few minutes. "I've heard this Martins is a nut."

Katzenbaum harrumphed. "He is, uh, rather abrasive, as I've already said. But his work is as elegant as he is crude."

"I agree with Lev's assessment," Cho said.

""Sam, there are some people who are really nervous about this. Particularly General Pilsher and the military."

"Why?"

"Because some of them were at that demonstration and saw what one of those holos can do. Martins scared the living shit out of them. You know how paranoid they are. Mainly they are frightened by what they found from that top-secret unmanned probe to the Alpha Centauri system. There's likely to be quite a bit of support from the military and the national security establishment for a manned mission."

Sam made a note to talk to General Pilsher personally about that. "What did they find out there Lev?"

Katzenbaum shook his head. "Top, top secret Sam. Only Pilsher knows and he's not telling."

The president bristled.

"Fuck Pilsher, who does he think he is? He wants my support for this manned mission and he's keeping me in the dark?"

"Not to worry Sam," Cho responded. "All you have to do is send somebody over to Langely and he'll tell all. They'll set up a meeting for you and your national security advisor anytime you want."

The president sat silently, drumming his fingers on the table. He'd send Munroe Whitehead over there with a list of questions. If Munroe gave the OK he might go along. *If* they were forthcoming and didn't try to bullshit him like they usually did. But there was a much more important issue to be settled first.

"In your opinion, does this manned mission warrant all the political messes I'll have to get myself in to weasel more money out of Congress?"

There were chuckles all around. The four friends knew that even before reading his briefing papers Sam checked the latest opinion polls.

"Sam, the political side is your business," Cho said quickly. "But purely from a scientific point of view it would be the most exciting thing since Apollo 12 first landed on the moon."

"I agree," said Bambridge. "It's been over a half century since the last Apollo mission. The shuttle is no more, the international space station is an afterthought. The manned mission to Mars never got off the ground. It's time to break new ground."

Sam was pleased. He was a politician first and foremost, and could imagine his popularity ratings going sky-high.

Bambridge must have divined something of the sort. "Sam, it would take a long time for a ship to get out there. Even with our new ion impulse engines."

Wheeler interrupted. "Not so, my friend. Monroe Whitehead tells me that a totally new and revolutionary propulsion drive has been developed. It's the result of decades of research in the misty black military depths of top secret research. That would shorten the trip to less than two years."

"But that still might be beyond the next election." Sam was dismayed. "I might never get any credit!"

The panel members all guffawed. The stars within reach? Who cares! It was Sam Rosen all the way.

"Think of your legacy Sam," Katzenbaum soothed. "The Rosen Mission is the first to reach the nearest star."

"Yeah," said Cho jokingly. "If you time it right the ship will arrive just before the voters go to the polls."

The president was a little embarrassed at his outburst. He had let down his guard a little in the presence of his old school friends. Just last night he had exited the White House and stood on the back lawn. He had looked up at the stars in a crystal clear black sky. For thousands of years human beings had done the same thing. Before the discovery of the telescope the starfield had been thought of merely as points of light in the sky.

"Do any of you really believe that the starfield is just a sophisticated hologram?"

John Cho answered for the Board. "Not really Sam. But I'd like to find out for certain."

"It brings up a lot of questions doesn't it?" Sam asked. "If Martins is right then who made this hologram? And why?"

No one answered. Apparently there was even some doubt amongst this group of hard-headed scientists.

"Who should I send to Langley for this briefing of Pilsher's? I want someone knowledgeable who can't be browbeaten by those double-dealers over there."

"Munroe Whitehead, your National Security Advisor," Dirk Wheeler said. "He's got a PhD in physics. He's trustworthy. And he can spot bullshit a mile away."

"All right gentlemen," the president said. "I think I might stick my neck out on this one. I'll send Munroe over there and get him to decipher all of that techno-gibberish so I have a clue what this thing is all about."

A spontaneous "Hooray!" broke out in the room. Sam was pleased. All he needed now was the Congress to feel the same way.

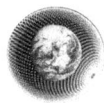

Chapter 7

PROFESSOR Martins was in the middle of his most boring lecture. Astronomy 135, the basic course. It usually drew freshman and sophomores. Or juniors and seniors looking to fulfill their science requirements. During his talk his eyes kept straying to a bright-faced girl in the front row with fine features, close-cropped red hair, and glasses. Jack recognized the signs right away. Passionate and probably good in bed. As he droned on he tried to catch her attention. She was having none of it.

Jack stopped speaking. He stood silently for a few moments at the lectern. The room slowly quieted. Someone coughed and it sounded like an explosion in the large auditorium. In the back of his mind Jack wondered if he could bottle this. Fifty kids sitting in a room, utterly silent.

He started a new thought. "The origins of the universe. What does it all mean?" He stared out into space and some of the students began to rustle nervously in their seats. What was the crazy professor going to do now? The tales of his erratic behavior were common knowledge on campus. Brilliant but volatile.

"We all know that a singularity is an impossibility. The gathering together of all of the matter and energy in the universe into one area of infinite density, therefore, cannot have occurred. Cosmological theories that postulate the universe coming from a singularity are wrong. In fact, the entire subject of cosmology is stunted. We already assume something exists but we never say how it got there."

Jack knew this was a basic review course. He was just supposed to present the standard material. Today he didn't feel like it. Today, he was going to expand their minds a little.

"We don't say it because we don't know, we can't know, and because speculation isn't science. But the fact remains that you can't get something from nothing. Right?"

No one responded. All eyes were on him, hanging on his every word and gesture. He had them.

"Metaphysical theories about the origins of the universe usually lead to circular arguments. They postulate forces or energies or data that must be logically prior. You know, the universe is really just an atom inside a larger universe. The simulation hypothesis, the Platonic idea of a higher but invisible source for all matter and energy. Where does it all end? Or begin?"

Jack was talking directly at the redhead, looking for a response. The lights were out in that skull. Oh well.

Jack returned his attention to the group. "One of the major questions in cosmology is, 'What is the size of the universe?' As some of you might have heard, I have postulated that the universe as we know it might just be a hologram, a total illusion. As far as we know intelligent life exists only on one tiny planet. The earth is an insignificant speck in an infinite universe. So why is the universe so immense? Why would anybody design something with all that wasted space?"

No one spoke until a voice from the back was heard. "Woop-de-fuckin-do."

Everybody laughed.

"OK people, lecture over."

Afterward three or four students gathered around, as usual. His classes were always crowded. Partly because of his new-found fame and the controversy that went along with it. But also because his lectures were usually entertaining and informative. Jack didn't particularly enjoy teaching but it was a strict requirement at Carleton. He usually warmed to the subject once he started. Many students had told him that his voice was compelling and easy to listen to.

Sex and cosmology, my two inspirations. That reminded him of Amara.

Later that night Jack drove over to Densingers and paid his tab before driving over to Amara's. As he entered Densingers the owner saw him and came over. Densinger apologized for his outburst but told Jack he had to behave himself. Jack was more afraid he'd get killed by the Hulkster. After the owner left the big bouncer came over and greeted Jack affably.

"Some kick you got there gramps. Where'd ya learn to do that?"

Jack grinned. "Learned it when I was at MIT. That's in Boston."

The man's eyes lit up. "I'm from Boston!"

Jack described his rich and spoiled upbringing in Exeter.

"That's a long way from where I grew up."

"I loved it in south Boston," Jack said. "The place has got character."

The big man held out his hand and they shook. "I'm Danny."

"Jack Martins."

Danny laughed. "I heard all about you, mostly from the prissy owner. You're more one of us than one of them." Danny was referring to street life versus academic life. Jack understood immediately.

The two men were pleased with each other and they chatted for a few minutes more. Jack bought Danny a beer. "Not supposed to circulate with the customers or drink on the job," the big man said. "This place is so big no one's gonna notice."

Danny got up to leave. "Whatever happened to that girl you rustled out of here?"

Jack's mind was blank for a second. "Oh, her." He screwed up his face. "She told me she didn't like me."

Danny laughed uproariously and waved goodbye.

Jack sat in the bar and drank a pitcher. He took out his letter-thin notebook, which fit neatly in his big jacket pocket. It was after 9 and he knew Amara was an early riser. Her number had been on his to-call list for weeks because of her help with the Review Committee. He knew that once reinvolved with her he would be committed and he wasn't ready for that. But he needed her.

The phone hadn't rung but once when he heard her voice. "Jack!"

"Hi Amara. Can I bother you tonight?"

The line was silent at the other end for a few moments.

"All right Jack, but you have to be out of here by 11."

Amara hung up the phone. She didn't know whether to jump for joy or kick herself. She remembered what her mother Naima told her. "Amara dear, never have sex with a man because you feel sorry for him. Above all, never let a drunk into your bed." She wondered nervously what kind of shape Jack would be in. Since that glorious night over a year ago they'd gone out for lunch and saw each other at the usual departmental meetings. But never a date. Her feelings for him had gradually subsided. But she knew that her heart and her feelings could quickly be re-ignited like a spark on dry tinder.

The doorbell rang and Jack stepped in. "Hello Amara." He tried to speak easily but inside he was vibrating like a live wire. They resonated to each other. He knew Amara felt it too.

Amara smelled the beer on his breath. Jack's clothing emitted the stale odor of alcohol and cigarette smoke. She should not have let him in, not in her present situation. But God, the man was handsome! His athletic build, fine black hair, the pale, square-jawed face with thick eyebrows and the intense black eyes looking into hers. Black and white, their story together. She had never met a gaze like his, ever. It went right through her. Behind that gaze she felt a vast intelligence and a passion for life and for her. There was also something broken and twisted. Tonight she must be very careful.

"Jack…"

"I know, I'm sorry. I've been meaning to call you for weeks …"

Tonight the alcohol did it for you, Amara thought.

"Could I have glass of water? I'm thirsty."

They went into the kitchen and she showed him the drinking glasses.

Jack saw nice cabinets with beveled glass fronts. The glasses were tinted dark blue and capacious. Functional and beautiful, just like the woman who purchased them.

Amara watched as he moved to the cabinet, opened the door, and took out the glass. His movements were graceful and purposeful with no wasted motion. From what she knew of the man, in complete contrast to the haphazard state of his life. But she remembered how he had handled her, caressed her. Despite herself she felt a growing warmth in her heart and a dangerous excitement in her loins. This was wrong. What would Leon say? She told herself that the relationship with Leon hadn't reached the serious stage. She hadn't committed to him yet.

"I'll have one too." Amara stood beside him and reached into the open cabinet for another glass. She measured her 5' 10' frame against his taller one, feeling his masculine presence.

They walked back into the living room. Jack noticed the deep bold colors on the walls and how tastefully the apartment was decorated. African sculpture, masks, and figurines were the dominant motif. There was some fine china and crystal in the glass hutch. The place was clean but not overly so.

It had a comfortable lived-in feeling. Jack sighed with satisfaction as he carefully sat on the couch next to Amara. He was embarrassed by his appearance but felt that a missing brick had been replaced in the foundation of his life.

Amara seemed to pick up on this, reading his thoughts and feelings effortlessly. She nodded her head. Without a word having been spoken there was between them a comfortable understanding.

For the first time Jack wondered what it would be like to be married to this woman. She knew him so well. So well that she left him alone. Amara knew the kernel of bitterness that lay inside him but that didn't stop her from loving him. Did he love her? It was a novel thought. Something inside him said marriage would be a bad idea.

Tonight she wore jeans that molded to her figure without being suggestive in any way, a light blue blouse, and her hair tied back in fuzzy corn rows. She was perfect, too perfect for the likes of him. The blood rushed to his face and Jack realized he'd make a big mistake. He didn't even know why he was here. He felt ashamed of himself for even thinking about using this exquisite woman for a night of good sex.

He rose to leave.

"It's OK Jack." Amara gave him a big smile.

He settled back onto the sofa. "Thanks for setting me up in that hearing."

"So you guessed then."

Jack grinned. "When I saw Matsui and Brundage I could almost feel your angelic presence from above."

Amara was pleased. She had pulled strings and called in favors to get those two on the board. She also knew that Jack had almost blown it. "You almost got expelled, Jack. Your conduct didn't help matters."

Somehow, when she said it, it didn't sound bitchy. "Yeah. Pollard and Krajicek were on me the whole time, the bastards."

"Brundage said that when you lit up outside the room he decided to erase you. Afterward he changed his mind." Amara was looking for his reaction.

"I'll remember that." Jack spoke in tones of grudging admiration. "Brundage is tough but fair." Jack knew that his was the most important vote.

"Jack, my name is going up for VP. Sather says I'm at the top of the list."

Jack was genuinely pleased. He spoke brightly. "Congratulations! You've got my vote."

"I'd rather not have it."

They both laughed.

Amara's face clouded. "Jack, I've been seeing someone."

It hit him like a body blow right in the solar plexus. He choked on his water. "You are?"

Jack noticed how uncomfortable she was. Her head was down and she fiddled with her glass. Then her head came up and she looked at him a little defiantly. "Met him at an interdepartmental meeting a few months ago. Works in the Admin building, assistant to the CFO. His name is Leon Whittaker."

Jack was silent and feeling a little sorry for himself. "That's nice." He wanted to take her in his arms and carry her to the bed He wanted to show her in the only way he knew how that he was the man for her. He was back to sex again, the preferred solution to many of his problems. That wouldn't do for a jewel that shone as brightly as Amara.

Time to go.

Jack rose quickly before he could change his mind. He held out his hand. "Thanks for seeing me tonight. I really enjoyed it."

Amara took his hand and allowed him to help her up. When his hand touched hers, both immediately felt a jolt of electricity.

Jack's heart raced. He had to get out of here now. Leon was the man for her, Leon would make her happy…

He said goodbye as cheerfully as he could and stumbled to the front door, letting himself out.

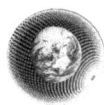

Chapter 8

MUNROE Whitehead entered the sealed conference room at CIA head-quarters in Langley. Sam Rosen had sent his most trusted confidante to get a final briefing from the Alpha Centauri Mission project coordinators. The Science Advisory Board had already given its approval for the manned mission but the decision to go ahead politically rested in his hands. The president was a practical man. Anything that was going to cost this much had to be able to be explained in terms a layman could understand.

The meeting started smoothly with greetings and handshakes exchanged. A NASA scientist was present along with Air Force General Thomas Pilsher, who ran the project. The general indicated four men seated at the end of the long rectangular table. "These men are observers. They represent the various interests of the intelligence community but will not participate in the discussion." Munroe knew that was code for, "These guys are recording everything we say and they already know what I'm going to say." Munroe ignored them. He had a list of questions to ask. Some of them were the president's. First and foremost was the skinny that a new space engine had been developed. Was it a radically new warp drive?

Lubomir Milicic, the NASA scientist, glanced over at General Pilsher. "The new space drive isn't propulsion at all Mr. Whitehead. It's much more advanced. The ship is cocooned by a ... field of energy ... that effortlessly moves the ship rapidly through space. That's as simple as we can say it in English. If you want to see the math..."

"No thank you. President Rosen is concerned about the secrecy surrounding this new development. Barely a mention of it in his briefs."

General Pilsher interrupted as Milicic was about to respond. "The new technology is part of a long-standing NASA–Air Force program investigating frontier physics and space travel. The new space drive has only been perfected within the last year. Certain ... ah ... developments have hastened its progress."

"You're talking about the Martins Sphere, general."

Pilsher nodded.

"The president and I thought that Martins' proposal was just an interesting theory. Or perhaps even crazy."

The general grimaced. "We asked our NASA scientists and mathematicians to assess the Martins concept. We expected to hear just like you thought." He glanced over at Milicic. "What we were told is that it is a coherent explanation for how the world actually works."

Munroe looked over at Milicic. "You're seriously saying that this goofball Martins could be right?"

"No rational person is going to believe that Martins' explanation for reality is the correct one," Milicic replied. "But—some of the finest minds in the world have torn his proposal to shreds, looking for errors. There are none."

General Pilsher broke in. "What we are saying, Mr. Whitehead, is that it is impossible to prove that Martins is wrong. Therefore his theory must be investigated. We have done so."

"I see," Munroe said. "That was the reason for the probe launch, was it not?"

The general nodded.

Munroe ticked off one of the questions on his list. "How fast can you go with it? Even the new ion propulsion drive that came online a few years ago would take several years to get to Alpha Centauri."

Milicic scratched his head. "We don't know what the drive's capabilities are yet. We've been able to attain a constant acceleration of over 800,000 miles per hour per hour with our test vehicles. All indications are that we can go much faster than that. With a manned mission we'd stick to what we've already established as safe. That's still good enough to get a spacecraft out to Alpha Centauri in about eleven months."

Whitehead's eyes bulged in disbelief.

Milicic was about to say something but Pilsher was ahead of him. "The technology for this mission has been under development for twenty-five years. It's been on, ah, a parallel track."

Munroe sighed. "All right general." His sources said that the new technology came from the special access programs, and was black. That meant it had been hidden from everyone. However, it was already proven and not just another attempt to grab more funding. He went down his list. "The president wants to know how can you go faster than light? My chart says that light can go approximately 5.875 trillion miles in one year's time. This distance is called a light-year."

Munroe saw the scientist nod in agreement.

"Alpha Centauri is about 4.3 light years from Sol, which is ... lets see ...about 25 trillion miles. If you are getting there in eleven months you are going faster than light can travel. It's impossible."

Milicic looked ruefully at the general. "Our national security advisor is well informed."

Milicic answered obliquely. "For a manned mission, the total trip time out is eleven months and eleven months to get back. Accounting for explore time in the Alpha Centauri system, a two-way trip would take almost exactly two years. Therefore, the spacecraft would have to travel more than four times the distance light could travel in that time."

"Precisely. It's fantastic, unbelievable. Faster-than-light travel is scientifically impossible."

General Pilsher shifted nervously in his seat. "It turns out that it is possible, Mr. Whitehead. You can tell that to the president." Pilsher glanced over at the four observers. "There are very sensitive negotiations ongoing with our counterparts in Europe, Russia, China, and others about sharing the technology. It's all highly classified material right now, for reasons you understand. But it works, we're sure of that."

Munroe wanted to throw the general off-guard. It was known that Pilsher wanted to lead the mission. "President Rosen will insist that any manned expedition be a non-military one, with an international crew."

General Pilsher flared. "I have made my wishes in this matter well known."

Munroe saw one of the observers grin. He ticked off another item on his list.

"Just so you know the president's will, general. We have been told that the services and the intelligence boys will be OK with a civilian run mission. As long as the secret talks are successful and work in the interests of U.S. national security."

Munroe noticed one of the observers look toward the other three and nod. He looked back at his list again. "The president wants to know more about the new technology."

Milicic brightened. "The engine has no moving parts and takes energy from the quantum vacuum. However, the new craft won't work unless you are free of the earth's magnetic field. So we need a simple rocket launch to get the ship out of the earth's atmosphere. When the ship returns, it goes into orbit around the earth and docks with a pickup vehicle. The astronauts come back to earth in a capsule just like the old Apollo missions."

Munroe was pleased. The president wanted a public launch and landing; something people would understand. Something you could have a ceremony at and give speeches.

General Pilsher summarized. "With the new technology there's no possibility of a breakdown or malfunction because the propulsion system is not in any way mechanical. It works faultlessly. All we have to do is turn the damn thing on and guide the spacecraft to its destination."

"All right general, we'll take your word on that. What about radiation? Our astronauts will be subjected to all kinds of gamma rays, cosmic rays, and the like during their voyage, won't they? And what about the lack of a magnetic field? Our bodies are tuned to earth's magnetic field. To become separate from it for any length of time is dangerous."

Pilsher and the NASA scientist exchanged glances. "The new drive generates a field that cocoons biological life safely inside it," Pilsher said. "We've done over one hundred tests so far without a fail."

Munroe had reached the last question on his list. "All right gentlemen. I'll inform the president." He walked out of the room and out of the facility. He was pleased that he didn't get any bullshit from Pilsher.

After the national security advisor left General Pilsher and Lubomir Milicic looked uncomfortably at each other.

"It didn't come up," the NASA scientist said.

"I'll have to tell him anyway," General Pilsher replied.

"Yeah. The probe made it out there just fine. When it got to the Martins Sphere boundary the damn thing disappeared."

Part II – MISSION

Chapter 9

Twenty years ago

TEAM Orsagh was in a top secret research station in the Nevada desert. The team looked at the strange craft lying upon the painted concrete floor. Just moments before the entire floor had been lowered from the surface by gigantic worm screws. Twelve of them, each the size of an 18-wheel truck. They had been flown into the facility on a black jet with armed personnel dressed in light-reflecting suits and glasses. Boris Orsagh wondered what he'd gotten himself into. He and his group of rocket scientists were supposed to discover the means of propulsion of an exotic spacecraft. He didn't know where it came from. He had not been given any instructions about how to proceed. The desert landscape outside the small window consisted mostly of scrub, and was dotted with a couple dozen sand-colored blisters.

A white-haired man addressed them on the plane. "You'll be sleeping and eating within the facility. You have four weeks to make your assessment. If by that time you have not succeeded in uncovering the craft's secrets another team will be sent in."

The speaker did not introduce himself. "We'll figure it out," Boris said. The man turned his back and walked away. There was something funny about that guy. At that moment the plane came to a stop within one of the blisters and the door opened. A voice said "Out!"

The big room with its ceiling about 100 feet high was well lit but there was no light source visible. The team walked along the floor toward a strange looking craft surrounded by equipment. This place was a fully equipped, underground analytical laboratory. Boris began to feel an inner excitement. Suddenly Jason Allison, their materials analyst, jumped. "There's no shadows Boris!" All of the team members stopped. "You're right Jason," Palmer Christenson said. "No shadows."

That was just the beginning of a series of anomalies that would confound Orsagh and his team, and make him question everything that he had ever known about science and aircraft.

The ship was egg-shaped. It had a smaller egg-shaped container sitting forward, toward the small end of the fuselage. The smaller egg was surrounded by snakelike tubing. This was probably the engine, Orsagh thought. He walked slowly toward the craft, motioning his crew to stay put. If there were any risks he would go first. It was a principle he'd followed throughout his career as a fighter pilot and now as a private consultant to the Air Force.

Orsagh got on a ladder and climbed up the fuselage of the craft. He immediately saw an opening that resembled the cockpit of an aircraft. But this was no aircraft. It had no wings, tail, or rudder. The fuselage appeared to have been painted with fifty coats of high gloss lacquer. He placed his hands on it. The material was soft to the touch. Boris lowered himself into the cockpit. He saw a small bench and a raised panel with several small egg-shaped indentations spaced equidistant from each other. A hemispherical opening appeared along the back wall at about head height. Behind that sat a tank about 4 feet by 6 feet by 4 feet deep. There were no controls, or none he recognized. Orsagh sat on the bench, which was only big enough for one person. He placed his head into the opening. Instantly the egg sprang to life.

"Palmer, get over here!" Orsagh shouted, but there was no need. The team had come running upon the instant. Light circulated within the egg in a figure-8 pattern of bright yellow. The tubing began to hum, emitting a deep blue glow. Boris pressed his finger into the first indentation. The light within the egg grew brighter and brighter. The glow emanating from the tubing, which twisted in seemingly random patterns around the "engine," became brighter as well. Boris Orsagh was not hurt. He felt no discomfort. He just sat there with his finger pressed lightly against what was obviously the control panel.

Palmer Christenson climbed up the ladder and checked on his boss, who raised a thumb in the "all OK" signal. Christenson stepped carefully out onto the fuselage and almost lost his balance. He braced his body against one of the tubes that curved back and forth and twisted around the engine. The tubes were of different diameters. Was it was one big tube or a series of smaller tubes? Palmer had worked on some pretty exotic aircraft. He was known as an expert in propulsion systems. But he had never seen anything like this. What was the function of the tubing? Where did the yellow energy source originate? By this time Jason Allison had clambered up the ladder. He stood next to Palmer, peering at Boris Orsagh.

Boris took his finger off the "button" and the engine slowly turned off. He pushed it again and it sprang to life once more. Funny way to design a ship! Do you have to keep touching the panel for this thing to work?

The craft was damaged. Boris had a feel for aircraft. It told him that some-one had already been through the thing with a fine tooth comb. It appeared to have been stripped of some vital components.

Boris increased the pressure on the first egg-shaped button. Christenson, crouching over the engine, observed that the light within the egg was shaped like a figure eight. The tubing began to glow again.

As Boris increased the pressure they were surrounded by a dark blue light, which expanded to touch the near wall. Some kind of energy field, Boris thought. The field resembled a fat doughnut with a tiny hole in the middle. The energy came forth from the very middle of the figure 8. A toroidal field. Whatever it was, it felt good. Nurturing, almost. The quality of this light was unlike anything he had ever seen.

Allison, standing on the ladder, noticed something very peculiar. The east wall, now touched by the field, seemed reachable. He stretched out his hand and felt the hard surface. How was this possible? That wall was well over 100 feet away. He tried it again with the same result.

The ship was situated in the middle of the room and slightly toward the east wall. The field touched only that wall and went through the floor. But the perspective of the room looked perfectly normal. The wall seemed to be about 100 feet away yet he was able to touch it with his outstretched hand.

"Mother of God," Palmer Christsenson said.

Orsagh climbed out of the cockpit and the field of energy slowly col-lapsed. The crew stepped down the ladder. Boris reached the floor and looked up at the engine, surrounded by the fine tubing. The damn thing looked a brain!

Boris Orsagh stared at the "engine." Clearly this was cutting-edge tech-nology. They weren't going to figure it out in four weeks.

The group sat on the gray floor and discussed what they had just observed. Boris gathered his team around him and they began to test...

After three weeks they were no further along in discovering how the thing worked. It became apparent that the triggering mechanism was tactile. This craft operated like a sophisticated touch screen. It would only activate when a living being occupied the 'cockpit.' Boris and the crew established that the craft was disabled. Every one of the team members had been able to enable the field and raise and lower its intensity. They could not get the thing off the ground even though the craft seemed to vibrate with a sense of power. Through simple trial and error Team Orsagh marked the sensitive areas, and their functions, on the control panel.

Team Orsagh looked for circuitry behind the control panel. They found a complicated nesting of wiring made out of the same substance as the tubing. Palmer Christenson would have called it a circuit board even though there were no resistors, capacitors, chips, or interfaces. The complex nesting of fine tubing looked organic to Boris. Jason Allison was hard put to identify the material of the tubing or the hull. It felt soft to the touch like living tissue, but it was definitely not organic. "Some kind of synthetic alloy. I have no idea how you'd manufacture it."

Exposure to the mysterious field of energy caused no harm to any of the testers. Boris Orsagh looked the scar on his right hand where he had sliced it open in a hunting accident several years before. It was gone. The skin was perfectly smooth there, as if the accident never happened.

Testing showed that the craft did not function well in the presence of strong magnetic fields. The yellow energy within the engine flickered on and off, causing the field to flicker as well. Perhaps that was how the craft crashed. Maybe it got tangled up in the earth's magnetic field.

At the end of each day the floor would rise, signaling the end of the work period. Each morning the walls within each of their cubicles would turn on. It was the signal to awaken, eat, shower, and shave. Food would appear on trays from inside a wall panel. The crew quickly learned to take all of the trays. The floor would not rise again for 16 hours. The team was not required to submit any reports and they did not see anyone, but each of them felt sure that they were under observation.

During the final week Team Orsagh finalized their pitifully few conclusions, most of which were just guesses. The engine's mechanism: unknown origin. Activation and control: initiated by brain wave activity and controlled by the operator's touch. Function: a local bending or warping of space through the generation of an unknown field of energy.

Present day, one year earlier, Vandenberg Air Force Base rocket launch facility

General Thomas Pilcher and Boris Orsagh, with his team, stood in the launch room at SLC-2W, West Pad. Over twenty-five years of research had resulted in the duplication of the engine and the design of a craft around it. The cigar-shaped probe was 25 feet long and 10 feet wide. It sat atop the specially designed Delta IV rocket and was the fruition of all their hard work.

Pilsher rubbed his hands together, excited as a child with a new toy. The engineers, although proud of their accomplishment, found little satisfaction. They were little more than idiot-savants, copying from rote a design that they did not fully understand. They had taken photographs of the engine from every conceivable angle and constructed a prototype. Materials analysts and chemists had analyzed the substance of the tubing and found a reasonable substitute. Then Orsagh and his team had constructed a 3 dimensional grid and painstakingly fitted the pieces of the craft on it. It was nothing more than a crude paint-by-the-numbers operation. Boris was a former Air Force pilot himself and a trained aircraft design engineer. He and his team, after 22 years, still did not understand the concept behind the design. Somebody must know because someone put the craft together. No one he knew did. It was the most frustrating project he had ever worked on. There was something about the design of this engine that eluded human thought. They were missing a vital concept; something that was outside the spectrum of human consciousness. But the damn thing worked!

Boris shook his head. The general stood beside him, mouth agape. His face was etched in an excited smile as the countdown went forward.

Boris felt something turn over in the pit of his stomach as the rocket lifted off successfully into space. A premonition of dread and death. He glanced quickly over at Palmer Christenson and their eyes locked. Palmer felt it too. Suddenly he couldn't wait to leave the building. He knew his involvement with this project was at an end, and his career as well. He felt as if someone had put a brick wall and a detour sign on his life. It was time to retire and play with the grandkids.

"Let's get the hell out of here Boris," Palmer said. Without another word or a backward glance at the excited general, the team marched out of the building and onto the waiting plane that would take them to the airport.

Eleven months after launch, two days after the probe went dead

General Thomas Pilsher, head of the Joint Chiefs of Staff and leader of the Alpha Centauri Project Development Team, gave a briefing to President Rosen in the White House. "We need to get a second probe out to the Martins Sphere as soon as possible."

"What happened general? My briefs for the past ten months have been uniformly positive."

"They *were* positive dammit! Excuse me sir, but I'm a little worked up. More than likely all systems just failed on that probe, Mr. President. It's happened before. But what if there's a threat out there? If there is we'd better know about it."

"What reason have you to suspect a threat, general? What kind of threat?"

"We don't know Mr. President. There was no reason for that probe to fail, no reason at all. Twenty-five years of testing has shown that the Pilsher Field is not mechanical. It cocoons or protects everything inside it, making a malfunction impossible. The only explanation is that someone or something...destroyed it."

"You don't think it had anything to do with this crazy theory of Jack Martins, do you?"

"Well, Mr. President, that's absurd of course ...not ...nobody in his right mind would even suggest it." Everything was fine after the probe left the Alpha Centauri system.

Sam easily read the general's eyes and body language. This man was afraid. It was one of the reasons he had him promoted to head of the Joint Chiefs. Pilsher was someone who wore his emotions on his sleeve. He could have no secrets from him. "Come now general, there's something else."

The general, like almost everyone who talked with Sam Rosen, felt at ease. There was a calmness and an innocence about the president that people opened up to.

"NASA was monitoring the probe's telemetry. Everyone there knew that Martins was full of shit but you could have cut the tension with a knife. As the probe got closer to the Martins Sphere limit we checked and triple checked all systems. Everything was go. Somebody said, 'approaching theoretical Martins Sphere barrier.' About a minute after that everything went dead."

Pilsher paused. "You could have heard a pin drop Mr. President. It was like somebody threw a blanket over everybody in that room. I don't know how to explain it, sir, but we all felt as if the universe itself had suddenly shrunk. Information was transmitted, a feeling...I can't explain it any better than that."

"What was it?" Sam asked.

"We aren't supposed to get to the stars."

Sam could see how agitated the general was.

"You had to have been there Mr. President, it scared the shit out of me. If you ask anybody in that room they'll tell you the same thing. Of course I imposed absolute secrecy on everybody there. They can't even speak to their dogs about it. The consensus among the Chiefs is that another probe needs to be sent out there yesterday."

The next day General Pilsher personally supervised the establishment of a special Command and Communications Center in the basement of the Pentagon. The CCC would receive the new probe's telemetry from NASA. The probe was nicknamed Cheesy-Poof after its tubular fuselage. It was packed with sophisticated instruments designed to measure gravitational effects within the craft, test relativistic effects, and measure the entirety of the electromagnetic spectrum during its approach to light speed and beyond. Systems were checked, rechecked, and checked again. There was to be no "instrument failure" on the Cheesy-Poof. The limits of the probe's propulsion system would be tested to get it out to the Martins Limit as fast as possible. It would then be rapidly decelerated. The probe would approach the Martins Sphere "barrier" at a mere crawl. Every foot of travel would be monitored. It was agreed that a probe failure meant confirmation of an anomaly and a possible threat to the planet earth. If that happened it would require a manned mission to directly contact or observe the phenomenon. Fortunately the NASA program for scientific exploration of the Alpha Centauri system was almost date and time coincident with a manned launch at this time.

General Pilsher asked Lubimir Milicic just how the probe kept contact with earth-based telemetry.

"We don't know sir. Even the generation of the Pilsher Field is not completely understood. The first probe has shown us that as long as the Pilsher Field is operational, transmissions from the probe are received in real time. It's as if the space between the craft and whatever it communicates with shrinks."

In order to test the new drive for the anticipated manned mission, human tissue samples and five lab rats were onboard. Tom Johnson, the rotund chief of telemetry responsible for naming the craft, included a package of cheese-puffs and three twinkies. "We're testing the ultimate boundaries of shrink-wrapping," he said.

General Pilsher briefed Munroe Whitehead the day before the second probe was to be launched. "The probe will be accelerated at the rate of about 800,000 miles per hour per hour. Relativistic effects are negated by the field of energy surrounding the propulsion engine. So the craft will attain the speed of light in 838 hours, or approximately 35 days. To get the spacecraft to its destination as quickly as possible we will accelerate for 7,800 hours, or 325 days. This will take it through the Alpha Centauri system. Then it will quickly decelerate the approximately 0.3 light years to the Martins Sphere boundary."

"What do you hope to accomplish with the second probe general?"

"It's all in your brief Mr. Whitehead." General Pilsher ticked them off on his fingers. "Critical mission objectives are (1), to maintain contact with the probe throughout its flight. (2), to determine whether life aboard the craft can comfortably sustain a long journey. (3), to observe any possible phenomena that could be a threat to earth. (4), a successful and uneventful flight to five light years, which is well past the so-called Martins Sphere barrier. (5), successfully turn the probe back inside the Martins Sphere to home."

Eleven months after launch the Cheesy-Poof reached the theoretical Martins Sphere barrier. All systems were functioning perfectly. A second later, all telemetry ceased at precisely the same spot as the first probe.

"Goddammit, I want answers and I want them now!"

General Pilsher's face was beet red. A pulsing blue vein stood out prominently on his left temple. The general's balding head was thrust forward only inches from Munroe Whitehead. The National Security Advisor stood next to President Rosen's desk in his White House office.

Monroe responded as coolly as he could. "To what do I owe the pleasure of this visit?"

"You know goddam well what I mean!" Pilsher was shouting and he shoved his face nose-to-nose with Munroe's. "You know how much I want this command."

"I'm sorry sir." Munroe was deferential. "You know that the mission has been packaged publicly as a test case for international cooperation and harmony. It has gotten surprising support from citizens of all countries precisely because it is non-military and open to anyone in the world." The general was out and he had known it for some time. Pilsher had just come to vent.

Munroe stood motionless as the general spun away and paced the small office like a bull ready to smash anything that moved. He would just have to weather the storm.

"The Joint Chiefs are *not* pleased. There is a potential enemy out there and we need military men onboard to handle this properly." Pilsher was shouting now. "This was our baby right from the beginning! We found the craft, we figured out how it works, and we built the prototype. Now the goddam Russians and the Chinese and even the Indians will have a hand in it."

"I'm sorry general. You know that we had to make the Alpha mission an international one. It's the biggest project planet earth has ever undertaken. It was the only way to fund the mission and keep the peace."

"Sure, that's the excuse anyway." Pilsher growled his reply, knowing the ascendancy of civilian authority.

"We all know what happened sir. When the world's militaries couldn't agree on how to share the new technology ... " Munroe met the general's eyes. Pilsher had been involved in those negotiations. "... President Rosen took over the sensitive Alpha Centauri Project negotiations. He soothed ruffled fathers and got the major powers to agree and participate. He got the reluctant backing of the minor ones as well. It was the most brilliant piece of diplomacy in history."

"That man is a gladhander," Pilsher said stubbornly. But it was true what Whitehead said. Sam Rosen genuinely liked people. He even tolerated pricks like himself, Yu Wa-shen, and that asshole Yuri Galinov, the Russian military chief. He knew precisely the concerns and personalities of each negotiator. Everything he said resonated in just the right way.

Munroe decided to throw the general a bone. "You want the truth general, I'll tell you. Sam Rosen knew that what he did would never become public because of the sensitive nature of those talks. That made him very upset. Also, he was so pissed off at you and the rest of your cohorts— "

"Those assholes aren't my cohorts!" Pilsher was indignant.

"I'm just telling you the president's thinking, general. He was so angry at the military, and you, for keeping everything so secret that in a fit of pique he insisted on a purely civilian mission. This is what he said: 'If I can't be acknowledged as the Guiding Light of mankind's first manned mission to the stars I can at least get my way in *something*.'"

Pilsher stopped his pacing and pointed a finger at Whitehead across the desk. "I don't give a fuck what the test results are, there had better be an American on board that ship."

"General, there are only six crew and a worldwide, open competition. So far there have been over 200 million applications."

Pilsher glared. "You tell that clown in the White House that we'll be watching. It's our baby, the world knows it, and we want an American leading this crew." The general stalked heavily out of the room.

Left unsaid but well understood by both men was the absolute secrecy connected with the two probe disappearances. Not even the intelligence services of other nations knew the significance of the two launches. The probes were just routine communications satellites, they were told.

Munroe wiped his sweaty forehead and called the president's private number.

"How did Pilsher take it?"

"He's really upset Sam. You owe me one."

Eight months later. Excalibur Convention Center, Washington DC

The ship had been built and was ready for launch.

It was officially known as the "Apollo's Arrow" but the builders called it the Cheesy-Poof 2. All that remained was the final crew selection.

President Sam Rosen stood at the podium in front of a huge crowd, basking in the glory. Sam was here to announce the winners of the worldwide testing for the mission to Alpha Centauri. These lucky few would compose the crew of mankind's first manned mission to the stars.

For over six months the Alpha Testing Commission had conducted the most rigorous mental, emotional, and physical testing that any human being had ever undergone in the history of space travel. There were six testing centers in North America, five in South America, seven in Europe, nine in China, and five in the rest of Asia. Ninety-nine percent of the applicants had been rejected before the testing even started. The six slots to be filled on the Orion Arrow required scientific training. The crew would be composed of a captain, an astrophysicist / navigator, an exobiologist, a mechanical and systems engineer, a physician, and a psychologist. Most of those who applied had no formal training. Those selected must be the very best of humanity in their profession. The testing criteria and procedures had been published on the WorldNet, along with the applicants. The entirety of humanity could follow the selection process.

A huge betting pool had evolved with brackets and applicants for each of the rounds of testing. This, Sam knew, had brought the human race together in support of the mission.

President Sam Rosen of the United States had been given the honor of announcing the Chosen Ones who would man the Alpha mission. The president felt slightly mollified even though he knew how far up he'd go in the polls if he could only have claimed due credit for mankind's first mission to the stars. Why, his second term would be assured!

Sam had worked up an ad-lib to the speech. He was seriously considering inserting it at the moment of the greatest applause. There he stood, at the podium of D.C.'s biggest convention center. Hundreds of the most influential names in the business world were in attendance, an international cast of political leaders, and dozens of big celebrities. He was the focal point of the entire planetary media. His words would be translated into over 100 different languages. Afterward there would be a big party. The whole world was watching. What a stage! What a moment!

"Ladies and gentlemen, citizens of earth, welcome!"

[applause]

In the back of Sam's mind he was estimating the worldwide percentage of those glued to their video sets. "It is my honor this evening to announce the results of the Alpha Mission testing. On behalf of the Commission, and the whole of humanity, we thank you for your interest!

[loud, extended applause]

"Ladies and gentlemen, the final bracket contained 96 applicants from 27 different countries. We now have the final results of the testing…" A loud roar of excitement erupted from the crowd. Sam could feel the tension in the air as several billion people sat on the edges of their seats. Now would be a great time for that ad-lib! "As you can see, there are six boxes in front of me, representing the winners. I will select a name from each box and read it aloud…" Now? No, the crowd had hushed. The first name read would be the captain of the crew, the person who had the scored highest of all the applicants. There were literally billions of dollars at stake here. His personal favorite was Robbie Evens, a tall, good-looking fellow from Texas with a degree in physics from the University of Michigan. Asian voters, who had the bulk of the world's population, had stuffed the ballot box for their favorite Liu Shen-chu of China. The Europeans favored Nigel Clarke, a physician from London. Clarke looked just like Robert Redford and had passed every one of the tests seemingly without effort. The South Americans also had their hero, the Paraguayan Oscar Lugo. Lugo was a short, compact, but brilliant astrophysicist. The Africans were enamored of Amara Mirembe of Nigeria, an exobiologist and one of 33 females to make the final cut.

In this moment of hushed silence, Sam had the entire world's attention. He slowly reached toward the box labeled "1" as hundreds of shutters clicked and lights flashed. He fished inside and brought the thick, gold-colored paper to his eyes. "And the winner is…" Sam paused, unbelieving. Here was a wild-card indeed! Sam forgot all about his ad-lib. The name that appeared had shocked him out of all thoughts of polls and second terms. "Katrina Antropov, Russian Space Academy," he intoned without enthusiasm. A woman? She wasn't even in the top 20!

The room had erupted into sound and not a few boos. "Who is Katrina Antropov? … She finished 38th! … The Commission is biased! …"

The three Russians in the audience exploded into applause. Soon everyone was politely clapping.

The President of the United States noticed that his audience was slipping away. That would never do! "Ladies and gentlemen, have you heard about the Muscovite who went to the doctor? Doctor: This medicine is for insomnia, this one is for nervous breakdown, and also take this one for depression. Patient: Thank you very much doctor. Don't you have anything besides vodka?"

Sam gradually calmed everybody down. "The WorldNet betting pool popularized the idea that the person who scored highest on the test would be the captain of the mission. It was also assumed that the six crew members would be the six highest scorers. But the Commission considered many other factors besides test scores ..."

Sam's stage presence was unparalleled and he soon had the audience in a festive mood again. "We want to congratulate Katrina Antropov for her win. She is the commander of the Apollo's Arrow!"

General Pilsher, watching at home, was disgusted that an American hadn't won the Big Prize. But Antropov was a good choice. He had met the woman in Russia on his visit to the Russian Space Academy last year. He was impressed with her character and her credentials. Easily 3 inches over 6 feet, she was an Amazon; mentally tough, and brilliant as well.

The president announced the five other winners: Sven Karlsson, engineer, from Sweden. Nigel Clarke, physician, from Great Britain. Liu Shen-chu of China, ship's psychologist. Rad Greenberg, exobiologist, from the United States. T'Munga Watanabe, the son of an African American military attaché stationed in Japan who held dual citizenship in both the United States and Japan.

The president could feel that the South Americans and the Asians were disappointed with the selections. "Ladies and gentlemen. The selection panel was composed of one member from each continent, assuring an objective choice. The winners were arrived at by physical and intellectual testing as well as psychological and emotional compatibility testing. As you know, the journey to Alpha Centauri and back will take two years. It is vital that the personalities of the crew members be harmonious."

A man strode quickly onto the stage surrounded by a phalanx of well-dressed guards. He handed the president a sheet of paper.

"Ladies and gentlemen, I have an announcement." The president paused and the room immediately went quiet. "Well, this is a real SNAFU. The Alpha Commission has decided at the last moment to include two more probes. In order to have enough cargo space for the probes that will bring back precious information about our nearest stellar neighbor, the size of the crew compartment has been reduced. One of the winners will be eliminated."

The room burst into loud, excited buzzing.

Two months later the crew was finally sorted out. The Apollo's Arrow was launched from the Jiuquan Satellite Launch Center in China with great fanfare. This was compensation for the elimination of the Chinese winner, and to save face for the Chinese. The Alpha Testing Commission had removed their representative from the crew, declaring that "a ship's psychologist will add more emotional and psychological tension to the group than will bring harmony."

Millions of people watched the launch from Tiananmen Square, where huge video sets were erected. World leaders congregated at Jiuquan. They congratulated themselves and felt as if the project had been their own brainchild. They all felt that they had been chiefly responsible for its successful completion. Especially Sam Rosen.

President Rosen gave a speech extolling the Chinese and telling the world how important their influence had been in getting the mission off the ground. Sam did this even though he knew that he was the guiding light behind it all.

Launch

All crew were strapped in to their padded chairs. The forward cabin was roomy enough so that the crew was not squashed together and had room to move. The captain sat in the center surrounded by her crewmates. Clear blisters in front, on both sides, and on the roof provided visual orientation.

The spacecraft's engine was activated as soon as the ship moved past the influence of earth's magnetic field.

T'Munga Watanabe sat in his navigator's station to the left of the captain's station and faced the front of the ship. He noticed a very faint blue light within the craft. As the Cheesy-Poof 2 began to accelerate he expected to be pushed back into his seat. But he felt nothing. It was like sitting on his couch at home watching TV.

Katrina Antropov, in the forward captain's chair facing the crew, was equally surprised. T'Munga immediately moved to loosen his restraint. "Belay that navigator!" she barked, and noticed the look of irritation on the man's dark face. Here was a man not used to taking orders from a woman.

T'Munga said nothing. On the large view screens fore and aft the earth shrunk rapidly. After only three hours it had disappeared altogether.

They were on their way!

Thirty five days into their journey the ship approached the speed of light.

All crew watched carefully. The light from the starfield had grown fainter and fainter as the ship continued to accelerate at 800,000 miles per hour every hour. The ghostly blue light within and surrounding the craft had grown more visible. Suddenly the starfield faded altogether. It was nothing like the old Star Trek movies. They had moved past the light barrier and were now cocooned within a dimpled sphere of light heading out into an unknown universe.

It took several days for the crew to adjust.

The stars were invisible through the blisters so they were closed. The blue light had faded. The ship was in a form of suspended animation traveling faster than light.

T'Munga had an instrument at his astro console that allowed the Cheesy-Poof 2 to know its current position relative to the starfield.

To Katrina Antropov it felt like they were flying blind.

A side effect of the Pilsher Field was the maintenance of biological life. Food did not spoil or rot, even when left unrefrigerated. As an experiment, Rad Greenberg left a bowl of ice cream sit for 24 hours. Although melted the sweet confection tasted as fresh as when it was made.

The crew spent their days checking and rechecking onboard instruments in preparation for their arrival in the Alpha Centauri system. They told stories and wondered whether evidence of life would be discovered. Most of all the crew debated what would happen when they arrived at the 4.618 light-year barrier.

The ship's logs and a full vid of the remarkable journey are available at ACMHQ in Brussels, and on the WorldNet. This account will ignore the journey out and concentrate on the disturbing and unexplained events that occurred after the Apollo's Arrow reached the Martins Sphere.

Two weeks after the launch the buzz had already died down on earth. Life quickly returned back to normal.

Alpha Centauri

Proxima Centauri, the closest star to Sol, was tired. It continued its process of fusion, converting the hydrogen in its core to helium. But inside it felt like a wheezing old man. It was a red dwarf star of spectral type M5 on the Main Sequence. The depleted solar nebula that birthed the star also threw out two deformed planets. These lifeless hulks moved in slightly erratic orbits which would, in a few million more years, send them crashing into their parent.

The star looked enviously across at Alpha Centauri A and B, its two binary companions 13,000 AU away. It also saw its cousin Sol, 4.3 light years away. All three were a picture of perfect health and functionality. Why couldn't it have turned out as well? Like a sickly and crippled child it had an almost stillborn birth. It was the result of a failed experiment in solar engineering. Yet it had labored on for billions of years, surprising itself.

Nothing could be done about its condition. Both its brothers were willing but unable to lend it the healthy stellar material it needed to repair itself. Even with such it was without the proper programming for well-being. Like a cancerous cell it would eventually succumb to its own deficiencies.

But life was precious. The star found a sort of satisfaction in its truncated existence. It loved to observe the goings on around its brother binaries even though the life forms on these planets had not yet achieved technological development. It was especially fascinated by its cousin Sol with its ten planets. Eight of them were teeming with life. It could almost forget its own troubles in its vicarious pleasure. It lost itself in the activities of the intelligent life which swarmed within the planetary cocoons. Especially upon the third planet.

It had already observed the two tiny craft which had shot forth from the frenzied surface of the third planet of Sol. It tried to capture them, longing to discover their secrets. But both projectiles had continued, hitting the Ring and vanishing. Now it felt a third canister being prepared. It knew that the fragile life forms within it would be coming close. Perhaps this time it would succeed. This delicious thought kept its furnace chugging away, almost joyfully…

11 months later

Rad Greenberg sat at his station gazing down at his instrument panel. His chores were done for the shipsday. The ship was now 0.3 light years past the binary system of Alpha Centauri A and B, approaching the anomaly. It had decelerated and was now traveling at sub-light speed. The stars were visible again and the transparencies were open.

They had spent a fascinating two months exploring the Alpha Centauri system before accelerating to the Martins Sphere barrier. The ship sent off two small satellites from her small cargo bay. One remained in a permanent orbit around Proxima Centauri. The other was placed in an orbit which would most optimally visit both binaries and their planets before it finally burned up in the solar atmosphere of Alpha Centauri B.

Alpha Centauri A is a yellow star of spectral type G2. Exactly the same as Sol and only slightly larger. Alpha Centauri B is also a possible candidate for supporting intelligent life. It is a slightly cooler and smaller orange star of spectral type K1. The Cheesy-Poof 1 discovered five planets orbiting A and four more around B. Rad Greenberg, the ship's exobiologist, spent his days analyzing the continuing stream of data from the satellites. To those on board the exploration of Sol's nearest neighbor had been the most exhilarating time of their lives.

In space nothing had changed. The star patterns looked exactly as their maps indicated they should. But that was to be expected. If the universe were indeed the holographic result of a boundary phenomenon then all should appear normal, even if nothing was out there. They were now entering the region of space that supposedly contained the information boundary. Their instruments detected nothing.

Yet two working probes had suddenly disappeared only a short distance from where they were now.

Rad Greenberg shuddered. What if there is an unknown phenomenon out here? Was the earth really in danger? General Pilsher thought so but Pilsher was scientifically ignorant. They had seen no sign of a hostile intelligence.

The crew had debated it endlessly on the trip out.

Nigel Clarke, the ship's eloquent physician, began the conversation one night. "I don't believe we'll see anything unusual. I think that the military is paranoid."

Katrina Andropov disagreed. "My training in the Russian Space Academy was more military in nature. We believe that Pilsher could be right."

Rad Greenberg shook his head. "I don't believe so Katrina." Everyone in the crew had long ago called each other by their first names. "Science has been collecting data about the universe for 500 years. There are 350 billion large galaxies, 3.5 trillion dwarf galaxies, and 30 billion trillion stars. That information cannot simply be dismissed with a theory, no matter how brilliantly it has been contructed."

T'Munga Watanabe snorted. "There's nothing out there at all. Martins' proposal is ridiculous."

He saw Rad Greenberg shake his head. "The problem is with religion, as it has always been throughout history." T'Munga spoke mockingly. "'See the magnificence of God's handiwork,' religion says. 'Such an infinite creation could not have come about unless by a Supreme Being or force, far beyond the pitiful understanding of mankind.' Then Martins comes along and blows holes in their carefully crafted belief systems. It's remarkable to me that religion has maintained its influence on the world stage despite most of its beliefs being countered by scientific truth. Religious influence is primarily behind this mission and they are going to be very disappointed when we find nothing." T'Munga's dark face brightened. "But it sure has been fun so far."

Karl Svenson, the little payload specialist, laughed. "I agree with you T'Munga. Jack Martins has turned the clock back 500 years! Martins' theory is purely speculative, based only on mathematics and a few clever simulations. People are offended that the universe might not be the vast and magnificent creation of an all powerful God. His suggestion that the universe might be a vivid hallucination, a sham, has pissed off billions of people. Not just religion. "

Nigel Clarke had made it clear during the trip that he was open-minded about the outcome. "I don't care one way or the other, really. Martins has attacked not only cherished scientific theories but the very concept of God. We have all seen his holograms. They are astonishing, more real than reality. I think that the mindset of everyone has been clouded by the sheer force of Martins' demonstrations. As T'Munga says, there is no reason to suppose that reality agrees with his theory. But it cannot be dismissed." Clarke smiled. "Jack Martins is quite possibly the most recognized figure on the planet."

T'Munga laughed. "Remember what Pope Clement XV said about him in that encyclical. 'Jack Martins is so arrogant he considers that he is a substitute for God Himself.' I've never met Martins but to those of us who are tired of the influence of religion, the man is a godsend."

Rad Greenberg shook his head, which always irritated Watanabe. "Your views on this matter are contradictory. You have resolutely dismissed the Martins concept. But your bias against religion requires you to support Martins' theory."

T'Munga shrugged. "I'm glad that Martins has pricked the silly bubble of religious belief and those who support such nonsense. On the other hand I am astonished at those who support the Martins concept without any proof. To me, that belief is similar to the unsupportable beliefs of religious nuts."

Katrina Antropov summed up. "Scientific curiosity and public support—including support from organized religion—got us out here. We should be thankful for that."

Everyone agreed.

As Rad Greenberg walked to his sleeping quarters he thought about his conversations with Sam Rosen, whom he met and befriended at university. Publicly the Alpha Mission was presented as mankind's first reach to the stars. A sort of modern-day Star Trek that would seek out new life and new civilizations. Behind closed doors Sam told him it was a different story. The military, politicians, religious leaders, and even some of the scientists were afraid that Martins' wild theory might be true. After rumors of the two lost probes had circulated their way along the corridors of power that feeling had intensified. "Most people are frightened by the idea that the universe could be so tiny," the president told him one day. "And I am too."

It would take two days for the Cheesy-Poof 2 to reach the Martins barrier. During those two days the tension in the ship increased exponentially.

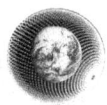

Chapter *10*

T'Munga Watanabe snorted in disgust. All looked normal through the clear composite material of the control room windows. Instruments indicated their position as almost 0.253 light years past the Alpha Centauri system relative to Sol.

The ship inched along now, very close to the so-called Martins Sphere barrier. There were no anomalies.

The Cheesy Poof 2 was shaped like an elongated cylinder and had three sections. The forward compartment contained the command chair occupied by the captain. The engineering and navigation sections were along one wall, and the scientific stations along the other wall. Katrina Antropov insisted that their view of space be unhindered as they approached the barrier, so all of the transparencies were open.

The second section contained cramped living quarters for each crew member and an exercise room. Gravity was maintained at earth normal but inactive muscles soon atrophied. Regs required each crew member to spend one hour in each 24 hour 'day' working out. This directive was ruthlessly enforced by the captain.

The back of the ship held the cargo bay.

"This is ridiculous," T'Munga Watanabe said, "but I wouldn't miss it for anything."

Rad Greenberg resisted the temptation to run through the same arguments again with his rival and colleague. "We'll see."

"Fifteen minutes till impact," Katrina announced. She gazed at a small holovid which showed the calculated view of Real Space, a tiny bubble 4.618 light years in radius from Sol.

T'Munga looked up, irritated. "Impact? With what?"

"Don't start," Greenberg said. Watanabe fired up to respond.

"Calm down mates," Clarke said. His words calmed the tall, muscular Japanese–American with the afro. T'Munga did not respond to Rad's taunt.

Katrina Antropov sat in the captain's chair in front of the control console. "Sixty seconds," she intoned. Was there something out there? A shimmering of some kind, indicating the mythical holographic boundary and the end of Real Space? Katrina looked once more, seeing nothing unusual. T'Munga was right! But then she remembered what had happened to Cheesy-Poof 1 and its predecessor. They were now approaching the exact same coordinates where the probes had disappeared.

"Full stop," she ordered.

The ship now stood in space approximately ten miles in front of the supposed barrier and as motionless as possible relative to it. The coordinates of the earlier probe's disappearance had been calculated as closely as possible but allowances must be made for error.

"Karl, launch the first probe."

One of the small rocket probes, filled with instrumentation, proceeded slowly out of the ship's side.

As the probe moved forward Antropov moved the ship, always keeping at least 1,000 feet of distance between it and the probe. After fifteen minutes Watanabe began to laugh mockingly. "Look at us. We're like a bunch of scared school kids afraid of the dark." Rad Greenberg was irritated but the excitement he felt was beginning to turn sour within him. He began to feel that he had been wrong all along.

Nigel moved next to T'Munga and laughed with him. Soon the crew was laughing and releasing the tension that was within each of them.

No one noticed that the little probe had disappeared.

Antropov looked up and shrieked involuntarily. "T'Munga, full stop." She was disgusted with herself. At the very moment when she should have been paying close attention she had allowed herself to lapse into laziness. It was an unconscionable dereliction of duty and she would mention it in her captain's log.

"Karl, where is that probe?" Katrina said.

Svenson scrambled to his station. "It's gone!"

"What do you mean it's gone?" T'Munga stepped to the little man's console and took a look for himself. "Shit on a stick."

Behind him Rad Greenberg smiled smugly.

"One precious probe wasted because of my carelessness," Katrina muttered. There were now five left in the cargo bay. The probe had sent back its telemetry to the ship's data banks but there was simply no substitute for human observation. "Launch another probe Karl," she commanded.

The probe began moving slowly forward. This time all hands kept their eyes peeled. T'Munga walked forward, just behind the captain's chair, and stood staring. After two minutes of tension everyone relaxed. Nothing was happening. Then the little probe gradually disappeared. First its nose vanished. Then, like James Earl Jones exiting the Field of Dreams, it was no more.

T'Munga stared in disbelief. Nigel and Karl, supposedly manning the data input stations, stood with mouths agape. Katrina slammed her palms down on the navigation console.

"Report!" she barked, a little too loudly.

Svenson glanced at the readouts in disbelief. He said nothing.

"Karl!" Antropov said. "Report!"

Svenson recovered. "Captain! I said nothing because there is nothing to report."

T'Munga strode across the cabin and looked at the display. "I don't believe it. Captain, the probe sent back …absolutely nothing. All instruments read null."

"Null? Explain!" Antropov was a non-scientist dealing with academic types. She sometimes found their behavior incomprehensible. One thing she was sure of: the biggest space mission in earth's history would not be a failure. Not under her command.

T'Munga turned and faced Katrina. "Our instruments have shown that the …holographic barrier, or whatever it is, is precisely 103.67 feet in front of us. Beyond that, instrumentation detects … not nothing, but an utter absence of anything."

"That's correct captain," Svenson affirmed. "It seems that what's out there is not out there at all. I mean it's not an emptiness but a complete nothingness. No space, no time, an utter lack of anything."

"Null space," T'Munga explained.

"So what does it mean?" Katrina asked.

"It means," Rad blurted, "that the universe as we know it is just an illusion."

Chapter *11*

Katrina Antropov stared blankly into space. She was unable to accept what she had just heard. "What happened to the probe?"

Watanabe shook his head. "To the best of my knowledge it no longer exists."

"But what *happened* to it?" Katrina demanded, not understanding.

Neither T'Munga nor Karl had a response. Rad Greenberg felt elation. He had seen that thing just vanish yet the starfield around them looked perfectly normal. "Martins was right!" he exclaimed. T'Munga was disgusted.

"Check for instrument malfunction," Antropov ordered. Karl went to work. Each of the crew was hoping to hear that their controls had somehow gone haywire. After about five minutes the little man nodded affirmatively to T'Munga, who stood next to him. "Instrumentation seems to be functioning normally, captain."

Katrina addressed Karl Svenson. "What is your recommendation?"

"Fire off another probe. I don't believe what I just saw. Perhaps the sequence of events we just observed was itself holographic."

"By gad," Nigel Clarke exclaimed.

T'Munga was sarcastic. "Yeah, and maybe we're just holograms too."

"Enough," Antropov said, glaring at her navigator and co-pilot.

There were still three of the probes left, might as well use them. "Go ahead," she said to Svenson.

"This time," Rad said, "look for boundary phenomena." Rad Greenberg seemed to be the only one who accepted the unfolding drama. His eyes were shining and he was almost jumping up and down in his excitement.

"Good idea," T'Munga said. "If Martins is right, IF he's right, there may be some turbulence or other physical evidence at the edge of this …whatever it is."

Karl quickly went through his checklist, preparing to launch the third probe. "Ready."

All eyes were on the tubular shaped probe that had emerged from the cargo hold. It was 20 feet in length and 6 feet in diameter. "Bring it up to just before the …barrier," T'Munga said.

Katrina said nothing, allowing the scientists to do their work.

Karl scanned the area and analyzed the data as it came in.

"There is no boundary phenomena," Svenson reported to his captain. "Or at least nothing that shows up on our instruments."

"So Martins is wrong," Watanabe said with satisfaction. Martins had reported a shimmering fuzziness around the periphery of every one of his spherical holograms.

"But he's right about the big picture," Greenberg said. Rad was not able to resist a rebuttal of Watanabe's assertion.

"That has yet to be determined definitively," T'Munga retorted.

"What happens if the third probe disappears as well?" Clarke asked.

"Then we might just have to go in ourselves," Antropov said from behind them.

Karl Svenson spoke. "I'm at a delicate moment here …Watch!"

The probe was now touching the "barrier" at its very tip, as closely as Svenson could bring it. Slowly it inched forward and the nose of the little rocket gradually vanished. There was no damage whatsoever to the rest of the craft. The barrier, or whatever it was, simply erased a portion of the fuselage without any mark at all.

"Don't go in too far," Katrina ordered. "Back it out before the forward thrusters vanish."

"Uh, right," Karl said.

T'Munga stared in disbelief. But he was a scientist first and foremost and admitted to himself that he had been wrong. "I'll make everyone here a bet. I say what has entered Nullspace is gone and our probe will return truncated."

"I agree," Nigel said. "And I," Karl agreed.

"Well," Rad said. "In Martins' paper …"

"To hell with his damn paper," T'Munga said. "Do you agree or not?"

"No," Rad said. "Nullspace will have no effect on the matter and energy of our probe." He said that just to contradict Watanabe but he didn't really believe it.

Karl began to back the probe out of Nullspace. To Rad's irritation it did not re-materialize.

T'Munga was smug. "You see, I was right."

Just as the probe was fully backed out it became entirely visible again.

"What the hell?" Nigel exclaimed.

Karl spoke. "I checked the data stream. The forward portion of that object was not there. Now it is."

"Are all devices in the probe's forward compartment still operational?" Katrina asked.

"Yes, it seems that way. Everything on board is within designed tolerance levels. Readings are the same now as before."

Karl repeated his earlier assertion. "What if what we're observing is itself a holographic illusion?"

No one had an answer.

After further experimentation it was discovered that only when the probe had fully exited Nullspace did it return to normal. However, a probe fully immersed was not recoverable. It simply vanished. But where did it go?

There were two probes left. Katrina decided to partially immerse one of them and to return it to the ship's cargo bay. Karl Svenson would perform a thorough analysis and inspection of the craft and its recording instruments.

"Now launch the last probe and set it just in front of the barrier," she ordered. "Earth can analyze its telemetry and continuously monitor the barrier."

"What do we do now?' Nigel Clarke asked, although he knew damn well. The eyes of all crew met for a second and quickly turned away. Silence held within the cabin. It was broken finally by the captain. "I say we go in."

The men blanched.

"You're the captain," T'Munga said. "But I think it's a foolish gamble. At the very least there'll be a hull breach and we'll lose our atmosphere."

"Yes," Nigel said, "but the Cheesy-Poof 2 has one advantage over the probes. We can measure the effect of this nullspace on the ship's Pilsher Field before we enter."

Karl Svenson snapped his fingers. "Of course! Good thinking doctor." Karl was excited. "The field is roughly spherical and extends approximately

100 feet around the ship. We can test the barrier's effect on the field without the probe actually touching it."

"All right," Katrina said. "Everybody get into your suits in case we lose our atmosphere. T'Munga, nudge the ship closer until the Pilsher Field contacts the barrier."

The men agreed and scrambled into their suits. All aboard knew they had to go in. Individually, none of them were strong enough to voice that course of action. But their captain had come through. She had overcome her fear and theirs as well. The men's respect for their lady commander went up a notch.

T'Munga began to inch the ship closer to the barrier, guided by the visuals and data from the RealSpace console. When the Pilsher field surrounding the ship contacted the barrier, the portion of it that entered nullspace simply disappeared. Nothing whatsoever unusual occurred within the ship.

"It's impossible!" Rad cried. "The Pilsher field should have lost integrity and coherence."

"Check your instruments," Katrina ordered. All consoles read normal, including the ship's life support systems.

"Gentlemen, we'll have to go in physically if we want to solve this mystery," Katrina said.

"We'll need to get permission from ACMHQ before we risk the entire mission," T'Munga warned.

"Fuck ACMHQ," the captain said. Watanabe grinned.

"Yeah, fuck 'em," Karl agreed, shocking his crewmates. The straight-laced little man had never shown anger or even used harsh language during the entire voyage.

After further debate it was agreed that Captain Antropov would have the honor of moving the ship into the barrier. Surprisingly, the ship's navigator did not argue the point. T'Munga admitted to himself that he was too nervous and excited to do it.

Slowly, Katrinav inched the ship forward while the crew held their collective breath. Sweat broke out on the captain's forehead as she manipulated the controls.

The ship touched NullSpace. Instruments and visuals showed an opaque gray oval 6 inches in diameter. The oval was in the shape of the ship's hull, at the bow of the ship. Antropov inched the ship in further. The oval increased in size as it moved toward them. "We've reached the environmentally sensitive portion of the ship," Katrina announced. "What say you?"

The four men glanced quickly at each other. Svenson spoke for them all. "Let's go!" Then he added quickly, "but slowly, OK?"

The men laughed nervously. "All right boys, here goes."

A dark gray oval appeared at the forward edge of the cabin, growing slowly larger. T'Munga closed his eyes, Nigel held his breath, Karl got out his calculator and Rad just stared. Absolutely nothing unusual occurred inside the cabin as the oval grew as large as the ship hull. The gray nothingness was now below their feet and above their heads and five feet away from the captain's control panel at the front of the cabin.

Katrina stopped the progress of the ship. Karl looked at his readouts. "No motion, no temperature, no atomic structure."

T'Munga opened his eyes and spoke mischievously. "I dare you to touch it."

Katrina was irritated at this boy's game but fascinated as well. She did not reply. She was thinking the exact same thing. She could almost lean forward from her captain's chair and reach it with an outstretched arm. If she dared.

The rest of the crew slowly approached the oval. Floor, ceiling, walls, and hull had simply vanished, replaced by a gray membrane hanging out into …what? Nothing was visible beyond or within or on the surface of the gray oval. It appeared to be of zero thickness. Nigel Clarke stared into it and he fell to the floor. "That thing …" he gasped, "it's …it's …*nothing!*"

T'Munga knew just what the doctor was talking about. It could not be but was. It possessed a cold and terrifying pristineness that stemmed from a complete lack of anything. At the back of his mind T'Munga wondered why it appeared gray to his eyes.

Antropov descended from her chair and stood directly in front of the oval. It looked to her a little like one of those lifeless skies in the middle of a Russian winter. But it was not cold.

The crew of the Cheesy Poof 2 stood spellbound before the unknown phenomenon. The four scientists had no more notion of what to make of it than a schoolboy upon encountering the Schroedinger wave equation. Karl Svenson looked sideways out of the cabin and saw normalcy. The stars all looked right.

Finally Katrina broke the silence. "We ought to do something. After all, the second probe was not damaged."

"So far as we can tell anyway," Karl said.

T'Munga stepped forward and was about to put his finger inside when it was slapped away. "Let the captain do it," Rad said. He was curious whether this hot-shot young lady was up to it.

Katrina felt the eyes of the men upon her. She took off her suit glove and hesitantly reached into the oval. The captain's index finger disappeared up to the knuckle. The captain gasped and a look of surprise came quickly over her features. She slowly withdrew the digit. The leading portion of her finger, as it exited the oval, was gone.

Nigel Clarke bent forward to look head-on at the stump. He expected to find a bloody mess. Instead, the cross-section of Katrina's finger neatly contained the same gray nothingness. The grayness covered the stump and sealed it perfectly.

Katrina exhibited not the slightest discomfort. The ship's physician continued to observe the truncated finger in fascination. As the finger was completely withdrawn, the severed portion reappeared.

Antropov laughed and the men burst into conversation. They peppered Katrina with questions.

"Protocol, gentlemen," she said. The men became silent. This was not a military mission but there was a chain of command. "Senior officers first," she directed.

Rad Greenberg said, "Sir, you did not seem to feel any pain during the insertion process. Would you please describe exactly what you experienced?"

Karl raced quickly over to his console and grabbed a recording device.

"When my finger went in I felt like the inserted portion was no longer part of my body." She looked puzzled. "I felt as if the part of my finger within that stuff had *never been* part of me. I don't know how to describe it. My memory of ever having that part of my finger was gone!" She stopped and put her hands to her face, astonished. "As I pulled out I never noticed that I was missing half my finger. It was only after it fully re-emerged into real space that my memory of it returned. Only after it did, my finger reappeared."

"Captain," said Nigel, "I observed the cross section as it came out and saw the same gray stuff covering your stump. It was like a perfect bandage. As if someone had cut off your finger with a knife of infinite sharpness."

"As I said, I have absolutely no memory of anything out of the ordinary the entire time my finger was in there."

After several more questions and answers T'Munga said, "Now the question is, do we go in all the way?"

"Are you still game?" Katrina asked.

The men all gulped but after an hour of debate, the crew came to unanimous agreement.

"Prepare for immersion," Katrina said. "But first, place the vid recording of this incident in a sealed container and place it in front of the barrier. If we don't come back it might be valuable to a future earth mission. I want everyone to write a report and put it on a message disk. Include any personal letters or communications to family and loved ones. We'll eject a separate canister with those."

Now that they were committed the crew began to have second thoughts. To enter Nullspace seemed sheer madness, but they had already committed to the action. The five crew members were a typical human group. Once agreement was reached on a course of action it was very difficult to turn back. Everyone felt that it would be cowardly to chicken out at the very end.

After a couple of hours all was in readiness.

Katrina activated the communication console. She beamed a short message to ACMHQ about their plans and a brief summary of their discoveries. Communication with earth was almost in real time inside the Pilsher Field (a phenomenon that made no sense whatsoever, and which no one could explain). There was a delay of about an hour, which made conversation impossible. During the flight out they had just beamed a summary of events at the end of each shipday.

"Hah!" T'Munga said with satisfaction. "ACMHQ won't like this at all."

Katrina grinned. "That's why we're just going in. If we let them decide they'd probably want us to turn back for home." Which is undoubtedly the sane decision.

Rad thought about what President Rosen would say about their proposed plunge into Nullspace. He almost burst out laughing. "No, don't do it," Sam would say. "Just think how much popularity I'll lose if you don't come back."

It was decided to just plunge in and get it over with.

"What could go wrong," Nigel Clarke joked just before they strapped in. "The worst that can happen is that we'll be trapped in Nullspace forever." Or cease to exist, in which case it didn't matter.

The crew laughed nervously, breaking the tension a little.

Katrina backed the ship a couple of miles away from the barrier and then accelerated as rapidly as possible.

The ship hit the barrier. For a brief instant a large gray oval was visible; then nothing. Only the last probe and the two canisters remained, silent and unmoving.

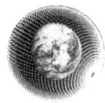

Chapter *12*

I NSTANTLY the crew found themselves sitting in a circle. They faced each other on a flat, smooth, gray surface that seemed to continue unbroken to infinity. Above their heads the "sky" was also a uniform light gray.

"Where are we?" T'Munga said.

Rad Greenberg just stared uncomprehendingly.

"Depressing place this," Nigel offered.

Rad laughed nervously but said nothing.

Katrina sighed. It reminded her of Moscow in the dead of winter. She didn't have a car and was forced to walk or take the subway. She never noticed her surroundings in the bitter cold. The great city was featureless in her eagerness to get to her destination.

Karl Svenson had never seen anything so perfectly flat. He concentrated, trying to find a reference point from which he could calculate a distance. But there was no recession of the barren landscape into the distance. It simply continued without end, in all directions, as far as he could see. In the infinite depths of outer space at least the stars served as a background. Karl realized with a jolt that the stars weren't really there. Martins had been right!

"It's not physically possible to have a perfect plain that goes to infinity," Karl said.

"In that case if we walk far enough we should come to the end of it," Nigel Clarke said.

"Yeah." Rad Greenberg was bitter. "We can walk off the end of the world."

"This place is clearly artificial," T'Munga said angrily. He didn't appreciate practical jokes. Their mission to the stars had turned farcical. "If it's artificial then somebody made it. I want to find these assholes."

It was T'Munga Watanabe all the way, Katrina thought. Nigel and Karl smiled and the depressing tension between the crew lifted a little.

Rad Greenberg was depressed. "The universe has turned out to be just a clever illusion." His arguments with T'Munga seemed trivial now.

Nigel tried to lighten the mood. "Why couldn't we have come to a desert island with lots of beautiful women?"

This attempt at humor was lost on Rad, but Karl Svenson laughed cheerfully. "My thoughts exactly."

Katrina saw that the physician and the engineer had already accepted their predicament. T'Munga was adjusting normally. Considering his abrasive personality, anger was a healthy reaction. She was a little worried about Rad Greenberg. His temperament, never cheerful, had taken an even more sullen turn.

Like Rad Greenberg, T'Munga was also bitter about the turn of events. He had imagined, upon their return to earth, stepping off the ship to the accolades of a good portion of the human race. He would write a book, lecture, and become the center of attention. And women! They would be falling all over him.

Katrina interrupted his thoughts. "C'mon, men. We're not solving anything by sitting on our butts." She began to stride forward, as if testing her continued authority over the crew.

The men got up and began to follow her.

"How do you know we're going in the right direction?" Nigel asked.

Katrina stopped and turned. "I don't. But we have no food or water. I intend to find the Cheesy Poof and get out of this godforsaken place." She knew she had to get them doing something, even if it was pointless. Her decisiveness spurred the men and all four caught up with her her. The crew seemed to accept the continuance of her authority by default.

Each was dressed in the standard gray mission jumpsuit, made of a light synthetic fabric, and athletic shoes. On ship two exercise periods were mandatory. One involving the lifting of weights, and the other aerobic. No one wanted to run the treadmill in a pair of heavy boots and the crew had insisted on light footgear. Since it was never intended that the crew ever leave the safety of their ship, it was an easy decision for the mission planners. They were dressed perfectly for their journey across the plain.

The crew trudged silently on and on, hearing only the rustling of their jumpsuit fabric. Nigel Clarke was seriously worried about provisions. After what seemed like several hours he glanced at his chronometer, curious to see how much time had elapsed. The instrument's display was frozen.

"Hold it!" he barked. His words sounded like a jackhammer in this utterly silent place, which was devoid of life or movement. Everyone came to a stop.

"What is it?" Katrina saw Nigel looking at his wrist. She moved the material of her parka and exposed her own timepiece. "The display isn't moving," she said stupidly.

"That's right Katrina." Nigel met her eyes with a smile. In those eyes she read understanding and a cool confidence, but there was something else as well. Her heart fluttered a little but she kept her voice calm. "We need to talk about this." She motioned for the crew to sit.

Karl Svenson continued walking, intent on something in the distance.

"I assume everyone has noticed that they are neither tired, hungry, nor thirsty," Nigel remarked. As crew physician, he was supposed to notice these things.

"Fuck," Watanabe said.

Rad Greenberg swore. "I was just noticing that myself."

Suddenly Karl Svenson shouted. "I've found something!" The others hurried over to where Karl was standing. "Watch." Karl slowly reached his arm out and his finger disappeared.

"Great balls of fire," Rad said. "Just like our entry into this place." He moved to stand beside the engineer. "Do that again." Svenson stuck his finger forward and part of it disappeared. Rad could find no evidence whatsoever to indicate that anything was there. The plain seemed to stretch out forever.

"Boundaryless," Watanabe said.

Katrina Antropov was beginning to get angry. Nothing they had experienced so far made any sense. She intended to solve this mystery right away. "Hold hands everybody. On the count of three, everyone move forward at the same time."

Karl, at the far left, grabbed T'Munga's hand in his right. Rad Greenberg grasped T'Munga's right hand and took the captain's left hand. Nigel, on the far right, held Katrina's right hand gently in his left. The group stepped forward.

The five humans found themselves back in the Cheesy Poof 2 They were all standing in the same positions as just before departure. Nigel quickly glanced down at his wrist chronometer and found that its hands again moved forward. "No time elapsed while we were in there."

"Look!" Greenberg pointed to the transparency. They were no longer in outer space. The ship rested upon a circular platform, level with the ground. Before them was the most beautiful scenery he had ever set eyes on.

Katrina smiled at Nigel Clarke, who came over and put his arm around her. She noticed that he was taller by an inch, and broad of shoulder. For some reason she no longer felt it necessary to maintain her status as captain. "Let's go out and see!" she cried, feeling a rush of childish joy.

The crew stumbled over themselves, laughing and shoving each other out of the exit portal. *I haven't felt this good since before Mansur left,* Rad Greenberg thought, as he jumped onto the grass of the meadow. The platform rested in a small glade surrounded by flowers and trees. Rad identified beech, birch, oak, maple, walnut, mahogany, Douglas fir, and redwood. He knew that these trees could not possibly have grown in such close proximity. Yet here they were. Overhead, clouds scudded in an aquamarine sky. A yellow sun, almost directly overhead, shone brightly. Rad looked directly at it without hurting his eyes. The meadow itself was high on a mountain and provided a spectacular view of a rushing river at least 3,000 feet below. A wide variety of trees lined the side of the mountain. Behind them the rock rose higher still. Rad craned his neck and saw a snow covered peak, impossibly high. This place sure looks like earth but it feels subtly different. Different in a good way. Rad broke out into spontaneous laughter. The tension and anxiety he had known for over a decade vanished into the atmosphere of this place. The ambient temperature was cool. Everything here seemed fresh and new but curiously ethereal. He took off his shoes and felt the living carpet of green underneath his feet. He felt the sun in his face. For the first time since he had stepped on board the ship he was surrounded by life. Life! Life is good. Now where did that come from? Ten years ago his wife, also Moroccan born, had left him for another man. After that a part of him had died. But now he felt utterly refreshed. "Hey Watanabe!" he shouted, waving his arms. "Explain this!"

"I can't my friend," his former adversary said. T'Munga walked up to Rad and gave him a hug. Greenberg was amazed. He stepped back and stared at the tall man with the fuzzy afro. "It seems right doesn't it?"

"Yes," T'Munga said confidently. "It does." Watanabe turned and began to inspect his surroundings.

Rad noticed that their little glade was separated from a larger meadow, which contained more of the circular groves. The meadow itself rested upon an outcropping from the side of the mountain. It was approximately a half mile or so in diameter.

Meanwhile Katrina had her arms around Nigel Clarke. His arms tightened around her and she was just about to raise her lips to his. Just then she noticed, over his shoulder, movement in the distance. She shoved him backwards to get a closer view and Clarke almost tripped over his feet. "My," he said, "you sure are strong." Katrina, intent on her observation, had completely forgotten him. Clarke tried again. "Perhaps you don't believe in kissing on the first date?"

Katrina turned to him and smiled. "Oh, sorry. I'm afraid my mission training takes over no matter what the situation."

"Is there something out there?"

"I think so."

"Well then, let's go into the ship and use our instruments to find out what it is."

"I can't believe I didn't think of that!" Normally she would have been disappointed in herself. In this cheerful and unthreatening place such an emotion seemed inappropriate.

As they were about to walk to the ship, Karl shouted. "Look!"

An airborne vehicle was rapidly approaching.

The craft, egg-shaped with the little end at the front and a bubble top, silently landed in front of the ship. The five humans waited expectantly for signs of life from the little vessel. But it just sat there.

T'Munga walked up to the ship and rapped on the door. "Helloooo! Anybody home?" An opening appeared in the hull and Watanabe stepped in. The ship had six seats but no controls. He sat down in one of the forward chairs, a simple bucket seat with no restraining strap. "Strange sort of ship. Can't see out of the damn thing." T'Munga tapped the hull with the tip of his finger. Instantly the curved wall became transparent.

"Nice trick!" T'Munga waved to his companions, motioning them aboard.

As soon as everyone was seated the craft took off. T'Munga showed everyone how to clear and opaque and clear the hull. The crew of the Apollo's Arrow gazed intently out of the window, inspecting their surroundings.

They flew away from the mountain and into the gorge a thousand feet above the rushing river. Then the world around them abruptly shifted. They were now traveling over a vast green ocean, with a whitish-yellow sun a pinprick in a yellow-green sky. There was no life here, no clouds. The water was perfectly still. "It's utterly foreign, but beautiful," Katrina said. She glanced at Nigel, seated across from her. After a couple of minutes their world shifted again with the same abruptness. The ship flew over an immense city with smoke bellowing up from uncounted factories. The sky was obscured in a polluted haze. There were no roads, houses, or any indication of human habitation. "This place looks completely automated," Karl Svenson remarked. "Ugh," Katrina said with disgust. It reminded her of some of the ugly, concrete housing structures built during the communist era in Moscow. Again, an abrupt shift and they entered a strange world of purple growths under a red giant of a sun that filled the sky, shining its soft red light everywhere. The plants swayed gently, rustled by a soft breeze.

The craft passed through several more worlds. Their craft moved through a small fishing village on a large bay. "Looks like the village where I was born," T'Munga said. Each time they shifted the weather often abruptly changed. They entered a frozen world of ice with a raging blizzard buffeting the sides of the craft. Karl let out a yelp but the little egg-shaped ship was unaffected. Nigel Clarke had been checking his wrist chronometer and announced that the shifts occurred every three minutes.

"Omigawd," Nigel said. Beside him Katrina stiffened. They had just entered deep space and saw themselves in the Cheesy Poof 2 just before their entry into Nullspace. The three stars of the Alpha Centauri system were visible in the background. The crew stared at themselves, frozen in time, as their little craft sped past the larger ship. Then they were out. Blazing sunlight filled the cabin, forcing everyone to shield their eyes. Three minutes later the scene changed again, and again, and again …

"This is pointless!" Katrina shouted. "Do any of you scientists have any idea what's happening to us?"

"Not a clue," Nigel said. "I've been lost since we exited the Martins Sphere."

"I say that we're experiencing a series of incredibly sophisticated holographic images," Karl said.

"Your solution to everything," T'Munga said, irritated.

Karl laughed. He was too used to T'Munga's moods to feel offended.

"I agree," Rad seconded. "The alternative is that we're jumping from world to world through some kind of wormhole. But there's no evidence of that."

"But why?" T'Munga exclaimed. He smashed his fist against the side of the craft in frustration. "Goddammitt, I want to know what's going on!" For him the fascination of this place had quickly worn off. T'Munga did not admit it, but when they entered Nullspace he had become almost paralyzed with fear. The idea that the universe was an illusion was to him absurd and fantastic, a madman's fantasy. Even though he was intrigued with Martins' theory he did not for even a moment seriously consider that it could be true. But when they arrived on the featureless gray plain he had felt the life force draining out of him as if in some horrid nightmare. As a scientist, the events of the past two days were utterly inexplicable. T'Munga Watanabe did not care for mysteries.

T'Munga left his seat and raised his arms upward, his fingers almost touching the bubble top. "Where are we?" he demanded. As if on cue the ship moved swiftly upward. In another abrupt shift they found themselves above an immense plain marked off in huge squares. It was like viewing farmland from an airplane except that each of the squares was actually a prism. The sky and the weather above the square landscapes reached several thousand feet above the ground. Some of the prisms contained clouds. Others had bright sun. Some were dark as night and others brilliantly lit. The variety of climates, colors, and atmospheres made for an astonishingly gorgeous feast for the eyes. "Like a gigantic city of beautiful skyscrapers," muttered the ship's astrophysicist.

Rad Greenberg, sitting in his seat to T'Munga's left, was numb with disbelief. He saw himself emotionlessly as from a distance, his trained scientific mind a calculator. He estimated the ship had reached a height of about 20,000 feet. The squares measured about ten miles on each side. The plain contained an astonishing variety of environments, some of which they had already visited. He let his eyes travel to the horizon and swore. There appeared to be no limitation to his line of sight. "No horizon line, just like in Nullspace," he announced. His companions were either too enthralled or too anesthetized with the panorama to even reply. The excitement he had felt in the glade now vanished. Rad felt just as depressed as he had during their walk in the grayness of Nullspace. He looked overhead through the transparent bubble of the ship. There was no sky or sun. A golden white light effortlessly illuminated this place.

To Karl Svenson's eyes the plain appeared perfectly flat and stretched out to infinity. He was astonished at how effortlessly the wildly different ecosystems blended together. "I wish we could get a closer look at these things." The ship again responded, lowering itself to afford a better view. The landscapes were illuminated with a sharpness that afforded easy viewing of even the smallest details. Karl became fascinated by an icy windblown arctic landscape with a dull gray sky. It was surrounded on four sides by desert environments. At the boundary a snow bank unexpectedly became a sand dune. It was impossible. The thermal disequilibrium should have resulted in violent atmospheric disturbances at the boundaries. Yet all seemed calm and well-ordered out on the immense plain even though the demarcation between each ecosystem was impossibly abrupt. Each environment was completely self-contained. Karl saw a white-furred animal dart out of a snow bank heading for a hilly, high desert environment adjacent to it. When the animal reached the boundary it disappeared.

"Excuse me captain. I think I might know what's happening out here."

"Go ahead Karl. My head is spinning!"

"This plain is composed of connected, orientable three-manifolds. But how it was done is incomprehensible."

"Explain," Rad asked.

"A three-manifold is a topological surface that has one or more sides abstractly 'glued' to another side," Karl explained. "Like one of those old computer games where the plane disappears off the screen on one side and reappears magically on the other side. It's the same in three dimensions. Imagine that the universe is a cube with the front side glued to the back side, the left side glued to the right and the top glued to the bottom. You would exit on any side of the manifold and come out on the opposite side. Same with a sphere, or any three-dimensional object like the prisms we see here. That might explain the abrupt changes we see below. It might also explain the disappearance of the probes and the absence of boundary phenomena. There is nothing 'outside' the self-contained structure of the manifold."

T'Munga was amazed. "So you're saying that each of these prisms is a self-contained little universe?"

"That's right," Karl said. "If Martins is right, so is our universe. And if that is so then maybe our probes just came out on the opposite side of the Martins Sphere."

"Karl, you're making me dizzy." Katrina held her head in her hands.

"Sorry boss. I'm an engineer and I like to have explanations for things." Karl was apologetic. This Amazon was completely self-sufficient but she was still a woman.

Nigel pointed to the plane of prisms. "How could this be engineered?"

Karl thought for a moment. "You can only do it in four physical dimensions. What we are seeing here is nothing short of an engineering miracle."

"Are you saying that we're actually in a four dimensional space?" NIgel asked.

"Very possible," Karl said. "A four dimensional hyper-object would have an extra dimension. You could have a whole bunch of three-dimensional universes sitting on it. Just like you have six two-dimensional planes sitting on the faces of a cube. Whoever designed this has technology far in advance of ours."

"That's a frightening thought," Rad said. "Maybe that idiot Pilsher was right. Maybe there is some sort of threat out here."

"But who made them?" T'Munga demanded. "And why?"

Karl shrugged his shoulders. "Your guess is as good as mine."

"Ship, set us down in that high desert environment," Katrina ordered. "We'll do a little exploring." The little craft obeyed.

The crew found themselves in a hilly land of browns. The barren ground was covered with rock and sparse vegetation. The sky was a deep blue. The sun, just over the horizon, lit the landscape with the bright clean light of early morning.

"This is incredible," Nigel declared. "I could have sworn that these prisms were finite little boxes. Now that we're down here it looks just like the surface of a planet."

"You were right Karl," Rad said. "This looks like a self-contained world." Rad looked up at the starfield, now fading in the silvery light of the rising sun. "The prisms couldn't be more than 10 miles on a side and five miles or so in the air. I see no evidence of a boundary anywhere."

"Just like the starfield before we entered the Martins Sphere!" Katrina exclaimed.

T'Munga's mind exploded with realization. "Or from earth itself!" Watanabe looked like a man who had just seen rabbits falling from the sky. "Karl said the prisms were self-contained universes. It appears that they are. But we know they are finite because we saw them from the air."

"Correct," Karl agreed. "Therefore, although we cannot see the boundaries of the three-manifold, they must exist."

"Yes. But when we hit the boundary of this prism do we emerge on the opposite side or jump into the next one?"

"There is only one way to find out," Katrina said. "We'll walk. Karl, how far to the nearest boundary?"

"I would estimate, from where we landed, that the next prism should be straight ahead. About 3 to 4 miles to the arctic environment adjacent to this one."

"Gentlemen, let's walk." Katrina bounded out of the ship, checking her compass and establishing a sight line. She knew there must be a boundary a few miles distant but her eyes saw nothing but hills far into the distance. The men all piled out and the crew began to walk together silently. The ground was hard under their athletic shoes, and covered with rocks and small pebbles. Occasionally a tumbleweed blew by in the cold breeze, which was fortunately at their backs.

After an hour Svenson spoke. "We should be coming up to the manifold boundary now."

Katrina, leading the group, disappeared.

"By gad," Nigel said, following her. He felt his foot over air and stumbled awkwardly into a small crevasse. He fell heavily into a pocket of snow and ice hollowed out by the howling wind. The captain lay ten feet away, her face a mask of pain. "Katrina!"

Nigel moved quickly to her. He saw that she held her left ankle.

"I can't get up or put any weight on it," she said.

Nigel quickly removed her shoe and felt the bones. The skin was unbroken but had already begun to show a dark purple bruise. "You've had a bad sprain." He took a bandage out of his medical bag and soaked it with arnica. He moved her trouser leg upward and gently wrapped her foot and ankle up to mid calf, providing support. "That feels good," she said thankfully.

Nigel slowly replaced her shoe and placed his arm around her, lifting her gently to her feet. She leaned heavily against the wall of their little snow cave. Nigel looked upward, studying a way out. They would have to climb approximately ten feet to reach the snow-covered ground above. Nigel dug his foot into the hard snow and managed to make a little foothold. "These shoes are not the perfect implement for this environment," he joked.

His calm demeanor pleased Katrina. It reminded her of his coolness during their short stay in Nullspace. Katrina stood against the hard packed snow as the cold seeped through her parka and her feet. She watched as Nigel calmly made holes in the snow. He stuffed his hands and feet into them and pulled himself slowly upward. She was thankful that this man seemed unruffled by even the most challenging situation.

Physical disability had always frightened her. She recalled the time she had broken her leg climbing a tree in the backyard of her apartment building when she was twelve. She had been bedridden for weeks. Her mother had soothed her and taken care of he, and she felt certain that Nigel would find a way to do so as well. Now he was out and climbed back down to her. "I'm just hopeful none of the others follow us or we'll have a lot more work to do!"

Katrina smiled. "If I can get on those broad shoulders of yours I think I can pull myself up if you support me from below."

Nigel smiled mischievously. "Oh, I'll be more than happy to do that."

The wind howled above. They were both freezing but she laughed. Nigel knelt down and Katrina stumbled over on one leg, straddling his shoulders with her legs. Nigel straightened and she jammed both her fists and her one good leg into the holes he had made and pulled with all her strength. Nigel moved his foot upward and pushed her toward the opening. After five minutes of struggle they emerged onto the ground and crawled slowly toward the barrier.

"Nigel!" "Katrina!" Rad moved swiftly to follow his two colleagues who had just disappeared.

"Wait!" T'Munga said, forcing the man backward. He had done enough mountain climbing to know that if a teammate got hurt you didn't immediately rush in to help or you'd find yourself in the same situation. "If they're in trouble we'll just find it too."

"But we can't just sit here!"

"T'Munga's right," Karl said. "We'll wait here until they come back through."

"And what if they don't?" Rad was irritated. His first impulse had been to rush in and save Katrina and be the hero. He didn't like the fact that Watanabe, his old rival, had physically prevented him from doing so. Even though his intellect told him that the bigger man was right. He glared at T'Munga and grumbled. "Yes of course."

They sat there for almost half an hour. Rad had made up his mind to run forward. At that moment their two shipmates appeared in front of them, on their hands and knees. Little icicles hung from their hair and their faces were red with cold.

Rad Greenberg was inordinately pleased to see both of them again. "Thank God."

"I didn't know you cared!" T'Munga said.

"Shutup you big jerk," Rad snapped. T'Munga laughed.

"Katrina's had an accident," Nigel explained, ignoring the unpleasant interchange. "She's severely sprained her left ankle."

Rad Greenberg thought quickly. "Two of us should go back to the ship. It seems responsive somehow to our commands. I'm sure we can get the thing to fly over here."

"Good idea," T'Munga said. They should have thought of that before. "Why don't you and Karl go and I'll stay here."

"Why don't you go and I'll stay?" Rad said, firing up. He was surprised at himself. Normally he despised anger and the irrational behavior it inspired. It was one of the reasons he found T'Munga Watanabe irritating. Now he was acting just like him and he didn't like it.

Katrina sat on the hard ground with her good leg stretched out for support. She took her lucky coin out of her pocket. It was an old Russian mint with the likeness of Peter the Great, given to her by her great grandfather just before he died. She flipped the coin high into the air. "Rad, choose heads or tails."

"Heads."

The coin landed on the hard ground, bounced a few times, and came up tails. "T'Munga? Your choice."

T'Munga was smug. "I'll stay."

"Karl, would you go with Rad?"

"Of course." The little man had already sized up the situation. The two combatants shouldn't travel together. Without further comment he got up and began to walk toward the little egg-shaped craft. In the clear sharp air he could just make it out. It sat there like a little pebble in the distance. Rad followed, grumbling.

Nigel wanted to put his arm around Katrina and kiss her. He refrained, seeing T'Munga's curious glances toward them. T'Munga turned his back and walked about ten feet away. Nigel noticed that he was still within easy hearing distance. Nigel met Katrina's eyes and she smiled. "Thank you," she said simply.

"You're quite welcome." There was a world of meaning in those three little words.

She took off her shoe. "It's starting to swell."

Nigel came over and inspected his handiwork. "Does it hurt?"

"Not too bad," she said, wincing a little.

"The arnica is doing its job. You've got a bad sprain there."

She smiled again. "I'll live." *Thanks to you.*

An hour later the little craft landed on a flat piece of ground a hundred feet away. Nigel lifted his fair burden to her feet and swept her into his arms. "No sense putting undue strain on that ankle," he explained, walking easily with her toward the ship.

Katrina lay her head on the big man's shoulder. After a year in command it felt good to let down her guard. Nigel stepped into the ship and set her down gently in one of the two forward seats. Everyone was already aboard. The men silently acknowledged the new relationship.

They waited for the ship to move but the little craft just sat there. After a few silent moments of silence T'Munga spoke. "Take us to your leader," he joked.

The ship took off immediately, once more flying over the plain. After about fifteen minutes it began to slow, banked right, and entered one of the prisms from above. It was a world of clouds in a deep blue sky. The ship banked into a beam of white light and followed it. After several minutes they landed. The sides of the ship opened, indicating to the humans that they should disembark. Katrina exited, supported by Nigel. The others followed.

"Now what?" T'Munga said. They heard laughter, softly at first, and then building louder and louder. The crew looked around them and discovered that they were at the bottom of a huge circular amphitheater. Row upon row of people reached far up, beyond sight. It seemed impossible that those in the topmost rows could even see them. "Will someone please explain what's been happening to us?" T'Munga asked.

A man strode towards them from a raised dais. He looked suspiciously like Dwight D. Eisenhower. "Welcome fellow soul mates," he said with a broad smile.

"Where are we?" Katrina asked.

"You're in heaven," the president said.

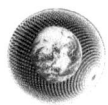

Chapter 13

Karl was the first to recover. "In heaven? Surely you must be joking."

"I have never been more serious," Eisenhower said. "If you knew me on earth you'd understand that I never jest about important issues."

Katrina felt like a woman who had just been told that her fiancee was really a frog in disguise. "But...but...heaven isn't real! It's just a metaphor."

"Feynman tells me that this...nullspace he calls it...is some sort of n-dimensional manifold. To me it feels more like heaven. I have no idea what a manifold is anyway. I am a politician, not a scientist."

"You mean you *were* a politician, don't you?" Katrina said.

The president looked solemn and slightly offended. "Am I real, young lady?" He waved his hand at the uncounted multitudes seated around them. "You see here every person who has ever lived on earth."

Rad Greenberg laughed. "Uh, sorry, I just don't believe in this Christian delusion."

Eisenhower smiled. "Well then, consider us to be the manifestation of what Jung called the collective unconscious. He's right up there if you'd like to talk to him." The president pointed to a white-haired gentleman in the front row who rose from his seat and bowed politely.

Rad stood firm. "I don't believe any of it."

Eisenhower ignored him. "We are assembled here because you are the first human beings to ever penetrate nullspace—the boundary between what-is and what-can-be."

"Even worse," Rad grumbled. "A new-age Christian!"

He fixed Dwight D. with his best intimidating stare, which had many times served to depress pretentious fools. "Why don't you just cut the bullshit and tell us exactly where we are and how we got here?"

"Oh dear," the president said gravely. "I've always hated foul language."

Rad Greenberg sighed. The others waited expectantly.

"You are the first physical beings to ever find your way here before normal life termination…"

"What is here?" Nigel asked.

Eisenhower frowned. "I misspoke when I referred to this place as heaven. It's more like Purgatory. But I digress. What you have seen here are templated realities. Perhaps a better terminology is potential realities. Many of them are not yet possible to live in physically."

"What the hell are you babbling about?" T'Munga asked. "We're real!"

"Are you?" The president was smiling. "When was the last time you drew breath? When was the last time you ate? The last time you went to the bathroom?"

The crew of the Cheesy Poof 2 stood fixed, staring at Dwight D. Eisenhower, their mouths open. Nigel had mentioned this back in Nullspace but it hadn't fully penetrated. Now the sudden realization of their condition hit them all like a ton of bricks.

"I was about to discuss this a number of times," Nigel Clarke said. "But I was afraid it might be too upsetting."

For once T'Munga Watanabe was at a loss for words.

"You mean…we're dead?" Katrina asked.

The president laughed. "Only in a manner of speaking."

"This is ridiculous," Katrina said, pointing to her ankle. "I just injured myself not two hours ago and…"

Eisenhower smiled. "Yes?" he said, looking down at her foot.

Katrina put pressure on the foot and it held. She bent down, removed the bandage, and found a perfectly healthy ankle.

"But…that's not possible!" Nigel objected.

"It's not possible for a physical being, that is true," the president said. "All of us, including yourselves, are part of the consciousness of earth. For millennia we have lived here in stasis."

Rad was intrigued despite his disdain for Christian metaphors. "Who made that fantastic plain of worlds? And how?"

The older man frowned. "We don't know. We have searched our memories. We do not have difficulty recalling anything, no matter how trivial or how far back in the past." The president pointed to several billion people ringed around them in this impossible amphitheater. "None of us can ever recall a time when it did not exist. We have learned how to construct more of these environments. It has been fascinating and enjoyable work. But we have never been able to solve the puzzle of our own origins. Nor have we found a way out of this place."

Rad suddenly thought of the Martins Sphere barrier. It was as if the solar system and everyone in it had somehow been quarantined. Were these the souls of the departed, throughout history? Was it possible to quarantine a soul?

During this conversation Katrina was looking about the huge stadium. She realized that it was possible to feel the identity of every one of the assembled beings.

"Mr. President. I can identify every individual present."

"That is correct my dear." Eisenhower's glumness disappeared and he responded with an admiring smile. Although he had stayed faithful to his wife during their long marriage he always had an eye for a beautiful woman. "If you allow yourself to become receptive for a moment you will be able to feel me and 10 billion separate personalities. Or souls, if you will. We are all gathered here and represent the collective consciousness of humanity."

"But how?"

Eisenhower shrugged. "It is how we communicate. We have had these abilities for so long we never question them. It's like breathing for a physical being."

Katrina became aware of millions of others. It was a strange but wonderful feeling. The sensation of joy and well being that she had experienced in the glade returned.

"You might say that we here are what is left after the death of the body," the president said. "You can call that consciousness, the soul, or a sophisticated holographic simulation. Whatever we are we aren't real! Without goals and dreams life becomes stagnant and hardly worth living. Decay and death then results, even for us. What you have seen are the dreamscapes of the collective consciousness, and from those who came before us." The older man became animated. "We have created thousands and thousands of environments. As fascinating as these are they are just dreams. Phantoms. Theoretical realities!" The president spoke passionately.

"They sure seem real to me," Karl Svenson said.

"Of course they're real," the president snapped. "But compare the feeling of this reality to your physical reality on earth. Isn't there something missing?"

Nigel Clarke gasped. Even when they had been in the crevasse he had not felt in any real danger. There was something a bit hollow about the experience. "Yes, dammit! It's…it's just a little shallow, less intense. Less poignant."

"It does feel wonderful here," Katrina said. "It's like looking at a beautiful picture instead of experiencing what's in the picture."

"That is correct," Eisenhower said. "Now imagine immortal beings living their lives out in dream realities, knowing deep down that it's all counterfeit. Knowing that they're really just pretending. We have been slowly dying. Even immortal beings can lose the will to live. If there are no real challenges there can be no real excitement. Unfortunately it is not possible for any of us here to reincarnate. Our numbers keep growing but we cannot go back to earth or leave this place. We are trapped."

"Or quarantined," T'Munga blurted.

"My thought exactly!" Rad said.

The president eagerly affirmed this idea. He was about to speak when someone approached from the stands and introduced himself. "I am Sir Isaac Newton." Newton wore a white wig and was dressed in the style of the early 18th century with white stockings, buckled shoes, a brown waistcoat, and knee breeches. He walked with a cane. Around his neck was a quizzing glass suspended on a black riband.

"Not now Isaac," Eisenhower said, irritated at the interruption. There was something the visitors desperately needed to know…

T'Munga laughed and turned to the newcomer. He had been following the conversation with more than a little disdain, as if this were a play staged for his amusement. "YOU are Isaac Newton? I don't believe it." Newton put up his glass and gazed haughtily at T'Munga, looking him up and down. Watanabe's face blushed fiery red and he stammered an apology. T'Munga recovered quickly. "If you are truly the author of the 'Principia Mathematica' then I would like to ask you a few questions."

The president ground his teeth. Didn't Newton understand the overwhelming importance and opportunity the visitors presented? Eisenhower himself found the great scientist to be boringly didactic. The man was an attention seeker. His lectures on religion always put him to sleep.

Sir Isaac just smiled and bowed slightly, indicating his acquiescence to this proposal.

"This concerns Keplers Second Law of Motion, you impostor. If an instantaneous centripetal force is considered on a planet during its orbit, what is the relationship between the area of the triangles defined by the path of the planet?"

Sit Isaac stamped his cane on the floor. "You dare to ask me such a trivial question? This is the subject of my Propositions 1 through 3 in Book One. The areas are the same."

T'Munga was impressed. "Proposition 6, Book one, Figure 2. How does the centripetal force vary in a body moving along a given non-circular trajectory?"

Sir Isaac tossed his head upward and gazed down over his chin at the upstart. "You fool, by the square of the distance."

Newton answered all of T'Munga's questions satisfactorily. The astrophysicist then engaged Sir Isaac in animated conversation.

Several more individuals came down from the stands and in turn were interrogated by the group. The president fumed. Katrina met her childhood hero, Yuri Gagarin, who was the first human to orbit the earth. Gagarin and Katrina became engrossed in conversation. Karl Svenson saw his beloved grandmother and threw his arms around her, crying like a little child. Rad Greenberg met the great Sufi vocalist Nusrat Fatah Ali Khan, and persuaded him to sing. Nigel Clarke, a history buff, spotted Queen Elizabeth I and engaged her in a lively discussion of court politics. He asked her about her relationship with Robert Dudley, first Earl of Leicester. Finally the visitors talked themselves out. Everyone returned to their seats in the gigantic stadium.

The president spoke again. "Now my friends, we come to the very important issue of your presence here. It affirms what we have always suspected: There is an outside force preventing us from departing this place. We want you to discover what it is and free us from this damnable prison."

T'Munga laughed. "We were hoping that *you* could tell *us*."

The president frowned. "I'm afraid not." Eisenhower indicated his fellow bound souls. "We are certain that this Martins Sphere is related to our difficulty. Remove it and we will be free."

"Why should we care if you stay here or not?" T'Munga said. "As far as I'm concerned you guys aren't my problem."

"But it will be your problem soon enough, T'Munga," the president replied. "Have you figured it out yet?"

Nigel Clarke spoke up. "We will also return here, our souls trapped, after we die."

"That is correct," said Eisenhower.

"So we aren't dead then?" Rad was skeptical.

"You are temporarily suspended between your physical selves and this world. That is why you are able to interface with this place and with all of us."

T'Munga snapped his fingers. "Of course!" The others turned immediately to him. "We've already seen ourselves in suspended animation just before entering Nullspace."

"Is it possible for us to return to our bodies?" Karl was excited.

The president nodded. "It is vital that you do so, for the reasons I've given." Eisenhower cleared his throat. "Your problem, my friends, is our problem. We have the capability to send your disembodied consciousness back to your bodies. Understand that your memories of this place may not be intact after your return. But you have now become sensitized to us and have the ability to return your consciousness here. If you have any questions don't hesitate to ask. We are with you all the way."

"But wait!" Katrina cried. "We have a million questions. What happened to our probes…"

The crew found themselves back in the Cheesy Poof 2.

"Did something just happen?" said Rad Greenberg. The ship rested motionless before the invisible interface to…what? "The last thing I remember we were all walking along on some kind of flat, gray plain."

There was something beyond, he just knew it. He could not remember what it was.

"We'll try again to go in," the captain said, glancing over at Nigel. Something was different about their relationship…. "But more slowly this time. Are we agreed?" Katrina surveyed each man and received no objections. "All right then, everybody strap in. T'Munga, move us in slowly."

As before a perfect gray oval appeared at the front of the vessel. As they advanced further into the grayness they found themselves intact, completely outside the barrier. After several more tries they discovered that it was impossible for the Apollo's Arrow to attain full immersion.

"I don't understand," Katrina said. "We lost two probes in there just before we tried it the first time."

"Perhaps the presence of life forms prevents immersion," Nigel suggested.

"Unsatisfactory," T'Munga interjected. "Recall that there were five lab animals and other living tissue aboard the first Cheesy Poof."

"Karl, scan the area for any evidence of an earlier probe," Katrina ordered.

After several minutes the engineer reported that this area of space was empty. "There's nothing within the range of our instruments captain."

"All right," Katrina said. "We've done all we can here. It is vital that we return to earth with the Alpha Centauri data and our verification of the validity of the Martins Sphere." The decision had come and the words were out of her mouth before she realized she had spoken them.

The scientists agreed and were secretly relieved. They had accomplished all of their mission objectives. T'Munga was heartily sick of celibacy and tired of shipboard life. Judging by the look on their faces whenever their eyes met, it was apparent to him that Nigel Clarke would be sharing the captain's bed before this voyage was over. T'Munga was not jealous. Katrina Antropov was definitely not his kind of woman. He liked them petite, soft, and pliable. Not Amazons an inch taller than he. His thoughts were interrupted by a command.

"T'Munga, plot a course back to earth."

The long journey back to earth passed uneventfully. The crew all noticed a peculiar phenomenon. They all shared, at one time or another, a vivid recurring dream. Nigel Clarke explained it by saying that they had all been cooped up together for months and had shared their thoughts on so many subjects. "It's a wonder we haven't all turned into clones of each other," he remarked to general laughter. This was after Karl Svenson had once again described his encounter with the former President Eisenhower. "I never liked the bastard from my study of history," said the ship's engineer, "or Republicans in general. So why am I dreaming about this guy all the time?"

"Probably because you're in love with him," Rad replied. "I'm almost ready to jump your bones myself."

Karl's face filled with loathing. He fled the forward cabin and retreated to his bunk. They all heard the click as he latched his cabin door. Rad shrugged and everyone had another laugh.

Eleven months later T'Munga Watanabe and his colleagues walked out of the Tubingen hospital complex in Berlin and into a barrage of bright lights and shouted voices. The crew had spent two horrible weeks being probed, metered, tested, and analyzed until tempers flared. They had, in unison, demanded to be released.

The international staff of physicians, psychologists, and psychiatrists had strenuously resisted their departure. "The international community requires your assistance and cooperation," said Dr. Helmut Grossklaus, Director of the Apollo's Arrow Medical Debriefing Team. It was the standard refrain used by all Tubingen personnel. "It's all in the contract you signed before your departure," Grossklaus told T'Munga Watanabe after another of the prolonged debriefing sessions in his small cubicle.

The emotionless Grossklaus seemed to relish their discomfort. After several days the crew learned to hate the flat monotone of his voice. His white, unbuttoned lab coat that swirled about him became a symbol of unwarranted intrusion into their bodies and minds. Grossklaus walked like a white Darth Vader down the sterile hallways of the complex, smelling of chemicals.

After almost two weeks of this T'Munga refused to be treated like a guinea pig for even one moment longer. "Fuck the international community." He began the walk down the long corridor of the hospital complex, toward the exit and freedom. T'Munga had been forcibly restrained. When the others found out a general mutiny resulted. Katrina Antropov spoke for the crew to the Tubingen staff. "We will not submit to even one more test." Outside, reporters and curious public had gathered. When the German authorities were informed of the ugly turn of events inside the facility they stopped issuing reports. This caused a feeding frenzy within the international media who immediately began sniffing out a possible story.

That night Rad Greenberg made a frantic call to Washington. President Rosen had been elected to a second term while they were away.

"Sam, this is Rad."

"Rad! What the hell is going on over there?"

"Sam, you gotta get us out of here. We can't take this probing and prodding any longer. They're treating us like lab animals." Rad quickly explained the situation.

"Calm down old friend," Sam said. "I'll get you out of there right away but you have to do something for me first."

Rad understood perfectly and broke into laughter, instantly dispelling his bad mood.

"Listen Rad. I want you guys to issue the most glowing reports when you meet the media. I'll write something for you to read out..."

The crew met the world media outside the Tubingen complex on a warm summer day in late June. Katrina read a prepared statement written by President Rosen. Then they answered questions for almost four hours.

"Is it true, then? Is the universe really an illusion?"

"What do you want to say to the people of the world after this historic mission?"

The questioning went on and on.

Finally they made their way slowly through the crush of media. The crew were grateful to President Rosen so they smiled and mouthed the appropriate platitudes. A limo was waiting for them outside the complex. Before they could reach the vehicle T'Munga stopped. The others were forced to halt as well. Nigel Clarke was extremely irritated. He had already made plans with Katrina Antropov and was in a hurry to return with her to London and the privacy of his home. Now they were pressed in on all sides. Rad saw that T'Munga was clearly enjoying himself. "Selfish bastard," he muttered. After almost two years of quiet and comfortable solitude aboard the Cheesy Poof 2 his nerves were not adjusting well to the noise and the throng of frantic humanity. So he hid himself behind Nigel Clarke. Rad comforted himself with the thought that after today, he would never have to spend another moment in the presence of T'Munga Watanabe.

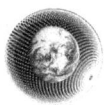

Chapter 14

Cardinal Che Rodriquez sat with the pope and the entire College of Cardinals. They were watching the huge flat panel display tacked to the wall of the big Vatican conference room. The discussion was about Pope Clement XV's latest encyclical, "Science and Religion." It was the church's official reaction to the remarkable video just released by the ACMHQ in Brussels.

"The Catholic church," the encyclical read, "commends the achievements of our valiant space travelers and is pleased that we have discovered five new planets that could eventually support intelligent life. The Church is not convinced that the visual evidence provided by the Apollo's Arrow conclusively proves the radical theories of Jack Martins."

Helmut Karl, the first German cardinal ever, expressed the sentiment of the group. "I believe that this film is nothing more than an entertaining science fiction video." Cardinal Rodriquez from Bolivia (known for his somewhat leftist and iconoclastic ideas) disagreed. "Explain then, dear Helmut, why 47 international governments would collude in such a conspiracy?"

The video in question had just been released by Alpha Centauri Misson Headquarters (ACMHQ) in Brussels. It showed the two little probes launched by the Apollo's Arrow disappearing into nothingness. It had also shown the finger of captain Antropov partially immersed. A small gray ellipse sliced perfectly into her finger. The film displayed the even more remarkable partial immersion of the ship itself. Captain Antropov described what happened in her slightly Russian accented English. "Here my finger goes through into what we call Nullspace. As my finger went past the barrier I lost all memory of ever having that portion of my anatomy. It was as if I had been born with only half a finger. When I withdrew the finger it became physically restored, as you see. Only after that did my memory of it return."

Rodriquez's sharp eyes detected the faintest of frowns at this. For a split second the Russian was struggling to recall something important. No one else noticed as Antropov continued her description of the remarkable series of events that had occurred at the Martins Sphere boundary. But Cardinal Rodriquez wondered. Transcripts of the crew's recorded conversations had been distributed by ACMHQ a month after the ship landed. The videos and transcripts of the voyage to Alpha Centauri and back mostly consisted of Nigel Clarke's stories and other personal conversation. Almost no one had bothered to read them or watch the videos. Che Rodriquez had. At the very end of those transcripts were some very interesting dream sequences.

"Could we go to when the Apollo's Arrow comes back through the barrier?" Che asked. The video operator obliged. "There! Stop there." Che could see the pope was getting irritated. "Go through it once more and watch what happens at the end of the sequence." There was a gap or a jerk in the video, as if something had been cut out of the action. "Do you see it? The Apollo's Arrow, partially through the barrier, suddenly returns whole. Something is missing in that footage."

The pope saw it. "That is very observant Cardinal Rodriquez."

"Your eminence, I now request we go back to the sequence where Captain Antropov inserts her finger into the barrier."

There was no gap.

An excited babble of conversation erupted. Cardinal Rodriquez became lost in thought as the conversation moved back and forth. There were rumors of bad blood between the crew and some of the medical staff at Tubingen. That would not account for the missing footage, if there was any.

The wording of the encyclical was debated and approved. Cardinal Rodriquez's observations of the video lent credibility to the Church's doubts about the validity of a crazy theory that destroyed the greatness of God and turned Him into something pitiful.

After the meeting Cardinal Rodriquez went to his private quarters and reviewed the video again. Was he just paranoid? No, there was something cut out. He reread the dream sequence transcripts once more, and wondered.

Meanwhile in Tehran, Baghdad, Damascus, and Riyadh, much communication had been sent and received in the offices of the highest officials in the Arab world. Ages old hatreds were being pushed aside. An historic conference was to take place between the two major factions within Islam. Sunni and Shiite Muslims began serious talks. They built upon the success of the Sam Rosen inspired peace process in Palestine. The Arab world had been mollified by the Israeli's agreement to formally recognize the Palestinian state. It was also agreed that the indefensible ACMHQ video was a desecration to Allah.

All factions within the Islamic world were in complete agreement with the Vatican's statement. It was agreed that the infidels had gone too far. As part of the Middle Eastern peace process the United States had withdrawn all its forces from Arab lands. Now, however, the Arab leaders saw an even more outrageous attack from the West. The assertion of Jack Martins that the glorious universe created by Allah was nothing more than a nonexistent phantom was of course dismissed contemptuously as foolish ranting. Then came the Alpha Centauri mission and the incredible video. On top of that the first-hand observations of the crew. All of them validated the nonsensical Martins Sphere concept.

Despite the best efforts of Arab leaders their countries had gradually become more and more Westernized. Their people had become more and more accustomed to material wealth and more attuned to Western godless popular culture. In the minds of certain leaders of the Arab world the assault on the very foundations of Islamic belief must be fought. ACMHQ had provided the perfect concept around which the masses could be mobilized.

The Arab street was much better informed through the WorldNet. Yet there was also heavy sentiment against Martins' theories, which were interpreted by many as an attack on Islam in general.

During the historic gathering the Arab leaders hammered out a statement. It was supported by Shiite Ayatollah Omar Shahin, Supreme Leader of Iran, and the Sunni Imam Husseini Fayood, from Baghdad. Support also came from the entire Syrian Parliament, King Fahd III of Saudi Arabia, and President Abdel Fattah el-Morsi of Egypt. The statement was read by Omar Shahin at a press conference in Baghdad:

"The outrageous assertion that Allah's magnificent universe is but an illusion is a pernicious assault on Islam and all true Muslims. All true believers, as well as men of sense, will reject the Martins Sphere concept for what it is: preposterous nonsense. The ACMHQ video proves nothing. It is obviously the product of someone's vivid imagination. It is more reminiscent of a very bad Hollywood movie than a legitimate search for truth. We call upon Muslims all over the world, in all walks of life, to find truth in the Koran. Muslims must reject the ridiculous assertions of the obviously paranoid and mentally unbalanced personnel of the Apollo's Arrow. Clearly, two years crammed into a little spaceship within the bowels of outer space has affected the sanity of the crew. We understand and sympathize. We hope that these well-intentioned but misguided persons will seek and receive guidance from Allah. God is great!"

A week later Ayatollah Shahin was seated in his private quarters in Tehran with his aide in attendance. He was pleased with the conference and his important role in it.

"Farshid, is the Arab world prepared for a Shiite leader from Iran?" Shahin asked.

"Ayatollah, I believe so," Farshid Madani replied. "Jack Martins and recent extraordinary events have galvanized sentiment on the street and in the corridors of power. Men are looking for a leader that can restore stability and order."

"Your thoughts mirror mine."

"It is an opportunity to reestablish the old ways," Farshid offered. "Excellency, as Supreme Leader of Shiite Iran and head of the Council of Guardians you have much power. Remember the old saying: 'power abhors a vacuum.'"

Shahin smiled. "That is so. The mullahs who compose the Council, with my help, have regained control of the *Sepah-e Pasdaran-e Enghelab-e Islami,* the Revolutionary Guards."

"The Guards are the largest military force in the country and are responsible for national security and law enforcement. He who controls the Guards controls the country."

Shahin nodded in agreement. "Because of Martins and ACMHQ the Council of Guardians has been able to replace secular members with those who have greater religious fervor. This plays nicely into my hands." Left unsaid was his goal to become leader of the entire Arab world. Farshid understood this.

Shahin smiled an oily smile and outlined his program.

"My first action will be to demand the immediate removal of the female Majlis members.[1] In every city and precinct, the strict religious review councils will be restored to their full power. Mandatory study of the Koran will be enforced. Women will again be required to wear the chador, as is proper."

"The people are ready for this, Ayatollah Shahin. They are ready for a strong leader with a strong hand."

Shahin smiled again. This man Farshid had the uncanny ability to precisely express his own thoughts. "Let's take a survey of the Arab world, Farshid. The decrepit King Fahd in Saudia Arabia will be easy to manipulate. Syria and Iraq will fall into line. The Iraqis especially, with their government now de facto controlled by the Shiites, will play right into my hands."

Farshid scoffed. "The Americans were fools. Their constitution for Iraq was written to deprive the Sunni majority in Iraq of influence. All the better for us."

"Yes. The Iraqis will follow my lead. That weakling in Syria will be putty in my hands." He looked intently at Farshid, wanting to get his reaction. "He who controls Syria controls Lebanon and can put great pressure upon the northern border of the Israelis. El-Morsi in Egypt is another weakling. The Palestinians can be brought round with a good dose of revolutionary and religious fervor. Their resentment of the West is still very strong even after the Rosen Accords were signed granting them their state."

Farshid nodded, agreeing with this. "Iran is now the strongest country economically in the region. This lends credence to the statements of the Iranian leader."

"Quite so." Shahin was brutally frank. "The Palestinians are not religious, but neither am I. I will capitalize on their emotions and use them for my own ends."

"And now the Vatican has issued its statement," Farshid offered.

Shahin laughed. "My call on the infidel pope and our subsequent discussions has brought the powerful influence of the Catholic Church to cover my back. The monetary support of the infidel church is welcome as well."

"Cardinal Tauron has many spies in Iran," Farshid pointed out.

---

[1] Majlis—The Iranian Parliament. In Arabic *majlis* means "a place of sitting." Here it is used in the context of a council.

"That cannot be helped," Shahin replied. "I need their money." Cardinal Tauron, the mastermind in charge of the Curia in Rome, was wickedly smart and cunning.

Omar Shahin knew that he was an uneducated man. The Arab world, and even Iran, had moved subtly Westward. Its culture and politics were much more secular since the days of his hero, Ayatollah Ruhollah Khomeini. His objective of uniting the Arab world under his leadership required subtlety, not brute force.

Farshid understood the direction of Shahin's thinking. "May I suggest, your eminence, that such an ambitious plan requires assistance."

It was as if Farshid had read his mind. "That is so."

Omar Shahin knew that he could never succeed on his own. He must eliminate his weaknesses and play to his strengths. As his aide watched Shahin listed his strengths: cunning, persistence, ambition, ruthlessness, and the ability to judge the political winds. These qualities had allowed him to reach the position of Supreme Leader. His weaknesses were impulsiveness, impatience, and an overbearing temperament that had made him many enemies. By himself he would alienate the very people he needed to make his grand scheme a success.

"A right hand man with intelligence and tact is required, Farshid. A man who can smooth the way for me. A man I can control."

Farshid shrugged. "Who better than Sheikh Izz-Al-Din? There is a man with acumen and strength."

"Such a man might have ambitions of his own."

His aide said nothing, letting Shahin mull it over.

"In my experience intelligent men are weaklings," Shahin offered. "When throat-slitting time comes they are likely to become squeamish."

"All the better then. Izz-Al-Din will be under your control."

Ayatollah Shahin patted his ample stomach with satisfaction. Sheik Izz-Al-Din was right underneath him. The sheikh had already supported him in the Council election that made him Supreme Leader.

Omar Shahin looked over at Farshid Madani. "Izz-Al-Din is known to you, is he not?" Shahin suggested.

Farshid nodded. "I went to university with his young brother."

In Tel Aviv Prime Minister Lavi Bar-Elet was watching the ACHMQ video from his private office.

The Israeli Prime Minister silently applauded Shahin's statement. He also looked with favor on the man's political ambitions. There would be no opposition to the Supreme Leader from Israel, despite what the Americans might say. He could work with Shahin or any of the current crop of Arab leaders that might emerge if the Ayatollah stumbled. He understood them far better than he did the Americans.

To astute students of Islamic politics such as Bar-Elet the true intent of the current Arabic love-fest was clear: the reestablishment of fundamentalist power. The Prime Minister was not himself wholly unsympathetic. He deplored the current trend toward secularism and away from orthodoxy in his own country. That is why he had introduced a motion in the Knesset. The motion called upon the Israeli government to encourage a return to core Jewish principles.

After his discussion with Omar Shahin, Farshid Madani spoke to his mentor, Sheikh Massoud Izz-Al-Din. "I was successful."

Izz-Al-Din smiled. "Report."

"The man is a simpleton. But useful. He will be contacting you shortly. A suggestion here, a suggestion there ... Shahin will take up your ideas if he sees how they can help him."

"You have done well. I will speak to the Supreme Leader about the Defenders of Islam."

Izz-Al-Din had already begun to organize his force. Sheik Izz-Al-Din had been consulted by political and religious leaders throughout Islam. With the Martins Sphere initiative and the manned space mission there was great concern that the Christian countries were once more planning to move against the Arab world. Everyone remembered the Persian Gulf War and how Iraq had been destroyed, how the entire Arab world had been forced to capitulate to the Americans and their lackeys. When the West struck it struck hard and without warning. The Arab world must be prepared.

Massoud Izz-Al-Din discussed it with Nasrin Pahlavi, an influential general within the Revolutionary Guards one evening in the general's quarters.

"The diabolical theories of Jack Martins has deeply shaken belief systems all over the world," Izz-Al-Din said. "But nowhere has that effect been more pronounced than in the Arab world."

"Something must be done to give the people hope," the general replied. "The Arab countries are becoming destabilized and directionless."

After a long discussion both men agreed that the Western countries were planning for war. "Behind this new space drive is a new weapon," the general concluded. "Something that will allow the Christian countries to once more gain ascendance in the world."

"It is a conclusion most Arab leaders have already reached. Including our own Supreme Leader, Ayatollah Omar Shahin." Izz-Al-Din was not so sure himself.

"We cannot afford to wait this time," the general said. "We were disorganized then, but not now. We must, as the Americans say, be proactive."

The general's belief suited Izz-Al-Din's purpose. "An Arab strike force must be prepared to counter the superior forces of the West. Our weapons will be the age-old tactics of fear, to be employed against their societies."

The general became excited. "This is what we have been hoping for."

Izz-Al-Din nodded. "We will go back into Arab and family history to organize our new force. I have been studying this and how it can be done. As you know, I am a direct descendant of Qutb-ud-din Aibak, the first Mamluk sultan."

The Mamluks were a slave army of elite fighters that had evolved into a warrior caste. This was well known to General Pahlavi. "But how can this be helpful?"

Izz-Al-Din explained. "The Mamluk system provided rulers with troops who had no link to established power structures. The slave-troops were strangers of the lowest possible status, making it impossible for them to conspire against the ruler. They could easily be punished if they caused trouble. This made them a great military asset."

Here Izz-Al-Din paused and smiled. "With your help, that is exactly how we can organize the Defenders of Islam. Each member should be carefully selected from the impoverished slums and streets of cities in the Arab world. The common denominator of all our fighters should be a sense of helplessness and dissatisfaction in their own personal lives. And a desire to strike back."

Pahlavi nodded. "Such young men are ready to strike at anything. They just need the right targets."

"My thought exactly general. But our force cannot be a military one. The Guards and the Army cannot be seen to be involved. The Defenders must be a quick-strike guerrilla force unassociated with the government. The targets must all be overseas." Izz-Al-Din's eyes hardened. "The Defenders must never be used for personal gain or against another Islamic state."

The general smiled broadly. "It is agreed. To sit and wait for events to overcome us again is irrational. We must learn from the lessons of history."

Izz-Al-Din nodded his agreement. But he wanted to make one point very clear to the general. "I will provide the religious dogma and the direction necessary to inspire our fighters. But understand that I am not myself religious." Izz-Al-Din shrugged his shoulders. "Neither is Ayatollah Shahin. It is a necessary subterfuge."

The general was satisfied. "We have no use for the irrationality of true believers. We will trust in Allah and our own ingenuity. In a year's time the Defenders will be ready."

Two days after he spoke with Farshid Madani, Izz-Al-Din conversed with Omar Shahin at a conference of Arab leaders in Riyadh. They sat in a private parlor. The two men were seated at a table covered with a brightly colored cloth on which prayers were inscribed. On the floor lay a beautiful Persian rug. The men drank tea and ate *khoresht-e-fesenjan,* chicken in a pomegranate and walnut sauce with white rice. Various fruits, pastries, and sweets had been placed on a sideboard. The men were served by young girls dressed in beautiful silks.

"Our force will be independent of any government, military, or religious organization," Izz-Al-Din said.

Shahin was a bulky and muscular man with a thick black mustache and thick lips. He leaned across the table and spoke confidentially. "You command, I will direct. Together we shall unite the Arab world and restore the glory of Islam."

Izz-Al-Din understood that should anything go wrong, as commander he would be blamed and cast aside. He did not let his contempt show.

"And how is that to be done?" Izz-Al-Din was hoping to discern more details of the Supreme Leader's thinking.

"This is what I have come to discuss with you," Shahin said, throwing the dolak back to the sheikh.

The men began to eat.

Ayatollah Shahin considered the man across from him.

Izz-Al-Din had very light skin, a remnant of his Caucasian Mamluk heritage. The Mamluks slaves had been recruited mainly from the Causcasus. This man was a direct descendant of the founder of that slave army. The sheikh's bloodline was inferior. He would not have to worry about this one.

Izz-Al-Din contemplated the Supreme Leader. He was a burly man with an unshaven stubble of beard. Shahin looked like one of those sweaty gunfighters in an American western. This man has probably not bathed today. Izz-Al-Din repressed a shudder.

Shahin was waiting for him to outline their plan. Izz-Al-Din did not tell him of his discussions with General Pahlavi. "It is simple. The Council of Guardians controls the budget and sets taxes. Your job would be to secure funding. The Libyans have already given us free use of their land for training."

At this Omar Shahin's eyes widened.

Izz-Al-Din continued calmly, repressing his inner excitement. He spoke as if giving a lecture to a high school student. "We recruit from all over the Arab world and build a unified force loyal only to us, completely independent of the Guards and the army."

Shahin's eyes grew bright.

"Like the Americans, we create a low-cost, quick-strike force. Within a year we can have 5,000 fighters trained and send them wherever we want." Izz-Al-Din would oversee the project personally and ensure that the force became loyal to him.

"Iran is now the greatest economic power in the Arab world," Izz-Al-Din continued. He would flatter the older man. "Our political influence is strong. It was largely due to your efforts that the Americans withdrew their troops from Islamic soil two years ago. Your influence forced the clown Rosen to accede to the creation of a Palestinian state."

Shahin nodded, accepting this.

"The puppet in Riyadh will make no trouble. Without the protection of the Americans he knows we will crush him. He exists only at our pleasure. The Iraqis have still not recovered from the attacks of the infidel. Syria and Lebanon are now controlled by Hezbollah and answer to us. The rest will follow where we lead."

Izz-Al-Din carefully read the countenance of Shahin and was satisfied. The man's eyes were bright and he listened attentively.

One of the serving girls entered in a swirl of silk and brought more food and tea. Izz-Al-Din regarded her youthful body appreciatively, but Shahin did not notice her.

"I suggest that our force be called the Defenders of Islam," Izz-Al-Din said. He wanted to see how far he could go with this man. "Our ostensible purpose will be jihad, but our real purpose will be to reassert Persian influence and control the Arab world from Tehran."

Shahin's face was now eager, his eyes wide with excitement. He was breathing hard. Small beads of sweat appeared on his forehead, although the room was cool.

This man is obsessed, Izz-Al-Din thought. A sexual energy emanated from the man and it disgusted him. He's also a homosexual, he realized with a shock. The rumors must be true then. He tried not to gloat, but kept an agreeable smile on his face. He now knew Shahin's weakness.

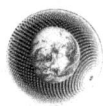

Chapter 15

All over the world religious and political leaders debated, argued, and defiantly rejected the idea of a truncated universe. The crew tried to find some semblance of normalcy in a world that seemed to be going crazy.

T'Munga Watanabe went on a whirlwind tour of TV, radio, and social media talk shows. He had begun his series of interviews with Kerry Hoff of NPR. He had spoken confidently. He recalled his reactions as the probes and then the ship itself had encountered the strange gray nothingness they called Nullspace. He discovered that the media had almost no interest in their fascinating exploration of the Alpha Centauri system and the discovery of five new planets. They wanted to talk about "the end of the universe" and "the controversy surrounding the verification of the Martins Sphere." T'Munga had at first enjoyed the limelight and the attention. But the excitement was wearing thin now. The women were mostly cardboard cutouts. They were shallow and interested only in being seen and photographed with him. The sex was great. But even great sex couldn't make up for the intellectually atrophied conversation. T'Munga Watanabe was discovering what many celebrities before him had discovered: fame had its drawbacks.

By the end of his tour, on the Olga show, he started to have serious doubts about the validity of his experiences. His words sounded silly. The more he described the events at the edge of Real Space the less he began to believe that they had ever happened.

The crew members were accused by religious leaders, some influential scientists, and conservative politicians as being slightly batty. Listening to himself, T'Munga almost began to believe it. On the Olga show he shifted gears from his set patter. "Ladies and gentlemen, sometimes I wonder if we ever experienced the events at the barrier at all. Everything is crystal clear in my mind until we approached the so-called end of Real Space. All I really remember is that we performed some tests. Then we headed back for earth. At that point we were all tired of the ship and each other. We wanted desperately to get home again. Perhaps we just dreamed it all up."

Olga objected. "But the video released by ACMHQ last month shows the probes clearly disappearing. The nose of the Apollo's Arrow was partially cut off by that…stuff."

T'Munga shrugged. "I suppose it does. But I don't remember anymore if it really happened like that." Then T'Munga Watanabe made his famous statement. If he had been thinking clearly he never would have said it. "Maybe somebody messed with the images."

After that, his last interview, the media had a field day.

"MISSION DATA FAKED?" cried the headlines of the *WorldNet Tribune.*

"DID ACMHQ FALSIFY MISSION DATA?" screamed the *Washington Post.*

"SERIOUS QUESTIONS RAISED ABOUT ACM AUTHENTICITY," said the *New York Times.*

After that T'Munga was not a popular man at ACMHQ in Brussels. Helmut Grossklaus at ACMHQ denounced him as "paranoid."

Katrina Antropov and Nigel Clarke lay in Nigel's giant four poster bed. They had just finished watching T'Munga's performance. Nigel had been recording his friend since his first appearance on America's National Public Radio. He clicked the remote and removed the disc from the recorder.

Katrina and Nigel had decided to remain silent. They didn't want to become the focus of media attention and remained holed up in Nigel's house. The two had arrived together after their debrief in Tubingen, weary in every cell of their bodies. The two had been greeted by a horde of British reporters snapping photographs. Paparazzi crowded round and fired questions at the top of their lungs. Nigel had stopped three feet in front of his front door with one arm around Katrina. He calmly answered their questions for over an hour. "Ladies and gentlemen, we have said all we are going to say. We do not desire the spotlight. You may discover the precise details of our mission from ACMHQ. I believe they are making available the more exciting parts of our journey directly from the ship's log. For the rest, you may read two years of transcripts. Most of these are my own boring and fantastical recitations. I imagine that any psychologist, after perusing my stories, would immediately conclude that I need professional help."

The seas parted amid general laughter and the pair was allowed to enter the house. There were always at least two people outside at any time of day or night, mostly curious tabloid reporters interested in the juicy details of their relationship. These paparazzi were always ready with cameras and filmed through any open window. Nigel, as ever, remained calm and urged Katrina to do so as well. "If you give them anything negative they'll be even that more persistent." After a week Nigel had to return to work and Katrina decided to go back to Russia and stay with her family for a while. Hopefully the next political crisis or natural disaster would take the crew off the front pages.

Nigel made a suggestion. "Why don't you live with me? I'm making enough money to support us both comfortably."

"That's fine for you but what am I to do?" Katrina responded. "I can't lie about the house like a housewife."

Nigel smiled. "No my dear, you weren't made for that." He looked her over appreciatively.

Katrina blushed. "The Moscow Space Academy is desperate for me to return and teach. They're planning a Russian mission to Alpha Centauri and they want me to lead it." The United States had already released full details of the amazing new space drive. It was part of the agreement to get international funding. It was now possible for individual governments to build their own ships. So far there were no military applications for the exotic new technology.

Nigel laughed but he was concerned. "You don't want to spend two more years in a sardine can, do you? Just think what it would be like without my stories to liven things up."

Katrina dimpled and spoke shyly. "I have no interest in going back to Alpha Centauri." No man had ever gotten her to show the childlike side of her personality. She liked it.

Nigel thought she looked adorable. From warrior-goddess to little girl in one second.

"I just don't want to lose you," he said.

She came into his arms and held him. "My family is anxious to spend some time with me. I want to visit some old friends in Moscow."

He sighed. "Our professions and our lives don't seem to be congruent."

"Buck up. We'll work it out."

Nigel spoke suddenly, kissing her forehead softly. "I love you, Katrina. After two years on ship you can't say that we barely know each other."

Katrina lowered her head to his shoulder. Did she have time for love in her life? For a committed relationship? Did she even want a relationship?

Nigel felt her hesitancy and thought it best to change the subject. "So what did you think of T'Munga's Olga appearance?"

"He's voiced what I've been thinking myself this last week." She was relieved that he had turned the subject. "I'm not so clear anymore about the events we experienced at the barrier." Katrina absently scratched her ankle.

"Got an itch?" Nigel asked.

Katrina frowned. "Not exactly. I don't know. I just feel a compulsion to touch myself there."

Nigel smiled. "Why don't I touch you in other places…"

Rad Greenberg went home to Midland, Illinois on the red-eye. He cleaned up and jumped on a plane to Washington early the same morning. Rad kept his head down and managed to avoid notice. His friend Sam Rosen had called the house the night he arrived and left a message. "I'd like you to come and see me for a personal debrief. We'll pay your plane fare and you can stay in one of the guest bedrooms in the White House." Rad agreed immediately. He knew he could return to his research position at the University of Illinois at any time. A few more days wouldn't matter.

Karl Svenson went quietly back to his hometown of Halmstad in Sweden. He did not give any interviews or speak to anyone other than his family. When he arrived at the airport he refused comment, referring all inquiries to ACMHQ. Fortunately for him Swedish reporters did not possess the irrational persistence of their British brethren. The little engineer was able to disappear into obscurity for a while.

Eight days later an event occurred that blew the minds of every single person on earth.

Part III – QUARANTINE

Chapter 16

Will Streeter was way off the beaten trail high up in the Colorado Rockies. He was looking for that perfect spot in which to test his formidable skills. Finally he saw it: a ledge of rock that stuck out 20 feet above a perilously steep downhill. The perilous slope was bordered on all sides with rocks and boulders. He made his way up to the ledge in the fading twilight knowing that he should wait until morning to try this slope. But Will was a loner and a daredevil. He would not wait. The brilliant white of the snow and the full moon were enough to guide him. The slope itself was not overly long. In less than ten minutes he could reach the bottom. Then a 15 minute ski to find his Jeep, parked on a little-used bike trail. He lived for moments like this.

Will made his way to the edge of the ledge and looked up at the sky. The stars were beginning to appear in the fading light. He breathed deep of the crisp cold air. After his run he'd get in the hot tub and soak, then get a good meal.

Will plunged off the slope.

Twenty feet in the air over the boulder-strewn slope, Will felt the familiar rush of adrenaline and then something turned his guts inside out.

The stars disappeared.

The night sky was replaced by a dull gray nothingness.

Will fell. His eyes stared in disbelief as the universe disappeared right in front of his eyes. The last thing he noticed just before his body was crushed against the unyielding surface of a protruding boulder was the moon. Its light appeared in the flattened gray sky like a bright lightbulb through a thin cotton bedsheet.

Sam Rosen walked on the grass in back of the White House. It was after midnight on a warm June night. He had just been briefed by Munroe Whitehead, his national security advisor. Hezbollah was busy planting bombs in what had become known as the neutral sector. They were trying to stir up trouble and block the establishment of a Palestinian state. Hezbollah were playing a dangerous game. On the Arab street sentiment had been shifting slowly away from conflict. The evil genius was of course Ayatollah Shahin, who dreamed of uniting the Islamic world under his leadership.

The president stretched his neck and looked north to find the big dipper. He tried to organize his thoughts. The stars had always fascinated and soothed him, though he had never bothered to study the constellations. As a child growing up in Illinois his bed was directly beneath the large double hung bedroom window. He had an excellent view of the starfield. How often he had fallen asleep gazing out at them.

Like a shutter in front of a camera lens, the beautiful pattern of lights disappeared.

The president stood stunned, not believing his eyes. The moon was still visible. Its soft light was visible through a compressed, two-dimensional grayness. The universe around him simply *flattened*. All 3 dimensional perspective was lost.

"What the hell?" The president ran into the White House and into the Oval Office. He heard the screech of tires and car horns out on Pennsylvania Avenue and along 15th street. The clamor of phones rang inside the building. Sam turned on the TV. A CNN reporter shouted hysterically, pointing to the heavens.

"The sky really *is* falling!"

Muhammed Abdul-Rahman slinked along an alleyway in a neutral West Bank sector settlement. He was just about to place his bomb when the sky went blank. Without thinking he armed the device and stared, unbelieving, at what used to be the night sky. "By Allah, have the infidels stolen the stars as well?" The bomb dropped to his feet. Every cell in his body screamed for movement but he stood rooted, his mouth agape. The explosion tore him to bits.

All over the world fear dominated the consciousness of humanity. Scientists could detect nothing different about the physical world other than the absent star field. Planetary commerce came to a halt for several days. Even during cloudy days the phenomenon was still noticeable. The gray of Nullspace penetrated the dome of the sky like a darker wall paint color underneath a lighter one. Curiously enough, plants and animals seemed to be unaffected.

The comforting idea of an infinite universe created by a Supreme Being was shattered forever. Many went insane, unable to believe the evidence of their own eyes. Others shuttered themselves indoors during the evenings and refused to venture outside.

Jack Martins became, overnight, a worldwide celebrity. Scientists began to explain the holographic principle to a terrified public.

Alex Krajicek, Jack Martins' department head at Carleton University, was quick to apologize. He made the talk show rounds and became an effective spokesman for the Martins Sphere concept. On the Tonight show he explained it to a frightened public. "A hologram contains all of the information necessary to recreate a 3 dimensional image. The holographic principle says that the reality of the material world can be completely described on the surface of a sphere. That's what Jack did with his spherical holograms, which everyone has seen on the WorldNet. The Alpha Mission showed us that there is a spherical hologram out in space, just past Alpha Centauri."

"That's great Alex," Daniel O'Connor said. "But why have the stars disappeared?"

Krajicek frowned. "I haven't the slightest fucking idea."

The day after the stars disappeared Jack Martins was given a leave of absence for the rest of the term by a frightened Dr. Spenser himself. "Jack, if you can make any sense out of this then have at it."

A week later Jack Martins demonstrated his spherical holograms to an astonished public in RFK Stadium in Washington DC. He toured the world's major cities on all five continents. "My sphere is only ten feet in diameter. The surface area of my hologram is about 28 square feet. So the amount of information recorded on this little sphere is only a tiny fraction of what is possible. The Martins Sphere itself is over 9 light years in diameter. It has a surface area of about 1,600 quadrillion miles. That's an area so large it's almost impossible for the human mind to conceive of it. You can see, ladies and gentlemen, how astonishingly real this image appears from my small spherical hologram. As the information content of the hologram gets greater and greater, the solidity of the images it describes also becomes proportionately more and more real.

Such a sophisticated hologram might be able to describe the physical world we see, hear, and feel around us."

The public got it. The politicians got it. The world was united now in understanding.

When someone asked Jack why the stars were no longer visible he paused for a moment. "The only explanation is that somebody must have turned them off."

People all over the world caught the disappearance of the stars on their phones and video cameras. All of that footage was gathered together. General Pilsher and a group of military scientists watched the videos in a secure room in the basement of the Pentagon.

"The universe doesn't just disappear, goddammit."

"I say we're under attack," said Colonel Bob Radigan, USAF. "Or this is just a precursor to an attack. Anybody who can turn off the universe's lights has got to have some heavy-hitting technology."

"Yes, yes," Pilsher said, waving his hand in the air dismissively. "That much is obvious. What I want to know is, HOW was it done? And what can we do about it?" He looked toward his college ROTC buddy, Jerome Williams.

"If what Martins said is correct we may be dealing with boundary phenomena."

"Explain," Pilsher said.

"If the physics on the boundary of the Martins Sphere is holographic it might be possible to prevent light from the outside universe to penetrate inside the sphere."

"Or," Radigan barked, "somebody may have built a fence around us!"

"My thoughts exactly," said Bruce Bowden, a NASA scientist on loan for the duration of the emergency.

"Aren't we forgetting something?" said Bill Hasterlin, an Air Force scientist. "All probe data and human observation shows that there's *nothing* out there. No boundary. Nothing visible or detectable."

"Maybe they missed something," Radigan shot back. "I say we go out there. This time, we go armed and ready."

"As far as we know," Pilsher said, "we're alone in the universe. If there is life out there why would they care enough about us to go to all that trouble?" He looked around the room at the five other men, making sure he had their attention. "We need to determine whether this phenomenon is a natural occurrence or whether there is intelligence behind it."

"The odds on this being a natural phenomenon are zillions to one," Williams offered. "It would be similar to the probability that all of the molecules of air in this half of the room, in their random motion, were to suddenly move to the other side."

"I agree," Bowden said. "This must be categorized as a threat to the entire human race."

Radigan slapped his palm on the hard granite table top, startling everyone in the room. "The only way to determine what's happening is to go out there again. Another manned mission."

"I agree," said Hasterlin.

"I've heard there have been improvements made to the drive," Williams said.

"Not improvements," Pilsher replied. "But we've taken the gloves off a little. We don't know what the upper limit of this thing is. We do know, from the flight of the Arrow, that the Pilsher drive is completely harmless to biological life."

"How long will it take to get out there?" Hasterlin asked.

"The ship can make it in about 170 days." The assembled men were flabbergasted. Williams took out his calculator. They all watched as he punched in some numbers. "That's a constant acceleration of about 3,034,170 miles per hour squared to get to the Alpha system. Assuming that the ship begins to decelerate just after exiting the binary."

"That's fucking impossible," Colonel Radigan asserted.

Pilsher shrugged. "The drive itself is impossible. We still don't really understand how it works but we're certain it can do even better than that. The damn thing isn't a propulsion system as we understand it. Somehow the drive interacts with the fabric of spacetime itself. We can get our people safely there and back in less than a year."

The men accepted Pilsher's statement. The previous flight of the Arrow and the probes before it had attained almost equally impossible speeds.

Jerome Williams spoke. "The previous mission data has shown absolutely nothing at the barrier. But that was before the barrier had activated. This time we should be able to detect something." Williams shuddered, thinking about the flattened grayness of the starfield. He could barely stand to look at it. It seemed to suck the life out of him like cold, inexorable doom. "There must be something detectable now at the boundary that is blocking the light from the stars."

Only the faint swish of the air conditioner could be heard as the men were alone with their thoughts.

"Every time I look up at night it scares the shit out of me," Radigan blurted.

"Amen to that," said Bowden.

"We need the same crew as before," Hasterlin suggested after a couple more minutes. "There's no time to train another."

"I hear Greenberg and Svenson have refused to even consider it," Williams said.

Radigan fired up. "They'll go, goddammit. If I have to personally escort each of them aboard."

Hasterlin laughed. Colonel Radigan's idea of an escort might not be quite what those civilians had in mind.

"Well, what are we waiting for?" Radigan said. "Let's get to it."

General Pilsher smiled. "I'll call Munroe Whitehead first thing tomorrow."

The decision to go back to the Martins barrier was made at a NSC meeting in the White House two weeks after Martins' demonstration tour ended.

Katrina Antropov, in her spartan quarters at the Russian Space Academy, thought about the return journey. At first she had been extremely reluctant. But when night fell she felt a rising anger. What should have been a beautiful starscape was now a soul-leeching, flat grayness. Someone or something was toying with the universe and with humanity and its evolution. That was intolerable.

She began to have extremely lucid dreams. Her hero Yuri Gagarin, as well as Isaac Newton and Dwight Eisenhower, urged her forward. Her left ankle was sore. That was also an anomaly for she never experienced 'aches and pains.' Nor had she ever damaged her ankles.

Nigel Clarke jumped at the chance mostly to be with her.

She'd been back once to England but her duties here kept her too busy to continue a romance that both knew could easily be rekindled.

Her former crew wanted no part of a return journey. But they had been browbeaten by public opinion and their sense of duty to the human race into joining forces once again. This time the trip time would be halved.

On impulse Katrina dialed up Nigel on her vidphone. His handsome blond head appeared on the small viewscreen. "Katrina!" He spoke in a voice that left no doubt of his feelings for her. "Are you ready for another voyage? I've been working on some more material to while away the hours."

"Nigel. Are you having...dreams?"

"Of course Katrina. We all dream."

"I mean, dreams about the barrier."

There was a pause. "Yes, Katrina, I have. But they don't make any sense."

"Do these dreams include the U.S. President Eisenhower and Sir Isaac Newton?"

"Well I'll be damned. You've seen them too?"

After an hour of conversation they confirmed several common dream threads.

"Let me call the others," Nigel said. "I'll get back to you."

Nigel Clarke had kept in contact with every member of the crew over the past year. Even the elusive Karl Svenson, who had buried himself in his hometown and refused to talk to the media.

Nigel called her back that evening. "Katrina, you're not going to believe this. I talked to every member of the crew today. I made a list of the common factors in our dreams. All of them include Eisenhower and Newton. And the most startling thing of all? You'll never guess."

"We were inside the barrier," she said quickly.

"That's right."

"Is it just coincidence that we all dreamed the same?"

"Medically speaking dreams are not well understood. However, we were confined together in a small ship for two years. We shared the same experiences. From a medical point of view I don't think it's terribly remarkable that we're dreaming similarly."

"I do. These dreams are opposite to reality. I've gone over and over those hours at the barrier in my mind. We never got in. But these mental images are so real! It's almost as if our minds have been wiped..."

Nigel heard her sudden intake of breath.

"Yes?"

"Nigel, you and I were trapped in an icy crevasse. You helped me out. I injured my ankle and you put arnica on it."

Nigel's face went blank for a moment. "Bloody hell. I *do* remember that. But it couldn't have happened. We were always within the ship."

"Maybe it did happen, Nigel. If it did we have to find out how and why." The images in her mind were not just those of a lucid dream. Katrina was sure of that now.

"Karl and Rad told me that they're convinced we *did* go in."

They both gazed intently at each other through the hand-helds. "I'll have Rad call President Rosen," Nigel said. "I want to get on that ship as soon as possible."

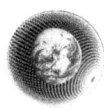

Chapter 17

The Cheesey-Poof 3 was lifted into orbit on a cold November afternoon. Once beyond the earth's atmosphere the voyagers stared into an empty grayness.

"We're enclosed in a shell," Rad remarked. "A container around our stellar environment. I see it but I still don't believe it."

"Opaque the transparencies please," Karl said. "That stuff, whatever it is, makes me nervous."

"Yeah, close the goddamn windows." T'Munga Watanabe pointed the ship toward Alpha Centauri. There was still a probe sitting at the barrier. Its sub-light telemetry would take over three years before its data stream reached earth. They would recover the probe and its precious data, and again attempt to solve the mystery of the Martins Sphere.

T'Munga was only too glad to be aboard once more. Within six months he had tired of the publicity and the fame. Not one of his female companions had been his intellectual equal or even close. He discovered, to his surprise, that it mattered. It had mattered a great deal. T'Munga realized that he was a much deeper and substantial person than he had thought himself to be. He'd built a fun-loving and carefree image of himself but it was only a mask. For two weeks prior to the call-up, he'd returned to the sleepy fishing town of his birth in Japan. He rented a house along the seashore and spent his days in meditation. He was trying to find a new direction for his life. When he received the call from Pilsher he said yes before the surprised general could even make his pitch.

As the ship accelerated past the speed of light the blue cocoon of light enclosed them once more. Even though the ship was accelerating twice as fast as before, T'Munga noticed absolutely no difference inside the spacecraft. Through the soft glow the gray of the Martins Sphere was still visible. By unanimous consent the transparencies were closed.

After three months the crew began to get cabin fever. Each had brought with them several holograms of nature scenes. One or the other was often activated, transforming the sterility of the control room. The crew spent almost all of their time together, telling stories, listening to music, reading, or meditating. When it was time for sleep Katrina and Nigel went together. The other men grumbled but the doctor's sunny disposition made it difficult for animosity to develop. The two were always on their best behavior during the day, usually sitting on different sides of the room.

After 168 days the ship began to decelerate. When the Arrow once again fell below light speed the blue cocoon of light vanished.

"Karl, set your panel to monitor realspace for signs of a hostile presence. Or anything that isn't us." Katrina was mindful of their orders to detect signs of any military threat to earth.

Katrina ordered the transparencies opened as the ship approached the boundary of the Martins Sphere. "I want to see where we are."

Karl Svenson moved to the engineering station. He kept his eyes lowered to avoid looking at Nullspace. The probe that was left from the previous mission was still there. There was no sign of a hostile presence, or of anything. Whoever or whatever had turned off the stars was invisible.

"This is ridiculous," T'Munga said. "Somebody is fucking with us."

"At least we have the probe, which should have recorded the entire sequence of the stars disappearing," Rad Greenberg said hopefully.

"Navigator, full stop at 1,000 feet before the barrier," Katrina said to T'Munga. She asked Karl to secure the probe in the cargo chamber. Everybody watched as it approached the hull and disappeared into the side of the ship. "Probe secured," Karl reported.

"All right Karl, ready another probe. T'Munga and Rad, I want every instrument we have analyzing the barrier."

"What am I going to do?" said Nigel Clarke playfully.

"Not a damn thing, doctor!" Katrina replied.

Karl stopped the probe just short of the barrier and everybody waited for his report. "Nothing, captain." The engineer was disgusted. "All readings zero, just like before. I don't know what we thought we were going to find different."

"There is no boundary excitation?" Rad asked in disbelief. "Nothing to indicate why the starfield has disappeared?"

"That is correct Rad. Readings are zero across the board."

"General Pilsher and the military people aren't going to be happy about this," Katrina said.

"Whoever is fucking with the universe, show yourselves!" T'Munga yelled. Nothing happened.

"It looks like the same stuff I stuck my finger into last time," Katrina commented. "Except that it now surrounds the entire periphery of the Martins Sphere."

"Our only hope now is that probe, as Rad said," Karl said. "When the barrier activated it might have left some kind of signature."

But when the probe's instruments were analyzed it too showed nothing. "No footprint anywhere in the EM spectrum," Karl reported. When the vid was played on the ship's big screen, the gray nothingness at the barrier simply appeared instantaneously out of nowhere. There was nothing to indicate how it was done or who had done it.

"Let's break down that vid," Katrinav said. "Even though it's probably useless."

The crew watched as Karl Svenson isolated and focused on a smaller and smaller window before and after the barrier's appearance. "I'm down to a delta of 10^{-12} second now. That's as fine a resolution as we have. If something happened, it happened so close to instantaneous that it's not worth mentioning."

"Crap," Nigel Clarke commented.

"So much for the glorious mission of the Apollo's Arrow 2 to save mankind," T'Munga said. "What a fucking waste of time."

Katrina was grim. "We're not done yet. Are you gentlemen ready for another plunge?"

The men looked at each other. "Oh what the hell," T'Munga said, speaking for them all. "Let's go."

The crew strapped in, nervous and anxious, fervently hoping that something definite would happen. Nigel tried to break the tension. "Are we in a time loop? I seem to remember doing this before…"

Then the ship touched the barrier and the gray shell of the Martins Sphere disappeared. An instant later, the Apollo's Arrow 2 found itself in blackness.

As far as the eye could see there was nothing visible. No light, no stars, no galaxies. But the depressing gray nothingness was gone.

"Where the hell are we?" T'Munga asked. His voice trembled a little. The utter blackness was much more terrifying to him than the gray shell of the Martins Sphere. That at least was finite.

Karl Svenson consulted his instrument panel. In the crew cabin there was absolute silence. After several minutes he looked up. "I have no idea where we are. My best guess is that we are now in the depths of intergalactic space."

"WHAT???" Rad shouted. He didn't know whether to laugh or cry. If the ship was in intergalactic space it meant that the universe was not a phantom after all. That was comforting. But it also meant they were dead. Karl must wrong. "Check your instruments again, engineer. You're jumping to conclusions."

The little man studied the board again, straightened, and sighed. "I'm afraid not Rad. There's nothing out there at all. Absolutely nothing."

Katrina was stunned. In her astronomy classes at the Russian Space Academy she learned that the distances between galaxies were unimaginably vast. It was about 2.9 million light years between the Milky Way and M31, the Andromeda galaxy. With a sinking feeling she knew that they were lost forever. The Cheesy Poof 3 was a death ship.

"Look for yourself," Karl said.

Rad studied the instruments. "My God. It's even worse than that."

"Explain, please," Nigel said anxiously. His normally sunny disposition and calm demeanor had vanished.

Rad straightened from his stooped position over the instrument console. "From these readings, or lack of them, my best guess is that we are in inter-sector space. I can't even find an atom of hydrogen."

"Fuck," T'Munga said. He expressed what everyone was thinking. "Galaxies are not distributed randomly throughout the universe but lie in clusters, filaments, bubbles, and sheet-like structures. Which means that there are large regions of the universe that contain no galaxies at all. That's where we are."

Svenson went back to the engineering panel. "I believe that Rad is correct. Our instruments cannot detect even a single photon of light or an atom of hydrogen. Even within the depths of intergalactic space we should be able to detect the light from distant galaxies. But there is absolutely nothing out there." Karl's face was ghostlike in the luminance from the console. "I'd estimate that the ship is at least 100 million light years from the nearest galaxy. We could be halfway across the universe." Karl was awed. "If there is a universe of course."

"Wait a minute," T'Munga said. "The mass density of the vacuum itself is approximately 10^{-28} grams per cubic meter, or 10^{-9} joules per cubic meter. That means that even in intersector space we should be able to detect some tiny bit of energy."

"So we're not anywhere," Nigel said.

T'Munga spoke again. "We have to assume that we're out in space somewhere if only to preserve our sanity."

"But how could this have happened?" Katrina asked. She was shocked to the core of her being but maintained a calm facade. That part of her captain's training had not deserted her. She went over what had happened at the barrier in her mind. "We approached the Martins Sphere slowly," she said, trying to keep her voice steady. "The ship hit the barrier. And now we're instantaneously millions of light years from earth? Why didn't that happen on our first mission?" She looked her question to Nigel Clarke, who just shrugged.

"Looks like I'll have a lot of storytelling time," he said lamely.

No one laughed.

T'Munga swore softly and bitterly. "We're a ghost ship, wherever we are. We're all as good as dead."

"None of that!" Katrina spoke harshly even though it was exactly what she was thinking. "We have to stay positive. Maybe there's a way out."

"A way out!" T'Munga strode angrily toward the captain. "Are you mad, woman? We're a million years from any hope of rescue even with this fancy star drive!" He was now only a foot away from Katrina and he was screaming. She felt he might strike her.

Nigel Clarke quickly moved toward T'Munga and placed his hand firmly on the other man's shoulder, drawing him back. T'Munga turned on the doctor. "Get your goddam hand off me, Clarke."

Nigel could see the man before him was at the breaking point. He lowered his arm back to his side. "It's not her fault," Nigel said quietly. "We all made the decision to go forward."

T'Munga raised his head and spoke quietly and very precisely. "Fuck you, doctor." Then he walked out of the room. Everyone heard the door panel close to his quarters.

"Well," Karl said. "What do we do now?"

"There's nothing much we can do," Rad said. He was feeling depressed again, and claustrophobic. He looked out into the infinite blackness and felt a smothering sensation in his brain and in his stomach. "I need a pill." Rad left the room.

Katrina could see that the crew was absolutely stunned. They were trapped with no way to get back, or inform humanity of their discovery. It wasn't fair! She felt herself falling into a dark pit, spinning down and down…then she felt a slap on her face. The pain brought her back to the present.

"Buck up, girl," Nigel Clarke said. "We're not dead yet."

"Thank you, doctor." Katrina kissed him lightly on the cheek.

Katrina stepped over to T'Munga's navigation station. "I'll plot a course." Even as she did so she realized how ludicrous it was. But the eyes of her remaining crew were on her, and her training kicked in. She remembered something Boris Kopitkin, her instructor in Command Psychology at the Russian Space Academy, always said. "Do something decisive even when the situation seems hopeless."

As her hands left the console she looked up to see Nigel Clarke smiling purposefully towards her. His face had lost all of its color.

The next shipday the crew gathered together and decided to push the ship as fast as it could possibly go. During the next several days the Arrow accelerated toward light speed. The crew barely spoke to one another. Each took a regular duty shift, as if everything were normal. The transparencies were opaqued. The crew spent their off hours activating holograms of earth in their private quarters. No one worried about food. Each crew member knew that the ship could manufacture food and that they could survive physically until a normal death. But what about psychologically? Rad Greenberg had already talked of suicide. T'Munga Watanabe was surly and unapproachable.

On the 17th day Karl Svenson was alone at his engineering station. He hadn't bothered to check his instruments for two days and had spent his shift time reading a book. What was there to see? Out of a sense of duty he made a routine check of all instruments and saw a blip on the scanner. Excitedly, he opened the transparencies. A tiny dot of light was visible at the forward panel. "Lights ahead!" he shouted.

Everyone tumbled into the control room. In the blackness it was difficult to estimate size or distance. There were no reference points.

"What do your instruments say, Karl?" Katrina said.

"Distance…approximately 0.0274 light years…about 10 days travel at lightspeed…size…approximately 100,000 miles in diameter."

Katrina felt an inner excitement and observed her crew. For the first time in weeks Rad Greenberg's face showed interest. T'Munga Watanabe's anger had vanished. He stood at Rad's side, looking like a little child about to open a present. Karl Svenson was emotionless but she could feel his suppressed excitement. Nigel Clarke smiled across the room at her, and she smiled back. She knew the doctor would stand, whatever happened. Although more subdued than normal, Nigel was by far the most well adjusted person on board. Katrina had been holding herself together mainly out of a sense of duty, but it had not been easy. During their nights together she cried on his shoulder more than once. A sense of black loneliness and emptiness filled her being. If it was this bad for her, how must T'Munga, Karl, and Rad be feeling? She had asked herself that question so many times during the past 17 shipdays that she could hardly bear to think about it. But now an eagerness and an energy coursed through her.

"How do we stop this damn thing in time?" T'Munga said impatiently. "Even if we decelerate at maximum we will shoot way past it. It will take days to stop and then change direction."

"What of it T'Munga?" Katrina said lightly. "It's not like we've got anything else to do!"

For the first time in a long time, T'Munga laughed. "That's right! I wonder what it could be?"

Katrina let the crew chatter a bit, watching them reestablish familiar connections. When she judged the mood of the group to be just right she spoke in her best command voice. "T'Munga, decelerate at maximum!" Now was the time to give the men something useful to do. "Karl and Rad, do a thorough analysis on that object. I want to know what it is and whether it could be harmful to the ship. After that I want all navigation and engineering systems thoroughly checked out. We've been lax around here for too long. Nigel, check all environmental and medical systems aboard ship. Give everyone a thorough physical."

"What will you do, captain?" Nigel teased.

Katrina laughed. "Not a thing. I'll just sit here and look pretty."

All the men laughed and got busy. For the first time in several days the little ship was filled with good vibes.

After several hours it became apparent that the pinprick of light, whatever it was, had grown larger.

"It looks like a multicolored ball of light," Karl remarked.

Rad Greenberg, the ship's exobiologist, was baffled and intrigued. No life could possibly exist where there was no matter or light. But to deny the evidence of his eyes was foolish. He threw himself without hesitation into the subject he loved best. "There are pulsating patterns of light in very complex geometries," he said, studying the object in the 3D view tank. "The character of the light and the changing patterns do not appear to be random...." Suddenly he drew breath. "Could this thing be intelligent?" Rad turned his head to look at Karl standing beside him.

"Intelligent? I think not, Dr. Greenberg. Probably some small nebula."

"No, not a nebula," T'Munga countered. He walked over to Rad's station. "A nebula is a diffuse mass of interstellar dust or gas or both, usually excited and caused to fluoresce by embedded stars." He raised his arm in a sweeping gesture. "There's absolutely nothing out here."

Nigel Clarke studied the display for a moment and met Rad's eyes. "It sure looks alive, doesn't it?"

The faces of both men lit up.

"Captain, look," Karl said. The tiny dot of light suddenly grew larger and larger. It was heading directly at them with frightening speed.

A brilliant light filled the cabin and the ship lurched suddenly, throwing the crew like rag dolls to the floor. *So this is what it feels like to die,* Rad Greenberg thought just before he felt himself losing consciousness. He uttered a silent scream and then there was nothing.

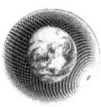

Chapter 18

Consciousness slowly returned to Rad Greenberg. He found himself sprawled on the cabin floor just beside T'Munga Watanabe's navigation station. The brilliant light was gone. The windows had opaqued but the cabin lights were on as usual. He must have been thrown out of his float when the ship listed. Pain shot through his right arm as he slowly rolled over. Nothing seemed amiss except for a large purplish bruise on his forearm, which was beginning to swell. No one else was awake. Antropov sat slumped and buckled in her captain's chair, forward in the cabin, her back to him. Watanabe was on his back in the middle of the room, his face a contorted mask of fear. Karl Svenson was hunched over at his engineering console with his head on the board and his mouth open. A little blood was trickling from a scalp wound. Rad couldn't tell if the man was alive or dead. Nigel Clarke was slowly coming awake at his medical station across from him. He met Rad's eyes and grinned painfully. "We're still above ground."

It was a preposterous statement. Despite his pain Rad laughed out loud. He wanted to tell the doctor how much he appreciated his humor and his light-heartedness throughout their journeys together. He couldn't find the right words. "Thank you doctor," was all he said. Rad knew Clarke understood.

The doctor went round to each of the crew, examining and treating each. He eventually pronounced that they were all none the worse for wear except for some cuts and bruises.

"Speak for yourself, doctor." T'Munga was embarrassed. In the end, when he stared death in the face, he had rushed from his nav float and thrown himself onto the cabin floor in a fit of madness. He had abandoned his post.

In that last moment someone had attempted to occupy the vacant nav chair, the most critical console on the entire ship. It must have been Greenberg who tried to do the duty he had shirked.

"Don't worry T'Munga," Katrina said. "I felt the same as you but I strapped myself in."

She straightened. "All right men. Let's find out where we are, shall we? Navigator, give us a position. Identify the location of that light source."

She watched carefully as T'Munga shuffled to his station. His shoulders were hunched as if expecting censure from his crewmates. No one said a word. The cabin was eerily silent as T'Munga checked his instruments. "No sign of the light source...by God!"

"Yes?" Katrina said. The navigator's voice conveyed an unmistakable excitement.

"We're back inside the Martins Sphere. That thing, whatever it was, must have flung us back inside the barrier."

Rad Greenberg groaned as he exposed the transparencies. "I don't know whether to laugh or to cry." He gazed mournfully at the flat dull grayness of nullspace.

T'Munga studied his board. "My instruments tell me that we are presently at coordinates 23.778 right ascension, declination 78.008, and exactly 1.618 light years from sol."

"Hot dog," Karl said. "It's a miracle!"

"But you can't travel hundreds of millions of light years in an instant," Rad said. He walked over to the nav station. After several minutes he confirmed Watanabe's findings. An almost angelic light suffused his face. "It is truly amazing. We are only a little over 1.6 light years from earth."

The crew, in an explosion of emotion, expressed their relief by dancing around the cabin.

The captain frowned. "Once again we've failed in our mission," she said. "*I've* failed, that is." Katrina gestured toward the depressing grayness that once again filled the transparency. "If I have to look at that stuff too much longer I think I'll go crazy. I'd almost rather be lost in space."

Rad silently agreed with her assessment of the barrier. "Don't be so hard on yourself captain. We are clearly dealing with forces that are far beyond our comprehension."

"But what are we going to say in our report? That we were magically transported millions of light years into space—we think—and then back again by some unknown force? Our mission was to prove, once and for all, whether there's a universe out there or whether it's just a holographic illusion. We were supposed to analyze the barrier and determine the forces that have caused the stars to disappear. We were to have determined whether there is a threat to earth. We have done nothing. In fact, we have another anomaly to explain! We're no further along than we were at the beginning."

Rad Greenberg suddenly burst into laughter. The sudden release from a slow death, combined with his imagination of the faces of the ACHMQ scientists when they all reported this fantastic story, was too much for even his sober temperament. Rad pretended to be Dr. Helmut Grossklaus, the most infamous of the ACHMQ debriefers. "Give us your report, Dr. Greenberg, of your analysis of the Martins Sphere barrier."

"Well doctor, we don't know a goddam thing about the barrier or why it appeared. We did meet up with an intelligent light source out in space that transported us 100 million light years to safety."

"'Qvickly!! 100 cc's of Demerol. This man is hallucinating!'"

The crew began laughing uproariously.

"Not bad, Rad," Nigel said after everyone had dried their eyes. "You just might have a future as a comedian."

"Astonishing, Greenberg," T'Munga said, fast recovering his equilibrium. "I didn't know you had it in you."

After the release of 17 days of nervous tension, the crew realized that they were utterly exhausted.

Nigel held out an inviting hand to the captain. "My prescription is that we all get some rest. I don't know about you but my nerves are shot. We've got six hours before next shift start. Let's all retire and get some sleep, if we can. Come, Katrina!"

Antropov did not move. "I'll rest at my post," she said. "T'Munga, before you leave, get us headed home."

Watanabe grinned. "We already are, captain. It's astonishing isn't it?"

The next day the crew played back the ship's vid and studied the instrument logs. There was no evidence of their encounter with the light source, which they had begun to call HAL.

"Check the time stamps Karl," Katrina ordered. "HAL, or whatever it was, must have been on our screens for at least an hour. And then it ran into us."

Svenson carefully checked the log. After several minutes he unbent from his board and shook his head. "Records show 0.0 seconds elapsed. No temporal discontinuity."

"Explain."

"Meaning, captain," said the little engineer, "that our encounter with HAL…er, that thing, never happened in real time. The logs simply show that our position changed instantaneously."

The crew was now arranged at their stations in the large forward control room. They sat there with their mouths open.

"But that is absurd," blurted T'Munga Watanabe. "Our instruments detected the light source. Therefore they must have recognized and registered it."

"Maybe we're all suffering from a mass delusion," Nigel suggested calmly. "We've been cooped up in this sardine can for months, and for two years previous on the first mission. We don't really know the long-term effects of exposure to Pilsher radiation."

Karl snorted. "My instruments must have suffered from the same delusion, doctor. We saw that thing. We're not crazy."

"Yes, yes," Rad said irritably, yesterday's humor forgotten. "The point is, that's what ACMHQ will say if we tell them the truth. With no physical evidence to corroborate our story they'll pronounce us all psychologically and mentally imbalanced. Our reputations will be ruined."

"That's true," Nigel admitted.

There was no answer to that. Everybody sat silent as the almost inaudible swoosh of recirculated air was heard through the ship's ventilation system. Katrina could see that their minds, like hers, were stretched to the breaking point. There was no proof whatsoever of the existence of a universe beyond the barrier. What had they seen, really? Blackness. No evidence of galaxies or other visible matter. No way to determine their position. It was impossible to determine what was reality and what was fantasy. That, Katrina knew from her Psych classes, was the definition of insanity.

"You're right of course Rad," Katrina said. "So what do we do?"

"If we tell the truth we'll look like crazies," T'Munga said. "But if we lie ACMHQ may eventually figure it out. We'll be disgraced anyway."

"Might not be a bad thing," Nigel said. "They'll not want us for any more missions."

"Our first translation to intersector space might be explained by an unknown force connected with our penetration of the Martins Sphere boundary," T'Munga said. "But the return?"

"Maybe some kind of boomerang effect," Rad suggested.

Karl grinned. "I think HAL did it."

"We had better figure out something plausible to tell those bastards at Tubingen," Nigel said. "They'll be asking a lot of pointed questions. Remember what happened last time."

This suggestion met with unanimous agreement. They all remembered how ACMHQ had pounced on every little inconsistency after their first voyage. The debriefers had harassed the crew and kept them locked up for weeks afterward.

Just then Nigel Clarke walked hurriedly over to Karl's station and whispered something in his ear. The little engineer straightened and his eyes opened wide. He began frantically fiddling with his panel. "OK, Nigel, all safe."

"What was that all about Karl?" Rad asked.

"Nigel pointed out, my dear Greenberg, that if we're going to lie to ACHMQ we'd better turn off the ship's vidlog while we talk about it."

T'munga swore. In the back of their minds they all knew that every moment of their lives was being recorded. But it never obtruded into their conscious awareness.

"We've got to think of something and think fast," Rad said. "Every gap in the ship's log will be cause for suspicion."

Katrina Antropov did not like the way things were progressing. Her training had imbued her with the necessity for integrity in all aspects of the mission. She regarded her command of the mission as a sacred trust, and she said so.

T'Munga did not like this. "I say we edit the vids and shut them down for the rest of the journey. You might not care about sacrificing yourself on the altar of duty, captain. Permit me to care about my future. I'm not going to have people calling me a lunatic."

You *are* a lunatic, Rad Greenberg thought to himself. He forbore to say anything. The others agreed with their captain's decision.

"The truth is going to come out sooner or later," said Nigel Clarke. "If we lie about it we'll just make it worse."

"It's not our problem," T'Munga said. "Let ACMHQ deal with it."

Rad replied testily. "But that's just the point. It *is* our problem because it directly affects our lives."

T'Munga gave up. "I can see that the sentiment is against me as usual." T'Munga understood the value of cooperation and how dangerous it was to disrupt their fragile coalition. He just liked to push and see how far he could go. "It's just like Katrina said. We have no evidence of anything real outside the barrier. We *think* we were in intersector space beyond the Martins Sphere but our logs show nothing. Maybe we *are* crazy, just like Ayatollah Shahin said."

Karl Svenson shrugged. "ACHMQ will debrief us and we'll tell them what we saw. They'll look at the vidlogs and make their own conclusions. Personally, I'm going to tell them the truth." Karl's face twisted into a reluctant smile. "Even though I think it's very possible that what we saw was a holographic illusion." He began to laugh at the absurdity of their situation. Soon the whole crew was laughing hysterically. Afterward, Katrina ordered Karl Svenson to turn on the ship's log.

A long debate that lasted far into the night then ensued about their experiences after penetrating the boundary.

"What actually happened on our first mission?" Nigel asked. "Instruments and ship's log show that last time we partially immersed into…whatever it is…but never fully penetrated it. Yet the probes we sent in disappeared. All of us have had strange but incredibly lucid dreams about a meeting with famous dead people. These dreams have too many points of congruence to be merely coincidental. This time, we seem to have penetrated the barrier and been thrown into the depths of space. Why?"

"The difference is that this time the Martins Sphere barrier was activated," Rad said. "Before it was dormant."

"But who activated it, and why?" T'Munga shouted, expressing their combined frustrations. "And who or what is HAL? What was we he doing out in the middle of nowhere?"

Everyone agreed that they had seen a light source and that the ship had collided with it. Rad Greenberg tried to convince himself that it had never happened. He didn't feel comfortable asserting something that he couldn't back up with cold hard facts. "There is no visual or physical evidence to indicate that those events actually occurred," Rad argued. "That is precisely what ACHMQ will conclude."

T'Munga snorted. "Except the little fact that our ship traveled uncounted light years in zero seconds."

Rad spoke loftily. "I would rather think that a more rational explanation could account for that. Unless you believe in light sources with magical powers."

"But we *saw* it," Svenson said.

"Did we?" Rad replied, looking directly into his eyes.

Karl broke eye contact. "Of course we did," he mumbled. "Maybe HAL erased the entries." It was lame and he knew it.

"Oh come now." Rad was testy. "We've anthropomorphized something into reality that might never have existed in the first place. We were beyond hope. We were looking for a miracle. It is not unreasonable to say that we dreamed it all up. Just like that famous racecar driver, Earnhart whatshisname, a few years back. Remember? He said that his dead father helped him out of a burning car. If that light source was real the evidence would have shown up in the logs. As an exobiologist my job is to investigate extra-terrestrial life, but that doesn't include fantasizing." Rad became insistent. "HAL doesn't exist. It is pointless to keep discussing this…anomaly…as if it was real."

T'Munga was still angry with himself for yesterday's failure. He took it out on Rad. "You call yourself a scientist and you can't believe the evidence of your own senses?"

Rad Greenberg controlled his anger with difficulty. "A scientist relies on observation and proof, not subjective speculation. Our translation back to the Martins Sphere probably resulted from some sort of boomerang effect. That is something our colleagues at ACHMQ will have to determine."

"I saw what I saw," T'Munga said stubbornly.

"Then you better unsee it," Rad snapped. "Weren't you the one who said ten minutes ago that we don't want our reputations ruined? That's what is going to happen if you continue to insist on the existence of HAL."

T'Munga knew that Rad was right. It was irritating. "You and I both know what we experienced even if we *have* to deny it."

Rad was gracious in victory. He nodded his head slightly in T'Munga's direction. "All right then, we'll agree on that." He stood up from his float. "Lady and gentlemen, further speculation on this subject is pointless. I'm tired. I'm going to bed."

In the duty-schedule morning, tempers had calmed. T'Munga Watanabe was feeling expansive. Every day was another day closer to the time when he would set his feet back on earth. Normally grumpy in the morning, today he had a smile on his face.

At their 0800 crew meeting, Katrina looked around the room at her crew and chuckled. "Are we still speaking? Or are we all so tired of each other that we can't stand the sight of each other?"

"The latter," Rad said, "would be pretty close to the truth."

"Do you mean to say that you don't like me anymore?" T'Munga spoke playfully.

"You big bastard, don't pretend you were ever fond of me. And you know I never liked you."

Watanabe's eyes twinkled. "Not even just a teensy, teensy weensy little bit?"

Rad looked into those eyes. Despite himself he felt his mood lighten.

Rad tried to hold back a smile. "Not at all you big lout."

T'Munga pouted and Rad found himself laughing.

"When we get back to earth I'll buy you a beer," T'Munga proposed.

Rad eyed him suspiciously for a moment, then relaxed. He could feel the crisp cold taste of a McEwan's Scottish Ale in his mouth. "I'd love to have a beer right now." It was strictly against regs to manufacture alcoholic beverages or drugs, although the ship certainly had the capability.

"It's settled then," T'Munga said. "As soon as ACMHQ lets us go I'll take you all out to dinner."

"You're on T'Munga," Karl said. "I'm going to order the most expensive thing on the menu."

Katrina smiled. "I get to choose the restaurant. Le Maisson Cherval, in Paris."

"Aye-aye, captain, anything you'd like."

"Just don't go blabbing to the media like you did the last time T'Munga," Rad said.

T'Munga's face clouded for just a second, then it cleared. "Not to worry. I've had my fling. I don't require any more notoriety."

"Rad has made a good point though," Nigel said. "We'll all have to be careful when we talk to the media."

Chapter 19

Jack Martins was down in his basement lab two weeks after the return of the Cheesy Poof 3. His livelihood and interests led him always to check the position of the stars and planets, but that was not possible now. It was a source of frustration.

The Event, as it was being called, was shocking to the world's greatest cosmologist even though everyone had been forced to admit the validity of his theory. Alex Krajicek had come into his office and apologized, although it cost him dearly to do so. Old Man Spenser, Carleton's president, had lately been obsequious in his attentions. His probation had been lifted.

Jack had been on his best behavior ever since the Event. But not from any desire to become acceptable to his fellow man. He had even quit smoking and had cut down on his drinking.

Jack Martins admitted to himself that he was afraid.

He remembered the night it happened as if it were yesterday. He had just finished drinking himself into oblivion at the Heavenly Bodies, the aptly named off-campus strip club. He pulled off the interstate and onto Plymouth Road just three miles from his house. Then the stars suddenly disappeared. A surge of adrenaline flooded his system. He managed to get the car over to the side of the road just as a car behind him came speeding by. He got a brief glimpse of the driver. The man was staring into space as his vehicle plowed into a ditch along the side of the road. Through Jack's whiskey-soaked brain he heard crashing sounds on the freeway. His mind was too dulled to do anything except turn off the ignition and stare upward in disbelief. He got out of his car and sat on the hood of the car. The moon shone through a flat, lifeless grayness. Jack forced his dulled mind to study the phenomenon and

155

felt his gorge rising. He crawled onto the dirt beside the road and emptied his belly. After several minutes he felt better and stood up, holding on to the car for balance. Clearly this was not cloud cover. The sky was completely uniform in appearance, like a piece of gray plastic. Jack noted how the moon's soft light lit the landscape as if this were just another normal evening.

After a few minutes a sense of excitement began to fill his being. The phenomenon was *behind* the moon, between it and the stars. Equations filled his mind as he got back in the car and raced home. Jack ignored his overflowing inbox and thanked God he didn't have a landline or a cell phone.

That night he had worked until 6 in the morning. He was about to hop in the shower when he realized that he hadn't checked the news. He flipped on the vid and saw panicked reporters pointing to the sky. On C–SPAN, Jack saw the ubiquitous mug of Sag Carlson. The pontificating and condescending scientist was explaining the phenomenon as "a temporary diffusion of the light from the stars." Jack flipped to channel 5, the local Midland station. An overexcited local reporter was exclaiming, "...and no one has heard a peep from Jack Martins, the famous scientist who proposed the Martins Sphere concept. Alex Krajicek, head of the Department of Astronomy and Cosmology at Carleton, says that Martins might have some answers. A delegation of scientists from Carleton is on its way right now to his home to speak with him personally. Apparently Martins doesn't have a phone and he isn't answering his email..."

Jack groaned and threw himself under hot water. Maybe they'd go away if didn't answer the door. Ten minutes later two news reporters with cameras, Krajicek, Spenser, and half the Physics and Astronomy Departments barged right in. They surprised him just as he stepped naked out of the shower.

Now, almost a year later, the world was no closer to an answer. Data from the second expedition to Alpha Centauri had been inconclusive. But it was clear that the cosmology that described the universe as they knew it had been altered. This implied some sort of super-intelligent agent or an unknown universal phenomenon.

If the Holographic Principle was correct, this had been accomplished by changing the information content on the boundary of the Martins Sphere. But how had that been accomplished? It was the question that beat in his brain every waking moment. The key must lie along the boundary of the spherical hologram out in space. The crew of the Apollo must have missed something.

Jack set up his equipment to display the famous cat hologram. For two years he had observed a subtle perturbation at the periphery. There was always a faint aura surrounding every one of his holograms, but he had never been able to determine exactly what it was or why it was there. If there was an aura surrounding the Martins Sphere it would be beyond the barrier. The Alpha mission crew would not have been able to detect it.

Jack adjusted the diameter of the spherical hologram display so that it was exactly 12 feet in diameter. It now occupied the central portion of his enlarged basement from floor to ceiling. There was still plenty of space surrounding the image for Jack to step away and observe it from the outside. He approached the hologram slowly, observing the boundary. Yes, there it was. A faint multicolored shimmering around the periphery.

Jack studied the phenomenon more closely. The periphery did not resemble an optical perturbation or an atmospheric disturbance. Perhaps it was an agitation in the fabric of space itself?

Jack stepped back and sat down at his desk. If crew accounts of both the Apollo's Arrow 1 and 2 could be believed, the key to the Event lay in a boundary activation. If the boundary of a Martins Sphere could be activated, what would the activating trigger be?

Jack rose from his swivel chair and placed himself into the holo. He cleared his mind of extraneous thoughts and imagined himself activating the periphery. Suddenly he was surrounded by a brightly colored luminescence. Jack jumped out of the holo and the light disappeared.

He had activated the boundary! The same phenomenon had occurred when the stars disappeared except on a much larger scale. All he had done was to make a clear visualization and use a strongly intended thought.

Could thought itself be the activating trigger? This made no sense to Jack. He was a scientist, not a philosopher.

Jack went back to his desk and replayed what he had just done. He recorded everything he did down here. He had terrabytes of recordings of all his experiments for the past 20 years. What he saw on the vid confirmed his perception of the event. The multicolored light came from slightly outside the boundary of the spherical hologram.

157

Jack repeated his experiment five more times from within the holo. He was successful each time in reproducing the multicolored light. He recalled his reading of the Cheesy Poof 1 mission documents. In that collection was an obscure report called "Tentative Conclusions from the Analysis of Unknown Craft" by Team Orsagh. The team leader described a figure-8 engine that responded to thought impulses.

Jack strode right into the holo and thought about a twinkie. Nothing. Then he thought about Amara. Immediately, the field colored and he was standing in front of her office desk, inside the hologram, surrounded by the multicolored light. She looked up, startled. "Jack?" He panicked and instantly found himself back in the lab at precisely the position he had left it.

"Balls!" Jack said aloud. "Did that really happen?"

He could check by calling Amara Thompson. Except that he had no phone. Amara…the shock of seeing her again, and the way it had come about, deeply unsettled him.

Jack Martins walked over to his desk and sat down. He began to laugh. First lightly, then louder and louder. Tears rolled down his face. Something within him was about to burst; a great, poisonous demon that had been living inside him for years. He began to cry. Great racking sobs shook his body. Jack jerked himself to his feet and his body slammed against the wall. He careened around the room, bumping into the walls, knocking some of his precious equipment on to the painted cement floor. He screamed. His voice was loud in his ears and sounded like a madman's shriek.

Jack found himself on the floor. His fists were smashing the hard concrete and his face was covered in his own sweat and tears. After several more minutes the spasming quieted, but he could not move. Occasionally he felt one of his limbs jerk.

That is how Amara Thompson found him half an hour later. Standing guard next to Jack's body was Ivan the cat.

Amara rushed to him. She petted Ivan reassuringly and then turned Jack over on his back. He smiled. "Amara," he mumbled. "I tried to call you but I don't have a phone."

Amara looked him over. "Stay here. I'll be right back."

"I'm not going anywhere."

Jack felt a curious, pleasant lassitude and a feeling of inner peace. It was strange to feel anything except a sort of self-contempt. His eyes closed.

"God I'm tired. But Amara is here so everything will be all right."

Just then Amara entered the room with a small plastic tub of hot water, a towel, and bandages. This is what she should be doing, looking after the man she loved. The only man she had ever loved.

Amara bathed Jack's bloody hands and wrists. She bandaged them and secured each wrap with two safety pins she found in Jack's medicine cabinet. Then she wiped his face and kissed him softly. Jack's eyes opened.

"Do you feel strong enough to walk up two flights of stairs to your bedroom?"

Jack smiled sleepily and nodded. "If you give me your arm."

Amara helped him to his feet and wrapped his arm about her waist. He leaned heavily on her. They began slowly walking up the basement stairs that led into the kitchen. Amara could see that he was almost sleepwalking. She said nothing, but enjoyed the feel of his body against hers. There was nothing sexual about this contact and she liked it a lot. She felt comfortable with this man. She knew he loved her. But she had never been able to draw him out of himself.

"I am very tired," Jack said as they went up the stairs from the ground floor to his bedroom. His head lolled to one side. He said it as a child might to his mother. Amara smiled.

"Yes Jack, it's going to be all right." She wished she was taller because his head was at an acute angle and looked to be in an uncomfortable position. She had the desire to prop it up somehow. She was a tall woman but she only came up a little past his shoulder.

They reached the top of the stairs that led to his bedroom. "I think I should go to bed now," Jack said.

Amara led him to the unmade bed and kicked a pair of athletic shoes out of the way. Jack fell onto the bed like a rag doll and was asleep as soon as he hit the sheets.

Amara walked down the stairs and let herself out the front door. Jack had experienced something life changing, she was sure of that. She hoped it was something positive.

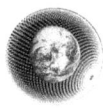

Chapter *20*

A desert camp somewhere in northern Libya

"The infidels have shut out the light from the stars," proclaimed Rizza Abd-Al-Aziz ("servant of the powerful"). He and a dozen of his Defenders of Islam sat around a small fire in the cold desert night. They occasionally stared with resentment at the evilness that had swallowed the sky. Technically, fires were strictly forbidden. The prying satellites of the enemy could see, it was said, a lit match anywhere on earth from outer space.

Rizza's statement met with no objections from his fellows. All were gathered here, and across the North African desert, for jihad. For revenge upon the Christian powers who insulted the glory of Allah. Each cell had a military leader and a religious advisor.

One of the young fighters spoke. "The infidels are somehow responsible for the disappearance of the night sky." This had been drilled into their heads over and over until it was an accepted truth.

Rizza replied. "Within us burns the blood of ancestors who have fought and bled in these deserts. They crossed them in their caravanserai, sharing life, love, and commerce throughout the Arab lands. The glory and magnificence of the desert, and pride in our heritage, sings in our blood and in our hearts."

Ishaq Hussein-al Najafi, the religious advisor, took up this theme. "For five centuries, before the Mongol uprising in the 13th century, the Arab world was the center of civilization. We were the leaders in philosophy, medicine, astronomy, and mathematics. For centuries the Christian countries of Europe were ignorant, flea-infested barbarisms. Our libraries were the world's greatest, with hundreds of thousands of volumes in Baghdad, Damascus, Alexandria, and Constantinople. The printing of books on parchment was known centuries before the European Gutenberg. How then have these Western barbarians taken over the world?"

No one had an answer.

"It is the duty of every true Muslim to restore the glory of Arab civilization!"

Each young man regarded the flat gray of night as a personal insult. Each was determined to be revenged upon Jack Martins who, it was said, was the evil demon behind the disappearance of the stars. These uneducated young men were ignorant of logic, mathematics, and the Holographic Principle. But they understood helplessness and frustration.

Organized by the growing power of the religious leaders in Tehran, each of the cells of the Defenders of Islam never numbered more than twelve fighters. Each had been assigned a specific target either in Europe or the United States. The object was simply to generate panic. Strict immigration and border controls had been relaxed in the Christian countries since the United States had finally withdrawn its troops from Muslim lands. Now was the perfect time to strike.

No one yet knew their assignments. But all were motivated by the Fatwa issued by Skeikh Massoud Izz-Al-Din, to cleanse the world of the threat to Islam. Izz-Al-Din means 'glory of religion.' It was said he could trace his ancestry directly back to the first Mamluk ruler in the 13th century.

All knew that in influence, Izz-Al-Din was second only to Ayatollah Omar Shahin, the Supreme Leader.

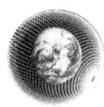

Chapter *21*

When Jack Martins woke up he felt different. He remembered that something extraordinary had happened. But the events of yesterday were a blur in his mind.

The sun was shining brightly into his window. That was odd, because that window has a western exposure. A glance at the clock on the bedstand told him it was 3:47 p.m.

Something inside him was different. He felt…relaxed, lighter somehow. Normally he'd get out of bed grumpy and jumpy. He'd be ready to attack the day and fend off all those idiots who just didn't get it, or get him.

Today Jack felt like part of the human race. He didn't know what to make of that. He was supposed to be the brilliant outsider. The iconoclast. The genius who saw things others couldn't or wouldn't. That separated him fundamentally from his fellow man, even his fellow academics. It was the source of his genius, was it not?

Jack walked into the shower humming a tune. For the first time in years he actually felt the hot water hitting his skin. He liked it. Why hadn't he ever noticed that before? "Because you were probably drunk," he answered aloud. Jack laughed. The old Jack Martins never laughed in the morning and rarely at any other time. Jack padded back to the bedroom and noticed the mess. Dirty clothes were strewn all over the floor. The bed sheets smelled of nicotine and coffee. When was the last time he'd washed them? A part of himself asked, *what difference does it make whether the sheets are washed? A bed is just a place to crash after a long night.* That made him laugh again.

He noticed the sun's rays through the window, illuminating the dark brown carpet and making it sparkle. It was going to be a nice day.

Who is this person? said the voice in his head. *It's the sun, idiot, get over it.* Jack laughed again, he couldn't help it. Like a gas escaping its container Jack felt as if he'd somehow gotten out of himself. Inexplicably there was now a new Jack Martins. One without an attitude.

Instead of picking something up off the floor, Jack walked into his closet and donned a fresh shirt and a new pair of pants. He grabbed a tie. Walking over to the full length mirror, he carefully tied it in a Windsor knot. He inspected himself and was not satisfied. He walked into the bathroom looking for his hair brush. His black hair was so thick it needed a special brush to get through it, which is why it was almost always disheveled. After rummaging around in a drawer he finally found it. Then he walked back to the mirror and brushed out his hair.

"Not bad, Martins. You're a good looking devil." After selecting a pair of dress shoes (instead of his usual athletic shoes) Jack walked out of the house very pleased with himself. The first thing he would do was talk to Amara.

Amara looked up as Jack walked into her office. "Jack!" she said, surprised and pleased to see him. Her eyes surveyed him and liked what she saw. "God you're a handsome devil."

Jack laughed. "That's just what I told myself this morning, er, this afternoon. I mean, when I got up."

Amara smiled. "Jack, has something happened? There's something different about you...I mean...I don't know, there just IS."

"We're both doing it."

"Doing what?"

"Being incoherent."

"Yes," she said, flushing slightly. Amara fumbled nervously with the pen on her desk.

"Amara, how did you know to come over yesterday? I don't remember hardly anything. You arrived at just the right moment." He was looking directly into her eyes and smiling.

Oh my God, she thought. That's the Jack I see behind the mask, and now it's coming out. Something *did* happen yesterday. Something good.

She told Jack about his sudden appearance in her office. "You were surrounded by a faint halo of light. It was remarkable. I thought it was one of your holograms. I went around looking for you but I couldn't find you. On impulse I came over."

"That's right." Suddenly everything in his mind was crystal clear. He had been analyzing the periphery. He had stepped into the holo and somehow been transported to Amara's office.

"Amara, would you come over tonight after work? I want you to see something."

There was nothing sexual in his request. "Yes Jack. I'd love to."

"Good. Meet me in the lab at 6. I'll get carry-out. We'll eat, and then go to the lab for a little experimentation."

"A exciting night on the town I see!" she said jokingly. "What sort of experimentation do you have in mind?"

"No tricks, Amara. There's something important I'm investigating and I need you to help me verify it."

Even his speech is different. More casual. She felt that it would be perfectly safe to be with him tonight. "All right, I'll be there. How about getting some of that Vietnamese noodle stuff?"

Two hours later they were in the lab.

Jack went to his small bench and activated the cat holo. He directed Amara to a spot ten feet away from it and stood beside her. "Just observe the holo for a minute and then tell me what you see."

Amara stared at the brilliantly defined bubble in the half light of the lab. "It's incredible, Jack." The black and white cat sat on the black granite bench in the act of licking his fur. It seemed to her that the cat in the bubble would spring back to life at any moment.

"That's just a picture of Ivan but it seems more like a stopped video. It looks even more real than real life." She walked around the bubble, inspecting it carefully. Then she stepped back for a minute and studied it. "Other than the incredible lifelike quality I don't see anything else. Well, maybe I see a fuzz around the outside of it. But it disappears every time I look directly at it."

"Describe the fuzz."

"It looks like some kind of hazy light you'd see around a soap bubble in the sunlight. There are lots of colors."

Jack nodded. "I thought I was seeing an optical illusion. Then I got in the damn thing and…well, you know what happened."

"It wasn't a holo of you?"

"Nope."

"Jack that's impossible. It must have been some kind of holographic projection. You weren't really in my office yesterday."

Jack opened his mouth to speak and then closed it. "I...I have no idea." He turned to look at her with wide eyes. "This is going to be exciting."

"What are you going to do? I don't want you killing yourself."

He laughed. "No danger of that sweetheart."

Her heart leaped. *Sweetheart. Yes, that's how I feel about you too.* "You're sure?"

He grinned. "Hell, I don't know. But I'm going to find out. If I get into trouble you can rescue me again."

"I won't know where you've gone!"

"That's true I guess, but maybe I just imagined it."

"I saw it too."

"The last time I just stepped into the thing ...I can't remember how I activated it."

She knew he was going to go in again, whether or not it was safe. "Try it again. If you get into trouble I'll call 911." She was trying to make light of her fear for him.

When Jack entered the holo nothing happened. "Do you notice any change in the periphery?"

"No, nothing."

"Shit. That was anticlimactic."

Amara smiled, a bit relieved even though she could tell Jack was disappointed. "Maybe we were both hallucinating."

Jack walked back into the holo. "No, there's something else. I was thinking about you when I walked in the last time."

At that moment the cat on the bench disappeared. Amara saw Jack in front of her office desk. Her office window was illuminated softly in the twilight just before darkness. Her desk lamp was on, throwing a beam of light onto the walnut surface and casting a fuzzy luminescence onto the objects in the room.

Amara didn't know much about photography. But she did know that it would be impossible for a camera to display the scene with such clarity. There wasn't enough light.

Amara saw Jack looking around the room in astonishment. He walked over to the lamp and bent to turn it off. Was this just a holographic projection of Jack or was he really there?

The lamp light disappeared, plunging the room into almost complete darkness. A little light still entered the room from a neon light at the end of the hallway. She could still see Jack faintly, moving around her desk.

Jack stepped out of the holo and the cat reappeared on the granite lab bench.

"What do you make of this?" Jack said, holding her blue pen inscribed with the words "Carleton University."

"I don't believe it. You must have really been in my office!"

"If so, it defies the laws of physics as I know them." He turned toward her, his eyes blazing. "I left a little souvenir on your desk. When you go in tomorrow morning call me and tell me what it says."

"You don't have a phone, dear," she reminded him.

"Blast! I keep forgetting. What's the matter with me? I don't have a way for people to get hold of me when I need them."

"You never needed anybody before, Jack. I thought that's the way you liked it."

"Well of course I like it…" his voice trailed off. A look of confusion passed over his face. "That's the way I used to like it." He looked down at her. "How did I ever go on?"

"You didn't, Jack." Amara spoke bitterly. "You have always been a complete loner."

"That bad, eh?"

"That bad."

There were several moments of silence. "Maybe I'll turn over a new leaf. But I'm not promising anything."

The corners of her mouth upturned in a little smile. "I like this new Jack Martins a lot better than the old one."

"So do I. I'm not sure he's real yet."

When Amara got to her office the next morning she found a piece of notepaper on her desk next to her computing device. Jack had scrawled, "I think I might be in love with you."

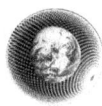

Chapter 22

Cardinal Che Rodriquez fiddled nervously with the silver cross suspended around his neck. He looked out of the window from his Vatican office. The moon was at the full but the stars behind it were no longer visible. The sky had been swallowed by a depressing gray blanket.

Cardinal Rodriquez remembered that fateful evening when the stars had inexplicably disappeared. When Pope Clement XV looked into the sky he began blubbering. The man had totally flipped out and it was thought at first that he might go insane. Fortunately the pope had gradually recovered his mental stability. Since the pope's unfortunate indisposition the other cardinals had been turning to him more and more for advice and counsel. It was said he might become the first South American pope.

The College of Cardinals had increased its influence within the Church during the past decade. Formerly an advisory body with no influence, it had chosen a sitting panel of a dozen of its brightest members. Even Cardinal Tauron had noticed and approved of its deliberations. The reclusive Tauron ran the Curia, the Vatican's intelligence service, with an iron hand.

Che had received disturbing news from him after their briefing yesterday. An unknown group called the Defenders of Islam had sprung up even as Arab leaders had publicly engaged in cooperative talks. According to Tauron this new group was convinced that Jack Martins and the Christian countries were responsible for the disappearance of the stars. Tauron read the statement released by the Defenders:

"Beware, Christian infidels! An attack on your societies is imminent unless the demon Martins returns the stars to us. Act now or face jihad from the Defenders of Islam!"

Cardinal Che shook his head in disbelief. The statement was irrational and obviously written by a fanatic.

"Could Arab leaders be behind the message?" he asked Tauron. "It seems unlikely. For over a year the Arabs have been coordinating more and more with the Israelis and the Vatican." Each religion had asserted the correctness of their beliefs. But all had agreed that without religion, the masses would descend into anarchy and barbarism. The Event had caused much fear and instability among the populations of all nations. "Religion is the glue that will hold humanity together," Che said finally.

Cardinal Tauron smiled, silently agreeing with the little Columbian. "Is it your opinion that Arab leaders are returning to the failed policies of confrontation and terrorism?"

"My dear Tauron, that is a question I should be asking you."

Cardinal Tauron had not been more forthcoming during the briefing, other than to say that Jack Martins must be protected.

Che was curious. "The Church has an interest in Martins?"

Tauron spoke blandly. "Over a year after the Event, a panicky Catholic community is losing faith in the teachings of the Church. If anyone can restore the stars to us, it will be Jack Martins."

Che remembered Tauron's curious wording, which sounded like the statement of the Defenders of Islam.

Just then the door to his office burst open, disturbing his thoughts. Cardinal Thorn flung himself into the room, his tonsure in disarray. "Have you had dinner yet Che?"

Che smiled. The maverick Cardinal Roderick Thorn, from the U.K., was known for his volatile personality. Thorn had converted suddenly to Catholicism after falling out of favor in the Church of England. He had risen rapidly in the Catholic hierarchy. It had caused some friction with the Anglican Church, Che recalled.

Cardinal Thorn grinned. "Let's go to the cafeteria and you can buy me dinner."

"All right."

Che put his arm around the larger man and they walked to the cafeteria. The two men found seats and ordered. Che ordered tea and an omelet. Rod ordered beef stroganoff.

"Have you heard anything about this new Islamic radical group, Che?"

Che was astonished. That information hadn't been made public yet. Cardinal Thorn never got anything first. "How did you hear about that?"

Cardinal Thorn sipped his coffee. "Damned hot this is."

"You didn't answer my question."

"Through the Vatican grapevine. There's a rumor going round."

"I will have another word with Cardinal Tauron about this," Che said. Had Tauron started the rumor?

"That is well. If the Islamic world is set on reverting back to holy war it would mean a setback for the Middle East peace process. And for international cooperation."

"Human consciousness is at a critical point, Rod. We have been fighting and killing each other for millennia. Now the human race is finally reaching toward global cooperation and an end to problem solving through violence. But it wouldn't take much, especially after the Event, to set us back."

"I wonder whether Cardinal Tauron is involved somehow with this new group," Cardinal Thorn said. "The brilliant cardinal has an eidetic memory and a personal network of contacts. Let's be honest and say spies, Che. He may be maneuvering for advantage somehow."

"Don't be fanciful Roderick. Certainly Tauron has used his network to maintain the Catholic Church's influence in world affairs. But causing an international panic wouldn't be in the Vatican's best interest."

Cardinal Thorn shrugged. "Perhaps, perhaps not. The Secretary of State for the Vatican has been around for 25 years now. Tauron has built the Curia's intelligence service to a level that rivals the Russian GRU. Who knows what machinations are going round inside that clever and devious brain?"

The food came.

Che laughed. "Eat your stroganoff, Rod."

After Cardinal Thorn left Che decided he would have a private word with Tauron about the Defenders of Islam. The secretive cardinal always knew much more than he disclosed in his briefings to the College of Cardinals.

Chapter 23

Jack Martins' classes were standing room only now. He saved five minutes at the end of his standard lecture for updates on his research, or general comments on current events. Many Carleton administrators and staff made it a point to squeeze into Room 233 during these summaries.

Today he said, "As you know, I have a sophisticated optical laboratory in my basement. Yesterday, with the help of a colleague, I discovered a potentially important phenomenon connected with the periphery of a spherical hologram. Whether this will have any bearing on our current difficulty I have no idea. Stay tuned for further details."

As he left the podium a crush of people surrounded him. Most of them were media. Surprising himself, he stood for over half an hour patiently answering stupid questions. Then he hurriedly ducked down the hallway and took the stairs outside into the cool September air. He would go to the Administration Building and see if Amara wanted to take some lunch with him. He walked swiftly along a secluded sidewalk at the back of the building toward Huron Street and the Admin building. A guy with a cameravid was following behind him. Jack heard a sharp crack and felt something whiz by his ear.

During his hell raising days in South Boston, Jack had been shot at. In those days heroin was the drug of choice. He had gotten involved in a small way with dealing until a rival outfit came after the gang he belonged to. After that the kid from Exeter decided to abandon a life of crime. Now he instinctively ducked and rolled to the ground, squeezing himself behind a thick hedge. He frantically crawled along the dirt and alongside the outside of the stone building, knowing that he was a dead duck. He heard a shout and then footsteps running away. Another bullet lodged itself into the wall several feet over his head.

Shaking, Jack got to his feet and saw the guy with the cameravid lying on the ground. His instrument was pointed at Jack.

"Are you all right?" the guy said, getting up. He was small and wiry, about 25 years old. As Jack approached he stuck out his hand. "Hi, I'm Bob Cameron."

"Mighty cool under fire, aren't you?" Jack grasped the proffered appendage.

Cameron grinned. "He wasn't shooting at me, he was shooting at you."

Jack smiled back. He liked this guy right off the bat.

"What was that all about?" Cameron asked.

"I don't know, you tell me. You had a better view of it than I did."

"Somebody shot at you from over there." Cameron indicated a little stand of trees about 100 feet away. "Don't know how he missed you."

"I'm sure as hell glad he did," Jack said. The rush of adrenalin had subsided. He now felt calm and cool.

"Taking it pretty well I'd say. I'd be scared to death right now if that happened to me." The younger man paused, looking carefully into Jack's eyes. "Hey, you're that Martins guy aren't you?"

"I would certainly hope that I am," Jack replied drolly.

"How about you take me out to lunch and we talk about it?" Cameron was hoping to get a story.

"Sorry kid, I haven't got time." Jack wanted to get out of the open. "I've got more important things to do."

"Let me guess: it's a woman."

Despite himself Jack grinned again. "You're a busybody kid. Unfortunately for the world you'll probably make a good reporter." He walked away quickly toward Huron Street. As he turned to look for traffic he noticed that the cameravid behind him was trained on him once more. Apparently no one else had noticed the altercation.

"Jack, did you mean it?" Amara said when he reached her office.

Normally he would have felt anxious about any expressions of love, and especially with this woman. Today he was strangely calm inside even after his brush with death. "I think I did."

"You think?"

Jack gazed at the only woman he would ever want to share his life with and felt a glow spread throughout his body. It wasn't sexual. Well, maybe a little, but there was something else. Something warm, something expansive, something mellow. It felt right.

Jack was honest. "I don't know what love is. But whatever this is it sure feels good."

She smiled. "It's a start." *And it's a lot more of you than you've ever given me.* "I'll take it." *For now.*

"Good! I want you to come down to the lab with me after work."

"Another hot date?"

"Yup. We're going to do some more experimentation with that holo."

Two hours later Jack got home. He flipped on the vid and saw himself on the 5 o'clock news. That bastard Cameron! "...someone took a shot at the famous Jack Martins as he came out of the Physics and Astronomy building at 3:30 this afternoon..." Jack groaned. It would be all over town and he'd have to answer a lot of questions. After he turned off the vid he began to wonder who would want to kill him. That first bullet had come very close. It wasn't more than twenty minutes later when he heard the door bell. "Amara! Maybe she decided to come a little early." When Jack opened the door two uniformed police officers were standing there, looking very official. "Excuse me Mr. Martins. Could we have a word with you?"

Jack reluctantly let the two men in. "I'm sorry officers. I have no idea who shot at me or why. And I've got a heavy date this evening. In an hour, to be exact."

One of the officers chuckled. "Don't worry sir. We just need to check on a couple of things and we'll be outta here."

Not two minutes after they'd left Amara burst into the room without knocking. "Oh Jack! I just heard about those killers on the news..." She was flustered and anxious. Jack cut her off.

"I won't have any of that," Jack said. "I hate it when people fuss over me."

"But Jack..."

"I can take care of myself. I've been shot at before you know."

"But Jack!" she shrieked. "That doesn't make it any better!"

"Makes it a damn sight better. Now we're going to go downstairs. I have the holo almost all set up."

Amara stamped her foot. "How could you think of stupid holograms at a time like this?"

"At a time like what?" Jack replied. He was confused.

"You men!" she cried. "You're so...you're all so *stupid*."

"Very well, Amara, I'm stupid." Jack was calm. "Now, are you ready to come downstairs with me?"

Amara was exasperated and stared at him in disbelief. Twice she opened her mouth to reply. She saw that he had no interest in discussing a measly little subject like attempted murder. She sighed. "All right Jack, but I don't understand..."

"I know you don't understand, sweet. Now..."

She grabbed his shirt and shook him. "Jack Martins, if anything ever happened to you I'd die." Jack saw the love in her eyes and her fear for him. His heart melted.

Jack took her in his arms. "Don't worry love. Everything will be all right."

She gazed up at him, her eyes wide. "You promise?"

"I promise."

Amara knew that was as far as she could take it. She relented and allowed him to lead her down to the lab.

Jack rubbed his hands together in excitement. "Now we're going to try it again. This time you get in."

"Me? I ain't gettin' in that thing, not for *nobody*. My mama didn't raise no fool."

Jack laughed. "Oh yes you are, darlin'. I'm going to fire this thing up and then you're going to walk your pretty little ass in there and see if you can activate it."

"You're serious aren't you?"

"Of course I'm serious. We're conductin' a scientifik expeerimint here, honey!" he said in his best redneck voice.

Amara giggled. "If I walk in there I'm going to need a reward."

Jack smiled. "We'll talk about that later." Jack walked over to the bench and fiddled with his setup.

Amara spoke teasingly. "That's a change. A Jack Martins who isn't interested in sex."

"I didn't say I wasn't interested in sex. Just not right now."

"We could do it on your big table."

"On my holo table!" Jack was shocked. "You're out of your mind, woman. That setup is so delicate and so expensive..."

He broke off as he saw Amara laughing at him. "You got me that time." He walked purposefully toward her. "I think I might have to spank that pretty little bottom of yours to teach you a lesson."

"Jack!" Amara stepped back toward the wall. "You'll ruin this brand new dress!"

Jack laughed. "Then behave yourself." He stepped back to the bench and activated the holo. "OK, we're ready. I want you formulate in your mind a clear picture of somewhere you want to go. Then step in."

"I'll imagine myself in Leon's bedroom. It's almost 7 and he's probably getting dressed for that University Musical Society concert tonight."

"Leon?" Jack inquired. "Who is that chump?"

"You know, Leon. The guy I was engaged to. And he's not a chump."

"Was?"

"We broke it off last fall by mutual agreement."

"Good. I want to have you all to myself."

"I thought you said you wanted to perform an experiment."

"I do. But you keep bringing up the subject of sex. Makes a man think you hadn't done it in a while."

"I do not!" she flared. "And I have!"

"Have what?"

"Have had sex!"

"See? I told you that you keep bringing it up."

They both broke down laughing. "Oh Jack," she said after a minute, "I haven't laughed that hard in years."

"Neither have I."

"Where were we?" she asked.

"We were talking about sex. Remember, you brought it up."

She stamped her foot. "I mean before that, stupid."

Jack made a sweeping gesture with his arm, indicating the amazingly vivid and beautiful spherical hologram of Ivan the cat that hung suspended in space.

They both gazed at it. "It's incredible," she said. "I don't think I could ever get tired of looking at it. I swear that cat looks alive and is ready to jump off the table."

"Indeed it does. The beauty of these things has kept me going for 25 years."

"All right Jack. I'm ready to try it."

"Good girl."

Amara straightened and took a deep breath. "Leon, I'm comin' for you, boy."

Jack laughed as she stepped into the holo. He stepped back about six feet from the holo, alert to any change around the periphery. For an instant he thought he saw the faint, multi-colored light self organize. Then Amara was standing in somebody's bedroom apartment.

"Jack! I did it!"

Just then the door opened and Leon Whittaker walked in. His jaw dropped. "*Amara?*"

Amara was panicking. She knew she had to visualize the lab in order to get back but she was so embarrassed she couldn't think straight. "Jaaaack." Amara turned to stare at her partner in crime back in Jack's basement. "Hel-llllllllp!"

In the middle of his bedroom Leon Whittaker gazed at a glowing sphere of light 12 feet in diameter. Inside the sphere was an incredibly lifelike vid of his former fiancée. Behind her, Leon saw a tall guy with black hair in some kind of laboratory.

"Jack, is it?" Leon was angry. "Hey fuck you buddy! What do you think you're doing? Is this some kind of a joke?"

Jack Martins was doubled over in laughter and heard nothing.

"Jack, get me out of here."

Leon's fists balled and Jack straightened. "So you're Leon, eh?" Jack spoke conversationally. "Didn't work out with her did it?"

Leon Whittaker was flabbergasted. His fists unclenched and his mouth moved open and closed like a fish gasping for air. Leon's features hardened in recognition and he pointed. "You're that damn Jack Martins aren't you?"

Jack executed a graceful bow. "I am he. Have I the pleasure of addressing Leon Whittaker, formerly affianced to my girlfriend Amara Thompson?"

In her holographic bubble, Amara giggled.

"Yeah I'm Leon all right. I've a good mind to call the cops on you. I know all about your little tricks, Martins. Your reputation precedes you."

"Call the cops?" Jack was mystified. "For what?"

"For trespassing, damn you! Can't a man even get dressed without people popping in on him?"

Amara laughed. "Leon, I didn't know you had such a good sense of humor. I might not have given you up."

"Who are you people, a couple of crazies?" Leon was a picture of outraged dignity. "Perverts, both of you." He looked at Amara, horrified. "I'm sure glad I didn't tie the knot with you."

"I always told you that you needed to lighten up a little," Amara said critically. "You're too serious."

In the lab, Jack was laughing again.

Leon swelled. "I'm calling the police." He reached over to grab the vidphone on his lamp stand.

"This is going to be interesting," Jack said.

"Hello, police? This is Leon Whittaker, of 1123 Pauline. Yes. I want to report an intruder...it's a she...no, a he! ...no, they haven't stolen anything...yet...no, no weapon, but...well, the guy is tall, I think, and has black hair...well, it's hard to tell how big he is...yes, he's standing right in front of me...I think...well, I can't be sure because she's in front of him and he's in some kind of laboratory...of course he's in my bedroom! I can see him from here...no, I don't have a laboratory in my bedroom. What a stupid question..."

Amara was laughing so hard she couldn't concentrate. She finally got herself together and mentally visualized the lab.

As magically as it had appeared the holo, and the two intruders, disappeared. The vidphone fell out of Leon's slackened grip and hit the carpet with a dull thud. "Hello?...Hello? Are you still there Mr. Whittaker? Do you want us to send someone over?"

Leon Whittaker decided that the concert was going to be too much strain on his shattered nerves. He went into the medicine cabinet and swallowed a sedative. Without taking off his clothes he lay down on his bed and was soon fast asleep.

Amara stepped out of the holo.

"So much for our scientific experiment."

Jack frowned. "Yes. We don't know a thing more than we did before. For instance, what would have happened if you walked out of the holo? Would you have appeared physically in Leon's bedroom?"

He looked at her closely.

"Think, Amara. Did it feel like you were physically present? Or did it feel like you were standing in the lab and looking at a vid of Leon?"

Amara sat down on her chair and took off her shoes. "Damn things have been pinching my feet all night." She thought for a moment. "I felt like I could step out and touch him."

"I felt the same when I was in your office. I was able to grab a piece of paper off your desk and write on it. That indicates I was physically present." He smiled at her. "Mighty small office you have there."

"When I'm VP I'll have a big one."

"So what have we gained from this experiment?" Jack asked rhetorically. "We've learned that I wasn't hallucinating and that this phenomenon, whatever it is, is real." Jack smiled. "And we have Mr. Leon Whittaker to corroborate our account!"

Jack looked down at Amara. "That guy's a stiff. How'd you ever fall in love with him?"

"He isn't a stiff!" Amara was insulted that he could have questioned her judgment. She was a little embarrassed at Leon's performance in their little play. "He has many sterling qualities."

"Name one," Jack countered.

"He's…loyal."

"Dogs are loyal."

"He's…steady."

"Phew!" Jack said. "That *was* a close call, wasn't it?"

Amara hit him with her shoe.

"I think we've had enough excitement for one night," Jack said. "Experiment over." He checked his recording vid. "Yup, we got all of it."

"You mean you recorded us?" Amara asked.

"I record everything I do down here. Scientific accuracy and all that."

Amara shook her hips. "You know Jack, you promised me a reward."

"God you're beautiful." Jack scooped her up in his arms. He lifted her easily and carried her up the stairs.

Chapter 24

"You had a good shot at him and you missed," complained Rizza Abd-Al-Aziz to his comrade. Rizza kicked the wall of the filthy room in the transient's hotel. The Fleabag, as it was known locally, was a decrepit building in the red light district. No questions were asked of any who entered. Only cash was accepted and no registration was required.

Rizza and his companion Rashid Sakhr were there the night after their attempt to eliminate Jack Martins. The relationship between the two fighters, however, was anything but amicable. Rizza did not like his companion. He asked too many questions and constantly debated the soundness of Rizza's decisions.

Rashid replied contemptuously. "I missed on purpose you fool."

Rizza growled and felt for the knife he carried inside his pant leg. Rashid spoke calmly. "I wouldn't do that if I were you." Rizza swore, for he knew that his unwelcome partner excelled in hand-to-hand combat.

"You missed on purpose?" Rizza was horrified. "You insult your sacred duty and your sworn oath!"

Sakhr spat on the dirty, stained carpet. "Enlighten me, O Wise One. If Jack Martins is the demon who prevents the stars from shining, and the glorious fighters of Islam from attaining Paradise, how will killing him remedy the problem?"

"When the devil Martins is destroyed Allah will restore the stars to us. It is stated in the fatwa of Izz-Al-Din." Rizza was confident.

"Have you read this fatwa, O Esteemed One?" Rashid asked. He stood in the center of the room, careful not to touch anything.

"I could not read the document even if it were available to me," Rizza flamed. "Would the great Izz-Al-Din lie?"

"Would he?"

"You are a heretic!" Rizza shouted. "I cannot understand why you were ever chosen for this sacred mission."

"There are many things you do not understand. If I were you I would keep my voice down. Do you want to draw these barbarians to us with drawn guns? All that is necessary is for one of them to overhear us and call the police."

This insult only further inflamed the volatile Rizza. Even worse, he knew that his subordinate was right. He sat on the bed in silent, sullen fury.

"You are a fool." Rashid spoke calmly, his lips curling slightly upward. "If the infidel police look for us where is the first place they will seek?"

"When our mission is complete I will find a way to kill you." Rizza wanted to smash that insolent face, the face with its high cheekbones and delicate features that spoke also of delicate breeding. It was a face that had mocked him ever since they were assigned as partners back in the Libyan desert.

"Would you have us sleep upon the filthy ground in the cold, like pigs?" Rizza asked.

Rashid waved a lazy hand around the room. "Are these not the unclean chambers of the unbeliever? These animals who contaminate all that they touch? Better to be cold than to lie upon these foul sheets."

Despite his hatred of Sakhr, Rizza felt the force of these comments. Then he remembered Rashid's deliberate dereliction of duty this afternoon and his hatred blazed once more. "Izz-Al-Din himself shall hear of your treachery!" he hissed.

"I think not." Rashid Sakhr then coolly palmed his weapon, an 8 round silenced PB / 6P9 Makarov pistol, and shot Rizza Abd-Al-Aziz right between the eyes. He then reached into his warbag. He carefully pulled out a pair of dress pants, a clean shirt, and a pair of nice looking athletic shoes. Quickly he changed clothes, stuffed the others into his bag, and calmly walked two miles to the Sheraton downtown. He smiled at the beautiful young woman manning the welcome desk and booked a suite on the top floor. He threw his duffel onto the elegantly made bed and looked around at the affluence of his surroundings. "This is more like it, as the Americans would say. Much more like it." Rashid Sakhr then stepped into the shower. He washed the contamination of the Fleabag, Rizza Abd-Al-Aziz, and, it seemed, months of sweat from his body. It felt like years since he had been truly clean. After scrubbing and rinsing he lowered himself into the whirlpool and soaked for half an hour in the deliciously hot water. Then he looked in the phone book for an escort service and arranged for some feminine companionship later that night. He found a custom tailoring service and bespoke a man to suit him first thing in the morning. Then he went downstairs and ate a passable dinner in the hotel restaurant. Only after this did Rashid Sakhr go to the stairs and call in to Cardinal Secretary Tauron on a special phone. This phone would route his communications back and forth several times, bouncing it through several satellites. It was traceable, of course. But he would speak only three words in Arabic, indicating the success of his mission.

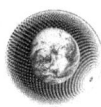

Chapter 25

Further experimentation by Jack Martins demonstrated that it was not possible to leave the hologram and remain at the desired physical coordinates. But it was possible to physically interact with anything at that location while inside it. He made that conclusion by envisioning his bedroom and translating to the second floor five times. Each time he attempted to step out of the holo he found himself back in the basement.

A week later Jack discovered something truly astonishing.

Both Alpha Centauri missions and his own experiences had involved movement in space and some phenomenon at the boundary. He postulated that any spherical hologram was itself a Martins Sphere. If that was so he could solve the mystery of the periphery using his little holos. It should be possible—theoretically at least—to solve the larger problem of the barrier around Alpha Centauri.

At the conclusion of his lecture yesterday he had hinted at such. Afterward he had been mobbed. On the Friday news at 5 a reporter blurted: "Jack Martins has made great progress in solving the mystery of the Event." He had to hold a damned news conference on his front lawn three hours later. He was shivering the whole time in the cold late October air. Jack called the reporters comment "a gross exaggeration."

The problem was that no one else had been able to make a spherical hologram. Jack had never published any formal papers on the technique. He had refused inquiries from curiosity seekers. There had been several break-ins over the years even though Jack had installed a steel door with a special security lock. Jack never bothered to use it mainly because it was a pain to keep locking and unlocking the thing every time he needed to go into the basement. After the Event the police had assigned a patrol car to watch the house and the neighborhood 24 hours a day. That had made him the most popular guy on the block.

Jack concluded that the periphery was activated through clearly defined and directed thought impulses. It was absurd, really. How this occurred was not possible to determine. It just *did*. The old Jack would probably not have been able to proceed on such a metaphysical leap of faith. The new Jack just shrugged and plunged in. Before stepping into the hologram he wrote down exactly what he would say in his mind.

Jack stepped into the hologram with a clear and simple idea. He would query the periphery, asking it to show him its function. At that moment the little holo expanded. Jack saw himself as someone in a house of mirrors. There were an infinity of replicas of himself all around him, radially. The replicas were all squashed toward the edges.

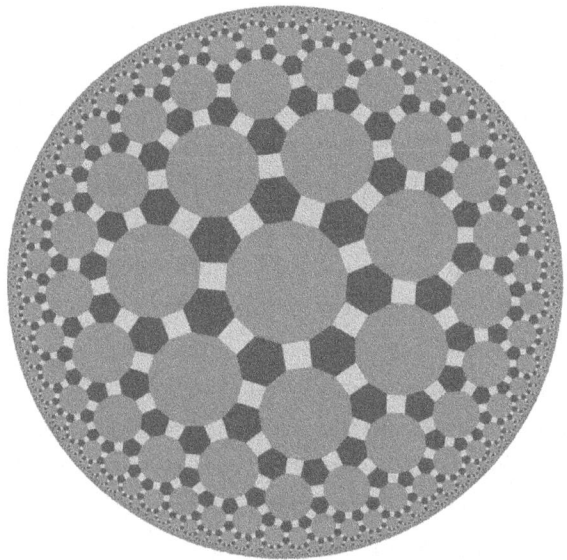

Each one of these replicas was slightly different, as if each Jack Martins existed in a different universe of possibility. One Jack was dressed in a very expensive suit. Another had scruffy clothes. Still another was wearing a sort of glittering high-tech sari. The Jack's went on and on. Did his life have this many probable outcomes? Apparently so! The space was curved hyperbolically. As he examined the structure more closely he perceived that the Jack's he was looking at were local 3 dimensional structures on the surface of a 4 dimensional manifold...

Jack swore and stepped out of the holo. Cold sweat beaded on his forehead. His mind (and his senses) felt like they had been twisted in some bizarre and frightening way.

He felt sick to his stomach and stepped out of the house for a walk in the brisk air. The sun was shining. Jack walked around the block, trying to clear his head.

After twenty minutes he felt a little better. His mind had stopped trying to figure out the impossibility of the 4-manifold. He went back into the lab for another try. He'd play back his vid and see what had been recorded later. Inside him he felt an eagerness, a freshening of his blood, and a feeling of adventure. He knew that his investigations had taken him way beyond science. Jack accepted it. Whatever he was experiencing it was real. He had one primary thought. His spherical holograms were crude imitations of the Martins Sphere beyond Alpha Centauri. The capabilities of a true Martins Sphere must somehow include physical transport.

"That would explain the sudden displacement of the Apollo's Arrow 2," Jack said to himself.

Jack stepped back into the holo and followed the same steps as before. This time he did not pay attention to the 4-manifold. He concentrated his attention on the local sphere of alternate Jack's. Which one should he choose? One of his replicas had a beard and a white lab coat...no, too boring. Another was dressed in rags and was sleeping in a filthy, unfinished basement...definitely not that one. Another was partying with several scantily clad women running around...that looked interesting, but no. Jack spotted the guy in the high tech sari...yes, that one.

He concentrated on that alternate Jack. Like a camera focusing the other Jack's disappeared along the outer edges of the manifold. He now stood about ten feet away from his alternate self. This Jack was even taller than he, and thinner. His head was bald. Baldie was seated on a floating cushion in front of a small table in the middle of the basement. Metallic shelves filled with bright silvery discs surrounded him. A library? On the table stood a small device that looked like a reader.

"Whoot be thees?" the man said, startled. His English was heavily accented.

"I am Jack Martins," Jack said.

"Hyou bee not me!! I bee Jacque Maarteens."

"You are frightfully ugly, my friend. I don't think you do too much credit to me."

The man was clearly puzzled but apparently got the gist of Jack's remarks. He replied in an affronted tone. "Hyou are a barbarreean."

Jack laughed. "All right. Why don't you put one of those discs in that device and show me what it can do."

"Hwheere commeth hyou hyeere?" said his counterpart.

Jack decided to treat his alternate self like a child. "I don't think you are too bright, my friend. Please put one of those discs in your viewer."

"I whass yusst habout to do so," the man said. He picked up a disc from the tabletop and placed it in the device. A holo of a deciduous forest filled the room. Birds sang and a small creek bubbled close by. Above the canopy of trees the sun shone, but that sun looked larger and more yellow than it should have. The effect was astonishing.

"Hey, that's pretty good! Do you know anything about spherical holograms?"

The man did not answer. Jack wanted to have a look at those discs and the reader. He tried to walk toward Baldie. Like a hamster on a treadmill he was not able to move from his present position. He was blocked, somehow, from actual physical contact. After several attempts Jack gave it up. Apparently these alternate Jack's were not accessible. But were they real or were they just a product of his imagination?

Jack stepped out of the holo and deactivated it. When he played the lab vidlog it showed everything. Which meant that what he had experienced was real. He now had visual proof that life existed elsewhere.

Elsewhere, but where was that? Were these alternate universes? Jack had no idea. He decided not to show these vids to anyone other than Amara.

Chapter 26

Two weeks after the first attack on Jack Martins a bomb went off in the London Underground at 3 a.m. The blast ruined three train cabs and killed two train inspectors. In New York, a similar incident destroyed two city cabs and their drivers as they waited at a cab stop. Another attack was made on Jack Martins as he came home from a visit to Amara. A bullet nicked his shoulder and put a hole in his driver's side window. Fortunately, a police car drove down Leland only seconds after the first shot and chased the assassins away. The men put guns to their heads before they could be captured. Each carried a laminated card that identified him as a fighter in the Defenders of Islam. In Washington DC, a taxi carrying all four members of the President's Science Advisory Board had its brake lines cut. Lev Katzenbaum suffered a broken collarbone. Dirk Wheeler had whiplash and a broken arm. A WorldNet broadcast by the Defenders of Islam claimed responsibility for the acts. "The Christian infidels, with their Godless science, are violating nature's laws. They are responsible for the disappearance of the stars. It is written in the fatwa of Izz-Al-Din. Only when the perpetrators of this heresy are destroyed will the stars be restored to us," the vid asserted. "Jack Martins must die for the good of humanity!"

The Vatican

Cardinal Che Rodriquez visited the Cardinal Secretary of State in his office for a private talk about the Defenders of Islam.

"The Supreme Leader, Ayatollah Omar Shahin, is clearly engaged in an attempt to unite the Arab world under his leadership. But why would the Iranians want to attack the United States and Europe?" Che was confused.

"There are several reasons." Cardinal Tauron ticked them off on his fingers. "One, primarily to send a warning to other Arab leaders. 'If we can strike across the Atlantic we can hit you anywhere and anytime we want.' We have it on good authority that Izz-Al-Din privately contacted the governments of the attacked countries beforehand. He assured them that their operations were isolated." Tauron folded his hands and leaned his chin on his fingertips. "Understand that such things are sometimes viewed as necessary at the highest levels of governance." Tauron was about to continue, but paused. Rodriquez knew that he had decided not to share something important. Che said nothing. He didn't want to interrupt the flow of information.

Tauron continued. "Two, to get a measure of revenge on the United States and Great Britain for the destruction of Iraq. And for the deaths of over 100,000 Arabs during the Gulf Wars and afterward. Shahin knows the US can't retaliate because the Middle East peace process will crumble. Britain is in no position now to assert itself militarily."

"And three, to test the effectiveness of their force. You see, Che, there are games being played within games. Our intelligence tells us that Izz-Al-Din and Shahin are involved in their own personal power struggle. Shahin was shocked at the efficiency of Izz-Al-Din's force. Even though they, ah, missed their prime target Martins. He rightly suspects that Izz-Al-Din has created an army loyal only to himself."

Tauron looked his contempt. "Shahin is a caricature. Too late, he sees that Izz-Al-Din holds all the cards. While Shahin stays in the limelight and receives the public glory, Izz-Al-Din is the éminence grise behind the throne." The Cardinal Secretary of State permitted himself a slight smile.

"Our Arab friends really are behind the times, are they not?" Che commented.

"Their societies are only now being modernized," replied Tauron. He spoke without criticism. "Old habits die hard."

"It seems odd to me that the Israelis escaped unscathed," Che said.

Tauron's lips curled. "The Israelis were not hit because of, ah, back-channel monetary flows from the Israeli government to certain well-placed officials. Also because Israel agreed beforehand not to retaliate for any attacks in allied countries. This, of course, is Bar-Elet's payback to President Rosen during the Middle East peace talks."

Che looked his question.

"President Rosen held firm during the most strenuous part of the negotiations between Israel and the Palestinians. He forced the Israelis to accede to more than they were willing to give. As a result the Israeli Prime Minister lost popularity. He barely survived a vote of confidence in the Knesset."

"I remember that. I didn't think President Rosen's character was that firm."

Tauron laughed. "The little man surprised everyone, including Bar-Elet. Rosen looked him in the eye during his visit to Washington. He said, 'withdraw from these negotiations and we'll cut off every penny of your funding.'"

Che was impressed. He also wondered where Tauron was getting his information.

"It seems that Bar-Elet is more subtle than I thought," Tauron said with approval. "When Bar-Elet agreed not to retaliate for attacks by the Defenders of Islam, Izz-Al-Din agreed to avoid Israeli territory."

"But how has Izz-Al-Din controlled Hezbollah? They have always been eager to attack the Israelis through their surrogates in northern Lebanon." It was confusing. "Hashim Nasrallah has always been a maverick."

"Good question, Cardinal Rodriquez. Here things become very interesting. You see, Izz-Al-Din has recruited the bulk of his fighters from the ranks of Hezbollah itself. Thus at one stroke he has accomplished two objectives. The diminishment of Nasrallah's power, and the transfer of Hezbollah's loyalty to himself. In effect, Sheik Izz-Al-Din has taken over Hezbollah and has also shown Shahin just how powerful he really is."

Tauron smiled and nodded his head slightly, as if respectfully acknowledging a worthy opponent for a brilliant move. "Izz-Al-Din is very clever, is he not? But I am beginning to think, a little unstable. He has set himself up for the end game, the fruition of all of his plans. But how will he play his hand?"

Milan, Italy

Biagio De Luca carefully inspected every millimeter on the recording surface of his hologram with his optical scanner. The silvery sphere sat upon his holographic bench, gleaming dully but uniformly in the subdued light of his laboratory. It was a bright sunny day. Biagio had fastened the black Velcro coverings securely to the four windows, blocking out the light.

He had built his lab and designed his equipment to the specifications sent by Dr. Jack Martins. Dr. Martins had three others besides himself and his assistant Burt Froebel working on the spherical hologram project. Dr. Collins in Australia, Chen Yu-Shao in China, and Rik Van Der Meer in Holland. He and Van Der Meer were young men in their mid-twenties. They were not scientists but were uncannily gifted in optics and good with their hands. The two men had access to money. Enough money to build the specialized equipment necessary to outfit a Martins Optical Laboratory. Jack had met all of them at various conferences over the past five years, and had enlisted their help. So far none of the others had been successful duplicating Jack's hologram. He, Biagio De Luca, had promised himself that he would succeed where the others had failed.

De Luca readied his equipment and then switched off the lights, plunging the room into darkness. At the center of his granite bench was a fake potted plant, the subject of the attempted hologram. He activated the optical equipment. Light beams, carefully targeted, bounced off mirrors forming two perfect semi-hemispheric circular wavefronts that simultaneously imprinted the recording surface of the sphere. Remarkably, according to Martins, a successful spherical hologram only required a 90-second burn for full resolution. De Luca paced the room impatiently. He turned his eyes from the bright lights surrounding the large holographic setup.

A minute and a half later Biagio removed the plant and adjusted the setup for playback. Here was the time of nervousness. De Luca always experienced a feeling of dread in the pit of his stomach at the idea of another failure. Martins had told them of the attempts on his life. He urged them to work night and day unless the secret were to be lost with him. It was important to duplicate the experiment and confirm this work!

De Luca activated the playback protocol. His potted plant appeared within a perfect sphere 10 feet in diameter in spectacularly vivid colors and sharper-than-life resolution. The holo took his breath away. Here was a Platonic, perfected representation of the actual thing! It made the "real" plant look like a drab, amateurish facsimile.

DeLuca was about to jump for joy and go to his favorite trattoria for lunch when he noticed something remarkable. Martins had sent a full report of his latest holographic experience. It read more like a science fiction story than a true account. De Luca studied the brilliant display before him. He observed a fuzziness at the boundary of the image, just as Martins had reported. Carefully, he followed the steps Jack had written down.

He found himself in a hall of mirrors. Duplicate images of himself faded into obscurity all around him. Martins had written, "My tentative conclusion, which must be confirmed by further experimentation, is that the boundary is thought-programmable. The boundary phenomenon provides access to a 4-dimensional manifold of alternate universes. You must have an absolutely clear image in your mind before anything will happen."

De Luca already knew what had happened to Jack Martins. Martins talked to his alternate self but Biagio De Luca looked at things from a broader perspective. What would an alternate earth look like? If other spatial dimensions exist, did the earth have a counterpart in those other realities? At that moment, the fabric of space and time itself began to morph. The walls of the lab dissolved and reality expanded. Biaggio saw 90 degree turns which appeared to his startled mind as extensions of the familiar three dimensions of height, width, and breadth. In each one of these higher dimensions was a different planet earth.

As his mind exploded almost out of control, De Luca swore as one only can in Italian, releasing his astonishment and his fear of the unknown. After several minutes he calmed down and stepped away from the holographic setup. The walls reappeared and reality asserted itself once more to his abused senses.

Shocked and excited, he used his nervous energy in taking down the playback setup and restoring the configuration for a new trial. Then he activated his dataset and sent a detailed report to Jack Martins.

Two months later

Amara sat in front of her holovid on a cold Saturday night. She was alone. Jack had abandoned her for this stupid conference in Milan, where he was to make "a very important announcement." Just when things had seemed to be going great between them!

For Amara, years of emotional disappointment had finally culminated in the relationship she had always wanted with the man she wanted. Now he was gallivanting around the world trying to get the stars back. Another attempt had been made on his life at a holographic conference in Germany.

Jack had stayed on a few days for sightseeing. The German authorities were never tolerant of foreigners shooting people on their territory. They killed the assailants, who again carried the laminated IDs of the Defenders of Islam.

Amara pleaded for Jack not to go to Milan. "Make them come here. I don't trust the Italian police."

Jack grinned. "Neither do I babe. I already promised De Luca that we'd all meet in Milan and have a few beers together."

Amara snorted. "A few beers my ass. You'd just like to go swimming on those nude beaches."

"It is one of the attractions of Europe, my dear."

Suddenly she threw herself into his arms. "Be careful Jack, for God's sake." She looked anxiously up into his black eyes.

Jack squeezed her. "Don't worry. I'll be all right."

Earlier she had shamelessly asked him to marry her. Jack said no.

"No? Why not?"

"Because…because I'm not good enough for you," Jack replied. He was at a loss for words.

"Don't give me that crap. You said we're perfect for each other."

"When did I ever say that?"

"The first night we made love." Amara spoke firmly, with a woman's infallible memory about matters of the heart. Her eyes softened. "Jack, you know you love me."

Jack met those eyes for a few moments, then broke off. "Yeah, I do. But I'm hell to live with."

"Let me be the judge of that. I'm a big girl. Besides, I know you better than anyone."

Jack acknowledged the truth of that. "The problem, my dear, is that I don't know myself well enough. Maybe if I have another fit I'll finally straighten myself out." Jack was joking but Amara didn't think it was funny.

"…and now, let me present Dr. Jack Martins," said the voice from the vid, startling Amara as she returned to the present. Jack sat at a long, curved wooden table raised upon a dais. Five other men were present in a huge lecture hall with a very high ceiling. Off to the side was a large holographic bench with one of Jack's gleaming silver spherical holograms suspended above it. It was surrounded by a complex setup of mirrors and optical equipment. Amara stared. It was the biggest holo she had ever seen, fully 20 feet in diameter.

Amara immediately recognized the geeky looking, almost effeminate young man seated to Jack's immediate right. Burt Froebel, Jack's long-time assistant. The other men were unfamiliar, known only to her from Jack's occasional reference to them in his work. In front of the panel were dozens of reporters with recording vids. An audience of several hundred spectators packed the auditorium.

"Ladies and gentlemen, we are excited to bring you Dr. Jack Martins and his colleagues, who have an important announcement. Later, Dr. Martins will be giving a demonstration. He assures us that it will rock our worlds." The Voice belonged to a short, thin man who seemed very excited. The man spoke heavily accented English. "So without further ado, let's get right to it." He waved toward the table and walked quickly off camera.

Jack briefly lowered his head and leaned in to the man on his right. He whispered something and nodded his head. "Good morning," Jack said. "As you know, five years ago Burt Froebel and I first demonstrated the remarkable properties of a spherical hologram." The crowd buzzed softly. All of them had heard about the famous demonstration in Washington DC. "Today, however, we have something even more remarkable to show you." Now the buzz became an excited babble. People began shouting questions from the audience. Jack Martins calmly held up his hand until they quieted down. "God, is that a handsome man!" Amara thought to herself. And completely, serenely in command in a way that the Old Jack would never be capable of.

"Today we are going to demonstrate the remarkable, programmable properties of the Martins Sphere boundary. Hold on to your seats!" The crowd buzzed once more, and Jack waited for them to quiet. Amara smiled. "Jack, you're getting to be quite a showman," she said to his image in the vid. She thought she saw him smile back at her.

Jack smiled playfully and his lips twisted in a shadow of what Amara recognized as the Old Jack Sneer. He rose slowly and walked over to the bench. The other men followed, ranging themselves around the table. "Please turn off the lights," he ordered. The room plunged into darkness except for one overhead on the ceiling, which provided illumination to the holo bench. The men fiddled with the equipment for a few minutes while the crowd looked on agog, and with bated breath. Jack told Amara later that you could have literally heard a pin drop.

Each of the men acknowledged their readiness and Jack nodded.

The room exploded with light.

The crowd gasped. A holo of Ivan the cat, 100 feet in diameter, floated in the middle of the huge auditorium. Jack had caught Ivan on his holo table just as he was about to spring. Even Jack was shocked at the impossibly life-like brilliance, sharpness, and detail of the image. Ivan was looking directly at most of the audience, his eyes locked on them in attack mode. A dozen people fainted on the spot but the audience was so mesmerized by the display that no one noticed. Every person there later said that it was the most breathtaking sight they had ever seen or would ever see.

After things had calmed a bit Jack began to speak. "Ladies and gentle-men, there is no danger. Ivan the cat is not really here, although your senses tell you otherwise!" There was nervous laughter from the audience. Jack acknowledged this with a couple of jokes to get everyone settled down in their seats. "Notice the periphery of the holographic image." At the boundary of the huge hologram was a brilliant, multi-colored fuzziness that roiled and moved in constantly changing patterns. "We have discovered that the boundary of every spherical hologram we have tested so far is programmable."

Another gasp from the audience.

"The purpose of this demonstration is to show you how this is done."

The crowd broke out once more into excited babbling. Jack said nothing more. He began to arrange six portable chairs in a hexagon. Each of the men took a seat. "Please pay close attention." Nothing happened for a minute. Suddenly, a gray nothingness surrounded the display.

"Does that look familiar, ladies and gentlemen?" Jack said rhetorically.

"What the hell?!..."

"How did you do that?..."

"It's a trick!..."

"Is this some kind of a joke?..."

"Omigawd..."

Jack grinned at his companions, who were very pleased with themselves. Within all of them was a sense of awe at what they had done.

"Now comes the best part," Jack said. He didn't respond to the questions and demands from the participants. The men concentrated. After two failed attempts the image reappeared.

The auditorium burst into pandemonium. People were shouting, cheering, and talking excitedly. Amara saw Jack and his crew walk calmly back to the holographic bench and deactivate the playback. The room was once more plunged into darkness, which had the effect of instantly quieting the crowd.

"Turn on the lights please," Jack requested. Before anyone in the audience could recover their senses Jack walked over to the discussion table and began speaking.

"Ladies and gentlemen, what you just saw was the interface of a Martins Sphere being programmed." Shouted questions were turned away. "Please address your questions to my colleague Dr. Collins, one at a time. Raise your hand and I will choose. Anyone who shouts a question will not be heard."

Immediately four score hands went up. Jack chose a man in a white lab coat. "Please tell us what you did, in the most concise language you can think of," the man said.

Jack grinned. "Good question." He looked over at Collins, who nodded. Jack stood up and gazed into the sea of faces in front of him. "To make a long story short, we have discovered two things. One, a properly constructed spherical hologram is a Martins Sphere. Two, the periphery of a Martins Sphere is programmable, through clearly imaged thought. Yes, you heard that right. After six months of experimentation we have discovered that a Martins Sphere contains what we are calling a zone of chaos. A zone of chaos is an interface between the world of matter and energy and thought impulses. We don't want to be accused of quackery so we demonstrated a very minor capability of this interface. A Martins Sphere has a basic "On-Off switch" that allows the programmer to deny the passage of specified electromagnetic frequencies. And to turn it on again."

Amara saw Jack pause, look down for a second, and then raise his head. He seemed to look directly into her eyes. "If our Martins Sphere model is correct then the implications for the current planetary situation are obvious."

Tehran

Massoud Izz-Al-Din watched the Milan demonstration from his private office. What he saw shook him to the core of his being. He knew that what had transpired was not fakery. Yet it was impossible. It *should* be impossible for a man, any man, no matter how intelligent, to play God. It was against the will of Allah. Izz-Al-Din was not religious. He had contempt for the fools in the Council of Guardians who enforced the so-called principles of the Koran so haphazardly. But he utterly rejected what he had seen as an abomination. Never should one man, or a group of men, have such power!

Izz-Al-Din fully comprehended the magnitude of the Martins demonstration. He understood the next logical step was to reprogram the Martins Sphere boundary. To bring back the stars! To get the people of earth to unite under Martins' leadership.

Izz-Al-Din apprehended the cold hard logic of it with a brutality that cut like a thousand knives into his psyche. His quest for Arab leadership was to be denied him. Who would listen to him when this infidel would restore the stars? And what of his people? To restore the glory of the Arab nations was one of his primary motivations. To actually help the people raise their standard of living. Not to fall victim to the decadence of the Christian nations and their degraded "pop culture." For him this was not a cheap phrase to appease the masses. Like all true adherents to a cause, Izz-Al-Din believed. And in that belief he found power and strength. But what of that dream once Martins gained control of the thoughts and beliefs of humanity on a world-wide scale? More Western and Christian dominance of the Arab world. No. It cannot be allowed to happen!

Izz-Al-Din rose abruptly from his desk and walked down the stairs into the cool Tehran night. Jack Martins must be stopped before it was too late. And those associates of his as well. He ticked them off on his fingers: Dr. Rimman Collins of Australia. Chen Yu-shao of China. Biaggio DeLuca of Italy. Rik Van Der Meer of the Netherlands, who was so tall and pale he looked like a ghost. And of course Martins' assistant Burt Froebel.

It may already be impossible to stop this new technology from spreading. But under no circumstances could a united population be allowed to perform this mass experiment. United in thought, aligned around the infidels, it would be a victory for Christianity. Once again Islam would be relegated to a secondary position. And himself as well. Therefore, the Defenders of Islam would have to create more chaos. A fragmented planet could never come together in the way Martins planned.

There had been three attempts on Martins' life already. All had been bungled. It occurred to Izz-Al-Din that Jack Martins was inordinately lucky. Did he perhaps enjoy the protection of Allah? The Defenders of Islam had successfully concluded almost every mission assigned, no matter where in the world. Yet Martins remained unharmed. Always through seeming coincidences. There would have to be a fourth attempt, and a fifth, or as many as necessary.

Moscow

Nigel Clarke and Katrina Antropov lay together on the bed in her 12th floor apartment in the Russian Space Academy complex. "Stay tuned for an important announcement!" screamed the vid.

Nigel rubbed his hands together in excitement. "This is just what we've been waiting for."

Nigel didn't care that much about the latest Martins announcement. But it had been a good excuse to break the ice. Katrina had called him last week and asked him to lecture at the Russian Space Academy. He jumped at the chance to see her again.

"I thought you'd forgotten about me." Nigel was unable to keep the hurt from his voice.

There was a long pause at the other end. He could feel her nervousness.

"No, Nigel, never that. We need to give our cadets some information on the medical and psychological aspects of long term space travel and I thought you would be the best because of all of your experience and..." Her words were running together. "Just come OK?"

Nigel jumped on the first plane out of Heathrow. He had knocked on her door at 10 p.m. Moscow time. There was no response from inside. He had a sudden fear that she was not at home. Above his head was the flat gray nullspace that some of the more well-adjusted had begun to call Duct Tape. Nigel didn't notice it anymore. He knew from his work that about 20% of the population had been driven completely bonkers by it.

He knocked again, harder this time.

Suddenly the door swung open. "Nigel! I didn't expect to see you so soon! I..." But she could no longer speak as a pair of strong arms pressed her to him. His lips crushed themselves against hers.

After a minute, Nigel held her at arms length. "There! That wasn't so bloody bad was it?"

She came into his arms again and he kissed her softly, tenderly. She sighed with happiness. Katrina looked shyly up into his eyes. "I'm sorry Nigel. I'm a good commander but not so good at the feminine stuff."

Nigel hugged her again. "You're doing just fine, dear." He was blissfully happy.

"Nigel, the door's open. It's freezing in here."

Nigel closed the door. "Turn on the vid. Supposed to be an important announcement from Martins right about now."

"It's just about my bed time," Katrina said. "I had a long day today and you're scheduled to talk at 8 a.m."

"Oh I am, am I?"

"Well, I hoped you would come," she said, turning back and forth on the balls of her feet. Nigel was pleased to notice how radiant she looked.

He wasn't tired in the least. Moscow was three hours ahead of London and it was only 7 p.m. London time. "You have two choices, Katrina. Either go to bed with me now or watch the conference."

"And after that?"

"You can go to bed with me."

She laughed, full throated, head thrown back. Her guard was down and he loved it.

"You're a beautiful angel," he said.

"Nigel…really?"

"Yes, really."

She smiled and he saw the love in her eyes. Finally. Finally, she's learned to fully trust me.

Katrina skipped over to the vid. "All right then, let's watch the conference."

Washington, DC

Jack Martins appeared with President Rosen, the U.S. Science Advisory Board, and five of Martins' colleagues in the Oval Office of the White House. Chairs had been arranged in a semi-circle in front of the famous desk. The president stood, his backside against it, leaving him slightly above the assembled scientists.

"Fellow Americans, and citizens of the world," Rosen said. Katrina could see the little man's suppressed excitement. "Today we have a momentous announcement and a proposal for all of you. As you know, Dr. Jack Martins and his group last week demonstrated the possibility of restoring the stars by a reprogramming of the Martins Sphere periphery. You've all heard about it. You have probably read the Special Report that the Martins team posted on WorldNet. You have probably seen the video. In cooperation with all civilized nations of the world and their governments, we are here to announce a worldwide experiment. A planetary experiment. At 12 a.m. midnight Greenwich Mean Time on Christmas day, December 25th, we want every person on earth to sit in front of your vid. Imagine, as clearly as you can, for five minutes, the disappearance of nullspace and the reappearance of the stars."

The president indicated Jack Martins, seated in front of him. "Dr. Martins, please tell our listeners a little more about the technical aspects of this proposal."

Jack Martins rose and faced the camera. Nigel flipped off the vid.

"Nigel, I wanted to hear what Martins has to say!"

"We know already, darling. We've both read the special report. We know exactly what to do."

The vid was off and the distracting noises were absent. In the quiet Nigel felt Katrina's body close to his, and the magnetic pull of her. He reached for her and she came willingly into his arms...

Midland, Illinois, the next morning

"Good morning, Midland Methodist church, Diane speaking."

"Hello Diane. This is Bob Abraham, Chief of Staff for President Rosen."

"Oh dear!" said Mrs. Cummings, almost dropping her handset. "What can we do for you Mr. Abraham?" Had something bad happened?

"The president has decided to hold a Christmas Eve celebration at the White House," the voice said without preamble. "He would like to know if your congregation would like to attend, all expenses paid."

Mrs. Cummings almost fainted. "*Would* we!" She placed her hand over the receiver to tell everyone in the crowded room, which was filled with Church members socializing after Sunday services. A few moments later she responded. "I think I can assure you of a 100% turnout."

"That's grand, Diane." The voice on the other end could barely suppress a laugh. If only the good people of Midland knew the impetus for their invitation! Abraham had received a call from the president shortly after Martins' Milan demonstration. The lame-duck president was now in the middle of his second term, and concerned for his legacy. Abraham knew how the president had yearned for the recognition denied him as the father of the Alpha Mission. But this was an even greater opportunity! What better way to secure his place in history than a Christmas Eve celebration at the White House. Just before he, Sam Rosen, restored the stars! And why not invite the congregation from the largest church in Jack Martins' hometown to witness the occasion? Robert Abraham shook his head, smiling. He didn't know how the president got away with it. The man's ego was enormous, but in a good way. He had the unique ability to get others to cooperate, even in tense situations. Sam Rosen was seemingly a man with whom disaster and bad luck had no issue.

"We'll make all the arrangements," Abraham said smoothly. "All you have to do is send us a list of those who will attend. We'll send you plane tickets and make hotel arrangements. We'll give you a detailed itinerary for the evening."

"We're so looking forward to it, Mr. Abraham. Thank you so much!" Diane Cummings hung up, more excited than she'd ever been in her life.

Tehran

"Attention Arabs and Muslims, Shia and Sunni, all those who follow the words of the Prophet and trust in Allah the beneficent, the wise!" The voice spoke off-camera. The screen showed the empty private office of Massoud Izz-Al-Din. The camera was focused on his desk. On the wall behind the desk, prominently displayed, was a picture of the Supreme Ruler, Omar Shahin. Izz-Al-Din was much more media friendly. The two men had agreed that Izz-Al-Din would give the speech. He would announce the new fatwa and pay homage to his superior with the portrait.

Izz-Al-Din strode confidently to his desk, dressed in traditional costume, and seated himself. His finely chiseled face oozed confidence, intelligence, and commitment. "Muslims and Arabs, you have heard the deluded proposition yesterday from Dr. Jack Martins. No one in possession of his sanity can believe that the stars may be restored simply by thinking about them. Can one create wealth merely through thought? Can one redress injustice merely by thinking about it? The idea is madness. If Allah wills, the stars shall be restored to us. But first the dog Martins must be erased from the face of the planet. The fatwa I issued last year still stands.

"World cooperation is code for continued Christian and Western dominance of the Arab world. It is a trick! Under the ruse of cooperation the oppressors, led by Jack Martins, seek to continue Christian dominance over the population of earth. Muslims must resist this domination. We must speak and act with one voice.

"Muslims all over the world! Today, with the approval of our leader, the Supreme Ruler Ayatollah Omar Shahin, I am issuing a new fatwa. We ask you to disrupt any gatherings of so-called world cooperation for the common good. We ask you to speak reason and common sense to those so deluded as to follow the fantasies of Jack Martins. You may find the new directive on the official vidpage at Muslim.ir.

"The Christian countries are mobilizing for the final strike against us. Freedom fighters everywhere! Our emissaries will be coming to your city. Join the Defenders of Islam. United, with Allah as our guide, we can defeat the Christian enemy."

After the broadcast Izz-Al-Din received a private vid message. It was from Harim Malakai, his most loyal officer. Malakai was head of intelligence for the Defenders of Islam. "Massoud, I have good news."

"Yes?" Izz-Al-Din's voice was tense with excitement.

"The Americans have blundered," Malakai reported. "We now have a chance to strike a fatal blow against the enemy. The American president has decided to have a celebration at the White House just hours before the great experiment. They have foolishly invited the entire congregation of the Midland Methodist church to the celebration."

Izz-Al-Din was astonished. "But the Americans have played right into our hands. How is that possible?"

"Allah is watching over us," Malakai responded. "The Americans have grown careless. All of their energies are concentrated on their great celebration." Malakai spoke with scorn. "As if they had already restored the stars. In their arrogance they usurp the power of the All-Wise and believe they are gods."

"This is good news indeed, Harim," Izz-Al-Din said. "We shall know how to respond, shall we not?" The face of Commander Malakai registered understanding and satisfaction.

Izz-Al-Din closed the connection. He thought how fortuitous was this latest development. Their plan would be a simple one, and safe. Over two years ago three Defenders had become members of the church's Midland's congregation. In Jack Martins' hometown. They pretended to be loyal converts to Christianity. These three kept an eye on the movements of Jack Martins whenever he was in town. They reported to Malakai every day and watched for a slip-up. Martins enjoyed police protection 24 hours a day now. But if a chance arose to take him out, these men would not miss. As a precaution the three joined the local Christian church to blend in with the community. Who would suspect three good Christian men? It had galled their Muslim souls to attend church every Sunday and participate in church fundraisers. Their gorge rose when the three went to Bible study groups.

The three men made it a point to be very helpful and unobtrusive in the community.

Now, Izz-Al-Din thought, they could finally be put to good use.

The Vatican

Cardinal Tauron, the Vatican Secretary of State, Cardinal Che Rodriquez, and Pope Clement XV sat in the Pope's private conference room in the Vatican.

The secretary spoke in a rare moment of candor. "Izz-Al-Din has gone renegade. I think he actually believes now in his own rhetoric."

Pope Clement was alarmed. "But you said that he was far too intelligent to fall for that pan-Arab hyperbole."

"Yes I did," Tauron replied. "But perhaps I am mistaken."

Both Rodriquez and the Pope gave an involuntary gasp. Tauron's omniscience was an accepted fact. The two were as shocked by his misjudgment as they were by his admission of it.

Tauron, however, knew his capabilities. As an intelligence officer—for that is precisely how he saw himself—he understood his limitations. It was one of the reasons he was so effective. Not every operation could go smoothly. Fortunately his special agent, Rashid Sakhr, had ensured the safety of Jack Martins. The idiocy of the Defenders of Islam, and its gross cynicism, disgusted him. But the speed with which Izz-Al-Din had assembled and trained his Defenders had greatly impressed him. The man was both intelligent and very capable.

Shahin and Izz-Al-Din understood how necessary Martins was to the lifting of the barrier. Shahin and now Izz-Al-Din were prepared to sacrifice the good of the entire planet for something as illusory as 'power.'

Power was information and the ability to use it appropriately. He was *certain* that he had read the character of Massoud Izz-Al-Din correctly. His judgment there could not be faulted. Yet somehow Izz-Al-Din had begun to backslide into religious fervor. He was therefore the more dangerous because he was now more unpredictable.

Cardinal Rodriguez interrupted Tauron's thoughts. "What do we do now, Cardinal Secretary?"

"We wait."

December 10th, Northern Israel – Southern Lebanon border

The sleepy Ben-Gurion kibbutz on the Israeli-Lebanon border baked in the searing heat. The settlers gathered in the community center for refreshment and a mid-afternoon break. Without warning, the building roof caved in. There were screams of anguish as a missile exploded on the hard packed earth, spraying metal everywhere...

December 10th, New York City Subway train #73, Route #1, 242nd Street Bronx to South Ferry, Manhattan

At 5:30 a.m. a man dressed in black clothing carried a briefcase to the 242nd street station stop. He boarded the train and walked casually to the back. His presence went unnoticed by the weary occupants of the bus. Three women and two men were both coming home from late work shifts and were eager for bed. The man placed the case casually on his lap and looked out the window at the false dawn. #73 gradually filled up along the route. At 145th street he opened the case and fiddled with something inside. He locked it and placed it underneath his seat. At 137th street, City College, he exited the train and walked south down Broadway. The man entered a small café and ordered coffee and a donut.

At the 125th street station a large group of passengers boarded. The suitcase exploded, blowing out the back wall of the train and spewing metal debris everywhere.

December 14th, Washington, DC

Yogesh Dalal entered the offices of Congressman Richard Dempsey in the Rayburn office complex. There were two desks in the front room. The Congressman's larger desk was in his private office at the back. Victorio, Dempsey's trusted aide, sat at the desk by the window. Dalal's desk was toward the wall and just in front of the door so that he could greet visitors. As usual he walked into the room with his head down, lost in thought. As he approached his desk he felt the piercing gaze of Victorio's eyes. The smaller man glanced up. Two black orbs sharply measured him, holding his attention like a magnet. Dalal knew that he could not have looked away until the Apache broke eye contact. Then he saw Victorio's wide smile. Dalal relaxed, but not before his body involuntarily shuddered. The man was a guru but didn't know it. Yogesh did not consider the Apache his friend. Victorio only rarely offered a glimpse inside to the man underneath. But he certainly would want him on his side in any kind of crisis.

Yogesh settled into his desk and began to read his email. He heard a knock on the door. He opened it to find a courier silently holding a packet with his left arm outstretched. Out of the corner of his eye he saw the Apache's eyes narrow. Yogesh felt the man's body tensing like a coiled spring. It was unusual for couriers to deliver items directly to a Congressman's office but it was not unheard of. There was nothing unusual at all about the young man's appearance. He was dressed in shorts, T-shirt, and athletic shoes, and wore a biker's helmet. The ID badge of his company, "D.C. Messenger Service," was pinned to his chest. Next to it the security clearance nametag required by anyone entering the Rayburn building. Yogesh accepted the package and signed for it. The courier disappeared down the hallway toward the elevator. He took the square cardboard package to his desk. It was marked "Baldwin Communications." Yogesh began to open the magnetic seal of the box. Suddenly, a black blur from the desk beside him grabbed the package and shoved him violently to the floor. Victorio hurled it out the window and onto the grass.

"Victorio, what do you think…"

An explosion rocked his world. The window shattered. Fragments of it exploded all over the room. Yogesh crawled from the floor to see the Apache's face covered with blood.

"How did you know?" Dalal asked.

"I didn't." Victorio spoke calmly while picking out little pieces of glass from his face. He wiped it clean with a towel from the bathroom. "I felt something was wrong."

Yogesh was amazed. "Do you always act so strongly on your feelings?"

The Apache stared back at him as if he were a child. "Of course." Victorio spoke as if it were obvious that a man's feelings were always a perfectly accurate indicator of the best course of thought and action.

That is the difference between you and me, Dalal thought. *Guru.* Out loud he said, "Thank you. You saved my life."

Victorio shrugged. "Did I?" The Apache walked back to his desk and went back to work as if nothing unusual had occurred. The red streaked towel lay on the desk beside him. The room was getting colder. Victorio went into the bathroom and taped a thick towel to the window frame with duct tape. Then he sat back down at his desk.

A moment later two uniformed D.C. police officers and a man wearing the insignia of the Rayburn security service burst into the room. "Is everything all right?" The speaker identified himself as Sergeant Davis. The sergeant stopped midway into the room to survey the damage inside and on the lawn. Victorio did not even look up from his desk. It was left to Yogesh to answer questions and fill out reports. The Apache was interviewed by Davis, a smallish man with a baby face and close-cropped hair. Victorio replied calmly, occasionally wiping his face with the towel as blood oozed from several cuts. Soon everyone felt as if the incident had been nothing untoward.

The investigators recorded their statements and took several images. "We'll send a clean-up crew right away." Davis nodded to Victorio. "I'll send a doctor up here for you."

Victorio waved him off. "Not necessary. Just a few cuts. I'm a fast healer."

"Mighty cool, ain't you?" Davis spoke tauntingly.

The Apache gazed at the policeman for a few seconds.

Davis looked away uncomfortably and cleared his throat. "Don't worry about the media. We've secured the building and the perimeter." Several minutes later the two staffers saw the sergeant and the security man snooping about on the lawn.

After the men left Yogesh was all eagerness to discuss the exciting events. Victorio just smiled. "I think we both have a lot of work to do on H.R. 343." This was the Apache's way of telling Yogesh to just get on with it.

Yogesh's mouth opened and closed but nothing came out. How could a person just sit there like a statue of Buddha after somebody had tried to kill them? His own heart was racing. He felt as jumpy if he had just drunk 10 cups of Masala Chai. Yogesh was a little embarrassed as he compared his own demeanor to that of Victorio. He, Yogesh Dalal, had done nothing except cower behind a desk. At that moment a maintenance man came to inspect the window. Yogesh rose quickly from his chair and walked toward the door. "I'm going out for a walk."

Victorio looked up from his workstation, surrounded by broken glass. He spoke absently. "Suit yourself." His attention was on the document on the vid screen. Remarkably, Victorio's vid and dataset were still working.

Yogesh shook his head. He wanted to ask Victorio if he was human but decided against it. He closed the door and left the room. Yogesh walked toward the Madras Masala for a meal and a place to calm down.

December 20th. London, Harrod's Department Store

A well-dressed man got off the Knightsbridge tube stop on the Brompton Road. He wore blue slacks, a white turtleneck, and a long winter coat. He carried a briefcase. The man walked into door #8 at Harrod's. The security guard looked him over and the man smiled. "Want to check my case?" he said cheerfully. "Gotta get some nice jewelry for the wife."

Harrod's was packed with Christmas shoppers. People streamed in and out. The guard smiled and waved him on, wishing he could afford something special for the wife this year.

The man turned right into the designer jewelry section. He placed his briefcase on the floor and inspected some of the brooches in the display case. "Find anything, sir?" The woman behind the sales counter was smartly dressed in an elegant black suit and a white blouse.

"Yes, I think this one will be fine."

The man prepared to pay but and discovered that he did not have his wallet with him. "Oh, drat. I'll have to go back to the parking lot. Will you save the brooch for me? I really do need to get my wife something she'll appreciate."

"Certainly sir."

The man rushed out of the store. He hurried past the guard, who noticed that he was not carrying the briefcase. The guard walked quickly into the jewelry section and spotted the briefcase sitting up against the display case. Just as he reached to pick it up, the case exploded.

Tehran December 20th

Massoud Izz-Al-Din was pleased. The attacks by the Defenders of Islam were producing exactly the sort of worldwide fear and tension that would prevent the success of Martins' absurd thought-experiment. But despite his public proclamations Izz-Al-Din was worried. What if Martins' experiment could actually restore the starfield?

For some reason not just the Christian world but many in Asia, Africa, and the sub-continent resonated to the idea of such a planetary effort. Unexpectedly (and irrationally) the Martins experiment was almost secondary to the idea of a world-wide gathering. Jack Martins had decided to throw a holiday celebration party and had invited the entire world. A significant majority had accepted his invitation! It was imperative that the experiment fail of course. It would be necessary to continue the attacks right up to the very moment of the event.

His old mentor, Ali Khamenei, was right. The Christian powers would never allow the Islamic world to exist on an equal footing. They arrogantly assumed that Christianity was superior and Islam was backward. Their self-important condescension to share dribbles of their technology when it suited them was galling.

The Defenders were an unqualified success. He had chosen his commanders well. They were fiercely loyal to himself and good soldiers who instilled discipline into the ranks.

Now it was time for the final blow. It was the strike that would demonstrate the power and the reach of the Defenders of Islam. It would strike fear into the hearts and minds of everyone in the Christian world. Shockwaves would be sent around the planet. Psychic havoc would be created and would prevent the cooperation that was a prerequisite for the success of the experiment. Fear was the greatest weapon of the downtrodden against the powerful.

Izz-Al-Din entered the code for Commander Malakai on his personal vid. The pudgy face of his right-hand man appeared. Malakai's baby-face in no way reflected his steely nature. Here was a man to rely on! "My friend, it is now time to implement our special mission."

Harim's eye's lit up. "Allah is great."

Izz-Al-Din could feel Malakai's suppressed excitement and knew he had been perfectly understood.

Malakai saluted smartly in affirmation. "We will strike at the very heart of the Christian world," the commander said fervently. "The White House itself will feel the wrath of Islam."

Izz-Al-Din then entered the personal code for his former friend and rival, the traitor who called himself Rashid Sakhr. Sakhr was the only child of the Moroccan ambassador to the United States. He had met Sakhr almost twenty years ago at the University of Michigan when they were undergraduates. Between them was a love/hate relationship. Each felt a strong attraction toward the other. But a competition had arisen that grew stronger and uglier as each had pursued his own path. Rashid had turned mercenary. Izz-Al-Din was in service to his people. Even now he felt a tug of sadness at the thought of Rashid's death, which was now inevitable.

The finely chiseled features of Sakhr appeared in his vid. "Well, well, well," Sakhr said lightly. The corners of his mouth were turned up slightly in a mocking smile. "I wondered how long it would be before I heard from you."

The man's arrogance was irritating and disturbing. Did he already know of their plans? If so, their scheme would certainly fail. Izz-Al-Din spoke disdainfully. "Dog! You may tell your infidel masters that another debilitating attack on a very important city in the United States will occur in less than one week's time." Let them sweat. The physical destruction of any terrorist act was as nothing compared to the psychological trauma it created. In this case damage and death must be kept to a minimum or the population would rally together. The attack at the crowded Harrod's department store had been a mistake. Too much loss of life had increased sympathy for the Martins Experiment in Europe.

Rashid looked at his counterpart with thinly disguised scorn. "You now believe the religious nonsense you spout? I didn't believe it when Tauron told me you had become mentally imbalanced." Sakhr sighed. "I am disappointed, Massoud. I always thought you were more intelligent."

Izz-Al-Din flared silently. Tauron! What game was that Catholic devil playing? What was Sakhr's relationship with the cardinal?

Sakhr smiled with cool hauteur as he observed Izz-Al-Din's confusion. Rashid had always been able to anger Massoud. It was now as it had been twenty years ago during their student days.

Izz-Al-Din admitted to himself that he had always felt slightly inferior to the Moroccan. This further enraged him as he saw Sakhr's disdainful sneer widen. Rashid had read his mind and acknowledged their mutual understanding of his superiority. Izz-Al-Din managed to reign in his temper.

"It was *you* who betrayed your trust as a Defender of Islam." Izz-Al-Din's voice was taut with anger. "It was you who protected the demon Martins while betraying your trust to me and your people. Hypocrite! Traitor!"

Rashid shook his head sadly. "So you have finally discovered the truth, Massoud. What took you so long?" Rashid locked eyes with his former friend. "Your vaunted Defenders of Islam will fail. It is inevitable."

"Cur! Go back to your kennel and deliver your messages." Izz-Al-Din's faced turned red. Within minutes the Cardinal Secretary of State and the Western intelligence services would know of the impending strike. But they would never guess where.

Rashid said nothing but continued to hold Izz-Al-Din calmly at gaze. He knew how much it galled Massoud.

Finally Izz-Al-Din broke eye contact. "I will arrange an accident for you Rashid. Do not congratulate yourself!" Izz-Al-Din pushed the "end" button.

The last thing he heard before the connection broke was the sound of his enemy's laughter.

The White House, Washington D.C., December 24th, "Christmas Celebration"

The three Defenders of Islam held a private meeting at their hotel in downtown Washington DC in preparation for their mission. The three were joined by Mohammed Al Saquami, Harim Malaki's most trusted operative. The four men discussed precisely what they would do upon arrival at the White House. The entire congregation would ride in two buses made available by the Rosen administration. The fighters finalized their plans and were saluted by the great Izz-Al-Din himself from Tehran.

The buses arrived at the White House. Al Saquami saw that security was lax, just as he had hoped. On this dark, cold, and festive night he had been able to board one of the crowded buses with his compatriots. Not a single question had been asked of him.

The Defenders were dressed just like their fellow parishioners. They blended in perfectly within the crowd of almost 100. The congregation entered the gates of the gaily decorated White House. Outside on the lawn a gigantic Christmas tree was lit. Despite themselves they were awed. Here they were in the inner sanctum of the most powerful, brilliant, evil, and destructive country the world had ever known!

The four Defenders were spread out in the crowd. They came together gradually and unnoticed. The group had just passed the East Room and were approaching the Green Room. The tour guide was speaking. "…we were to have visited the West Wing, which contains the Oval Office. This is the most famous room, perhaps, in the world, where President Nixon resigned in 1974. President Rosen signed the Washington Accords there, which formalized the establishment of the State of Palestine. Unfortunately we will not be able to enter today. President Rosen is having an important meeting relating to tonight's great experiment…"

Mohammed Al Saquami realized that their dream of annihilating the Oval Office was not possible. Already they had begun to attract some attention as the four were behind the main party. The Green Room would have to do.

Al Saquami quickly signaled his fighters and they gathered round him. He gave them a last second pep talk. "Here we are in the very den of the infidel, on the eve of their great Christian celebration. Now is the time to perform our sacred duty and reap our reward in Paradise! Strike, my brothers. Strike for the glory of Allah!" Seeing that all were with him, Al Saquami threw a pack of explosive gum against the wall of the Green Room. The others followed suit. Some hurled their explosives against the walls of East Room and some threw forward toward the Blue Room, causing a huge explosion. Almost immediately each of the fighters smashed two sticks of the volatile explosive together, sending blood and body parts down the hallway amidst the wreckage.

Izz-Al-Din sat at his desk in his private office in Tehran along with Hakim Malakai. The two men gazed at Massoud's holovid. Fortunately individual vid comm was almost impossible to monitor. This had led to a decrease in the power of security and intelligence services all over the world and an increase in individual freedoms. It had also made terrorist activities easier to accomplish. But after the withdrawal of American troops from Islamic soil such actions had been deemed unnecessary. Until now.

Izz-Al-Din was waiting for the signal breakup that would indicate the successful accomplishment of the suicide mission. The hero Al Saquami, a Saudi Sunni, would not fail. Nor would his warriors. He could hear the fatuous commentary of the tour guide. He could see nothing. The commander Al Saquami's personal vid was stuffed into his coat pocket on this cold December night in the infidel capitol. Izz-Al-Din permitted himself a smile. It was only fitting that a church group from the home city of Jack Martins should be responsible for the destruction of the most sacred building in the country. It was a fitting payback for decades of Christian occupation of Islamic soil. Now the infidel would share how it felt to be vulnerable in their most private parts.

After the success of this mission he would also arrange for an accident to befall that dog Rashid Sakhr.

Suddenly Izz-Al-Din heard a tremendous noise from his vid, and then silence. He and Malakai exchanged glances of complete satisfaction. Mission accomplished.

In twenty-four separate locations around the world the Defenders of Islam launched further attacks. They were designed to cause the maximum amount of chaos and publicity hours before the scheduled world-wide experiment. Both Omar Shahin and Izz-Al-Din watched with satisfaction as panic spread across the globe. Martins' thought experiment would fail utterly in a milieu of panic and anxiety, Izz-Al-Din thought. The next step was to depose this fool Shahin and take complete control of Iran. And then the entire Arab world.

They must first wait to see whether their efforts would result in success or failure.

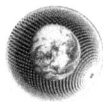

Chapter 27

At 12 a.m. on the 25th of December, GMT, the whole world gathered around their vids. Even those who decided not to participate wanted to be a part of the most monumental event in world history, if only as observers. But the screens were filled with death and destruction.

The attacks of the Defenders of Islam were successful, and generated enormous fear. Many simply turned off their vids, horrified and disgusted at human nature. The time approached for the unprecedented experiment. Some who were on the fence recalled the words of Izz-Al-Din: "Are we to bring back the stars merely by thinking about them?" Many who were in favor declined to participate. Many of those who had been excited now felt foolish and stupid as the time for action was upon them. Just as one might become enraptured by a new, untested idea and then shrink from acting upon it.

Yet there was also an unanticipated back-reaction. A Londoner who had been injured in the Harrod's blast later said, "Why should we let a few dictate the actions of the vast majority?" A sense of shared burdens and suffering united all who participated, estimated later at several hundred million. And who could tell whether a person contributed or not? This was a thought experiment, legitimized scientifically by the great Einstein. But the stage for this thought experiment was the entire planet and the return of the stars. It had a practical objective, not something that tested an abstruse theoretical concept. Jack Martins' demonstration had fired the imagination of the entire world, both for and against.

The *New York Times* wrote in its front page story on the 26th:

It was a festive, barbecue Christmas block party in Midland, Illinois. This college town is the home of Jack Martins, the discoverer of the Martins Sphere. An entire city block gathered in the cold on the spacious front lawn of Miles Jamison, professor of History at Carleton University. Mr. Jamison rigged his 100 inch vid and audio system just off the sidewalk. Floodlights lit the frozen front yard as bright as day. A brightly decorated Christmas tree sat in front of the big picture window. Children raced around throwing snowballs while dogs barked and ran excitedly underfoot. At least forty adults chatted and played with their children. Some stood over hot gas grills and cooked barbecue chicken, steaks, hot dogs, and hamburgers.

I walked up to Professor Jamison's station at the front of the house, where he had arranged an electronic control center under a tarpaulin stretched across four poles. "Welcome!" he said when I introduced myself as a reporter form the New York Times. "Join the club!" The professor had to fend off a snowball thrown by one of the neighborhood children. Professor Jamison laughed as snow fell, exploding onto his grill.

"What prompted you to have a Christmas party outside in the cold?" I asked.

"Here in Midland we're hardy folk," Jamison responded. "The cold doesn't bother us." He pointed to a man in a brown fur coat. "That's my next door neighbor, Bob Hudler. He wanted to get everyone together for the thought experiment. Here in Midland we're big supporters of Jack Martins. Like almost everyone we saw the demonstration in Milan, or videos of it. We were impressed to say the least." Jamison called Bob Hudler over and put an arm around his shoulders. "Bob suggested that we have a block party and let the children celebrate along with us. Most of them understood the idea immediately. So here we are!"

"I said, we could have a winter barbecue, just as a joke, you know. But the idea got around. So many people wanted to do it that we said, why not?"

Honestly, I couldn't tell the difference between this party and a real summer barbecue. Other than the snow and cold, of course. I'm from Louisiana and I have lived in New York for two years. But I don't think I'll ever get used to winter. Midlanders, apparently, delight in it, like those crazy people who jump into freezing water without any clothes on.

The tome for the Great Experiment approached. In Midland this was 6 p.m. because Midland is 6 hours behind Greenwich. People stopped eating and the children quieted. This was a minor miracle all by itself that boded well for the bigger one. Candles were lit. All eyes turned to the vid. President Sam Rosen led the festivities along with the Science Advisory Board in the Oval Office. Dr. Jack Martins was somewhere in Midland with his fiancée.

The moment was subdued, uncomplicated, and utterly profound. "And now, my fellow Americans and citizens of the world, let us pray. Imagine, in your mind, the Martins Sphere barrier dissolving and the return of the stars."

Like the wizard of Oz Professor Jamison raised his hand and switched off the lights. Everything plunged into darkness. As I stood on the porch I saw dozens of little points of candle light shining in the darkness. A vigil of hope.

Everyone knew about the attacks from the Defenders of Islam but no one here paid attention. An almost palpable longing filled the air. Adults and children closed their eyes. In ways personal to each individual everyone sent their intention and thoughts to the heavens. Some meditated, some chanted, some prayed, others were silent. And then the most astonishing thing I have ever witnessed or will ever witness occurred. The sick gray patina that covered the sky dissolved. The stars! Oh, the glorious universe! I looked north and spotted the Little Dipper. To the east I saw Betelgeuse and Orion's Belt, just where they should be.

It was over in barely five minutes. People broke down and cried. Some shouted with glee. Some kneeled and offered thanks to God. One woman swooned. "Daddy, look!" a child cried. "I can see the sky again!" That was the signal for a grand celebration. Bob Hudler went into his house next door and came back with a magnum of champagne. People drank and hugged and yelled and clapped each other on the back. Even the children were allowed to drink a little out of small paper cups.

As I left the scene to return to my hotel people were back at the grills. Almost everyone I saw glanced upward regularly, as if to assure themselves that their work had indeed been successful. I raised my head to the sky in silent thanks to all those who were a part of this historic event. I recalled the words of Marcel Proust: "Let us be grateful to people who make us happy; they are the charming gardeners who make our souls blossom."

This glorious accomplishment set off a series of cataclysmic events that brought the planet earth, and all of humanity, into mortal danger.

Part IV – UNIVERSE

Chapter 28

65 million years ago

The scout ship was way off the beaten track. It had been sent on a mapping mission to a deserted section of Gudalur. The ship was in sector 3, at almost the very northern tip of the universal sphere. The civilizations of this sector were unknown. It was the job of the Survey Patrol to periodically check up on even the remotest backwaters. The ship had cataloged over 10,000 galaxies so far. Eventually it entered the local group of galaxies and the Orion arm of the Milky Way galaxy. The ship eventually found its way into our solar system. Soon the crew saw a beautiful water planet in orbit three around the single yellow dwarf. The ship sent an immediate report of its discovery. Once it entered the earth's magnetic field the little scout immediately began to wobble out of control. The captain fought her down. The ship crash-landed on the soft sand of a beach on the northwestern coast of Gondwanaland, only fifty feet from the tropical sea. The land sloped gradually upward from the sea to about 5,000 feet above sea level. A tropical forest gave way to hills and a cooler climate in the snowless mountains. The ship was beyond repair. The crew abandoned it and set forth into a new and exotic land. All hope of rescue had been abandoned. It was one of the risks of the Survey Patrol. Many ships and crew had been lost on backwater planets millions of light years from civilization.

The small colony grew quickly in the favorable climate. The crew members were Adam Kadmon human, and were able to adjust to the new world. Food was plentiful. But the high oxygen content of the atmosphere speeded up their metabolisms and shortened their life spans. The crew had their data sets and savagery was not an option. Each member was part of a cultural lineage that went back billions of years. Even so, life spans grew dramatically shorter over the course of twenty generations. Temperaments became more volatile. The dream of Gudalur, however, would not die.

Five hundred years after the crash, Tapaka went for water to the olla that hung from the rafters of her open air porch. The olla caught the fresh sea breeze. She was dressed in a light, colorful robe made from plant fibers. The colony now numbered over 10,000 members. Today was the Meeting of the Elders. This would be followed by the launching of a rebuilt spaceship. The new craft was modeled after the original, which still lay on the beach. It served as a monument and an inspiration for a return to the stars. The precious datasets had been handed down from father to son and mother to daughter. In them was the technology that had launched space faring civilizations upon billions of less resource-rich worlds than this one. It was to be a great day of celebration. A scaled down version of the original scout craft would carry 25 colonists. It was capable of traveling the approximately 19,000 light years to the edge of the galaxy in less than 10 orbits of the planet around its sun. There it would enter the Ring and proceed quickly to Miralet at Gudalur Central. A rescue craft would then be dispatched to take all who desired off this volatile and unpredictable world.

It was hot and humid. Tapaka dipped her hand into the clear, cool water. A dark shadow appeared, blotting out the sunlight.

The meteor was almost a mile in diameter. It plunged to earth in a terrible explosion of sound, earth, and water. In a matter of seconds the colony was erased from the face of the earth. The impact penetrated deeply into the planet's crust, scattering dust and debris into the atmosphere. Huge fires raged. Tsunamis and severe storms with high winds and highly acidic rain pounded the coasts. Seismic activity and volcanic activity multiplied. The impact caused chemical changes in the Earth's atmosphere, increasing concentrations of sulfuric acid, nitric acid, and fluoride compounds. The dust and debris thrust into the atmosphere blocked most of the sunlight for months. The temperature of the planet lowered globally. Almost all higher life forms did not survive.

Following its time honored schedule, the Survey Patrol sent out another ship to the sector a million years later. It too found the planet, and crash-landed. There was something about the planet's magnetic field that disrupted the ship's drive.

50 million years ago

Koori stood at the head of the command and control center within the Sword of Victory, the flagship of the galactic fleet. The commander was a short, muscular man with a deep chest and a flat, cruel face. He was dressed ceremoniously in a white robe hemmed in black. At his waist a dress sword hung in a bejeweled scabbard. On his chest was the symbol of his galaxy, a holograph showing the known universe with a sword through the middle of it. The immense fleet numbered over 100 million ships and over 500 billion soldiers. Today it would embark on the greatest military campaign in history: the subjugation of an entire universe.

Under the leadership of Koori, head of the Earthian Planetary Council, an entire galaxy had been organized for a war of conquest. Koori stood within the bow of the ship and gazed at the fleet. He thought about the coming campaign. One galaxy was tiny indeed when compared to the over 1.5 billion galaxies with intelligent life represented in Gudalur. But Koori knew the very concept of war was an anachronism. Long ago conflict had been a tool of diplomacy. But this was billions of years in the past and before the discovery of the Rings and the organization of intergalactic commerce. Such barbarism had been unknown for eons. One aggressive civilization on Earth had been able to conquer an entire galaxy using physical violence. It was something no longer understood or even contemplated. The subjugation of the galaxy had come from a planet hidden within an obscure solar system with a single sun. The shock and terror of such tactics generated fear and instant compliance amongst the settled and ordered civilizations of the Milky Way. It was comparable to a ruthless killer let loose on a school playground. These tactics would do the same in every galaxy in the universe.

Koori remembered his first trip into space, when he was 16. The Grand Tour took him to fifty of the most important galaxies, using the universal Ring system. Surrounding each galaxy was a portal that shrunk the distances between galaxies to nothing. No one knew who had constructed these portals or whether they were simply a part of the fabric of space. He knew that the Rings were not machines or devices. Each galactic Ring was a sophisticated universal navigation and communications system. Each Ring connected to every other Ring in the universe. A Ring is a programmable interface. The technicians called it a manifold. The Ring system was a part of the double-torus geometry of space. A double-torus surrounded each and every object in the universe. Koori knew that he could use this ancient system to his advantage.

What he had seen on his tour was a universal civilization so ancient that no one could even remember when it had begun. Like a hardened warrior entering a children's nursery, he had seen how ripe was the universe for conquering.

The Rings surround each galaxy and are necessary for intra-universal travel and communication. Therefore major civilizations grow at the edges of galaxies, not at the center. Nevertheless, each galaxy had a capitol sector, a hub, from which commerce, art, and communications flowed. Galactic civilizations were organized like a spider's web. Destroy the center and the web weakened and died.

Each of the 100,000 sectors of Galaxy Six had been required to build 100 ships and send 500,000 troops. This was a trivial task. The technology of space flight had been understood for eons. The population of each sector was in the hundreds of billions. Koori was amazed that it had never been thought of before. Now they would use the Rings to translate to each strategic galactic capitol sector. Like a knife through butter, each ship with its complement of 5,000 trained soldiers would easily take over the key galactic webs. And most important, Miralet itself, the central hub of Gudalur. He who controlled the web controlled the galaxy. He who controlled the galaxies controlled the universe.

It was said that to look into the eyes of the earthian was to know fear and an almost hypnotic compulsion to obey. Koori gazed around the room, which contained beings of every physical description from every sector of the Milky Way galaxy. He knew he was in complete command. The fleet stood poised in space. Koori gave the order to attack.

2,500 years later

The Universal Council met in emergency session for the first time in over 2 revs (500 million years). The setting was the Capitol planet of Soyopa, a desert planet of reds, browns, and yellows. The planet had a very thin atmosphere and a bright white sun, which was just a pinprick in a dark purple sky. Soyopa, instead of the central planetoid of Miralet, was used for the most important ceremonies and meetings that affected all of Gudalur. The dry, arid environment perfectly suited all of the council members. Their meeting was held on top of a mesa in the open air. The proceedings were broadcast to every planet in every galaxy in the known universe. All members sat, stood, or rested at the famous council table, which was in the shape of a crude ellipse. It was made of ironwood and over 1000 feet on its long axis. The table had been handed down from generation to generation for the past 5 billion years.

Nacori led the meeting. It stood upon the thick stumps of Its three legs, supporting a triangular shaped body on top of which rested a cylindrical head. This being was an Oorant, and known for Its very high intelligence and imperturbability. Its three eyes swept the huge table, gathering everyone's attention. Over 5,000 members were present, each representing the major sectors of the Universe. The Universe is known as Gudalur, which means "the meeting place."

All citizens of Gudalur immediately recognized Okitoa, who resembled an earthian sparrow hawk. Directly across the table from Nacori towered Senokipe, whose name meant "hollow tree." At the far end of the table sat Matape, a squat being who looked like one of the mesas of Soyopa with a large black boulder of a head. Matape, whose name meant "red cliff," came from sector Malpais. Sector Malpais had borne the brunt of the fighting, and many deaths. Next to him Chimala and Kiburi, a race of beings who were physically and psychically dependent upon each other like a binary sun. These two would die if ever separated. Above the table floated the huge canister of Origin [0,0,0], the almost mythical entity from galaxy 6 in the earthian sector. These gaseous beings reproduced by extrusion. In the middle of the table an amoeba-like being lay sprawled out like a raw egg in a pan. A small dog with a huge head and forepaws ending in flexible digits scampered upon the table, carefully avoiding it. Those who watched numbered in the quintillions and were from every sector in Gudalur. They represented a diversity of species that is simply impossible to describe.

"Fellow citizens of the universe, the earthian threat has been extinguished," Nacori said gravely. "But at such a cost of lives and infrastructure that it is difficult to contemplate. That such a thing as war could manifest itself upon the universal landscape is unthinkable. That it could even be contemplated is terrifying." It paused. The slit that was Its mouth turned down slightly, indicating severe disapproval. It gestured to his right. "Batuco, please give your report."

Batuco rested upon the table top in a large container of the seawater of his home planet. She was a fishlike being with four appendages ending in flexible cilia. The bright, hot sunlight warmed the water in her tank and the hot sun was exactly the same spectral type as her home star. All members spoke Muripa, the universal language. Muripa had, eons ago, become the standard for all diplomatic exchanges, commerce, and communication between galaxies.

"Fellow citizens of the universe, welcome!" she said, opening with the customary greeting. "The threat to Gudalur came from sector 3, an obscure sector in an almost unknown and deserted area of the Universe. It has been a severe shock to us all. Let us now stand silent for a few moments. We remember our brothers, sisters, hatchlings, extrusions and other loved ones who lost their lives during the recent conflict."

Several minutes later, Batuco continued. "A careful study of sector 3, the earthian planet, and Koori, its barbarian leader, was made. We conclude that conditions upon the earthian planet are not duplicated anywhere in Gudalur."

An excited buzz, and not a few objections, arose around the table. "That is impossible," said the representative from a sector halfway across the universe from earth. It raised a polyp with an eye attached. "All planets and life forms are unique but each follows the universal laws of Planetary and Species Development. It would be absurd and outrageous to suggest that among the billions of civilized galaxies and hundreds of trillions of planets in Gudalur, there is only *one* planet that is so unique."

Batuco turned in his water tank to face the speaker. The statement had been brashly stated. It was a serious breach of protocol, a not so subtle denigration of the integrity of the speaker. Batuco knew that the beings from this sector were incapable of sarcasm or insult. He also knew that the delegate had voiced the opinion of the majority of attendees. Therefore he responded calmly and quietly. "Yes, these laws have been tested and confirmed for billions of years. We have studied the earthian planet intensely for 100 standard planetary years. We have reviewed every record relating to this place, which date back several hundred million years. The Special Commission has concluded that the earthian planet is an exception. In fact, we consider this little orb to be a complete anomaly. There are…certain unexplainable, even mysterious phenomena associated with the planet that make conditions there utterly unlike any other planet in Gudalur."

Now the noise level increased and Batuco felt the tension and excitement in the room increase. All present knew the legend of the Old Ones, a race of ancient Superbeings who had supposedly designed and created the Rings. The Old Ones departed Gudalur for a higher plane of existence billions of years ago. The legend was of a mysterious object that connected Gudalur to a fantastic structure of other universes. All were united in a complex multidimensional configuration.

"There is something you aren't telling us," said a delegate from a Ring in Cluster Sagittarius, known for their psychic abilities.

Batuco, in his water tank, fidgeted uncomfortably. "We have prepared our interactive report. The Commission will be placing it upon the universal Network for all to understand. But here is a short summary. The earthian planet exists within a solar system with a single sun, violating the Law of Binaries. The earthian planet is a water planet but exists within a solar system that does not support such development. Each of the inner planets in this solar system are dry, barren worlds, devoid of life. The outer planets are gas giants. The earthian planet could not possibly have arisen naturally within its stellar environment. The planet's ecological and species diversity is unmatched anywhere in Gudalur by a wide margin. Its sun is a yellow dwarf and is unstable, just like the planet. The sun sends out massive pulses of solar radiation which regularly disrupt the planet's weather systems.

"Exobiologists, climatologists, archaeologists, and anthropologists from all over Gudalur have come to the planet to study. The norm for the earthian planet is cyclical, dramatic, and catastrophic upheavals. We have documented periodic but unpredictable flips of the planet's magnetic field, which exhibits peculiar and unknown properties. Many scout ships that have entered the vicinity of this world have malfunctioned and crashed.

"The planet's crust also shifts from time to time, causing widespread destruction upon the surface. Periods of glaciation move back and forth upon the surface in an unpredictable fashion. The planet's climate is influenced strongly by ocean temperature and circulation patterns, which also change unpredictably. The planet's atmospheric composition shows an unusually high concentration of oxygen, over 23 percent! But the most remarkable feature is the planet's wobble. It is like a spinning top that begins to lose its speed of rotation. All of these factors contribute to the planet's remarkable volatility. In short, fellow citizens, the earthian planet seems to exist outside the laws of planetary and species development. We have discovered archaeological evidence of at least ten major warlike cultures prior to the present one. All of them without exception were wiped out by one of the planet's periodic natural disasters. For those who doubt this, you may experience the full report in your data tanks.

"Therefore the rise of Koori to prominence we conclude to be an anomaly. Koori was the product of an extraordinarily violent and volatile planetary environment. The science group has made its recommendation. The earthian Ring must be programmed to permanently quarantine all spacecraft and communications to and from the earthian solar system. The planet, and any civilization that happens to develop on it, will be isolated from the Network. The contamination of earthian memes, like a bacterial culture, will be contained within its Ring. We are saddened that this Ring will not proceed along the normal lines of species and planetary development. We feel that this is the only way to protect Gudalur from the earthian scourge."

This suggestion met with unanimous approval from the Council, and with sighs of relief from all citizens of Gudalur.

Miralet, Gudalur Central (planetoid orbiting the binary star Orpheus, sector (0,0,0)), present day

"Alteration in Ring, coordinates (5.93757GP, 141.00098, 0.30000)." This was stated by a being with three stumpy legs, a triangular torso and a very large head with three eyes. It transmitted a full report of Its observations through the headset to Its observer twin. This being was from Ring (344677P, 23.44598, 178.11300), a Ring very close to Gudular Central. This entity possessed an extremely large brain and consequently demonstrated phenomenal information processing capabilities. Fifteen percent of all inhabitants of Miralet were Oorants. In Muripa this translates to 'wise one.' They were Gudalur's premiere intellectuals (excluding the Illirians, the ephemeral and frightening intelligences from gas giant planets in Galaxy 6).

"What? That is the Critical Ring!" cried a fishlike being with hundreds of sensory cilia protruding from its tubelike body. These beings came from stellar systems with water planets. They are perfect telepaths but known for their emotional volatility. All observers, even Oorants, were assigned twins for observational accuracy. Each pair would agree on any information sent within the gigantic and sensitive Miralet communications network.

The three eyes of the Oorant blinked, indicating irritation. An Oorant, unlike a human, kept its eyes open at all times because they evolved genetically from prey animals. "Your communication is redundant," the Oorant said. "You need only confirm my report of Ring status so that it may be transmitted immediately to Node Zero."

"Of course!" the telepath cried. "But is this the beginning of another intergalactic war?"

The Oorant could feel the panic and excitement of the creature through Its headset. The Oorant suppressed Its irritation with another of Its partner's irrelevant and emotionally packed transmissions. The assignment of twins was purely arbitrary, under the maxim that all on Miralet were the finest minds in the universe. But sometimes It wondered.

"It is a mistake to theorize in advance of the facts," the Oorant said, doing a passable imitation of Sherlock Holmes. "Merely confirm the report."

The fish gesticulated angrily by flopping up and down on the workstation with its cilia. "Do not patronize me, fat-head."

The Oorant blinked twice, indicating extreme anger. It was the height of ill-grace and a violation of protocol for any being to personally insult another. It felt like taking one of Its three thick, trunk-like arms and beating this silly creature to a pulp.

The Oorant performed the equivalent of a guided meditation, calming Itself and restoring mental equilibrium. As it did so, the Oorant gazed around the immense interior of the facility. It remembered the guided tour It had received after being admitted to Miralet.

Millions of technicians sat inside the gigantic planetoid, which monitored the status of every Ring in the known universe. An immense 3 dimensional replica of Gudalur called The Bowl hovered in the middle of the planetoid. The Bowl is a sphere 100 miles in diameter, with every Ring cataloged and marked. This display is in the shape of a double-torus. The bottom and top hemispheres rotate in opposite directions. The majority of the galaxies and superclusters concentrate around the center and less in the upper and lower regions. No visible matter surrounds the poles.

The universe itself is a closed orientable three torus, a topological entity with no boundaries. The Oorant knew that each planet in the universe saw itself in the center of this structure. When one looked past the "edge" of the universe one simply encountered the other side. The orientation of the planetarium's display is from Miralet, of course. Each technician on Miralet has complete access to the display, which can be zoomed-in for analysis in the minutest detail to any coordinate in the universe.

Miralet itself is a gigantic, hollowed out planetoid approximately 10,000 earthian miles in diameter. It contains the Bowl, living quarters for millions of beings from all over Gudalur, and immense recreational spaces for athletic activities, music, and the arts. Miralet also has spaces for walking, meditating, and communicating with all of the galaxies, stars, and planets in Gudalur. No walls or ceilings exist in this immense space. One can see up, down, and to the sides in all directions.

When the Oorant first entered Miralet to be assigned Its position in the research facility (34, 6778, 90012), It suffered an acute case of Ulia. For humans this is similar to severe nausea and dizziness. Each structure within Miralet is suspended in mid-air, held rigidly in place by directed fields of force. All workstations and any enclosures such as the many research labs occupy a coordinate within the interior's immense structure. All structures within the immense facility appear to have no visible means of support. The distances, even for a being of the Oorant's mental stature, are appalling. But It had adjusted.

The Oorant flicked one of Its three eyes to observe the fish, which was still gesticulating wildly at him. It would have to wait another time period for the being to calm down.

The Bowl is part of a research facility called the Network, which allows communications and Ring travel throughout Gudalur. Ring travel was first discovered over 10 billion earthian years ago. A communications network evolved gradually from a local group of galaxies and quickly spread over the next 100 million years to encompass the entire universe. The Network is actually a sophisticated holospace—a virtual reality that allows beings to communicate in full visual and audio. The holospace also allows the transfer of emotions and feelings. Communicating within the Network is as good as being there. Therefore all beings can know firsthand the experiences of any other being, anywhere in the Universe.

An expanding universe does not affect the Ring system, for it is not dependent upon the characteristics of space and time. (Gudalurians long ago discovered that our universe is what earthian science would call a steady-state universe. Local areas of space-time expand or contract in harmony).

What distinguishes Ring travel is its immediate-ness. A physical space ship can travel instantaneously from one Ring to the other at any point within it. Even if that Ring is on the opposite side of the universe. Destinations are mapped precisely, depending only upon the exact coordinates of entry. Over billions of years a detailed three-dimensional image had been constructed showing the exit and entry points on any Ring to any other Ring in Gudalur. This programmable manifold is the most complex structure in all the universe. Even the collective Illirian Supermind of mental giants cannot encompass all of the data.

Miralet means "mind" in Mirapa, the Gudalur Standard spoken language. It is the universe's central communications hub. Imagine a spider's web with literally quintillions of filaments stretching 13 billion light years across in all directions. Each of the approximately 8 trillion galaxies has a Ring. There are smaller rings around each star, used for inter-stellar travel. In Miralet are projections containing the sub-Ring system for every galaxy. These are incredibly complex maps that require all 100 miles of the Bowl to properly display.

The fish seemed to be calming now but the Oorant decided to wait until the creature's mind became less turbulent. It began to meditate. An Oorant's mind needed calm to operate effectively. Acute emotion strongly affected their mental equilibrium, which was sacred to them.

The technology used on Miralet (and in Gudalur) is billions of years old. It evolved from the merging of science and consciousness, which is the primary requisite of any sane civilization. This eons old technology had resulted in the identification of thought energy and the means to work with it. Data storage and retrieval used sophisticated holograms that are activated with targeted thought impulses. Even a small storage hologram can store over 10^{120} bits of information. This makes possible the recording and transmission of thoughts and emotions as well as the accompanying imagery and other perceptics. Information technology on Miralet requires a precisely targeted thought impulse directly matching the vibrational envelope of the requested information. An envelope surrounds each separate storage hologram and acts like a primary key to a table in a database. Mental discipline is of the utmost importance. Only one in 10 billion applicants are ever considered for assignment on Miralet. The planetoid is truly an intellectual's ideal of the best and the brightest.

At all times the special Earthian Ring is monitored. A repetition of the events surrounding the Koori Incident was unthinkable. After the first earthian spaceship penetrated the barrier the Council had ordered its reprogramming. Anything that made contact with the earthian Ring periphery would now be hurled over 1.5 billion light years into the depths of inter-sector space. The Oorant felt distinctly uncomfortable with this decision. Even the fastest Gudalurian spacecraft would require over 70,000 standard planetary years to traverse that 100 million light year distance. There were no Rings in inter-sector space.

When the earthian mass experiment altered the Ring's programming, the system registered the change immediately.

As the Oorant finished Its meditation, It saw the fish digesting Its report.

"Your report is satisfactory," the fish said condescendingly. By this time the Oorant had entered Annea, the state of mental serenity and clarity.

"Very well then," It said calmly. "I will send the report."

When the report reached Council Headquarters it caused great upset and turbulence. A standing committee called the Supreme Adjudicators is always in session. 99% of its business is the mediation of the most intractable trade disputes throughout Gudalur.[1] This day the panel was thrown into total confusion. It frantically called for the Gudalur Universal Council to assemble in emergency session.

After agonizing consideration, the result of their deliberation was the destruction of the earthian Ring. The earthian solar system, along with the clos-

---

[1] The High Council and the Supreme Adjudicators have branches in every Ring, galaxy, and stellar system. Only the most intractable and egregious problems or disputes ever reach Ring 0. Unless the issue is of monumental importance (like the Koori Incident) the participants are almost always dead by the time the case is heard on Miralet. These cases are heard because there is always a vital legal, economic, or philosophical issue of widespread interest that affects a significant portion of Gudalur.

est binary, would be moved into intergalactic space between its home galaxy and M-31, the Andromeda Galaxy. Each Ring exists symbiotically with all others in a synergetic balance. The removal of the earthian system from its natural position would upset the balance of forces that allowed life to flourish. Therefore, the decision of the Council was a sentence of death.

The decision sent shock waves throughout Gudalur. It was a violation of principles held sacred for almost 10 billion years: that the sanctity of life was paramount. However, the Council decided that the threat of another earthian attack would not and could not be borne. Those opposed managed to extract a promise. A delegation to the earthian planet would be sent from Miralet. These observers would gauge the conditions on the planet before it was thrown into the depths of inter-galactic space. Only after their report would action be taken.

Earthian Ring, coordinates (5.93757GP, 141.00098, 0.30000)

Three beings were on board the information gathering craft. The Oorant, an Adam Kadmon humanoid from the Orion system in the earthian subgroup, and the Universal Council president himself. This being resembled a gigantic praying mantis.

The craft instantaneously negotiated the immense distance from Gudalur Central to the Earthian Ring, which was literally halfway across the universe. The ship, a highly sophisticated communications and data gathering center, appeared within the planet's atmosphere over the North Pole. It was immediately spotted by the U.S. tracking station in Nome Alaska who reported it immediately to NORAD.

"It's huge!" said an excited voice over the voice channel. "Nothing like I've ever seen. It may definitely be an alien craft. Unless the Chinese have come up with something we've never heard of."

"Calm down lieutenant," NORAD replied. "Scramble your aircraft and give us a visual."

Fifteen minutes later an elliptical UFO appeared on the huge Hi-Def display in the secure NORAD communications center.

"By God it's alien all right." Major Anselm was an expert on the world's fighting aircraft. "But what the hell is it *doing* up there?"

The craft measured approximately 6000 feet on its long axis and 2500 feet on its short axis. It floated serenely above the frozen arctic. The outer hull was perfectly smooth and glowed softly white. The scout craft was actually a floating palace and could accommodate several thousand in luxurious comfort. Gudalurians believed that you should always travel in style. Each Gudalurian ship, no matter how large, could be operated by a single person.

Inside, the three crew members stared wide-eyed at the frozen wasteland. They were here, on the earthian planet, the most famous planet in all the universe! Even Xttlzttl, the Universal Council president, was awed. The earthian planet had an appeal and a terror for all citizens of every Ring. Here was the source of the Great War. Billions had been killed by the evil and unspeakable Koori, whose name was etched boldly in every history book in Gudalur. Xttlzttl's voice had been loud in support of the destruction of this nefarious world. But as he surveyed the surface of the planet he was astounded at its incredible diversity. His training in exobiology told him that this planet truly was unique. To destroy this world would be a crime far greater than the damage inflicted in all of the Great War. It troubled him immensely. He turned to his Orion assistant. "Please give me a preliminary report on the human population of this planet."

Regat Toor was also astonished. His instruments told him that fully 10 billion of homo sapiens covered the surface, most of them in densely packed cities. Toor was the 2,567,101st descendant of the Orion ruling family in an unbroken line that went back almost a billion years. Toor reported the billions of other life forms present upon the surface to his crewmates. He too realized that the destruction of this planet would be criminal.

The Oorant was overwhelmed. Never had It seen a world with such a large biomass and teeming with such a fantastic variety of life. The Oorant worlds were water planets. They had hot and wet climates but very little biomass. Several edible plant species existed on and around the small landmasses that dotted the planet's surface. Half a dozen predatory carnivores prowled the ocean depths. The Oorants had learned to survive on the flourishing plant life. They had no competition from other land species. With plenty of food and an agreeable climate the Oorant had developed a contemplative lifestyle that emphasized mental and philosophical achievement. That lifestyle had not changed in several billion years. But this planet was radically different!

It felt deeply troubled. It had agreed to the mission, hoping to convince Itself that the elimination of the earthian planet was justified for the greater good of Gudalur. Now It was trapped. It had given Its word to do what was necessary. Overwhelming sentiment within Gudalur favored the planet's destruction. It would now be required to give Its consent. The Oorant knew that Its participation in this mission would result in Its excommunication from all Oorant civilization. It was a steep price to pay for Its unwarranted curiosity, which had gotten It in trouble before. It had been categorized as a maverick.

The scout ship completed a polar orbit, leisurely exploring the planet from the skies. The craft observed every continent and ocean. The three scientists studied the earthian ecosystems and its weather and geology. They scrutinized the human civilization. It also catalogued the position of every rock, tree, and grain of sand on the surface, storing it into a 3D holographic map.

What they discovered was both horrifying and exhilarating.

"This planet did not evolve normally," Xttlzttl said through the headset. He was stating the obvious. To a human being, the giant mantis would be a terrifying sight. Xttlzttl was over 7 feet tall and humanoid. He had two legs, four arms, a torso, and a great triangular head with large multi-faceted eyes and huge mandibles. Each arm ended in a claw-like hand with four digits. Where a human thumb and forefinger would be, the species had evolved a powerful pincer which could instantly snap a man's neck. The mantis spoke with others of its kind by opening their jaws and moving short, fuzzy upper arms together. These rasping and clicking sounds functioned as their language.

No words were actually spoken on board the craft. Communication was provided through the headsets. These consciousness-assisted devices transferred thought impulses, data, complex imagery, and even emotions accurately from being to being on the infinite landscape of the mental plane.

"Everything we have seen is a violation of the laws of planetary development," Xttlzttl continued. "This combination of environments and species is far off the main sequence. I cannot even plot data points."

"Truly remarkable," Toor agreed. "This world has been carefully pieced together like a zoo collection of diverse species and ecosystems. I cannot understand how it was done. An extraordinary accomplishment."

"Perhaps I can shed some light on the matter," the Oorant said. Its powerful and serene thought impulses came through crystal clear. "My analysis of the earthian magnetic field and its planetary grids[2] shows an impossible level of sophistication and integration. From our surveys I have constructed a map of the earthian grids and its magnetic field. As you can see, it is extraordinarily complex."

The three saw the planet earth from the mental plane. Their consciousness was filled with a glowing, dynamically interacting tapestry of trillions of brilliant filaments of light. These filaments self-organized in astonishingly complex and beautiful geometric patterns. There was a collective gasp.

"It's impossible," said Xttlzttl softly, awed.

Even the jaded Orion was amazed despite his upbringing in a wealthy, elite ruling family with a billion year history of privilege. To think that this planet existed in his own stellar neighborhood! It had never been fully investigated.

The Oorant, studying the pattern, suddenly uttered an oath. It choked in Its excitement.

"What is it?" Xttlzttl cried.

The Oorant could barely contain Its enthusiasm. The others, knowing the stoic nature of the species, knew that It had understood something truly remarkable.

"It will take me several hours to demonstrate my discovery," the Oorant said. "It will require the full capabilities of the ship's information systems. Please refrain from using them until I give the word."

"But what *is* it?" the Orion exclaimed in irritation.

The Oorant was already deep in thought at Its personal console. It did not respond.

The others, exasperated, strode through the luxuriously appointed ship. They ignored the beautiful gardens, waterfalls, miniature lakes and forests, and other luxuries provided for their entertainment. Each Gudalurian craft, even small scouts, were floating worlds. This one was named for the fourth planet in the famous Celebron system in Ring Orban, known for its beautiful vacation planets. The theme was chosen by Xttlzttl himself. But he could not enjoy the spectacular scenery. The Council president gazed out through the interior of the great ship, lighted by an artificial sun that spread its light

---

[2] The planetary "grids" are holographic templates of subtle energy that program the planet's ecosystems, weather patterns, and also the DNA for each species, and which record all events that occur within, upon, and around the planet.

uniformly throughout the vessel. He could think only of the Oorant and Its unusual behavior. The race was known for its avoidance of uncomfortable emotion. Even though this one was unusual, Its conduct had animated the crew. Something of monumental importance was about to be revealed.

Even the head of the Gudalurian Universal Council could not hurry an Oorant.

Xttlzttl wandered the ship for what seemed like a day. Eventually he stopped in a little food court suspended at the upper front of the ship. The court was surrounded by fountains, gardens, and ferns. It closely resembled his home world of Kzttztt, a hot, humid planet resembling the Jurassic period on earth. Everything on the ship, just like on Miralet, was held in place by invisible fields of force. Gudalurian technology allowed for independent mini-ecosystems to exist within their own bubbles of energy, complete with atmosphere, variations in gravity, and complementary species. Traveling in one of these ships was so much fun that a small but significant portion of the population of Gudalur chose to spend their entire lives on them. They traveled from Ring to Ring, enjoying all that the universe had to offer. Some of these ships were as large as small planetoids and were literally self-contained civilizations unto themselves.

Finally Xttlzttl received an impulse through his personal headset. He rushed back to the ship's control room. An air of palpable excitement filled the mental plane as the Oorant prepared to reveal his discovery.

"Here is the earthian planetary grid," It said calmly. A complex display of light exploded into their consciousness in breathtaking detail.

"Observe now the Gudalurian Network." The Network was the relationship between each and every Ring in the universe.

"No, it cannot be!" cried Xttlzttl.

The Orion swore. "By the great god El-Hath!"

The Oorant relaxed his tripod and leaned Its head back in satisfaction. "As you can clearly see, the earthian grid system is modeled after the Network itself."

The crew was astounded. For Xttlzttl, it was proof that this backward planet was not backward at all. Some vast intelligence must have created it. An intelligence that would have predated the 10 billion year history of Gudalur.

The Oorant continued. "When the grid patterns of this planet are fully understood, if that is possible, the subsystems will closely resemble intra-Ring geometries."

No one said anything, no one even thought anything. The Oorant had arranged the two displays side by side. Their beauty and complexity was too astonishing to even express through thought.

The Orion abruptly left the room and ran into a water closet, regurgitating the contents of Its stomach. The thought of destroying this planet sickened It. It could not, would not, take part in it.

Chapter 29

The appearance of the Gudalurian scout ship predictably caused a sensation on earth. Major world governments had received cryptic communications from the spacecraft. It had identified itself as a representative of a universe-wide civilization that had been sent to open talks with the human race on a matter of great importance. That had calmed some frantic minds and excited others.

For six weeks the ship orbited the earth, studying the planet and its inhabitants. From observations of the planet's grids, a preliminary assessment of how the earthians had managed to reprogram the Ring emerged. Several warplanes took shots at it but their missiles vaporized in the white light surrounding the hull of the ship. A small nuclear weapon was launched on a rocket but it too was neutralized. Attempts to communicate were ignored.

Then each of the three representatives of Gudalur transported to the surface.

It was agreed that the Universal Council president should talk to the leaders of the Western nations and the discoverer of the Martins Sphere, Jack Martins. The Oorant would speak with the leaders of the most populous culture, and most powerful economic power. The Orion would visit with those who best represented the fundamental energy of the earthian planet.

Therefore, the Oorant landed inside the Forbidden City in Beijing, the mantis arrived unexpectedly on the front lawn of the White House, and the Orion touched down in Lagos, Nigeria.

Beijing

The Oorant was led into the inner sanctum of the Chinese Elders. It noticed that these earthians were slightly taller, but noticeably thinner than an Oorant. The planet's gravity was approximately normal and so It felt little discomfort. However, the unusual nature of the planet's magnetic field caused It to feel slightly disoriented. It probed the ethers and quickly withdrew. Disturbing thought streams of hatred and violence were embedded there. The Oorant hoped that Its time on the surface would be limited, for It did not know how long before It would begin to feel severe discomfort.

Wang Shao-Lin glanced quickly at his compatriots. For this historic meeting, only himself, Liu Bo-Li, Wen Hung, and the Flower, Hun Shi-Chu, were present across the ancient table. A formal tea ceremony was presented using a delicate Song Dynasty set.

The Oorant watched, fascinated, as the ritual was performed. Each movement was executed with grace and dignity. An aura of sacredness permeated the ethers surrounding the humans. Here was true ceremony. The tiny, steaming cup of liquid was presented to him. All four of the humans bowed. Not deferentially, but respectfully. As was proper, It thought, in welcoming a guest. These primitives were neither awed by the great ship in the skies above them nor revolted by his appearance. Something in him resonated warmly to these supposedly barbaric earthians.

As It prepared to reach for the cup, in the back of Its orderly and complex mind a tendril of remembrance rose to conscious awareness. There was something about this rite that resonated strongly within It…The ceremony reminded It of the ritual opening to all gatherings of the Universal Council. But how could these backwater primitives know anything about that? The planet's history showed periodic upheavals upon the surface that destroyed all life. Therefore, there could be no continuity of culture from the time of Koori, 50 million years ago, to the present. It was a mystery and something that needed further study.

The Oorant prepared to bring the steaming liquid to Its mouth with one of Its three tendrils. Each tendril had nine dexterous appendages longer than human fingers, which were used for gripping and which were capable of extremely delicate work. Under the intense but polite gaze of the four humans, It analyzed the brew by delicately inserting one of Its digits. The tea was a vegetable mixture surprisingly resembling the Eneat, the dominant plant species on Oorant planets! Pleased, It used the same grace in Its movements, sipping as It had seen the others do.

Wang Shao-Lin glanced quickly at the Flower. They both smiled. All four humans nodded with approval toward the Oorant. It knew that It had quickly (and unexpectedly) succeeded in gaining a level of communication and trust with the barbarians.

Quickly, the Oorant brushed that thought out of Its mind. It had determined, during Its intensive six-week study of the planet, that many earthians *were* barbaric. But not these before him. It knew that no culture on this planet had existed for more than 5,000 planetary revolutions. But It sensed that a deep and eons-old wisdom existed here. Its conscious mind said that this was not possible. But the Oorant never denied Its intuitive understanding.

As the ceremony unfolded, the Oorant found Itself actually enjoying the ritual. The scripted movements relaxed Its mind. At the end It beamed Its pleasure. Somehow the humans understood. All four again bowed and from their expressions and demeanor, the Oorant knew that It had communicated Its enjoyment and satisfaction.

A beautiful young girl in a brightly colored silk robe silently and reverently cleared the implements. Then the four humans relaxed back in their seats. The Oorant understood clearly that It had the next move. It reached into the pouch tied above the base of its tripodal leg system and removed four headsets. These devices would allow for accurate communication through thought impulses. The earthians stared at the delicate devices. Each headset consisted of a thin band of a shiny, silvery substance, and two delicate pads that fit over the temples. Each of the pads glowed with a bright multi-colored light.

The Oorant placed Its specially designed set over Its large brain case and gestured toward the humans. Wang Shao-Lin was the first to pick up one of the devices, placing it around his head. His three companions quickly followed his lead. When all five beings had their sets on the Oorant enabled the devices. Everyone was now connected to the ship's systems and the mental plane.

In that moment, all five present gasped in astonishment.

For the humans, an entire universe of possibility opened before them, like an unfolding flower. Their minds flowed through the Network. Each of the humans explored its depths and stared at the Oorant, and themselves, in wonder. The devices were a gateway into the entire Gudalurian universe of art, science, and philosophy!

If the humans were amazed and delighted, the Oorant was shocked to the core of Its being. It had been prepared, as with all new visitors to Gudalurian culture, to painstakingly introduce them to the basics of the system and conduct a rudimentary discussion. However, the humans had learned the system almost instantaneously. It saw how their minds quickly invaded the system. Never before had It experienced such startlingly quick mental adaptation. These creatures were clearly raw and untrained, however. Like little earthian kittens they knocked things over and made a big mess. But their mental agility and adaptability were off the charts.

Something of the Oorant's amazement must have communicated to the humans. As one they stopped their explorations and gazed at their visitor.

"Is something wrong?" asked the one they called the Flower. This earthian was a small, delicately built female with (for earthians) huge black eyes, high cheekbones, and aristocratic features. The fascinated Oorant observed her long, jet black hair tied in an enormous braid that curled elegantly around her head. No Oorant, or any species on their planets, had hair of any kind.

The Oorant smiled mentally. "No, children, I am just amazed at how quickly you learned our communications system. It seems that you have prior or inherent knowledge of it."

The Elders were not insulted by his use of the word 'children.' They mentally gazed at the Oorant in awe. Its mind was of a strength, depth, and sophistication that amazed them. The humans and the Oorant engaged in the small talk that inevitably accompanied diplomatic missions. The Oorant was learning a great deal indeed, far more than the earthians suspected. It carefully and subtly explored the depths of the Elder's minds without the earthians even suspecting.

The overwhelming surface impression It received from the humans was their satisfaction with this type of communication. There was no possibility of deceit. The Elders longed for all diplomatic, cultural, and business transactions to be conducted with integrity and transparency. This was built in to any system of mind-to-mind communication.

The Oorant made a decision: The destruction of this planet was an impossibility. It decided to violate the parameters of the mission. It informed the Elders of the decision of the Universal Council.

"For something that happened 50 million years ago?" Wen Hung was angry. "There were no humans on earth at that time! Only dinosaurs."

The Oorant did not argue, but directed their attention to the 'Koori Period' in the ship's holographic database. As the humans began to inspect the earth history section they were convinced the alien was telling the truth.

"Everything we know about our planet's history is essentially incorrect!" Wang Shao-Lin exploded.

"What you are showing us here has the ring of authenticity," the Flower concurred.

The Oorant smiled. "That is because these impressions are taken directly from the grids of subtle energy that record every event on your planet. All experiences, all thought, all events are recorded and stored within this matrix. It is somewhat like one of your holograms, but even more sophisticated."

The Oorant opened that compartment of Its mind that contained all of Its knowledge and experiences regarding the earthian situation. In an instant the Elders knew everything the Oorant knew about Gudular's relationship with earth. And, Wen Hung acknowledged to himself, a whole lot more besides. Tantalizing sidebands of thought opened up to his awareness. He saw impressions of the Oorant's culture and home planet and Its scientific knowledge. He received knowledge of the mental enhancement and disciplinary protocols of the Oorant. These were so common to all members of the Oorant that they were left unshielded. In a few seconds, Wen Hung understood that he was now sitting on a goldmine. He now knew these protocols as well as did the Oorant.

"So what do we do?" Wang Shao-Lin asked.

In another breach of mission directives, the Oorant showed the earthians some of the Ring Programming protocols and algorithms. "With these," It said, "you should be able to discover counter-measures."

The Oorant knew that Its discovery of the true nature of this hidden planet would far outweigh Its divulging of a few Ring programming protocols. It was clear that the earthians would rapidly ascertain them anyway.

Washington D.C.

The mantis appeared suddenly on the lawn of the White House and clanked awkwardly toward the front entrance. Immediately, a security detail rushed toward it. Fearful at the sight of such a menacing carnivore, the men instantly aimed their weapons and fired. The bullets passed harmlessly through the walking figure.

"Hold your fire!" a voice shouted authoritatively. "Just a projection!"

"The damndest realist projection I ever saw," replied a burly man with a brush cut as he lowered his weapon.

The creature then reached into its carapace and brought out several headsets. The men were fascinated by the devices, which glowed with a multi-colored light. They watched as the mantis placed one on the top of its bony carapaced head. Projection or no projection, Sergeant Tokolowski's guts turned to water as he confronted the gigantic, evil-looking insect. Tokolowski gamely stepped forward and took the proffered headsets. He placed one over his head and noticed that the pads fit snugly to his temples. The other men did the same.

"That's better," Xttlzttl said. "Now we can talk."

Unlike his counterpart in Beijing, the president of the Universal Council of all Gudalur perceived that the intelligence of his auditors was not first-rate. So he simply stated his request. "Please let me speak to your president. I am here from Gudalur on a cultural exchange visit."

"I would also like to speak with Dr. Jack Martins, of Martins Sphere fame," Xttlzttl added. "I believe he is in your city at a conference of holographic scientists."

Through his shock, Sergeant Tokolowski was amazed by the warmth and depth of feeling he received from the grotesque figure in front of him. This creature was not threatening. The sergeant was even more amazed by these cool headsets. This was technology far above anything he'd ever seen.

"Uh," the sergeant stammered. This couldn't be a joke because he was hearing the thoughts of this creature inside his head. He reverted to his old Sears customer service voice. "Why don't you wait right here sir and I'll inform the president."

The sergeant reached to his waist and spoke into his vid. "Visitor here from…uh…Gudalur, to see President Rosen." As soon as he said it he felt like a fool. But how else could he put it? Out of the corner of his eye he noticed that people walking along Pennsylvania Avenue were beginning to stare. A news van was whipping along K Street.

"Escort the gentleman in," he was told.

In the most bizarre moment in his life, Sergeant Tokolowski, secret service agent, found himself walking next to a 7 ½ foot tall praying mantis up the steps to the White House. Later, this picture would be broadcast around the world and Tokolowski would find himself making the talk show rounds.

Xttlzttl was shown in to a conference room on the first floor of the White House. Along with the president was Lev Katzenbaum and John Cho of the Science Advisory Board. They just happened to be in the building at the time. The president grabbed them with the astonishing story that an alien visitor was here for a cultural exchange visit.

"I gotta see this," Cho cracked.

Katzenbaum was a little worried. His friend had been under a lot of stress lately with the falling dollar. Just then Sergeant Tokolowski entered with the mantis. Cho jumped out of his chair and Katzenbaum hid underneath the table. President Rosen maintained his cool and greeted the hideous looking creature with a bit of humor. "Do you have an appointment sir, or will you call back later?"

Cho laughed and sat down. Katzenbaum sheepishly clambered from underneath the table to take his seat at Rosen's right. The joke was lost on Xttlzttl but the Council president perceived that he was in the presence of beings who might be perceptive enough to understand his mission.

The security detail ringed themselves unobtrusively about the room, standing against the walls but ready for action. Tokolowski watched as the alien clanked his carapace uncomfortably onto a chair. He then thought better of it and stood. When it moved it sounded like the tin man from the Wizard of Oz. The sergeant saw the mantis throw three of the headsets onto the conference table. His men had taken theirs off. At a nod from the sergeant each man slipped the devices quietly onto their temples. No one noticed. Tokolowski and his men were going to be flies on the wall to a very interesting conversation.

As soon as the president and the scientists had their headsets on Xttlzttl began to speak. "I am here as a representative of Gudalur, a universe-wide civilization of every galaxy and sector in the visible universe." Xttlzttl opened a compartment of his mind, allowing the humans to see the immensity and magnificence of Gudalur. For President Rosen, it was a revelation. Katzenbaum and Cho were shocked. As scientists they could accept the fact that there *might* be microbial life on Mars.

To see the entire universe teeming with intelligent life was difficult to accept.

"Our mission here is to determine exactly how you were able to reprogram your Ring," Xttlzttl said.

Xttlzttl saw that President Rosen was eager and interested. The two scientists just stared at him uncomfortably.

"What is a Ring?" the president asked.

"A Ring is a programmable interface that surrounds all planets, stars, and galaxies. A Ring allows communication and travel between star systems and galaxies."

The two scientists shook their heads in disbelief. They had checked out of the conversation.

The president was amazed at the tenor of Xttlzttl's thoughts. The creature emanated a feeling of affinity and love. The terrifying mantis was harmless. "Is that how your ship got here?"

Xttlzttl nodded. He was reading the president's mind and saw that the earthians had removed the Ring barrier with a planetary thought experiment. It should not have been possible. "Ring programming is a terribly precise business. It requires intimate knowledge of the Ring Matrix."

"The Ring Matrix?" the president asked.

Xttlzttl sent an image of the Gudalurian Ring System on Miralet.

"Oh my God," the president said. "Lev, John, pay attention," the president said to his two friends. "Look at that."

"The Ring Matrix is a complex three dimensional manifold that contains the templates that direct the Ring to perform specific tasks," Xttlzttl said. "To enable each of the templates requires a thought template with a precise footprint and geometry. The smallest deviation and nothing will happen. It is similar to an earthian programming language where a minor mistake in a variable declaration could cause the entire program to fail. Rings can be programmed to perform a variety of tasks. To move themselves within the Gudalurian matrix, to send targeted communications or materiel anywhere in the universe."

"I don't believe it," Lev Katzenbaum said.

"Science fiction," agreed John Cho.

Xttlzttl read from Sam's mind that a human named Jack Martins was responsible for the thought experiment.

"I would like to communicate with the human Jack Martins," Xtllztll said.

President Rosen pushed a button on his desk, calling his chief of staff. "Peter, get Jack Martins in here. He's in DC at some conference."

"You're in luck sir. He's right here in the building talking to Peter Bambridge and Dirk Wheeler."

Five minutes later Jack Martins walked into the Oval Office. When he saw the alien Jack took a step backward. He recovered and said cheerfully, "Welcome to planet earth! How do you like it so far?"

Xttlzttl handed him a headset, curious as to how the earthian would react. The earthian placed it on his head. "Yes," Martins said, nodding in satisfaction. "Yes, indeed, this is more like it." Suddenly, Xttlzttl saw the mental envelope of the earthian shape itself into the precise key needed to unlock the ship's communications system. In a flash he was in and probing the holographic data banks. It had happened so swiftly that Xttlzttl couldn't follow it, and he was a Class Three Ring technician.

Xttlzttl attempted to close him off but the earthian was too quick. Several minutes later Jack emerged from the system. Xttlzttl was shocked to see that the earthian's mental profile had grown radically larger in power and sophistication. He now understood that Martins himself must have provided the mental key to reprogram their Ring. But how did he do it?.

"Thank you for the introduction to Gudalur," Martins said as he took off the headset. "Mind if I keep this? Thanks." Jack walked out, leaving the mantis speechless.

Later, back on ship, the mantis reviewed the ship's holographic logs. Fear stabbed through Xttlzttl's consciousness. Martins' profile had a disturbing similarity to that of Koori, the dangerous earthian lunatic who had begun the Great War.

Lagos, Nigeria

Regat Toor touched down in Lagos and took a deep breath of African air. The energies in the psychic space of this planet were uncomfortable. But Toor felt an underlying warmth that seeped into his bones and relaxed him.

The Orion's presence on the hot, dusty streets caused no comment whatsoever from passersby. He closely resembled an earthian Caucasian. Toor was an experienced traveler to hundreds of planets. He recognized immediately the resemblance of these dark-skinned humans to the Denebians, Galaxy Six's greatest intuitives. Regat Toor took in his surroundings as he walked. He was struck once more by an unidentified feeling that this backwater planet was more than it seemed on the surface.

Toor had embarked four blocks from the presidential palace from one of the ship's transport bubbles. The transport was an invisible, molecule-thin transparency that could fold up into nothing and be stored in a tiny pouch. All Gudalurian travelers carried these bubbles with them, and so were never lost. For security purposes Toor kept the periphery of his bubble activated. It was always tuned to the ship's hull, which would open automatically when the bubble touched its surface.

Toor walked unhurriedly down the street toward the palace. This building was an ostentatiously columned affair made from native stone. As Toor turned toward the entrance the guards immediately raised their weapons. One of the men stepped forward. "Halt and state your business!"

Toor was not worried about the guns, for the transport bubble monitored his coordinates and protected him with an invisible field of force.

"Please take me to see your president. I am here on a diplomatic mission from Gudalur."

"Never heard of the place," said one of the guards. The man nudged him with the barrel of his AK. "Get lost."

Toor sighed and walked through the men, who began firing wildly at him. After their weapons were discharged President M'basa himself ran out, gesticulating wildly. "What are you doing, you fools? Do you think to destroy my brand new palace?"

The men threw down their weapons and abased themselves. M'basa pointed to Toor. "Who is this person?"

The sergeant of the guard answered. "An intruder sire. He would not halt when requested and tried to force his way in. So we shot him."

"You *shot* him?" M'basa cried, pointing to the bullet-ridden facade. "Idiots! How could you have missed from point-blank range?"

"We didn't miss, sire!" the sergeant cried. "The bullets went right through him."

"Fools! Incompetents! I will deal with this man. Reload your weapons and resume your duties."

Toor could barely contain his laughter. During the ship's six week survey he had analyzed the planet's holographic database. To his delight he had discovered slapstick comedy and had spent many hours watching Charlie Chaplin and the Three Stooges. Toor could discern little difference between those recordings and the present situation.

M'basa gestured toward him and Toor followed the man inside. They walked down a marble-floored hallway, decorated with African art. M'basa led him into a large air-conditioned room that was covered with woven rugs. On the wall hung African masks, spears, and photographs.

"My private office," M'basa said, by way of introduction. He looked up at his visitor. "Please state your business. I am a busy man. A delegation from the European Union is expected within the hour."

What was this cracker doing here, anyhow? M'basa wondered. Apparently he had wandered in from off the street. But anyone who could get past his guards so easily deserved scrutiny.

Silently, Toor handed M'basa one of the headsets. M'basa stared at its quiet elegance. Although not technically inclined, it was obvious to him that the instrument exuded power. He placed the device over his head. When the two pads touched his temples the universe exploded.

For a second M'basa sat, stunned, as he gazed at the mental landscape before him. To enter was child's play. There was a door, and beside the door was a key. M'basa fitted the key into the lock and he was in.

M'basa experienced the immensity of the universe-wide Gudaluian Network. He now understood the legends of his people. The stars were populated with races and civilizations of every description! His mind opened and his heart sang with joy. Oh, to join his brothers and sisters in the heavens! It was as if a drowning man saw a pool of crystal clear water. He was Home.

Aboard the Gudalurian ship

The President of the Universal Council of Gudalur, the Oorant, and the Orion met twelve hours later aboard their ship. All three were subdued as each told their story through the headsets, sharing their experiences. They placed their data into the standard Summary Information Matrix. It was even more clear that the destruction of this planet was impossible. But all of Gudalur was against them.

Xttlzttl was president of the Universal Council and his opinion would carry great weight. Nevertheless, the three missionaries approached their conference call to Miralet with trepidation. Sentiment was strong within Gudalur for the elimination, once and for all, of this noisome and odious cancer. Especially now that the earthians had once again shown themselves capable of mastering Gudalurian technology.

The missionaries remained hopeful. Their data, experiences, and impressions of this place should be sufficient to convince their colleagues that the earthian planet held secrets that may be important to the further evolution of Gudalur.

The ship moved out of the solar system to the Ring boundary. It deactivated the Ring programming that would have hurled the ship into inter-sector space. This enabled it to connect to the Network and communicate with Miralet in Ring 0.

A conference with the Gudalurian Universal Council was held in holospace. To the subjective experience of the participants, there was absolutely no difference between the holospace and reality.

"We have been eagerly awaiting your report," said the Council Vice President, an Oorant. Oorant's did not assign themselves names because each was instantly recognizable to others of its kind. The VP gazed at Its counterpart aboard the ship with hauteur and disdain (for an Oorant). Through the ship's Network It had already analyzed the treasonous actions of the maverick Oorant in Beijing. The other thirty members of the Universal Council reclined in floats within the Inner Chamber. This demesne is ornately decorated with spectacular artifacts from all over Gudalur, reflecting the universe's cultural diversity.

The maverick Oorant sighed, understanding at a glance that the Council had already come to a decision. After It made Its report, It summarized. "And so, Dear Ones, an objective analysis shows clearly that the grids of this planet reflect those of the Network itself. This is a monumental discovery which shows that this planet may have a direct connection to the Ring Creators. Certainly, this planet needs further investigation. To destroy life here is not only a violation of the First Principle but a crime against all life everywhere." It noticed that several of the Council members expressed their disapproval at Its strongly worded statement. "Of course these earthians are barbaric, untrained, and undisciplined. Yet they hold the key that may finally unlock the greatest mystery of all: 'Who created the Ring Network and how did they do it?'"

The Orion was next to give his report. "This planet is both terrifying and beautiful. These earthians must be welcomed to Gudalur. They must be trained to harness their extraordinary mental capabilities. To destroy this planet would make mockery of all that we stand for. Do we abandon our principles when the going gets tough? Are we hypocrites to proclaim the sanctity of life and then destroy an entire planet, and billions of life forms?" The Orion gazed pointedly at the council and spoke defiantly. "I, for one, will have no part in this insanity. I will remain here on the earthian planet and work with my friend, the Oorant. I will resist any attempt to reprogram this Ring. If you intend to destroy this world you will also extinguish a fellow member of the Council."

The members exploded out of their floats. "You violate your sacred word of cooperation and defy the will of Council?" shouted a lizard-like being from Ring (2378P, 12.0998, 4744866). "Such is the word of an Orion."

This was a gross personal insult and an egregious violation of diplomatic protocol. It caused the members to become even more agitated, arguing and shouting amongst themselves.

The VP grabbed Its ceremonial mallet and banged the sacred Gortu, an ancient metallic bowl that resonated harmonious musical frequencies.

After a few moments the group quieted. It said, "Is it not obvious that the very ethers of the earthian planet contaminate the peace and serenity of Gudalur?" The others acknowledged the truth of this statement, even the three in the scout ship. "Its very existence causes divisiveness and conflict," the VP continued. "The earthians are on the verge of another outbreak." The VP gestured contemptuously toward its fellow Oorant. "My colleague's treason has given these savages the fundamental protocols with which to sabotage our efforts to maintain universal peace and harmony!" The Oorant was speaking now with unaccustomed emotion. "Are we to allow one insignificant planet to despoil and infect all Gudalur?"

It realized that It was now emotionally out of control. It steadied Itself, using the standard Oorant meditation. Then It said, "My dear friends, we all know how delicate is our Network. We all understand the power of thought. It is clear that these earthian memes have infiltrated the consciousness of even the Council, the most spiritually and mentally developed beings in all Gudalur. Just as did the despicable Koori 50 million standard years ago. Left unchecked the earthian thought forms will quickly travel the length and breadth of the Network at the speed of thought. This will instantly pollute the entire universe. It will incite hatred, violence, and war. No my friends! We cannot risk the entire universe for the sake of one planet. Even a planet that might or might not hold a key to some unsubstantiated, hypothetical connection to a race of beings who have been dead for billions of years. Dear Ones, for the good of all, the earthian menace must be extirpated once and for all. Before it is too late."

Applause and agreement rang loudly through the chamber.

"I agree with our illustrious Vice President," said a partially disembodied being of light. This being, a neural network in a nutrient solution, was able to project its consciousness into a plasma sphere. The sphere reflected its thoughts in trillions of multicolored points of light. Those who understood this form of communication could tell its mood by observing the geometric patterns and their colors. These beings were considered to be the most spiritually advanced in all of Gudalur.

"It saddens me to see how quickly our own psyches have been influenced by the earthian thought forms. It saddens me even further to understand that these earthians are indeed unique. They are uncontrollable, dangerous, and too volatile to ever merge smoothly into Gudalurian civilization. For me to sanction the destruction of any life form must result in my immediate suicide, for I could not live with myself. But I can see no other alternative. It is my sacred duty to protect Gudalar and all life within it. Therefore, I hereby cast my vote for the elimination of the earthian planet."

The nutrient bath and its container then imploded, a soft mist rising from the blackened shell. The lights within the plasma sphere died.

The entire council was shocked. No one spoke, thought, or moved for several minutes. Such a thing had never occurred in the eight billion year history of the Council. The members, shaken, could only stare in horror and despair at the remnants of its dear friend.

The VP gazed around the room, trembling with grief and sickness. It finnaly got the attention of the members and called for a vote.

"Wait." It was the voice of Xttlzttl, Council President. "I have not yet delivered my report."

The VP turned respectfully to the mantis and inclined Its great head, giving Xttlzttl the floor.

"Dear friends, I am in excruciating pain. Having the seen the potential of the earthians first hand, I am much more aware of the promise of this planet's linkage to something spiritually greater than anything in Gudalur."

To the Council this was a powerful statement. Gudalurians understood their spiritual nature and celebrated it. The search for higher levels of consciousness was a powerful motivation, even for the average citizen.

"It was my intention to vigorously oppose the intent of the Council." Xt-tlzttl avoided the eyes of his fellow missionaires. "I now find myself in agreement with the majority. I vote for implementation of the Universal Council's plan for immediate termination of the earthian Ring."

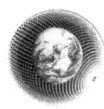

Chapter 30

Confrontation

Sergeant Tokolowski and his secret service crew took off their headsets and stared at each other in the subdued light of a desk lamp. In a gross breach of duty each had abandoned their posts this night. They met in an unused conference room a short distance away from the presidential bedroom. From their study of the scoutship's holobanks they had discovered the date and time of the conference. The men were able to hear all that transpired.

"What the hell are they talking about?" asked agent DeShawn Williams.

"It's an invasion!" cried agent Filpulla, Tokolowski's good buddy.

"Shut up Valteri!" the sergeant said quickly.

"Sorry."

The five secret service agents sat silently for several moments. Each of them knew that their planet was in grave danger but did not know what the next step should be.

Finally, Williams expressed the common consensus of their thoughts. "Nobody fucks with the human race."

"Goddam right D," Filpulla said angrily. Everyone murmured their agreement. "No aliens are gonna destroy us."

"What do we do?" Williams asked. All eyes turned toward the sergeant.

At the presidential palace in Lagos, President M'basa threw down his headset in disgust. "The bastards!" he cried. Along with Tokolowski and his men, M'basa was able to know what happened on the ship through the headsets.

At that moment the door flung open. The sergeant of the guard appeared. "Is everything all right sire?"

"Yes you fool."

The man hastily closed the door. "Wait!"

"Yes sire?"

"Get me Ademola, the Communications Director. Quickly man."

Sergeant Mirembe shot out the door. M'basa thought of the others who had these sets. The four Elders in China, President Rosen, and Jack Martins. The ship's holobase told him that.

They would have to talk, and quickly...but why did he have to wait to speak through diplomatic channels? The headset might be unsecure but he picked up the device and placed it on his head. "Calling China, calling Jack Martins or President Rosen, are you there? We've got a big problem in case you haven't heard already..."

Sergeant Tokolowski and his men heard M'basa's call through their headsets. "What if it's a fake?" Tokolowski asked the group. "I don't want to wake the president for some crazy in Nigeria."

Deshawn Williams spoke. "I got it covered. I'll call Rad Greenberg. He knows the president. Let Rad wake him up."

"How do you know Greenberg?" Tokolowski asked.

"Long story. He's an irritating bastard. Amazing the crew of that ship didn't kill him."

Agent Williams gleefully made the call.

Hun Shi-Chu put down her headset on the silk bedspread. BETRAYAL!!! was the word that screamed within her consciousness. It did not seem possible that such an advanced civilization could even contemplate the destruction of an entire planet. But she knew she was wrong. The Flower was named for her personal beauty, but inside she was hardened steel. In a world dominated by men she was known and respected for her intelligence and her courage. She placed the delicate headset back on her head and called her three companions.

In the presidential bedroom, the president's vid chirped. "Goddam, it's 3 in the morning," Sam muttered. Fortunately he was a light sleeper and always awoke fully conscious, a trait necessary in his job. His heart raced, expecting another report of a terrorist attack. To his surprise it was his friend Rad Greenberg.

"Rad! To what do I owe this honor? You don't need any money do you old pal?"

"Ha ha, Sam. You'd better call Jack Martins right now, I don't have time to explain. Here's the number. Got that?"

"Rad, what the hell is this all about?"

"No time Sam. Just call Martins right away."

Jack Martins, lying in bed with Amara, heard his personal vid activate. The chubby face of President Rosen appeared.

"Jack, it's the president!" Amara exclaimed.

"Damn right it's the president, honey-child," Martins said. The president explained the situation.

"We've got important things to discuss," Jack said to Amara. "Guy stuff."

Amara fired up. "Don't patronize me Jack Martins."

"That's no way to talk to a lady Martins," said the president.

"Thank you Mr. President," Amara said.

Rosen gazed appreciatively at Amara, clad only in a transparent cotton robe. "Martins, where did you find her?"

Amara jumped out of bed cursing all men. Jack and President Rosen smiled.

"I thought I'd call you," the president said. "Rad told me something about the ship and a situation that needs attending to."

Jack quickly put on his headset and entered the Gudalurian ship's holospace. In a second he saw the entire Council deliberation at the speed of thought. M'basa in Nigeria hadn't exaggerated.

"All right sir, we've got a serious problem. Do you still have that headset the alien gave you?"

"Yes, I stuck it in my desk drawer. An amazing device, isn't it?"

"Yes sir, and it's going to get even more amazing. To make a long story short, the earth is about to be destroyed by this alien culture."

The president laughed nervously. "You must be mistaken, Dr. Martins. My conversation with the alien showed me a very advanced culture, both spiritually and politically. Apparently there's something called the First Principle. It forbids the destruction of life."

"That's true sir," Jack acknowledged. "But things have changed radically. Our deactivation of the Martins Sphere boundary has totally freaked them out. Orders have been given to fling our entire solar system into the depths of inter-galactic space. That would almost immediately destroy all life on earth."

President Rosen was afraid of the calm certainty and authority in Jack's voice. It was obvious that the scientist understood much more than he did.

Jack was working with the ship's information system as he spoke. The Oorant suddenly came online and Jack devoted some of his attention to talk with It. "If you have your headset, I want you to put it on as soon as you hang up. These devices provide access to a virtual holographic communications, data storage, and retrieval space on their ship. I have collected all of the images, events, and data surrounding the visit of the aliens to our planet. I've encrypted the area with a password. Here it is."

Jack gave President Rosen the password knowing that the aliens could retrieve it. But time was of the essence.

"My summary will give you all the data you need. Give the set and the password to anyone who needs to know. Do whatever is necessary, Mr. President. I'll handle things from the scientific sector. I am in communication right now with everyone who has one of these sets, including the Chinese."

Rosen sat on his bed. He was stunned and said nothing.

"We have two allies, sir, among the aliens," Jack continued. "The one you met, the mantis, is our enemy. But there are two others. One of 'em's an Oorant, a strange looking three-legged creature with an IQ of about 800. The other one's an Orion. He looks just like that old actor George Clooney except his head is bigger."

"Oy gevalt," Rosen muttered.

"One more thing sir. The Oorant is manufacturing a bunch more of these headsets. He says...It says...that It can get several thousand of them to us within the next planetary revolution...er, the next 24 hours."

President Rosen could hardly make sense of anything the scientist was telling him.

Jack felt his uncertainty and smiled. "Don't worry Mr. President. You'll understand everything in a couple of seconds after you put on that headset. Good luck! I trust in your judgment."

Martins rang off, leaving the President in a state of shock. But he placed the headphones over his head and gave the password. Instantly he was in the holospace. An explosion of imagery, data, and thought impinged on his consciousness.

A silent battle raged in the skies over earth. Two hundred ships had been sent from Miralet in an attempt to coerce the scout ship home. Xttlzttl had been allowed to transport off ship but the two renegades remained on board. As long as the scout ship's holographic communications system remained enabled the earthians could use it to access the Gudalurian Network. They would be able to communicate telepathically with each other and gain access to the Ring programming protocols. Xttlzttl and his comrades realized that they couldn't shut down the Network to stop the earthians. It was the lifeblood of the entire universe.

The Council VP called his Oorant counterpart aboard the scoutship, attempting conciliation. "Dear One," It said, "you have admirably defended the First Principle in your desire to help the earthians. But it is now time to act for the greater good. Abandon this madness and come back with us to Gudalur."

Implied was the understanding of ex-communication. Not only from Oorant culture, but from the universe itself. Even if all went well the Oorant understood that It would be forevermore stranded on the earth. It would probably live the rest of Its life aboard the scoutship within the earthian Ring. The sense of isolation It felt was shocking, but It could not abandon Its principles. The Oorant bowed to the VP. "I thank you for your consideration. But my mind, along with my Orion companion, is made up."

The expression on the VP's face hardened, the thin lips tightening around Its feeding orifice. "Thy will be done." Then It cut communications.

The VP wondered whether the fleet would scuttle one of their own ships. For an Oorant that would truly be an act of madness, a violation of everything It stood for. But in order to completely cleanse the earthian contamination from Gudalur the scout ship may have to be sacrificed.

It saw now the slippery slope toward conflict and war. The Council VP was appalled. What was the destruction of one scout ship when compared with the extermination of an entire planet? What was the termination of life in one solar system in comparison to the greater loss of life represented by the earthian threat? It suddenly felt ashamed. For a fleeting instant It longed to join Its companion aboard the rebel ship. Rebel! There, you see? It told Itself. The divisive earthian memes had now contaminated Its own consciousness. It would have to meditate for many hours to remove the stain.

At 4 p.m. in the afternoon of the next day, the gigantic elliptical vessels of Gudalur disappeared from the skies above earth. All but one.

Chapter 31

Ten humans stood on board the Gudalurian scout craft wearing headsets. President Rosen, Wen Hung, the Flower, President M'basa, Sergeant Tokolowski, the Science Advisory Board, and General Pilsher, Chairman of the Joint Chiefs. All were awed at the ship's beauty and power. The four scientists of the Science Advisory Board, at first skeptical, were now convinced of the threat from Gudalur.

"Where is your weaponry?" General Pilsher asked.

The Oorant was disgusted. "We have no weaponry other than the ability to manipulate the planetary grids and program the Ring. In Gudalur, war has been unknown for 5 billion years." Except for Koori, It thought.

General Pilsher nodded. "I thought as much." To communicate in this fashion was extraordinary. Absolute transparency. No lies or even half-truths possible. And the imagery! It was a virtual reality with the ability to relive events and send thoughts complete with sound, pictures, and emotions. And all at the speed of thought. In comparison his vid was like communicating with two tin cans and a string tied between them.

President Rosen spoke first. "The first step, as I see it, is to get people immediately learning the Ring programming protocols. The Gudalurians are going to move this entire Ring out of its proper position using these protocols. I've got Jack Martins on that right now. He's searching for talent as fast as you can manufacture these headsets and test prospective candidates. Lots of gamers and musicians so far, Jack says."

"We are also testing our people," Wen Hung said. "We've passed several dozen so far. The question is, how many do we need in order to counter the Gudalurian programmers? They've got an entire universe to choose from."

"Lots of brilliant people on Miralet," Tokolowski chimed in. "Hard to defeat the best minds in the universe."

"Thank you for that sergeant," Pilsher said, irritated.

"He's right," said Hun Shi-Chu. "How can we compete with people who have been doing this for billions of years?"

"Dr. Martins is very confident," replied the president. "He says that we have an edge. It's one of the reasons we are perceived as being so dangerous."

"What edge?" M'basa said.

The Oorant stepped in. In one sense It was now appalled at Its decision to stay with these earthians. Their thought patterns were rough and undisciplined. Every time one of them spoke it felt like fingernails on a chalkboard, to use an earthian expression. It was necessary for It to spend several hours a day in meditation. Nevertheless, there was something exhilarating about Its association with these beings.

"Let me demonstrate," the Oorant said. It replayed the earthian's experiences when first contacting the scout ship's comm system. It showed their thought patterns and the ship's holographic interface as geometric and mathematical entities. "Now watch carefully," It said. The Oorant showed M'basa as he first picked up his unfamiliar headset. The ship's holo interface was now an enormously complex, three dimensional matrix. "Mathematically and geometrically your intellects are not capable of solving the matrix. Even if you spent an entire lifetime of study none of you could do it. Now watch what happens." The earthians saw the mind of M'basa almost immediately derive the proper identities and the system opened.

"Do you see?" the Oorant said. "Intellectually, none of you are even remotely close to myself. Or indeed, any Gudalurian on Miralet, or even one of our average citizens. Yet each one of you was able to solve an enormously complex encryption within milliseconds. That kind of intuitive ability," the Oorant paused for emphasis, "is what they are afraid of."

"I don't know anything about mathematics or geometry!" M'basa protested. "All I saw was a key fitting into a door lock."

The Oorant rocked back and fo4rth on Its tripod, indicating bafflement. "What all of you have done is simply not possible. Apparently, earthians have extraordinarily powerful intuitive capabilities. We do not comprehend their origin or why you have them in such great measure."

The Oorant paused once more, lost in thought. "Your latent abilities are what frighten my compatriots," It continued. "Fifty million years ago another earthian, who called himself Koori, harnessed these abilities and began a Great War. The objective was total domination and control of the entire universe. And he almost succeeded after great loss of life and property. That is why your planet has been quarantined, you see. Now you may understand our shock and fear when you managed to remove your Ring's Nullspace barrier. Without even knowing any of the Ring programming protocols!"

The earthians were amazed at their accomplishment even though none of them knew how it had been done.

"Observe the one you call Jack Martins," the Oorant said. "Here is something that frightens even me." They watched as Martins walked into the conference room and directed a joke at the president. Martins sat in front of the mantis and put on the headset. Instantly his mind was in the system, unlocking sub-sections of the holographic matrix. Martin's mind decoded and absorbed information so rapidly that the system could hardly keep track. "Here is a mind that combines both intellectual and intuitive abilities. If this earthian were on Miralet he would be instantly promoted to the head of the technical section."

The assembled earthians were pleased with the praise from the Oorant. But It then dampened their enthusiasm considerably.

"When Gudalur saw that performance, all objections to your demise evaporated. For 36 of your hours our ships analyzed the earthian grid system and imaged its Ring. I estimate that within 100 planetary rotations Gudalur will begin the process of moving your Ring to the depths of inter-galactic space. That estimate is, of course, only my educated guess. But it is fairly accurate. You do not have much time. My suggestion is to make the most of it."

With the Oorant's advice and that of Regat Toor, the Ring Control Group frantically began to develop a plan for defense of the earth. The Cheesy Poof space travelers were asked to participate. Karl Svenson was coaxed out of retirement to join the effort.

The recruitment process was presented as a scientific experiment to test the capabilities of human intuition. It was presented to the public in the same spirit of competition as the testing for the manned Alpha mission. The true purpose for the contest was never explicitly stated but an underlying sense of urgency permeated the project. This lent it an air of mystery and excitement to the general public. Literally hundreds of millions took the aptitude test. This test was a virtual reality testing regimen hosted in the scout ship's holospace. It was connected, through Gudalurian magic, to the WorldNet. Even those who had no desire to participate took the test just to find out their scores. Test results were posted on WorldNet, further escalating the sense of excitement.

The media-friendly General Pilsher was appointed spokesman for the Ring Control Group. The governments of the world were only too happy to allow a select group of individuals from the private sector to take the lead (and the blame for failure). It was a lose-lose situation for governments because those in the know understood that the odds against humanity were billions to one. The following bulletin was issued and read by General Pisher on WorldNet:

"The Ring Control Group needs the best and the brightest to participate in an experiment vital to the safety of earth. As you know, we have been visited by beings from the stars who represent a vast, eons-old, universe-wide civilization. These beings, we now know, were responsible for the Event. They have made us aware of an impending crisis facing the earth. Two Gudalurian representatives have been sent to help us in this crisis (images shown). Here, ladies and gentlemen, is the Oorant, from a sector halfway across the universe. This gentleman is Regat Toor, from our very own stellar neighborhood of Orion. Regat is from Anlinam in the constellation of Orion, which is one of the three stars in Orion's belt (image provided). As you can see, our Orion friend looks just like one of us. Despite the Oorant's strange appearance It is a gentle being and enormously intelligent. It has volunteered to help us in our time of need. A holovid of the Oorant and Its home planet has been provided for your information, as well as a personal message from It to the people of earth (Oorants are asexual). We encourage all of you to take the aptitude test. Your skills and abilities may be vitally necessary to the future of humanity, and to our planet! The twenty thousand highest scorers will be invited to participate in this vital project."

In the holospace the Oorant showed the earthians their Ring and the precise locations that needed to be programmed. It demonstrated the correct energetic signatures necessary to activate them. "Once these templates have been activated," It said, "your Ring will begin moving out of its assigned section of space. Your job is to neutralize these templates by devising ones that are its exact opposite," the Oorant said. "When the two templates collide, they will dissolve harmlessly into one another. This is very fortunate because you do not need to be expert Ring programmers. All you need to do is learn specific protocols for a tiny sub-section of your Ring."

"What is this Ring anyway, and how do these templates interact with the Ring to cause it to move?" President Rosen asked.

"A Ring is contained in the double-torus structure of space itself," the Oorant answered. "Billions of years ago it was discovered that stars and galaxies were surrounded by a subtle but programmable manifold of enormous complexity. These manifolds are responsive to targeted vibrational impulses. Soon after that we learned how to manipulate these templates with amplified thought forms. Universal communication and travel then became possible.

"Each galactic Ring contains billions of these energetic templates. Each has a specific function. Mostly they are simply used for space travel, communications, and commerce. Then came the launching of your first manned mission to the Ring. This was recorded on Miralet. The Gudalur High Council knows the warlike nature of your societies. It determined that you had become too dangerous and activated a strict quarantine protocol on your Ring. This caused what you now call the Event.

"A Ring is the programmable interface to spacetime itself, similar to one of the user interfaces in a computer program. Each template acts like a menu item except that the menus are activated by targeted thought impulses. These templates literally control the physics, and the physical attributes, of the matter and energy contained within them."

Rosen gulped. "Uh…thanks. This is a little over my head."

"How much power will be required to enable the Ring movement?" Pilsher asked. "We'll need to match it."

"Examine the signatures on the marked templates," the Oorant said. "Begin to experiment within the ship's holographic training facility. This is where all Ring training takes place, even on Miralet. Rest assured, you will be able to generate enough power. IF you can master the protocols that activate the templates. I estimate that you will need at least 5,000 trained individuals and probably as many as 20,000. There are only approximately 100 days left. This effort will be nothing like the simplistic success you had with the thought experiment and the Ring boundary. That was a trivial exercise. You must work fast."

For the earthians, the entire project was unreal. No one could believe it possible until Toor showed them a holo of the famous Argent Ring episode. An entire stellar system became convinced that the Ring Creators were about to return to raise all devotees to another plane of existence. They moved their local Ring to the Zero Point and perished.[1] That holo sent chills down the spines of everyone present and radically increased their motivation.

President M'basa had a question. "What will happen if the Gudalurians are successful programming our Ring?" M'basa functioned as Communications Liaison for the group. The petty concerns of power and control in Nigeria now seemed like child's play in comparison with his new duties.

"Your people will notice nothing at first," Toor replied. "Except that the heavens will gradually alter their appearance. Slowly at first, then more rapidly, your constellations will become unrecognizable. The bonds that hold your Ring balanced within the cocoon of gravitational forces will be ripped asunder. Your planets will gradually lose their orbital positions. Rotational velocities will alter unpredictably, throwing the delicate balance of earthian ecosystems into chaos. More than likely, all life upon your planet will have been destroyed before your Ring even reaches inter-galactic space."

M'basa gulped. Those on the Gudalurian scout ship would be safe, of course. An emergency plan had already been worked out in case of failure. Twenty thousand of the most important human beings on earth, as well as two of every available species, would be taken aboard the scout ship. This had been named Cheesy Poof 3 by the earthians. A new Ark, but one that traveled the spaceways.

"How will we know when the attack begins?" M'basa asked.

"Jack Martins is in charge of that," the Oorant responded. It was beginning to identify more and more with earthian thought patterns and rhythms of speech. These beings were raw, untrained, and unpredictable, but eager and excited about life. It felt Itself on a great adventure. It was now mentor to a gigantic horde of untamable but brilliantly eccentric children just coming into their adolescence. It had not felt this young, or this excited, in decades.

---

[1] The Zero Point is a completely barren, 20 million light-year patch of space at the center of the double torus, that is known for its mysterious properties. Ships that travel too close suddenly disappear, never to be found again.

"The ship is connected to the Network and will be able to immediately ascertain the moment of attack. We will also know the precise footprint of the incoming thought forms."

Jack Martins took a day off from his work on the scout ship. He briefed a special Joint Intelligence Subcommittee of representatives and senators. Congressman Dempsey and his aides, Yogesh Dalal and Victorio, attended. Both could hardly believe their ears. But then, it had been equally as difficult to believe that the stars had disappeared and been restored. On an impulse Jack asked both men to take the Martins Aptitude Test. This exercise had been designed by the Oorant to measure mental aptitude and intuitive ability. Dalal scored at the lower end but Victorio broke the record on the intuitive parameter. He had the highest score recorded so far, even higher than Jack.

Jack was curious and walked over to the Apache. When the man turned to face him Jack received an impression of quiet power and physical strength. Time was short and he did not hesitate. "I'd like you to come up to the ship. We've got important work for you in the coming battle. I'll clear it with your boss."

The Apache's eyes lit up. "Battle? What kind of battle?"

Jack grinned. "A battle of mental willpower, intention, acuity, and strength."

The man's eyes were literally burning with eagerness. Here was a fellow to have on your side in a fight!

Victorio measured Jack and liked what he saw. The Apache stuck out his hand. "Then I'm your man. If we have to take a few scalps, all the better."

"My sentiments exactly," Jack said. "If we have to kill a few of the bastards, we'll do it." Jack grinned and took the Apache's hand, which held his in a gentle grip. As he met the man's gaze Jack received the distinct impression that this guy could crush his bones like a vise on balsa wood. He had met only one other whom he felt was his physical superior. One of his roommates in college who, although of only average height and build, possessed superhuman strength. Victorio was the same.

Jack walked over to Congressman Dempsey. "I'd like to borrow your aide for a few weeks sir," Jack requested. "It seems that he's broken the record on our aptitude test."

Dempsey eyed the scientist shrewdly. "He's yours, Martins, for the next ten weeks," the Congressman replied. "But only until the start of debate on H.R. 734."

"There might not be any debate, Congressman, if the aliens win this battle."

Dempsey winked. "You stick to your area of expertise Dr. Martins. I'll stick to mine!"

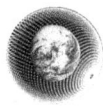

Chapter 32

Miralet

Xttlzttl and 143 Gudalurians stood within the immense bowl that was Council chambers on Miralet. The 144 performed the song khur, the ceremony for the dead. Song khur was the most solemn ritual in the universe. These brave beings were to sacrifice themselves for the good of all Gudalur. They would be forever excommunicated from it.

For almost ten billion years, beings throughout the universe communicated telepathically through the Network. They forged an intimate connection that made even the concept of war unthinkable. To destroy an entire civilization, even though it might threaten all Gudalur, was a crime against all life everywhere. This act was so heinous that it would indelibly stain the soul of anyone who consciously participated in it.

On the other hand, to volunteer for such a mission was the ultimate selfless act for the good of all. The kuhr is the act of soul sacrifice. It simultaneously dammed the soul of a being for all eternity yet raised it to an almost mystical level of purity. Such was the glorious and horrible contradiction of the kuhr. Thus was the song kuhr, the Acknowledgment of Sacrifice and Damnation, the most sacred ceremony in Gudalur.

Each of the 144 Tukhir, which in English would translate loosely to "dead men walking," wore ceremonial garb. They stood, gazing upward, in a circle upon the floor. This is a holograph of a rising sun spreading its rays into the darkness. The Tukhrati, or Acknowledgers, sat suspended within the gigantic auditorium. To describe this gathering is impossible. The variety of life gathered here was beyond imagination. Xttlzttl's carapace was elaborately painted in greens and reds (the colors of celebration and death in his culture). The Council president weaved in and out through the assembly with his fellows in a ritual pattern that had been established over 8 billion standard years ago. Every one of the 10 million Sectors within the known universe either sent a personal representative or a live holographic projection. No sector was absent from the powerful ceremony. Each Tukhir sat (or swam or stood or perched) on a float decorated with the colors of its sector and the personal accouterments of its culture. Each of the 144 was personally acknowledged by each of the Tukhrati. It was their way of saying goodbye and of honoring them and the sacred duty they had agreed to perform. Never again could they access the Network, nor communicate with any Gudalurian citizen in good standing. The destruction of the abominable earthian civilization was imperative. But the psychic contamination would be passed on to anyone they met or communicated with at the unimaginable speed of thought. Therefore their isolation from Gudalur was an absolute necessity. Not even Zurg received such treatment, Xttlzttl thought. But then again, neither were they in any way as dangerous.

Xttlztttl floated to and fro, gazing into the space of each Acknowledger. He received from each a personal holograph of his or her or its home sector, native planet, and a personal message. It was a poignant reminder of all that he had experienced in Gudalur, and what he was going to miss.

After the ceremony the Tukhir again gathered together in the circle on the floor of the auditorium. The Tuhkrati faced them and bowed. Then all 10 million turned their backs. The condemned exited the chamber, outcasts forever from Gudalur and civilized society throughout the universe.

The Battle for Earth

The battle was unlike any ever fought on earth. The scout ship was now crammed with over 20,000 carefully selected candidates. Each sat with a headset at curved, cream-colored tables, manufactured on-ship. The tables fitted together like pieces in a 3 dimensional jigsaw puzzle. They were suspended in mid-air so that the total volume of space occupied by the team was minimal. The ship could have handled over 500,000 if required.

When the candidates arrived on the ship they were informed of the true purpose of the mission. Each was sworn to secrecy and was offered the chance to go back to earth. No one did.

Amara, tired of not seeing Jack, had on a whim taken the aptitude test. She had qualified and was now part of the team. "I'm eligible and you have no right to refuse," she had said, insisting upon being part of the action. Jack objected strongly. "No babe. We've already been training for almost eight weeks now. You can't get up to snuff in time."

"Oh I can't, can't I?"

Jack groaned. Wrong! He should have known by now never to challenge this woman. It was one of her sensitive areas and it sometimes irritated the hell out of him.

Jack retreated. "It's too dangerous."

"If it's too dangerous then why are you doing it?" she asked.

"That's different. I'm a man. Men are used to fighting."

"Don't give me any of that chauvinist shit! I've got just as much right as you do!"

"The right to die? If anything ever happened to you…"

"How do you think I feel?" she flared. "What makes you so damn special?"

Jack had no answer for that and gave it up. But he knew, somehow, that this battle would be to the death.

Now Jack and Amara walked hand in hand on one of the ship's suspended walkways that snaked through the complex. Like everything in Gudalur the path hung in mid-air without any visible means of support. Amara surveyed the group and noticed that most of the participants were young people. They either sat at their stations in mental concentration or chatted easily with each other. An aura of power, confidence, and affinity surrounded this complex. The people here were all geniuses just waiting to strut their stuff. She felt sorry for the aliens who might have to go against this team.

"Who is that guy?" Amara asked, pointing to a stockily built man with long black hair who sat slightly apart. He was in one of two floats set within the middle of the group.

"That's Victorio," Jack said. "Our Strike Leader."

"Who's the other float belong to?"

"Yours truly," Jack said.

271

Amara smirked. "I thought you'd wangle your bossy way to the top of this somehow," she joked.

"I scored the highest on the technical aptitude portion of the test!"

Amara smiled. "I'm sure you did, Jack. Who devised this test, anyway? You?"

Jack snorted. "Nope, not me babe. You see that odd looking creature off to the left there? The one at the float above everyone else?"

Amara looked out over the space and saw the Oorant, with one of the ubiquitous silvery headsets on Its great cylindrical dome. "That's the guy who made up the test. Actually, the test was devised more than 5 billion years ago. It just adapted the test for our uses."

"Why do you call him an it?" Amara wondered. "He looks like a guy to me." A very strange guy, but the idea of an alien did not startle her. Certainly, that Oorant was less fantastic than this magnificent space ship.

Jack smiled. "Oorants are asexual."

Amara grinned and swung her hip into his leg. "How unfortunate for them."

Jack was worried for her. But he was proud that Amara had qualified. He felt a sense of love and happiness walking her to her station. But soon things would be different. The alien strike could come at any time and they had better be ready. Or else their beautiful planet would be dead, a frozen lifeless husk floating in space.

"Goddamit Amara. We're going to win, we *have* to win!" Jack was passionate.

"Is it really that bad, Jack?" Amara was frightened.

Jack never pulled any punches with her. "It's that bad, sweetheart. You'll find out when you see the introduction." Jack led her to her place within the floating complex, at a chair about 500 feet from his.

"But I'm so far away from you, Jack!"

He smiled. "Don't worry babe. When you put on that headset for the first time we'll be connected in the most intimate fashion. And you'll connect with everyone here in the same way." Jack's eyes lit up. "You have to experience it to believe it. It's really, really good."

"Better than sex?" she teased.

"It's…awesome," Jack said fervently. "In the short time we've been here we've already had 160 marriages."

Amara looked around the floating complex and became excited. "There's as many women as men."

"That's right. Nobody knows how or why it worked out that way. Not even the Orion or the Oorant."

Amara had dozens more questions.

"No time, Amara." Jack kissed her softly and seated her in her assigned position. "Here, put these on and give this password. You'll get your instructions and then get right onto learning and practicing the protocols. The alien attack could come at any time now."

Jack left her and practically ran to his seat next to Victorio, putting on his headset. He felt Amara in the holospace and she snuggled up to him quite nicely. There were thousands of other pairings just like theirs. Each pair gathered into pods of 12, and then into larger groupings of 12, and so on. It had worked out to exactly $12^4 = 20,736$ persons in all. And it was an amazingly tight fit, like a band or an orchestra that had practiced and played together for decades. The sense of camaraderie here was like nothing he had ever experienced.

Jack asked the Oorant why everything had worked out so perfectly. It had been completely baffled. "It exemplifies the vast intuitive potential of your species. I simply do not understand the high incidence of conflict and war on your planet. I have attempted to model the situation on your world with the most extensive and sophisticated matrices known in Gudalaur. You simply don't fit."

It was as close as the Oorant had ever come to the display of a genuine emotion, Jack thought.

Jack then spotted the blond heads of Nigel Clarke and Katrina Antropov. He went over to say hi. Nigel's head was on a level with his own, and Katrina's only an inch lower. "Where are the other two?" Jack asked. Katrina giggled. Nigel smiled. "Karl is hiding again in Halmstad. T'Munga couldn't be bothered." The man in person was as sunny and bright as everyone said. Looking at the couple, it was clear to him they were made for each other. It would be a shame if anything happened to either of them.

"Battle practice!" Victorio shouted. The team groaned. Over twenty thousand volunteers, including himself, put on their headsets and entered the virtual reality of the holospace.

273

Jack saw the Ring as a shell surrounding the nine-light-year section of space. Within that shell, fields of interlocking energy created a beautiful but deadly landscape of mountains, hills, valleys, and meadows strewn with boulders and trees. The programmable energy templates appeared as golden-white spider-webs. The templates functioned just like complex computer programs. Each node within the spider web contained programmable energy codes. The Gudalurian goal was to locate the correct template and overlay a matching template that would activate all of the codes at the same time. These codes would activate the appropriate Ring functions, hurling the earthian Ring into the depths of inter-galactic space.

The Oorant identified the location of the target template deep within a massive cave. The cave was in one of the energetic meadows, on low ground surrounded by hills. The attackers would have the high ground. Therefore the defenders would be exposed. But the attackers must enter the cave to activate the template, which meant that his team knew precisely the point of attack. No energy weapons of any sort were allowed, or guns. Such gross disturbances might damage the templates or make it impossible to insert the correct energetic signatures. Therefore the battle would be hand-to-hand, with swords, lances, rocks, or anything else that came to hand.

Jack stood on one of the hills overlooking the cave and considered their position. He did not like what he saw. To bunch up within the cave was suicide but their force was too numerous to hide within the shelter of the trees. To occupy higher ground left the cave defenseless. *It's hopeless.* Suddenly he felt the presence of the Apache and bucked up a little. In the holospace, the man was a mental giant. Victorio exuded confidence and power.

Jack felt mentally exhausted by their constant training. After weeks of practice the defenders were bunched into two broad camps. The strikers, led by Victorio, and the techies, led by Jack. The strikers were the group's power sources. The techies would analyze the enemy and detect the patterns of their attack. They would bear the brunt of the assault and slow the enemy down while the strikers would use their mental energy to destroy them. The problem was that no one knew who the enemy was. No one knew how many of the enemy there were, or how they would fight. By now, however, the defenders were intimately familiar with the ground. Victorio made them go over and over it, identifying every bit of cover, every exposed position, and the likeliest places for a successful ambush.

"Our goal is to make the enemy fight on the ground we choose," he said. "Then we have the advantage."

The team had naturally evolved the best use of their skills. The techies were like Marines. First in, and hoping to soften the enemy up for the strikers' killing blow.

Victorio placed the team in their positions for the coming drill. Jack sat on his unicorn, fidgeting. During their eight weeks of training the Apache had conducted drill after drill, with every imaginable scenario his versatile mind could devise. Fighting was in his blood. Victorio had an instinctive understanding of strategy and tactics. The man was adept at shielding his mind and not allowing stray thoughts to escape. He wondered what they would drill today. Victorio had devised hundreds of unique and interesting training exercises, keeping concentration and morale high.

Victorio hovered above the team as a glowing blue-white ball of energy. "If the enemy attacks with overwhelming force we are lost," the Apache thought to himself. But like a good commander he exuded confidence. They were fighting blind.

For Jack, the holospace was a high definition extension of physical reality. The coming battle would be just as deadly as real conflict, but much, much quicker. Everything moved at the speed of thought. Colors seemed much brighter and crisper. Even the subtlest sound was audible and every feeling was amplified. Every time you thought something it manifested instantly. During their training exercises several serious incidents had occurred as fighters, in their exuberance, accidentally injured their teammates. It was quickly discovered that holospace injuries mirrored themselves in the physical body. After that it was not difficult to enforce discipline in the ranks. Every team member either learned to adequately master his or her thoughts or was dismissed.

Jack looked up and saw their commander, glowing and sparkling with electrical energy. He shook his head in wonder. During their long hours of drilling it was discovered that a person's holospace persona was a perfect mirror of their fundamental personality, character, and mental ability. This caused not a little consternation among those who had never looked closely within themselves. Jack first appeared on a unicorn with sword in hand and surrounded by a brilliant blue halo. He almost laughed. It was confirmation of what he had sometimes suspected. He was a romantic at heart. Amara appeared beside him as a warrior queen on a huge white battle horse.

Jack looked around at the assembled team. Each defender had their own holospace persona, but most fell into certain categories. Hun Shi-Chu's persona was a black leopard. There were several hundred animals such as panthers, lions, and tigers. Even a few dinosaurs like Tyrannosaurus Rex, Allosaurus, and Pterodactyl. Others appeared as mythical beasts such as fire-breathing dragons or terrifying monsters. Many of the gamers appeared as Transformers, some as comic book heroes or heroines, and some as machines. The techies were mostly robots with the computing power of giant supercomputers, or Star Trek characters like Mr. Spock. Some of the team were shape-shifters. The military types were Terminators. A few hundreds, like Victorio, existed as balls of luminous energy. These were the team's power sources. The team appeared to Jack as a perfectly integrated and indomitable army who must defend an indefensible position.

The opponents they faced had billions of years of training in these same protocols. The alien's sophistication and mental advancement was far beyond theirs, was it not?

He suddenly felt a calming presence like aloe-vera on a skin burn. It was the Apache. "He who occupies the field of battle first and awaits his enemy is at ease. He who comes later to the scene and rushes into the fight is weary," Victorio said. Sun-Tzu! Jack recognized the phrase, from 'Weaknesses and Strengths.'

The Apache spoke confidently. "We occupy the battlefield and force the enemy to come to us." The flat planes of his face were like slabs of granite. "We will not fail."

Looking into those eyes, Jack's confidence rose.

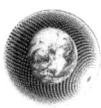

Chapter 33

Xttlzttl linked together with his 143 companions in the cruiser craft's holospace. The holospace allowed the consciousness of a being to be projected to an actual physical location. Their football-shaped ship was 20 miles in length and 12.36 miles wide. It had been designed as a fully self-contained world because it could never again alight upon any planet nor enter any stellar system connected to the Network. It broadcast a signal designating it as a death ship. Its occupants were persona non grata and its holospace, although connected to the earthian Ring, was blocked from any access to the Network itself.

"Here we are, my beloved friends," Xttlzttl said. "How could we have possibly gotten ourselves into this situation?" The former Universal Council president echoed perfectly the feelings of the others.

They had gathered on the rocky surface of an uninhabited desert planet near the center of the Al Niyat galaxy in Sector Jedda. This world had a deep blue sky that faded quickly to black. From horizon to horizon a spectacular, brightly lit collection of stars shone brilliantly, day or night. Exploding supernovae created a misty background of blues and greens. It was one of the most famous and beautiful sights in the universe.

"Let us examine this dangerous planet in more detail," Xttlzttl said. He hoped to find ample justification for their distasteful mission. Before them floated a brilliant representation of the earthian planet from approximately 100 miles out in space.

A collective gasp went through the group. "It's beautiful," said Ueelee, a being that could best be described as a mobile fern.

"But dangerous," replied a creature who closely resembled a blue jay, but with highly developed feet and two arms with flexible appendages. (It is impossible to render this being's name into English, as their spoken language is composed of high pitched chirps.)

"Examine these earthians," said a spider-like being with eight legs and four arms and covered with a soft down. It indicated a downtown city street in North America in which a robbery was in progress. The group looked on in horror as two men punched a woman, stole her purse and valuables, and left her bleeding on the street. Then the spider pointed with one of her arms to a dozen fighter planes screaming toward a village in central Africa. A woman with a bowl of water on her head ran swiftly for cover just as a bomb tore her limb from limb. The display shifted to a small child in Asia torturing a cat, and then to a CIA interrogation camp in Afghanistan where a man was hanging from his wrists while another jolted him with electricity.

"Stop!" cried an erect panda bear, who gestured with her forelegs. Tears ran down her furry face from huge round black eyes. "Enough of this, I cannot bear any more."

"Consider," said the spider. "These are the creatures we have been sent to eradicate from Gudalur. Is it not for the best?"

Then the Shai-Lin, a very tall, thin humanoid with bright white skin, focused the display upon a different scene in central Africa. The group saw elephants, giraffes, zebras, antelopes, hippos, and birds flying from tree to tree. Ueelee looked around at the group. "These creatures look like us!"

The Gudalurians made an intensive study of the planet and discovered that it was, remarkably, a microcosm of Gudalur itself. There was strong sentiment then and there for abandoning their mission altogether. Some said that they should destroy their ship with all aboard.

Upon further study it became apparent that a barbaric, unregulated consciousness was predominant on the planet. It was a far cry from the harmonious self-regulation that characterized intra- and inter-species relationships upon Gudalurian planets.

"We now understand how it works on the earthian planet," the spider said with disgust. A vid showed baby turtles moving swiftly into the water, only to be gobbled up by predators. "Species count is regulated by competition and death from other predator species. Clearly, the entire psyche of this planet and all of its species is insane."

"Our decision to eliminate this Ring is the correct one," seconded the blue jay.

Ueelee objected. "Is it rational to destroy all life because of a few flaws?" Ueelee then showed a man who jumped into a swollen river, risking his life to save another. The scene then shifted to a classical music concert where a violinist played with extraordinary skill. Each of the members saw and felt the transports of the audience into the higher artistic vibrations of aesthetic creativity and beauty. At the conclusion of a violent hockey game the participants put down their sticks, gathered in separate lines, and shook hands. Two parrots groomed each other, smiling joyously.

The group was divided. A great argument ensued, each side not lacking for examples to prove their point. Eventually Xttlzttl interrupted the discussion. "This debate is pointless." The mantis was irritated that he had begun this colloquy, which had devolved into the lower emotions. "Our duty is clear. The sooner we get to it the sooner we can begin to heal ourselves and forget the unspeakable criminal act we are about to perform."

"I agree," concurred Lledren, a sleek, silver-furred feline with a very long tail, which it sat upon. "This planet has many species like myself. The thought of destroying my own kind blackens my soul. So let us get it over with!"

This met with unanimous agreement. The blue jay summed up the feelings on both sides. "It is astonishing how even the slightest connection with the earthian planet leads to grotesque and twisted thinking."

"It is time to commence our work," Xttlzttl said. "First let us examine the earthian position within the Ring. We can then determine the best course of action to activate the correct Ring templates."

For several weeks Xttlzttl and his team surveyed the earthian position from the safety of the holospace.

"These earthians are taking no chances," the spider said. "They have sent their personalities directly to the correct Ring coordinates."

Xttlzttl had hoped that the earthians would make the beginners mistake of merely defending from the holospace. The Gudalurians would then have been able to easily activate the Ring template long before the earthians could get into action. Was it luck, or had the barbarians done this consciously? Then he remembered that the Oorant and the Orion had remained with the scout craft. The traitors! Xttlzttl was already dismayed at the tone of his thoughts. Once fully committed to destruction he could not stop his mind from descending into the gutter.

The spider had made her decision as soon as she was asked to participate. When a Cttrx makes a choice she does it without reservation and never looks back.

Ueelee inspected the array of gladiators before her. She felt dismay at the primitive and tawdry nature of their raiment and their attitude. Most of them were cloaked in the garb of war, yucking and joking lewdly, or making light of their future murders. She had thought that at least these elite earthians would have proceeded further in their development. Ueelee inspected the Trans-formers, killing machines, warriors, and other killers arrayed before her. She steeled herself for the coming action. They would perform the Allia Protocol, which was unlikely to be known by the earthians. They would make them-selves psychically invisible, undetectable even through the ephemeral nature of thought itself. Perhaps, she thought buoyantly, it could be done without inflicting harm to the defenders. She was glad to be finally proceeding along the chosen path that would lead to her psychic ruin.

It was necessary to continuously occupy the holospace with fresh minds. The earthian team devised a duty schedule of three eight hour periods. It was dis-covered that holospace work was even more tiring than physical labor; only the strongest could stay alert longer than that. The targeted Ring templates were therefore guarded by at least one-third of the group at all times, and sometimes more. No one knew what the size of the attacking Gudalurain force would be. Were they mental giants who could dispose of the earthians with only a few? Or would they attack with millions?

Two days later they found out. The Gudalurians appeared as wraiths, visible for a few milliseconds, then gone. They blinked in and out of existence. Within a couple of seconds they had darted through the earthian defenses.

Just as the team was beginning to mobilize the enemy disappeared.

"How did they get past our defenses so quickly?" Jack asked anyone who would listen.

"This was a foray to test our strength," the Oorant said. It was familiar with Gudalurian procedures. "They did not carry with them the activating template." It would not participate in the battle, and shuddered at the thought of inflicting harm upon another being. "A scouting party," Victorio said. "We still do not know the true size of their force. Like good generals they hide their strength for the major battle."

Six hours later came another attack, this time from a different direction. Jack was about to muster his forces when Victorio spoke. "Ignore this. It is merely a feint."

"The Apache is correct," the Oorant confirmed.

Jack stood down. "How did you know?" he asked his partner.

"My people were masters at guerrilla fighting. It is in my blood."

"Remember that in order to activate the proper holographic codes the enabling template must arrive at the precise location and enter the Ring at the precisely correct angle," the Oorant advised. "Therefore, the battleground of any genuine attack must be the Cave." It referred to the earthians name for the holo coordinates of the target templates. "The object for the Gudalurians is to win the battle without fighting. To harm another being is as distasteful to them as it is to me."

The struggle for the future of earth was being fought 4.618 light years away, directed from a virtual holospace within an alien space ship. The team members were now completely devoted to each other and their mission, even though the people they fought for could not appreciate their work.

A 25-year-old keyboard player from Ann Arbor, Michigan summed up the feeling of the defenders. "To be a part of this group is the greatest experience of my life. It's not just that we're aboard an exotic spaceship light years from earth. That's really not relevant at all because what we have experienced could have happened anywhere. It's the relationships and the shared intimacy of our work. I know all 20,736 people better than I know my own mother and father. It might be crazy to say it, but within an hour every one of my team members felt like a beloved and trusted old friend. Almost like a lover, actually. I'm in love with all 20,000 of these wonderful people. And the two aliens too!"

Jack Martins now understood why war had not existed within Gudalurian civilization for billions of years. Once exposed to the pure, unadulterated thoughts and psyches of your fellow man, you saw and felt their quintessential nature. That nature was something admirable. There was no way around it. He knew he could never go back to thinking like a human being again. This experience made you transcend your humanness.

"How can the Gudalurians sanction the destruction of an entire solar system?" Jack asked the Oorant. "It doesn't make sense from their perspective."

"Gudalurians remember the destruction and psychological trauma of the Koori Incident," the Oorant explained. "They are determined that it should never happen again. When they discovered the energy of the one you call Victorio, they saw a direct descendant of Koori. It is a matter of protecting the whole and sacrificing a few. Those who participate in this war will be forever excommunicated from society." It spoke solemnly. "It is the ultimate sacrifice. Their names will be honored and despised for millions of years to come."

Jack did not understand. "How can they be honored and excommunicated at the same time? On earth, those who sacrifice for the good of all are heroes."

If the Oorant could shrug, It would have. "It is not possible for you to understand. The psychic pollution that results from participating in the murder of other beings can never be removed. Infection would inevitably result from association with anyone who has done so. This psychic virus would spread throughout the Network at the speed of thought, dredging up buried memories and precipitating ancient quarrels that have been long forgotten. Our civilization would rapidly descend into barbarity and chaos. Just as yours has done so often in its history."

"But that means that you and the Orion can never return to Gudalur!"

"Yes, that is correct." The Oorant was sad. Its refusal to participate in the battle did not spare It from psychic infection. When it chose to stay and help the earthians It had literally signed Its Gudalurian death warrant.

Three shipdays later the Gudalurians attacked for real.

The Gudalurians performed an exhaustive study of their previous foray to the earthian position. The spider expressed the group's findings. "It is impossible to carry the activating template past the earthian guard or create it on the spot without unacceptable losses on our side."

There was only one solution. Everyone knew it.

"Mercenaries," the Cttrx said firmly.

"No!" Xttlzttl and the group cried in unison. "We must execute this distasteful duty ourselves," Xttlzttl said. "We cannot shunt our responsibility to others." This was the common sentiment.

"Impossible," the spider replied. "Review the projections. We shall need 144 of us just to activate the template. Our helpers must perform the work of disabling the earthian resistance."

"Helpers!" Ueelee shouted, against her nature. "Murderers. Killers for hire."

The panda seconded Ueelee. "To resort to such degradation is simply unimaginable."

"We are all open to a better solution," the spider said.

The civilized veneer was slowly being pulled off the barbaric nature of their mission. Xttlzttl was still the nominal leader of the group because of his rank as former Council President. But he was deferring more and more to the Cttrx.

Ueelee could think of no alternative. "Yes, all right. But no Zurg."

"Yes, Zurg," Xttlzttl said, backing the spider. "It is the only way we have now."

The Gudalurians identified the proper Miralet Ring coordinates for entry into Ring Zurg. After a twenty shiphour journey their ship emerged into the Zurg stellar system.

Xttlzttl, the blue jay, and the Cttrx all gazed out of the holoviewer into the desolation that was Ring Zurg. The history of this blighted system was displayed within the viewer. Images from the planet's evolutionary history were shown, as well as the system's association and relations with Gudalur. What they saw was not pleasant. A great galactic nebula slowly broke apart 13 billion years ago, forming the solar nebulae that would create the solar systems of Galaxy 6 in Sector (4GP, 23.3445, 9.33799). During this process of star formation a stray cloud of dust and gas broke away. Isolated in space, it's nearest stellar neighbor was almost 200 light years away. There was nevertheless enough hydrogen in the cloud to begin the process of fusion and form a pale, cool, and weak sun. Three planets orbited this star. The inner two were barren and lifeless rocks. The third planet was a dark, cold, and arid world of grays, browns, and blacks.

The dominant life form evolved from insects that crawled beneath the ground. They eeked out an existence from grubs and worms that aerated the almost sterile soil. Cactus-like vegetation grew that provided water and food for the evolving species. Because resources were so scarce, species members often fought each other for the little food that existed. These conditions bred a culture of hatred and divisiveness. Balancing this emotion was the necessity for cooperation in locating and storing food for the period when the planet's orbit took it too far away from their sun. Gradually the race learned a brutal sort of efficiency. Other members were tolerated simply because their labor was necessary.

Zurg are controlled with implants placed in their sensitive neck areas. The species has a hard exoskeleton, with vital organs on the inside. Each Zurg is about five feet tall and possesses powerful mandibles capable of crushing anything remotely edible. Each has two very long arms and two legs. The arms end in huge, razor-sharp pincers that can quickly snap the hard exoskeleton of krag. Krag are scraggly six-legged insects that most closely resemble an earthian spider. They are the main food source for the Zurg. The legs of Zurg end in feet with six digits terminating in sharp claws that can dig into the hardscrabble surface of their planet for edible subterranean creatures.

The three Gudalurians and their shipmates studied the Zurg historical record. Those who came into contact with Zurg could not help but feel an utterly cold emotionless-ness. They read the accounts from visitors to the planet. Almost all feeling had been bred out of the species from millions of years of brutal survival upon a world almost entirely devoid of beauty. No trees grew and no birds sang. Weak sunlight from the pale star rarely broke through a dense cloud cover. The wind whipped and blew the sustaining vegetation, which is the only feature of the barren landscape. The pitifully few insect species, including krag, survive on the vegetation and provide sustenance for the planet's dominant species.

The record showed that Zurg society is hierarchical and controlled always by the Dominant. The Dominant is an absolute ruler who dispenses work assignments, food, and death. Its word was unquestioned. Zurg liked it that way. It suited their feeling of contempt for their fellows.

Pirates and other criminals from backwater stellar systems outside the Gudalurian Network often raided the planet, using Zurg either as slaves or as mercenaries.

The species was hopeless, Xttlzttl thought. And this is what we have descended to! The idea of having these brutes aboard their wonderful ship was disgusting. Their presence could only foul its pristine beauty. Each Gudalurian ship was crafted with loving care and blessed with a ritual ceremony upon launch, infused with the higher spiritual vibrations. But this was the only way to perform their sacred duty. It was clear that the nature of the earthian planet would always be volatile. Its periodic and catastrophic upheavals would always destroy life before it could attain the proper emotional and mental maturity.

What kind of a planet had adults that would turn on their own children? Raping them, brutalizing them. Earth is a rogue planet! A sick, twisted, and psychotic planet that could only breed violent and perverse species. A small cut above the Zurg perhaps. Yes, it was much better that the entire earthian system should be eliminated. It was fitting. The Gudalurian outcasts would use one hateful species to eliminate another.

Xttlzttl felt the presence of the Cttrx and was comforted. The blue jay, Lledren, and the panda watched at the ship settled down in front of the underground hive that housed the Dominant, his ruling elite, and their dependents. The history vid showed them that negotiating with these creatures was simple. One merely approached the Dominant and negotiated for the rental of whatever quantity of Zurg was needed.

The Cttrx volunteered to be their representative.

"That is not possible," the blue jay said. "Recall that your species closely resembles krag. You would instantly be regarded as inferior. You would have no bargaining position."

"I will go," Lledren said, fully aware of what he was in for. In order to communicate effectively with Zurg he must speak to them on their level. That meant embracing, for a time, the extremely uncomfortable emotions of hatred, contempt, and cruelty. "Of all of us I am the best qualified to deal with these creatures." Lledren shielded his reluctance from the group. "I will take the Shai-Lin as my assistant, if he will be so good as to accompany me."

The Huarag were master psychologists. Lledren's suggestion was readily accepted by the Shai-Lin. So the cat and the Huarag disembarked from the ship carrying three headsets. Each was encased in a protective bubble of force. They merely stood before the hive, waiting. The two shipmates observed Zurg feeding, fighting, and moving seemingly haphazardly along and within the rabbit warren of corridors that composed the hive.

The Shai-Lin shielded his mind from the psychic onslaught. A great wave of compassion and pity rose within him. Within a few minutes a Zurg slowly emerged from within the hive and approached. Behind him two smaller creatures trailed submissively.

Lledren slowly brought a headset forward with his long tail. He flung it at the creature. The Zurg picked up the delicate instrument gently within its huge pincers, placing it on its head. The Shai-Lin was amazed at its dexterity, for its pincers were deadly sharp. The Shai-Lin could see that these creatures knew the devices well. He donned his own headset. When his mind met that of the Zurg he was careful not to show the shock and disgust he felt. The creature's psyche was like an earthian chain saw gleefully chopping its way through bloody flesh. He was able to ascertain that it called itself the Dominant. It was the ruler of all Zurg upon the planet. The Shai-Lin transmitted this data and other cultural information to Lledren.

"How many of my scum do you wish? What have you to bargain?" the Dominant said aggressively. The creature's mind was filled with its needs: more krag or other tasty flesh, a fresh supply of electronic implants, and slaves. The Shai-Lin almost lost it here, for he regarded the eating of meat unthinkable.

Lledren was also shocked but was able to adjust his thoughts perfectly to communicate effectively with this primitive. The cat straightened its magnificent body and preened, as if to say, 'Look at how beautiful I am and how ugly you are.'

Lledren replied harshly. "We require 5,000 of your loathsome vermin. In exchange we offer valuable trinkets that you may use in trade with the other reprobates who visit you on this dunghill planet."

The Zurg was impressed with this peroration. It looked closely at the two off-worlders. These were not the usual lot of brigands and criminals. It knew how to deal with that scum. Both the sleek, silvery furred cat and the tall, pure white humanoid were appetizing morsels indeed. Each emanated a sense of refinement and beauty. The Dominant sensed instinctively that behind this refinement was raw power.

The Dominant stood before these magnificent beings. From some long-buried ancestral memory it suddenly felt a sense of powerlessness and rage. The Zurg took a step forward, intending to eviscerate these soft creatures and consume their tasty flesh and organs.

The Shai-Lin immediately ascertained the Dominant's intention. He warned his partner through the headset, mind to mind. Lledren pulled out a weapon. "Malignant, let but one atom of your vile person come nearer and I will obliterate you."

The Zurg stifled its rage and held itself completely still. One leap forward and it could still slash the throat of this furry animal, which was covered with a down that slightly resembled a krag's. It decided not to test the creature's reactions. It took a step backward, still seething inwardly.

"How much?" it demanded.

"Silence, excrement!" Lledren thundered. "You presume to dictate to us? If there is any more of your presumption I will destroy this planet and all of the filth upon it."

The Dominant eyed the great ship floating above and concluded that the visitors were not bluffing. It was satisfied. The Dominant bowed its head in a sign of submission, a trick it had learned from a slave trader. These were beings it could deal profitably with. Great power also meant great wealth.

The downy one spoke. "We offer you 5,000 pieces of pure Lamanite, each 150 Gudalurian grams, for the rental of your vermin for as long as we require. If there are any left we will return them to you."

This confirmed its assessment. Pure Lamanite, in exchange for a mere 5,000 scum? A rich haul indeed! It would have offered 20,000 for such a treasure.

Lledren turned and began to walk away. The Shai-Lin, stunned at his friend's amazing performance, belatedly followed. After the cat had taken a few steps, Lledren turned and again faced the Zurg. "Assemble your miscreants at exactly 0800 Galactic Standard Time in front of this dung-heap," he commanded. "If you are late by even one minute I will slag this hive and everything in it."

Lledren and the Shai-Lin then floated slowly upward within their transport bubbles to the ship.

After the hull had closed upon them, Lledren collapsed to the floor, shaking. "It was all I could do to remain upright," he told the assembled group, who had watched the display from the holovid. "We have our assassins."

The next shipsday, precisely at 0800, five thousand Zurg assembled in front of the Dominant's hive. Lledren was accompanied by four transport robots. He threw bags of Lamanite coins toward the assembled Zurg. One of the bags broke, spilling the precious metal onto the bleak, rocky ground. Zurg broke ranks and scrabbled for the loose valuables, fighting amongst themselves.

The Dominant was enraged. He slagged the offenders and a dozen more for good measure. The stench from their smoking bodies was terrible.

Lledren strove to keep up appearances. He shouted at the Dominant. "Reprobate! You have destroyed my property!"

The Dominant promptly marched out replacements. Lledren opened the ship's hull to a special sealed chamber that would house their mercenaries. The entire group had an overseer, whose job it was to rigidly enforce discipline through the implants. This Zurg assured Lledren that any who disobeyed would die instantly.

The cold emotionless hatred of the creature almost overpowered him but Lledren steeled himself to conclude his mission. "You will feed on nutrient solution," the cat commanded. He directed the Zurg commandant to a large tub of liquid. "We do not eat flesh aboard this ship."

The overseer nodded, even though it was enraged. Nutrient solution? When it deserved fresh krag meat? But it was impressed by the silvery-furred creature and his great shining ship. It was by far the largest it had ever seen.

"Tell your scum that there is plenty for all to gorge. But remember this: there is to be no infighting. If I see even one scratch on one carapace during your stay here, your implants will be removed and you will all be exquisitely tortured."

The overseer was now thoroughly cowed and bowed low in submission. The greatest fear of any Zurg was the removal of its guiding implant, which would render it as helpless as a krag larva.

Lledren exited the Zurg holding area and walked, exhausted, to his private chamber. They should be able to control these creatures. Like automatons each Zurg would simply obey any order transmitted through their implant. A command to the Zurg overseer should be all that was required. But he would no longer have anything to do with them. He had gotten Xttlzttl his mercenaries. Let someone else direct the beasts in the coming conflict.

After his ordeal Lledren activated his favorite holo. He settled into his favorite float and spent four hours in meditation in a futile attempt to purify his consciousness.

The attack on the earthians would begin tomorrow.

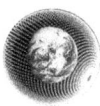

Chapter 34

An immensely powerful shockwave of predatory hatred suddenly burst upon the earthians stationed at the target template. "Zurg!" the Orion shouted. "They've sent those monsters to do their dirty work!" The terrifying creatures tore through the earthian defenses, destroying flesh, robot, and machine alike. In the middle of their battle formation the Zurg carried the precious template that would reprogram the earthian Ring.

Their emotionless and single-minded annihilation was shocking to the now sensitive and close-knit earthian defenders. Jack saw one of the black-carapaced creatures use its pincers, literally decapitating the head of one of his techie robots. Too late his unicorn ran it through with its long, spiraled horn. Chaos and death was all around him. So desperate was his plight that he did not have even a moment to look for Amara.

The Orion called immediately for reinforcements. "All hands to the holospace! We are under attack!" Men and women flooded to their stations, picked up their headsets, and joined the fight.

The Oorant had already fled. The Orion, unable to watch the devastation, also removed himself from the holospace.

The earthian front line buckled. The injured quickly went to the back while stronger and fresher minds replaced them at the point of attack. Another wave struck, and then another. Only the heroic effort of Victorio and his strikers prevented the earthian defenses from crumbling altogether. Thousands were forced to withdraw from the battle, crying or screaming in pain, throwing off their headsets. After an hour the Zurg withdrew, repulsed for the moment.

The earthians were dazed, and suffering psychically and physically. They gazed dully around at the quiet, comfortable ship, unable to believe that the vi-

olent battle they had just experienced had taken place. Then their fallen comrades were recognized. Some of them were slashed and gored, others sliced
open. Groans and cries of anguish filled the air.

Jack was sick to his stomach and barely able to walk. He made a rapid
survey of their losses with Victorio. Over two thousand of the team had died,
unable to withstand the Zurg offensive. Thousands more would be out of action for the foreseeable future. Jack frantically searched for Amara. He saw
her seated at her station, her head in her hands, completely shattered.

"Oh Jack, that was so terrifying," she wailed. She pointed to three of her
teammates, whose grotesque features in death showed the horror of their experience.

A slow anger burned in Jack's gut as he made the rounds. The Apache
was stoic. "These brave warriors have died well," he said with approval. He
pointed to a young man of about 23 with a blood soaked hole in his chest.
"That one took two of those fiends with him."

"The Gudalurians will not attack again for at least a shipsday," Victorio
announced.

"You can't know that," Jack replied. "If I were them I'd get started right
away."

Victorio spoke disdainfully. "Their enlightened minds are sickened by
what they have done. They will need time for rest and recuperation." The
Apache had only contempt for those who sent others to fight their battles.

The Oorant reappeared, ignoring Its personal psychic trauma. It conducted the wounded to the ship's Meditation and Healing Center, where It
personally directed their physical and psychic recovery. Victorio organized
a burial detail, laying the bodies out in a private chamber next to the Center
with as much dignity as possible. A stasis field surrounding the flesh would
ensure that the bodies would not decay. A formal ceremony would be held at
a later time. Then the bodies could be sent back to earth for funeral arrangements.

The Oorant spoke. "Unless life force has permanently left the body or the
will to live is gone, a complete recovery is assured."

Jack breathed a sigh of relief and cursed himself for allowing Amara to
participate. But there was little he could do about it now. If they failed all of
humanity would soon be extinct. Why not die quickly and gloriously in bat-

tle, instead of slowly and helplessly? Jack could now appreciate the Apache's stoicism. It was a way to blunt the emotional pain of losing beloved ones.

Jack felt completely wasted by the assault. He took his treatment in the Center along with Amara, who had suffered only a few bruises. She had come late to the team and had been in the rear.

Victorio had the fighting man's gleam in his eye. "Let them come again," he said, the black eyes hard as flint. "I, Gian-nah-tah, will show them how The People deal with their enemies."

A short time later the remaining fighters met at their stations to discuss what had happened during the battle, and to let off some steam. Regat Toor explained about the Zurg.

"Zurg are emotionless, predatory, insect-like humanoids who evolved upon an isolated, barren, almost lifeless planet. Zurg are still used as mercenaries in backwater areas of Gudalur."

"So not everything in Gudalur is sweetness and light!" Jack exclaimed.

Toor was slightly miffed. "The universe is a very large place. But no civilization of any importance whatsoever resolves their difficulties with violence."

"Coulda fooled me," Jack said.

"Zurg evolution was stunted by an unprecedented anomaly of planetary evolution. It is a miracle that the species survived under such impossibly harsh conditions. Unfortunately, their spiritual growth has been permanently stunted. They are to be pitied, not hated."

Victorio glanced quickly at the alien. His eyes were hard. "You pity them. I'll kill them."

Toor shuddered.

After another hour or so Victorio addressed the group. "Our only option is to attack. We will give them a taste of their own medicine."

"But it's suicide!" cried Amara, who spoke for many of the team members. "We leave the Ring undefended."

"We have lost over half of our force," Victorio replied. "Another attack like the last and we will be destroyed. Our enemy knows this and waits only to recover his strength and gather more of those fiends. We face certain ruin if we continue to defend. But there is a chance if we risk all on a bold and daring strike."

None of the remaining fighters could doubt Victorio's truth. After discussion his suggestion was approved unanimously. The group's laughter, good fellowship and lighthearted feeling of adventure had completely vanished. There was now a feeling of grim desperation, and hatred for those who were trying to destroy them. "We go to defend our women, our husbands, our children, our entire civilization," Victorio said.

Jack, Victorio, and five others with military experience planned the earthian strike. Through the ship's interface, the location of the Gudalurian ship was known. "We shall not attack on the battlefield," Victorio said. "We will destroy the Gudalurians in their own holospace before the battle has begun."

This met with unanimous approval from the strategy group, who were eager to avenge the deaths of thousands of their fallen comrades.

"Attack where the enemy is unprepared; sally out when he does not expect you," Victorio said.

"That is Sun-Tzu again," Jack said.

"Sun-Tzu was an Apache," Victorio replied.

"We have about 4,500 able fighters left," Victorio said. "There are only 144 Gudalurians. Without direction, their fiendish troops can do nothing. Even though the Gudalurian minds are probably more powerful than ours, we will overwhelm them with numbers. Victorio spoke with contempt. "They are cowards. They have no stomach for a real fight."

It was decided to leave 500 of the team on the battlefield as a token guard, and attack with 4,000. Through the magic of Gudalurian thought-based technology, both ship's holospaces were in instantaneous contact. Fortunately the Gudalurians kept their headsets on continuously except when sleeping, as did the Oorant and the Orion. Apparently Gudalurians relished the intimacy of mind-to-mind contact. The earthians only donned the headsets during training exercises. Therefore, the Gudalurians would not know of their plans as long as the earthians kept their headsets off. Until it was time to attack.

Jack briefed the team members an hour later. "We will strike the Gudalurians directly in their holospace, before they can mount the attack that will finish us off. There are 27 of us for every one of them." Jack pointed to Victorio and Major Rafe Lienau, a stocky man of about 40 with prematurely white hair and the look of a combat veteran. "Victorio and Rafe will organize teams and assign each team a target. Our alien friends have identified each of the 144 Gudalurians and prepared a profile for each one. Each of you will study these profiles until you are familiar with them. Your mission is to destroy that target, no matter what. Remember that you fight not only for yourselves but for the very existence of our planet. As soon as Victorio gives the signal, put on your headsets and attack simultaneously. Good luck!"

Ninety minutes later the Oorant, with infinite subtlety, probed the Gudalurian ship and reported that all aboard were connected to the holospace. They were all still resting. In unison the earthians, on Victorio's signal, put on their headsets and attacked…

Jack and Major Rafe Lienau led their team into the Gudalurian holospace, shouting.

Jack sat on his unicorn and carried his sword and energy weapon. Rafe's holospace persona was a Terminator with an energy weapon. Their target was Xttlzttl himself, the Gudalurian leader. The mantis was resting comfortably a quarter mile away underneath a hot, bright white sun next to his ancestral hive. Jack knew that the holospace was as vast as the imagination. To enter without scouting the ground was an act of great courage, even suicide, for his 27 fighters. But it was the only way to assure complete surprise, their only asset.

A Pteradactyl and a fire breathing dragon raced overhead. Transformers, terminators, and beasts of every description rushed the prone mantis. There were no others present on the hot, dusty landscape. Major Rafe Lienau gestured toward Jack.

"Halt!" Jack commanded. The team, excited from a rush of adrenaline, broke off. Everyone was confused, and milled about.

"Around me!" he said, raising his glowing blue sword.

The team gathered round, breathless. "Why is there no resistance?" Jack said.

"Approach the target slowly in groups of three," Major Lienau said, giving directions to surround the mantis. He was concerned about an ambush. The ground was open, with a few red and brown buttes in the distance. But he knew well that a dip or hollow might exist that could swallow an army. The team discovered nothing on the way.

Rafe carefully approached the mantis and touched it. His metal claw went right through!

"A trick!" cried a lioness.

Jack cursed himself for a fool. "A sophisticated holographic projection!" How the hell did the Gudalurians do that? Toor had assured him that all was in order!

A dragon landed on the sandy surface with a roar of fire. "If this is just a projection, where is the real Xttlzttl?"

"The Ring template!" the lioness cried, jumping up and down and vocalizing what everyone now knew. "They've gone to the Ring!"

Jack and Major Lienau exchanged grim glances. Failure! They had been duped like boot camp cherry's. But there was no time to feel sorry for themselves. "To the Ring!" Rafe shouted. "All at once. Find the target and destroy."

Creatures of every description exited and returned to the scout ship's holo. They found themselves back at their stations, in their bodies once more. To go anywhere in holospace it was necessary to first exit any holo coordinate spaces by going home first, then re-entering. The team hurried to the Ring to find several teams already on the ground and a number of injured lying about. Jack saw a black panther with a mangled ear, a terminator with a big hole in its arm, and several dozen others.

"They fooled us!" Amara cried. She had been looking frantically for him, and threw herself into his arms from her battle horse as he rode up to the cave on his unicorn. She pointed to the target templates, which were glowing brightly. "Look." The templates were rapidly sending out billions of tendrils of energy throughout the Ring. "We don't know how to stop it."

"How many more casualties?" Jack asked grimly.

"None, thank God." Amara patted her horse. "But a number of injured, as you can see." She pointed at the great white battle horse, whose coat was stained with blood above the back leg. "Jack here was clawed by one of those brutes. Other than that I'm OK."

Jack smiled, appreciating that she had named her horse after him. He felt hopeless. What did it matter now how many were injured?

Victorio appeared with the Oorant and the Orion. The Oorant and the Orion did not have a separate holo personality and appeared as themselves. Was that because they were more spiritually advanced and knew themselves better?

Jack wandered around in a daze, feeling completely detached from reality and from himself.

Victorio was unruffled, accepting reality as he found it. "It was a beautifully executed strategy. They played on our emotions and used our anger against us."

"How did it happen?" Rafe asked.

"Thousands of Zurg quickly overwhelmed our guard," said one of the injured. "A quick strike, with those beasts carrying the activating template. They could have killed us all had it not been for the insistence of Xttlzttl. It was over so quickly we hardly even put up a fight." The man spoke bitterly. "We were outmaneuvered at every turn. Xttlzttl himself directed the proper placement of the Ring template."

Jack felt the bitter, crushing failure of defeat crash over him, knowing that he was responsible in part for it. "Is there any way to deactivate the templates?" he asked the Oorant.

"No. These templates affect the entire Ring. Once activated, it triggers others it needs and neutralizes the rest until it completes its programming instructions."

There was no sound but the silence of the defeated.

"What do we do now?" Amara asked finally.

"Go back to earth and die." Jack was apathetic. "Those poor souls probably don't even know what is about to happen to them."

But Jack was wrong.

Chapter 35

"Jack, will you marry me?" Amara asked as they lie in her bed after making love. The smoke from Jack's cigarette filled her nostrils. She was on her back and Jack was on his back next to her. She could feel the hard muscles of his leg and the soft hairs of him brushing against her left leg. They had exited the scout craft immediately, determined to die with their fellows. A few days would pass until things started happening. It didn't take long for them to get back into their lives. It was difficult for Jack to believe that they were all shortly going to perish.

Jack laughed and turned on his side. "The earth is about to be annihilated and you want marriage? Whatever for?"

"Because…because I want you all to myself for what little time we have left."

"You already have me all to yourself."

Amara propped herself up on her elbow. "Do I? What were you doing in Milan last summer? Or at any of the other conferences you attended all over the world?"

Jack met her gaze without breaking eye contact. "My prowess is over-rated. Of course I went to the beach and looked. But I didn't do anything."

She probed him for a few seconds and was satisfied. "What makes men look at other women when they already have one they lust after?"

Jack laughed. "Good question." He looked her over from top to bottom with satisfaction. "Yes, I certainly do lust after you."

She said nothing, waiting for an answer.

Jack shrugged. "Women are the most beautiful things in the universe. Forget about cars and nature scenes and sunsets and all that stuff, there's noth-ing more attractive to a man than a beautiful woman. Beauty is something we all yearn for. It's in our souls to want to experience as much of it as we can. Beauty itself is encapsulated in the body of a woman."

"I don't think you answered my question," Amara said.

"Looking at other women doesn't diminish my desire for you."

"Do you really love me Jack?" As soon as she asked, she knew it was a mistake. He had already told her, but she wasn't *sure* of him. What if he said no?

Jack spoke without hesitation. "I love you as well as I can love anybody or anything."

"Then let's get married. To hell with the world and the universe. If we're going to die, let's do it together."

Jack grinned. "Will it really make you happy? What difference does it make? We're together, married or not."

"It matters to me."

"Ah, you're old fashioned."

"Damn right I'm old fashioned," she said, pulling him to her.

Then the lights went out on the universe.

Xttlzttl, the Ctrrx, the Shai-Lin, Lledren, Ueelee and the 144 watched as the earthian Ring programming took effect. As the energy from the activated templates spread throughout the manifold, Xttlzttl contemplated with despair how far he had fallen. Not two Gudalurian Standard months ago he was on Miralet, presiding over a routine Council meeting. Now he was a criminal known throughout the universe. Images and personal histories had been placed on the Network immediately after the song khur. All aboard were persona non grata in civilized society. Damned and purified. He felt more damned than anything else. A blackness had settled in upon his consciousness, never to be removed.

Never again was he to see his own hive. Never again to help with the larvae, to commune with his fellows, to mate with attractive females, to feel the hot sun upon his carapace. Never again to see his home planet Zlrrrk!

The mantis returned his attention to the rapidly spreading energy pattern as it contacted billions of other templates, programming them or neutralizing them. At this rate it would take several earthian planetary rotations before the Ring became fully enabled. Xttlzttl threw off his headset and clanked his way toward a transport vehicle, which took him to his chambers.

Ueelee spent every moment within the holospace, morbidly fascinated at what she had helped to set in motion. She watched as the activated templates rapidly gobbled up system resources, sending their codes throughout the manifold, programming relevant templates. Tendrils of light flew forth like a rapidly spreading disease. Within a few earthian planetary revolutions the Ring manifold was glowing and pulsating with subtle energy. This was clearly observable within the holospace, but not to primitive earthian scientific instruments. All was now prepared for Ring movement out of the earthian coordinates to the programmed ones.

How would life die? That was the disgusting and fascinating question that coursed through Ueelee's consciousness. Here was a unique opportunity to see and record the annihilation of billions of diverse life forms.

How would the earthian humans react? Would imminent death result in a spiritual awakening? Or would it cause a barbaric, violent struggle for survival, desperately clinging to life for as long as possible?

As the time for the denouement approached, Ueelee was joined by the others.

"The earthian Ring is now fully activated," said the Ctrrx.

"Soon the journey will begin," seconded the Shai-Lin. His psyche trembled for the fate of the earthians. Like Ueelee, he was fascinated to be present at this historic event.

"Will not Ring movement disturb the fabric of space and cause damage to other stellar systems?" Lledren asked.

"That is impossible," Ueelee replied. "Each stellar system has a sub-ring. Each Ring and sub-ring resemble a living entity. Ring travel is more like the cooperative movement of a school of fish as each element harmoniously makes way for those surrounding it."

"Yes, that is what the science report says," Xttlzttl confirmed. "I couldn't sleep last night and I immersed myself in the Network records. Theoretically the earthian Ring could survive indefinitely, even in the depths of intergalactic space. But the protocols for self-sustenance have been deactivated."

"Monstrous!" the Shai-Lin cried, confronted now with the grim reality of something that had heretofore been theoretical. "Is it not enough to remove the threat of earthian contamination from Gudalur? Must we murder billions of life forms as well?"

The Ctrrx had no patience with this reasoning. "And what if these earthians, who have proven themselves diabolically clever as well as violent, develop space travel? No my friend, we must destroy this rabble and save all Gudalur from this pernicious infection."

Xttlzttl was saddened. "Once the earthian Ring begins to move, its sun will rapidly destabilize. The planets will fall out of their orbits and the earthian planet's rotational wobble will become more pronounced. All life within the Ring will suffer a slow, painful death."

"And here we are, watching like debased earthians at a Roman arena as innocents are thrown to the lions." Lledren was disgusted.

"Innocents!" the Ctrrx cried. "You forget Koori the Barbarian. How many deaths was that earthian responsible for?"

"That was 50 million years ago," asserted the Shai-Lin. "This is now."

The Cttrx rubbed two of her furry forelegs together in irritation. "We have been through this already. Let us not squabble amongst ourselves. We must be content in the fulfillment of our duty."

Suddenly the pulsing Ring manifold glowed brightly, then went dark.

"Here it is," Lledren said. "The moment we've all been waiting for."

Very slowly and deliberately, the earthian Ring began to accelerate, moving out of the place assigned to it by the complex of gravitational forces acting upon it. The Ring inched along on its path out of the galaxy. Soon it would gather momentum, accelerating faster and faster, until the Ring positioned itself between this galaxy and it's nearest neighbor, over 1 million light years away.

But suddenly space itself began to morph, twisting and bending grotesquely. The Ring and everything in it disappeared.

Within a few seconds the Ring returned to visibility and its acceleration stopped. The Ring and everything within it began to flicker on and off, as if a titanic battle were being waged between monumentally powerful forces.

"What is going on in there?" Lledren asked.

Massoud Izz-Al-Din's vidphone chirped and he activated it. The face of Harim Malakai appeared, excited. Malakai was jabbering. "Massoud! The aliens! I have just had word that a great battle was fought out in space. The aliens have destroyed us. It was all a trick, Massoud. The aliens tricked the Chinese and the Americans, led by the traitor Martins…"

At that moment the world literally blanked out. Terror sent a knife through Izz-Al-Din's guts. His mind imploded as the walls, ceiling, and everything in existence disappeared, replaced by a dull gray sanity-sapping nothingness.

Cardinal Che Rodriquez gazed out from his Vatican office window at the stars. It had been a long day. Cardinal Tauron had just briefed the College about the Gudalrian attack and their imminent deaths. Of course it was impossible. Was it not a mere seven months ago that the Martins Experiment had cooperatively united the majority of mankind?

Then the desk upon which his elbows rested disappeared. The walls disappeared, and the stars as well. He looked down at his body, and that was gone too. Only a sort of phantom image, like a limb that had been cut off. Everything, every molecule of visible matter, was gone, replaced by the same gray nothingness that had obscured the stars.

Nullspace

President Dwight D. Eisenhower, Sir Isaac Newton, Yuri Gagarin, Nusrat Fatah Ali Khan and Queen Elizabeth I were playing a game of gin rummy when they suddenly felt a jolt within the fabric of spacetime. The circular light oak table, the cards, and the recreation center that looked out on a forest of tall white pines began to flicker. One moment they were playing cards. The next, the five friends found themselves on a featureless flat gray plain, the sunny blue sky replaced by the dull grayness of nullspace.

"What is happening?" Queen Elizabeth said, startled by the appearance and disappearance of reality.

Sir Isaac got up slowly from his chair. "Our deliverance, perhaps," the scientist said. "Let us go to the planetarium."

The planetarium was Newton's 18th century conception of a sophisticated observation platform, which allowed a glimpse into anywhere in Heaven or on earth. The five jumped in a small transport ship and flew over the spectacular plain of worlds. It was a strange flight. The ship, the plain, and everything around them continued to flicker in and out of existence. Yet somehow they continued along the flight path without mishap. When they reached their destination it was already crowded. The planetarium was a great domed auditorium with a ceiling several hundred feet high, and projection apparatus in the middle. Outside, it was surrounded by a 50 foot wide walkway overlooking an ocean. Every 50 feet or so was a viewer.

"Look here," Sir Conan Doyle said to Newton, pointing to one of the viewers. These devices looked like something you'd find on a beach, with dials for zooming in and a more sophisticated array of controls that allowed the user to focus on a specific target.

Sir Isaac put down his enameled walking stick and looked through the viewfinder. His mouth dropped open as he gazed upon an entire section of space that had begun to move. But the entire solar system, and the binary star system closest to earth, was somehow anchored. There were millions of earths, one in front of the other, like a slow-motion stroboscopic image. The planets were moving outward as if a gigantic rubber band were attached to them, pulling and straining the fabric of space. With every movement reality turned off, then on again.

"I am unable to understand this phenomena," said the author the Principia Mathemetica, circa 1676. "Perhaps someone with a more modern weltanschauung, as my friend Leibnitz would say, can decipher this." Sir Isaac stepped back and saw Richard Feynman, who was juggling four rubber balls. As he threw in a fifth, they all fell to the ground. "Rats!" Feynman shouted. "That fifth ball is always my undoing."

"Come come, sir," Sir Isaac said impatiently. "Put down your toys and tell us what is happening here."

Feynman, unconcerned, gathered up his balls and placed them carefully into a large pocket sewed into the side of his athletic slacks. Then he casually strolled to the viewer, bent over, and looked in for several minutes. The famous physicist twiddled several dials and occasionally grunted. He said nothing.

"Well man, have you anything to tell us?" Sir Isaac said. The great physicist straightened his lanky form.

"Yes!" Feynman said. "Whoever designed that damn viewer didn't make the thing adjustable. My back is killing me."

"You bloody fool, I'm not talking about the viewer," Sir Isaac shot back. "You modern types are remarkably flippant and undisciplined."

"You wouldn't say that if you saw me at my juggling," Feynman replied. "I worked for six hours straight yesterday."

Sit Isaac's face had gone red. "It's no wonder the world went to pieces after I died. Such frivolity! Such irreverence!"

"Oh shut up Isaac," said President Eisenhower, who had come up, eager to hear what the great physicist had to say. He looked up at Feynman and smiled. "You'll get that fifth any day now."

"You think so?" Feynman was anxious.

"I'm sure of it," the president said with a wink.

Feynman relaxed. "Well then, that's all right." He was just about to walk away when Eisenhower spoke. "Your thoughts?"

"Yes of course. Well, all of the matter in a section of space approximately 9 light years in diameter surrounding the earth is moving…or trying to move. There is a force holding it in place and that is causing spatial and temporal discontinuities within the affected area."

"In plain language, sir, what does that mean?" Doyle asked.

"It means that powerful forces, almost certainly of intelligent design, are fucking with the earth and the solar system. And I have no idea who or what is causing it."

"I just want to get out of this purgatory," Sir Isaac moaned.

"You and 12 billion others," Doyle replied.

T'Munga Watanabe sat upon the sandy Pacific Ocean shore just before dawn. His legs were crossed in the lotus position. He had unknowingly chosen the busiest spot on the beach. Fisherman silently walked past and around him as they readied their vessels for the day's catch. Amid the bustle of ships preparing for the day's labors, he heard the zing and slap of lines. Sailcloth flapped in the wind. Occasionally the sound of an engine made its way into the edges of his consciousness. Fish were still plentiful in this isolated, sleepy village within its small bay on the south western coast of Hokkaido. The big trawlers did not find it worth their while to venture here. For centuries, the village had taken from the sea only that which was needed. Environmental balance had been maintained.

Within him a vague discontent had recently blossomed into a feeling of anxiety. He had returned to his mother's birthplace to find peace and mental clarity.

Deep in meditation, Watanabe did not at first notice the complete dissolving of reality, even when terrified villagers began to shake him awake.

"T'Munga!" they cried. "The world has vanished!"

The famous voyageur was not even aware of their presence. He began to notice something interesting though. As in a very lucid dream, his old buddies from the Apollo's Arrow appeared before him. Nigel and Katrina, lying in her bed in Moscow. Karl Svenson, seated at his kitchen table in Halmstad and looking out his window at the foaming North Sea. And Rad Greenberg, his old antagonist, lecturing before a crowd of now panicking students.

"Greenberg," T'Munga said. He reached out his hand to touch his former crewmate. "This is remarkable. I seem to have reached a new level in my meditation."

"Watanabe!" Greenberg cried. "What are you doing here?"

T'Munga felt expansive and serene. "No my friend. The question is, what are YOU doing HERE!"

Katrina Antropov sat up in bed. "T'Munga! I see you sitting on a beach!"

"Yes, T'Munga, I see you as well...and Karl!" Nigel Clarke said. "Are you still in Hamlstad?"

Svenson started. "The world..." he sputtered in confusion. "It's gone. What is happening?"

T'Munga laughed. "I know nothing about that, Karl. I must have fallen asleep during meditation. I think I am dreaming."

"Dreaming! Thor's spear! The world—-reality itself—-is flickering on and off like a strobe light."

Katrina and Nigel had dressed quickly and were sitting on the side of the bed. "I thought we were both going crazy," she said, trembling. "I am very glad to hear that you are experiencing the same as we are."

"Ha!" T'Munga said. "I think all of you are crazy."

T'Munga opened his eyes for a peek. His body, the beach, the fishermen, the ocean, and the sky had vanished. All he perceived was Nullspace. Then, a few seconds later, everything reappeared. He gulped. "Uh...OK, I believe you." He paused for a few moments. "But...if nothing exists, why do I see you guys?"

"You're asking us?" the other four said almost at once.

It was as if the five companions had closed a circuit that enabled a network of connections. Others joined the crew. Families, social groups, and vid networks suddenly materialized in Nullspace. Antropov saw President Eisenhower, grinning from ear to ear, and an astonished Sir Isaac Newton.

Professor Feynman appeared, juggling five rubber balls. Cardinal Che Ro-driquez spotted a dumbfounded Massoud Izz-Al-Din, staring in disbelief at his dead father. Rizza Abd-Al-Aziz confronted Rashid Sakhr. "Traitor! Mur-derer!" Sakhr just smiled, understanding that something deeply metaphysical was occurring. Rashid felt in no way threatened by his former comrade. In ever increasing numbers, millions more joined T'Munga's dream.

T'Munga Watanabe spotted Sir Isaac and walked up to him. "Don't I know you from somewhere, sir? I seem to recall a conversation we had about your second law of motion…But no." T'Munga shook his head. "I must have been dreaming."

Sir Isaac smiled. "In a sense you were," said the great scientist. "I'll explain it all to you someday."

"Am I dreaming now?" T'Munga asked.

Sir Isaac banged his walking stick on the ground. "I just do not know."

Millions of similar tableaus were being enacted, all at the same time.

"Jack, what is happening?" Amara said. Millions of people, it appeared, were gathered in their bedroom.

"I don't know honey but it looks pretty big," Jack replied.

Jack heard a voice. "There he is!" A young man ran up with a vid camera, panting, surrounded by a lot of excited people. "Excuse me Jack Martins. I don't mean to intrude. For the record, can you tell us anything?"

"Who are you?" Jack asked, irritated.

"You don't remember?" He made his fingers into a gun. "Bang bang."

"Oh shit." It was Bob Cameron, the reporter from the *Midland Times*. The one who had recorded the first attempt on his life. "Not you again, kid. Go away."

"I thought you, of all people, would have an explanation."

"What explanation is there for this?" Jack said, waving his hand at the growing parade of beings, both dead and alive. There were millions and millions of them, and getting larger by the moment.

At that moment Victorio appeared, grinning, along with Yogesh Dalal. "So this is your woman." Victorio gazed at Amara.

Amara laughed despite her fear. "Who is this handsome fellow?" she said to Jack. "He's a typical man though. In a time of crisis he's thinking about sex."

"My people say that when the end of the world is near…"

This discourse was interrupted. Within the gray emptiness of Nullspace a tiny but brilliant point of light appeared far in the distance. The character of this object was so arresting that it drew all attention to it. All conversation stopped. The point grew very slowly as if it were tearing a hole in the grayness. To Jack Martins it resembled a singularity. But it was the opposite of a black hole, for light emanated from it. The edges of the object were impossibly sharp. When he looked carefully, trying to discern its boundary, he detected movement. Suddenly the object expanded very rapidly and its event horizon advanced toward them. They were about to be engulfed.

"It's that light source!" Rad Greenberg exclaimed in sudden recognition. "HAL!"

"I'll be damned," T'Munga said. "You're right Rad. It certainly does look like the same entity that ran into the Cheesy Poof."

Jack felt Amara's grip tighten on his arm. He put his arm around her waist and pulled her close. The wavefront of light passed through them like a gigantic but soundless explosion. The space around them was now brilliantly lit with a complex, shifting tapestry of light. Every twenty seconds or so reality would flicker back on. Just for a moment Jack would find himself alone with Amara. Then the scene would return to…whatever this was. Jack was too astonished to be terrified. The crew of the Orions' Arrow was now standing next to the bed, deep in conversation. Jack had no idea how they had gotten here.

Rad Greenberh was speaking. "My eyes don't hurt when I look into this stuff, but it's as bright as the sun."

"It's beautiful," Katrina said.

The 144 Gudalurians huddled to themselves. They were perfectly aware that they were surrounded by billions of earthians, and were directly responsible for the imminent death of their planet. They were ignored in the earthian's amazement of meeting friends and loved ones both living and deceased.

"Our quarantine has finally been broken," declared Conan Doyle. "But where do we go?"

The entirety of Gudalur was also watching on the Network, for each Ring is a sophisticated communications and transportation device. It was the greatest show since the trial and imprisonment of Koori the Barbarian, almost 50 million Standard years ago.

Richard Feynman was unimpressed. He continued to juggle. Actually he was in shock, for these events went so far beyond even his great understanding that he felt completely numb. The physics that he had been taught was clearly inadequate here. His mind groped for answers that weren't there. So he juggled, all the while furiously trying to make sense of this madness.

Isaac Newton just stared, unable to utter a word or think a thought. Everything inside his head seemed to be frozen.

Billions of beings waited, breathless, as reality flickered in and out of existence...

Chapter 36

THE toggling of reality stopped and Feynman stopped his juggling. "I see it now," he said.

"As do I," Newton remarked. "We are finally free!"

The 144 Gudalurians were in awe. The mantis turned to Jack and said sadly, "This battle was entirely pointless."

"Explain," Amara said.

"The earthian Ring cannot be moved," Xttlzttl said.

Newton was curious. "Why?"

Xtllzttl moved his bony carapace up and down, which passed for a shrug. "Apparently the Old Ones who created this Ring made sure that it would always stay in place."

"So that means we are safe!" Amara said.

All present were listening intently now. The buzz of millions of conversations had gradually faded.

"Yes," Xttlzttl said. The mantis was bitter. He and his companions were now outcast without having completed their mission.

But the trapped and quarantined souls of earth, all 12 billion of them, began to see a beautiful white light.

"Look!" said Isaac Newton. "Heaven beckons."

Even the imperturbable and irreligious Feynman was impressed. He turned and smiled at Newton. "Our ticket Home."

Jack was confused. "I don't see anything."

President Eisenhower appeared. "Only those souls who have completely terminated their association with the physical body can enter the gates of heaven. Or even perceive it."

Jack snorted. "You can believe that if you want, Mr. President."

Amara noticed that something was definitely happening.. A great vortex was forming. The personalities of Feynman, Newton, and Eisenhower, along with the other 12 billion souls in Purgatory, were floating up into it. The vortex ascended and finally disappeared altogether. At the very last Amara saw Feynman reach into his pocket and begin juggling, with a smile on his face.

Amara turned to Jack. T'Munga, Karl, Nigel, and the other crew members, along with the rest of humanity still alive, were gone. She looked around at the familiar solid reality of her bedroom. After the great battle, it had never looked so good.

Amara smiled up at Jack. "We have a life together now!"

All of the tension went out of Jack's body. For the first time in his life he felt totally relaxed. "Yes honey, we do. And I plan to do a better job of it this time."

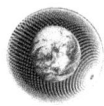

Chapter 37

Afterword

On Miralet and on the Gudalurian ship, the battle had been observed carefully.

"The earthian scourge still exists," the Ctrrx said angrily.

"The planet is clearly protected," the Shai-Lin remarked.

"Yes," Xttlzttl agreed. "It seems as if we will have to find another way to deal with the earthians."

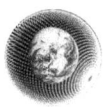

Appendix A

Story Notes

This book is based upon the assumption that it is possible to accelerate at the rate of 1,600,000 mph^2 and eliminate relativistic effects. I use a typical SF gimmick by describing a "field" of unknown energy that conveniently takes care of this little difficulty. But hey, none of our spacecraft has ever even come close to traveling at the speed of light, so no one really knows what would happen!

It is interesting, however, to contemplate a mode of space travel in which not just the ship, but all within it are affected by the propulsion system. This mode of travel would not be a propulsion system at all, for it would have to cocoon life safely within it, like the Pilsher field. Such a means of travel would simply be beyond our present level of consciousness, and our present understanding of natural laws.

The level of consciousness of any species determines the subset of natural law that it is aware of. Right now, our species is confrontational, and we think of solving problems by "fighting" its opposite. We fight cancer, fight poverty, fight injustice, etc. Looked at objectively, the idea of improvement by fighting its opposite is insane, for it focuses attention and resources on the unwanted thing.

Therefore, as a result of humanity's limited awareness, the subset of nature's laws that are available to us is at the lower end of the spectrum. Is it any wonder that our energy systems are based on the forced combustion and expolsion of primitive fossil fuels? Is it any wonder that our methods of problem resolution ultimately devolve to conflict and war?

Until mankind raises its level of awareness, we will continue to be mired in the same difficulties that have been with us for over 5,000 years. But if we can somehow transcend our constricted and myopic way of perceiving the world, and our fellow man, I am convinced that such technologies as are described in this book will somehow become available to us.

Using the classical equations of motion:

$$V = Vo + at \tag{A.1}$$

$$V_a v = (V = V_o)/2 \tag{A.2}$$

$$X = Xo + V_o t + 1/2at^2 \tag{A.3}$$

$$V^2 = V_o^2 + 2a(X - X_o) \tag{A.4}$$

All calculations ignore relativistic effects!

Calculations:

- How long will it take for a spacecraft accelerating at a constant rate of 800,000 mph^2 to reach the speed of light?

Speed of light $= 670,000,000$ mph
   Using (A.1),

$$t = (V - Vo)/a, t = 670,000,000/800,000 = 838 \text{ hrs, } 35 \text{ days} \tag{A.5}$$

- How many miles does light travel in one year?

$$1 \text{ light year} = 5.8730124 * 10^{12} \text{ miles} \tag{A.6}$$

- How many miles is 4.618 light years?

1 light year $= 2.7121771 * 10^{13}$ miles $= 27.121771$ trillion miles. (A.7)

- How many miles is 4.3 light years?

4.3 light years $= 5.8730124 * 10^{12}$ miles $* 4.3 = 25.2534$ trillion miles (A.8)

- How many miles from the Alpha system to the Martins Sphere barrier?

1.86782 trillion miles

The mean distance of the midpoint of the orbit of the binary's Alpha Centauri A and B are 4.381966013 ly from Sol. The Martins Sphere barrier turns out to be 4.618033991 ly from Sol.

- How long will it take a ship accelerating at a constant rate of 800,000 miles per hour to reach the Martins Sphere barrier?

  Barrier $= 4.618$ light years $= 2.7121771 * 10^{13}$ miles $= 27$ trillion miles. Using (A.3), $2.7121771 * 10^{13} = 0.5 * 8 * 10^5 * t^2$, $t = 343$ days.

- What rate of acceleration would be required to get the ship to Alpha Cebtauri in 170 days?

  Using (A.3), $x = 1/2at^2$, $2.5254 * 10^{13} = 0.5 * a * (170 * 24)^2$, $a = 3,034,170$ mph^2

Appendix B

Information in the Holographic Universe

From the *Scientific American* article "Information in the Holographic Universe – Theoretical results about black holes suggest that the universe could be like a gigantic hologram"

By Jacob D. Bekenstein August 2003 issue:

"We can now answer some of those elusive questions about the ultimate limits of information storage. A device measuring a centimeter across could in principle hold up to 10^66 bits–a mind-boggling amount. The visible universe contains at least 10^100 bits of entropy, which could in principle be packed inside a sphere a tenth of a light-year across. Estimating the entropy of the universe is a difficult problem, however, and much larger numbers, requiring a sphere almost as big as the universe itself, are entirely plausible.

"This surprising result – that information capacity depends on surface area – has a natural explanation if the holographic principle (proposed in 1993 by Nobelist Gerard 't Hooft of the University of Utrecht in the Netherlands and elaborated by Susskind) is true. In the everyday world, a hologram is a special kind of photograph that generates a full three-dimensional image when it is illuminated in the right manner. All the information describing the 3-D scene is encoded into the pattern of light and dark areas on the two-dimensional piece of film, ready to be regenerated. The holographic principle contends that an analogue of this visual magic applies to the full physical description of any system occupying a 3-D region: it proposes that another physical theory defined only on the 2-D boundary of the region completely describes the 3-D physics. If a 3-D system can be fully described by a physical theory operating solely on its 2-D boundary, one would expect the information content of the system not to exceed that of the description on the boundary."

Also see the *Scientific American* article at

http://www.scientificamerican.com/article.cfm?id=sidebar-the-holographic-p

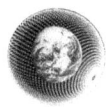

Appendix *C*

Holography

From Steve Michael's website at http://www.3dimagery.com/:

"Holography is one of the most significant discoveries humankind has ever made. Its discovery has had such a profound effect on our lives, that the person who discovered the process in 1947, Dr. Dennis Gabor, received the Nobel Prize in Physics in 1972. Holography is the only visual recording and playback process that can record our three-dimensional world on a two-dimensional recording medium and playback the original object or scene, to the unaided eyes, as a three dimensional image. The image demonstrates complete parallax and depth-of-field. The image floats in space either behind, in front of, or straddling the recording medium."

Appendix D

About the Author

Kenneth James Michael MacLean is a writer, book editor, and web tech. He has written 8 books, over 100 essays and three movies.

Ken was born in 1951 and lives with his wife of 30 years, Jennifer, and their 3 cats, in Ann Arbor Michigan, home of the Michigan Wolverines.

For a complete list of Ken's books and movies, go to

http://www.kjmaclean.com/Products/MainProductPage.php

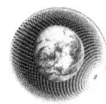

Appendix E

Other Books by the Author

Dialogues: Conversations with my Higher Self
Beyond the Beginning
The Vibrational Universe
The Manchild
Miracles Can Happen
A Geometric Analysis of the Platonic Solids and Other Semi-regular Polyhedra. With a Discussion of the Phi Ratio
I Love You Dad

www.ingramcontent.com/pod-product-compliance
Lightning Source LLC
Chambersburg PA
CBHW060946030726
47503CB00003B/744